ARU SHAH AND THE TREE OF WISHES

Roshani Chokshi

SCHOLASTIC

Published in the UK by Scholastic Children's Books, 2020
Euston House, 24 Eversholt Street, London, NW1 1DB
A division of Scholastic Limited

London – New York – Toronto – Sydney – Auckland
Mexico City – New Delhi – Hong Kong

First published in the US by Disney • Hyperion, an imprint of Disney Book Group, 2020.

ISBN 978 0702 30353 1

A CIP catalogue record for this book is available from the British Library.

Printed by CPI Group (UK) Ltd, Croydon, CR0 4YY
Papers used by Scholastic Children's Books are made
from wood grown in sustainable forests.

1 3 5 7 9 10 8 6 4 2

www.scholastic.co.uk

For my parents, May and Hitesh, who always insisted on making sure we read the "real" versions of myths and fairy tales. Thanks for the delightful trauma. Love you.

CONTENTS

ONE

Aru Shah Is Not Spider-Man

Aru Shah had a gigantic lightning bolt, and she really wanted to use it.

"Please don't, Shah," begged her friend Aiden. "If you electrocute the targets with Vajra... we've blown this Pandava mission."

"Puh-*leeze*," said Aru, hoping she sounded more confident than she felt. "I'm the daughter of the god of thunder and lightning. Electricity is practically my thing."

"Yesterday you stuck a fork in the toaster," pointed out Aiden.

"It was just for a *second*, and it was holding my breakfast prisoner."

A gust of wind hit the back of Aru's head, and she turned to see a huge eagle with sapphire-colored feathers swooping toward them. The bird dove to the ground and in a flash of blue light transformed into Brynne, her soul sister and the daughter of the god of the wind.

"No visuals on the targets," Brynne said. "Also, Aiden's right. I seriously don't trust you around electricity."

"You weren't even part of this conversation!" said Aru.

"Still heard it." Brynne tapped the side of her head. "I had eagle ears for a second, remember?"

Beside Aiden stood Mini, daughter of the god of the dead. She clutched Dee Dee, her Death Danda, and looked around anxiously.

"You could've electrocuted yourself with that fork!" scolded Mini. "And then you would've—"

"Died?" guessed Aiden, Aru, and Brynne at the same time.

Mini crossed her arms. "I was going to say that you would've suffered severe burns, cardiac arrest, possible coma . . . and yes, potentially, death."

Brynne rolled her eyes. "Enough about toasters. We need a plan to rescue the targets, and *quick*."

The three Pandavas and Aiden stood on the street, gazing up at the illuminated Ferris wheel that crowned downtown Atlanta. Beyond the wheel loomed the bright, jagged skyline. Cars honked and inched their way through rush-hour traffic on the street behind them, completely oblivious to the four kids holding glowing weapons.

Earlier, Hanuman, their monkey-faced war instructor, and Boo, their pigeon mentor, had told them that somewhere on the Ferris wheel were two people in need of rescuing. The Pandavas had no idea what the targets looked like, but they knew one of them was a clairvoyant.

Why would someone hide a clarinet? Aru had asked.

Boo had sighed. *It's not a clarinet.*

Oh.

Turns out a *clairvoyant* was not a musical instrument,

but someone who could see the future and prophesize. The Otherworld had been waiting for centuries for an important prophecy to be uttered. If the rumors were true, it would hold enough power to determine the victor in the *devas'* war against the *asuras,* who were currently being led by the Sleeper. But prophecies were sensitive things, Boo had explained. They would only reveal themselves in the presence of certain beings—usually those whom the prophecy was about. Boo believed that in this case only the Pandavas or the Sleeper's soldiers would be able to hear it. And each side's success depended on making sure that the other side didn't.

Aru eyed the lengthening late-winter shadows. So much had changed in the past year since they'd ventured into the Ocean of Milk. She was fourteen now. She had grown a couple inches, her hair now fell to her shoulders, and lately she could fit into her mom's shoes . . . but she still preferred walking around barefoot. In the light of early evening, dogwood blossoms gleamed like stars caught on dark branches. Cherry trees lining the streets shed pink petals, and the damp pollen on the streets looked like flakes of gold.

"I tried flying up to spot the targets, but some of the booths are dark and shut tight," said Brynne. "I just don't understand why anyone who can see the future would choose to hide out on an amusement park ride."

"Especially a stalled one, with no operator," added Aiden.

"Maybe he or she wanted a better view?" suggested Mini.

"Who knows, but first we need to get the Ferris wheel moving so we can access the closed booths," said Brynne. "If I blast it with wind—"

"The whole thing could topple over!" said Aru.

"And if we try to start it with Vajra, we could fry the clairvoyant!" said Brynne.

Mini bit her lip, looking from Aru to Brynne. "Maybe... there's another way?"

Aiden nodded. "Bee can use her wind mace to—*gently*—get it moving. I'll take the perimeter and—"

"We don't have time for gently!" cut in Aru.

"How 'bout you and I climb the Ferris wheel, and I use Dee Dee to scan the booths?" offered Mini.

"Climb the Ferris wheel?!" echoed Aru. "Do I look like Spider-Man to you?"

"Well, you sometimes wear those pajamas..." said Mini.

Brynne snorted.

"What pajamas?" asked Aiden.

Abandon conversation! screamed Aru's brain. *Abandon conversation!*

"Let's get moving," she said quickly.

Brynne grinned widely, then swung the wind mace over her head. Bright blue light burst from the weapon. A screech of metal tore through the air. Up ahead, the towering wheel slowly began to turn.

"Go!" said Brynne.

Aru ran toward the Ferris wheel—a nearly two-hundred-foot-tall contraption with rotating enclosed booths. Her nerves bubbled with tension as she dashed up the exit stairs and reached for the first inner rung. The metal bars were slick with recent rain and smelled of iron. Normally, there was no way she would agree to climb this thing, but her customized Pandava kicks came with enchanted suction cups on the bottom that promised she wouldn't fall.

The Pandavas had been preparing for this all week, and they knew what was at stake. Not a single day had passed without Aru hearing about increased demon activity in the mortal world. But no one had caught sight of the person behind the chaos: the Sleeper. Her father. Aru wished she could only see him as the monster that he was. But certain memories kept messing with her head, and sometimes she didn't picture the Sleeper as he was now, but as the dad he had been in the past. The man who had cradled her. If just for an hour.

Aru faltered, her hand slipping. A cool wind hit her face as her gaze fell to the ground more than a hundred feet below. From here, the lines of streetlights looked like faraway strings of stars and the groups of trees resembled clumps of mashed-up broccoli.

"You okay?" called Mini from the spoke below.

Steady, Shah, she told herself.

They'd trained for this.

She could *do* this.

"Nope. I'm Aru." She smiled weakly and reached for the next rung.

Another cold gust lashed her hair into her eyes.

You're climbing a Ferris wheel, thought Aru. *You know who does that? SUPERHEROES. And that guy from* The Notebook, *but mostly superheroes.*

"Super*heroines*," she whispered to herself, and reached for another bar.

Quietly, Aru started singing. Her hands ached and her teeth

were chattering. When she looked up, she realized she was eye level with towering skyscrapers.

"Are you singing?" asked Mini, who was getting closer.

Aru quickly shut up. "Nope."

"Because it sounded like *'Spider-Man, Spider-Man . . . does whatever a Spider-Man does,'* which I'm pretty sure aren't the right lyrics."

"The wind is messing with your ears."

Mini, who had always been more agile than Brynne and Aru combined, moved past her.

"I thought you were scared of heights," said Aru.

"I am!" said Mini. "I'm scared of lots of stuff . . . but exposure therapy is helping. Maybe for my eighteenth birthday we'll all go skydiving."

"We?"

"Look, Aru! First closed booth!"

About fifteen feet away, across a slender metallic bridge, was a glass-encased compartment big enough to hold two people. Its red door was shut tight, and the inside was dark. Aru flicked her wrist, and Vajra turned from a bracelet into a spear. Her lightning weapon sent a shiver of electricity up her arm.

Don't fry the mission, Aru muttered to herself.

The entire fate of the Otherworld was depending on them. Aru aimed at the door, then let her bolt loose. . . .

Bang!

The lightning hit the door's hinges. The door swung open with a screech, to reveal . . . nothing. The booth looked totally empty. Mini held up Dee Dee in its compact-mirror form. Its reflection could show the truth behind enchantments.

"No one's hiding in this one," said Mini.

Aru opened her hand and Vajra rushed back to her grip. "Onward," she said.

They slowly picked their way back across the bridge to the wheel's hub, then hauled themselves up to the arm above. As they navigated the spoke to the next booth, Aru winced at the sound of her shoe suckers squelching on the damp metal. She zapped the enclosure open, and Mini scanned it with Dee Dee.

"Empty," she said with a frown.

The third was the same: empty. In the fourth, Aru nearly leaped back as a pair of sneakers, tied to a seat belt, dropped out and dangled in her face....

But it was just a prank left over from whoever had been in there last.

The booth's door swung shut with a heavy thud.

Aru looked above them. There was only one more booth to check. Her pulse ratcheted up. She closed her eyes, imagining she could hear the hum of unspoken prophecies echoing through the night. The air felt colder, weighted down somehow.

"Last one," whispered Aru.

She rose on her tiptoes to see better, her shoe suckers letting go of the slick metal bridge. As she adjusted her grip on the lightning bolt, the Ferris wheel lurched violently, pitching her to the right. Weightlessness gripped her belly as she swung out, her hand just barely catching a metal bar while her legs dangled over a steep drop.

Mini screamed and held on for dear life.

Demons have found us! said Brynne's panicked mind message. *Be careful!*

Aru's legs dangled uselessly as she kicked for purchase. The

Ferris wheel gave another jolt, just enough to allow her to swing her legs upward and hook a bar with the insides of her knees. She twisted herself until she was crouching on top of the spoke before she shakily rose to her feet, her shoes reattaching to the metal with a *slurp!*

Aru risked one glance below... and quickly wished she hadn't.

Now the demons' attention wasn't on Aiden and Brynne—it was on *her and Mini.*

"You still with me?" Aru called to Mini. "We're running out of time!"

Mini's eyes went even rounder with fear, but she bit her lip and nodded. Aru stepped carefully down the spoke that led to the last booth, not ten feet away. It looked empty, like all the others, but the air around it seemed strangely warped. Mini snapped her compact shut.

Someone's definitely inside, said Mini's mind message. *It* has *to be the targets. Do we warn them we're gonna bust down the door?*

Aru shook her head. *Their abductor might be with them.*

On the count of three?

Aru nodded.

One... two... three!

Aru threw Vajra, and the lightning bolt sliced through the hinges before returning to her hand. The metal groaned as it burst open, revealing a mass of black vines that writhed like snakes.

"Release the clairvoyant!" shouted Mini. "Oh, and the other person! And don't try anything, because we're armed!"

Aru brandished Vajra, on the verge of declaring *And dangerous!* But the Ferris wheel teetered and she ended up yelling, "And danger-ahh!"

The writhing mass of vines went suddenly still. A green light broke through the middle of the tangle, like a hairy monster blinking open one eye.

"'*Danger-ahhh*'? Is that even a word?" demanded a haughty feminine voice.

"Are you the clairvoyant?" called Mini over the howling wind.

There was a beat of silence.

"Maybe."

Aru swayed, even as her shoe suckers gripped the bridge. She held out her arms for balance, and Vajra wrapped around her wrist in bracelet form. "Then come with us . . . if you want to live."

Another pause.

"We're fine here," said the haughty voice. "Thanks, but no thanks."

"Seriously?" said Aru. "We're here to save you! You should be *way* more grateful! How'd you even end up in a Ferris wheel?"

From deep within the vines came the sound of whispers.

"We were hiding," said a different, softer voice. "Are you Aru Shah?"

Aru paused. "Yes?"

The vines parted, revealing a pair of identical dark-skinned girls who looked about ten years old. One of them was wearing a flower-print dress with a shiny blazer over it. A small tiara nestled in her dozens of tiny braids. The other wore a striped T-shirt and dark jeans, and her braids fell straight to her shoulders. Instantly, Aru *knew* them. She'd seen them in a dream.

"You . . ." Mini breathed, before Aru had the chance to open her mouth. "I've seen you in my dreams!"

Aru whipped her head around. "Wait, *what*? You've seen them, too?"

The girl with the tiara huffed impatiently. "We paid a visit to all the Pandavas."

"We'll discuss this later," said Aru, holding out her hand. "For now, you've got to come with us."

Tiara Girl narrowed her ice-blue eyes at Aru and Mini.

"First you have to save us. That's what you saw in your vision, right, Sheela?"

"Uh-huh," said Sheela distractedly as she counted down on her fingers—*three, two, one.*

"Save you from—" started Mini, but before she could finish, a sound like a wet slap echoed on the metal rung right above their heads.

Aru reeled back. A *rakshasa* with the body of a man and the head of a bull swung upside down and let out a terrible roar. Tiara Girl coughed lightly, crossed her arms, and pointed at the demon.

"From *that*."

TWO

That Time Brynne's Shoes Got Ruined

The bull-headed rakshasa advanced on them.

"That prophecy belongs to the glorious vision of the Sleeper," he growled. "Deliver the clairvoyant to me, and I might spare your young lives."

"Might?" repeated Aru. "Not exactly a bargain."

The rakshasa laughed. "Little girl, your luck has run out. Give her to me."

Aru's gaze darted to the lightning bolt, now in the form of a sparkling bracelet. If she could just get the demon into the right position...

Aru was distracted by a moan from Sheela, who was clutching her stomach. Her ice-blue eyes began to glow. "Nikita! It's coming soon!"

Nikita grabbed her sister. "Are you sure?"

Sheela began to tremble. "Y-yes—"

"Hold it in," pleaded her twin.

The rakshasa gave a ghastly smile. "*Speak,* clairvoyant. What do you *see?*"

Panic shot through Aru. *No, no, no!* she thought. No one was supposed to hear it but them.

"Don't tell him!" Aru yelled.

Brynne's voice called out over the Pandava mind link: *BRACE YOURSELVES!*

Mini dropped into a crouch. "Hold on!" she shouted to the twins.

With a flick of her wrist, Nikita created a protective screen of black vines over the open door.

Aru's jaw nearly dropped. *What the—?*

"Aru!" yelled Mini.

A powerful gust of wind flattened Aru to the outside of the compartment. She grabbed hold of the nearest vine and gripped it hard. Out the corner of her eye, she caught the glimmer of traffic hundreds of feet beneath her and her stomach swooped. Mini, holding tight to a metal support beam, changed Dee Dee from a compact to a stick. Violet light erupted from the tip, ready to make a shield to protect them, but the rakshasa was now nowhere to be seen.

The wind subsided, and Brynne's voice sounded in Aru's head: *Did I knock him off?*

I'M *the one who almost got knocked off!* replied Aru.

I said brace yourself!

Well, I was NOT *braced!*

A low, menacing growl filled the air, and the hair on Aru's neck prickled. On the spoke she and Mini were standing on, Aru saw a series of dents appear, as if left behind by very strong invisible fingertips.

The rakshasa materialized once more, one hand clutching

the bridge as his body dangled in the air beneath them. "You will regret that."

He flung out his other hand, and an S-shaped piece of onyx came hurtling toward Aru. The weapon writhed as it flew, emitting shadows that obscured her vision. Mini swung Dee Dee over her head, and a ray of violet light cut through the blackness. As the glow washed over them, Aru caught sight of something else—tendrils of shadow. One wrapped itself around Mini's ankle while another slipped under her sneakers, trying to dislodge her shoe suckers.

"Mini, watch out!" screamed Aru.

Aru reached for Vajra, but she was too late. One moment, Mini held Dee Dee. The next, her arms pinwheeled as she fell backward, screaming.

Without hesitating, Aru dove off the metal beam she'd been standing on, cold air rushing into her lungs as she fought to breathe.

Above her, she heard the rakshasa laughing. "Good-bye, Pandavas!"

You just jumped off a Ferris wheel! screamed Aru's brain. *WHY WOULD YOU DO THAT?!*

Aru squeezed her eyes shut, then clenched her hand into a fist. "Vajra!" she called out.

Heat clambered up her arm as Vajra activated and leaped off her wrist, transforming into a crackling hoverboard made of lightning. Electricity snapped in the air as Vajra zoomed beneath her and Aru's feet touched down on it. She opened her eyes, and together, she and Vajra accelerated through the evening sky.

Mini spun fifteen feet below them, caught in a vicious

downward spiral. Her panicked thoughts blared through the mind link.

I'M SORRY I DIDN'T FLOSS MY TEETH YESTERDAY. I PROMISE I'LL NEVER FORGET AGAIN! AND I'LL EAT ALL THE VEGETABLES ON MY PLATE! PLEASE, PLEASE, PLEASE—

Look up! Aru called through their mind link.

Aru stretched out her hand, trying to grab hold of Mini's outstretched fingers, but her sister kept pinwheeling just out of her grasp. With every second that passed, the ground surged closer to meet them. The streetlights came into focus, as well as the red taillights blinking down the highway.

With one last burst of speed, Aru tilted Vajra forward, slicing through the air until the girls caught each other. Mini hugged Aru fiercely as the Vajra hoverboard shot back up toward the Ferris wheel.

"What're we going to do?" asked Mini. "You heard her! The clairvoyant can't hold in the prophecy much longer, and the whole mission will be ruined! The Council will—"

A panicked gasp choked off the rest of her words. Aru followed Mini's horrified gaze up to the rakshasa. He twisted his hand, and a giant sword manifested in the air. He grabbed it and started hacking away at Nikita's vines. The moment the rakshasa captured Sheela, the Otherworld would be doomed. And Aru refused to let that happen.

Time seemed to slow. Her senses turned diamond-sharp. She could feel the cold light of distant stars, hear the crunch as the rakshasa's sword hit metal—even smell the tinny residue in the air from the thunderstorm hours ago.

"I've got a plan," she said, thinking of Mini's illusion

abilities. "Mini, can you make the clairvoyant's booth look like all the others?"

Mini's hand tightened on her shoulder. Through the mind link, Aru sent a message to Brynne: *We're going to need one more powerful gust.*

Aru felt a gleeful answering tremor from Brynne. *Done and done.*

A flash of blue came from far below. At the same time, Aru heard Mini whisper the command "Hide" as a violet shimmer burst in the air like colored sugar crystals. The twins' battered compartment blinked back into view as the Ferris wheel began to turn—slowly, then fast and ever *faster* until its lights blurred. Even Aru couldn't tell anymore which booth held the twins. The rakshasa's grip loosened and he tumbled, his bull head knocking against the metal spokes as he dropped from one rung to the next.

"Hold tight!" Aru said to Mini.

She urged Vajra through the sky, and the lightning board took a sharp dip, careening toward the earth. Aru and Mini jumped off the hoverboard, and Brynne and Aiden raced to meet them. Brynne twirled her mace like a baton, and the Ferris wheel screeched to a halt.

The rakshasa had hit the ground near a compartment and was sitting up, shaking his head. "Feeble effort," he growled, slowly rising. "I know they're here, and you're too *late*."

Aiden brandished one of his scimitars, but Brynne held back her friend. The demon hobbled over to the booth, and when he reached it, Aru shifted Vajra into a spear and pointed it.

She waited for Mini's quick *go-ahead* nod, then took a deep breath, aimed, and let loose. Electricity rippled around the door just as the rakshasa grabbed the metal handle. He howled as a surge of lightning shot through his arm, sending him crumpling to his knees. Vajra rebounded into Aru's outstretched hand. Instantly, Aiden, Brynne, and Mini had their weapons pointed at the demon.

The rakshasa raised his head, clutching one arm to his chest. Behind him, the compartment was smoking and the door had been blown off, revealing nothing inside.

"What did you do to the seer?" he screeched as he struggled to his feet. "I *need* that prophecy!"

Once again he wielded his S-shaped stone, but Aru was quick. Her lightning bolt erupted into a crackling net and sprang toward the demon, covering him completely. The rakshasa tried to pull out his sword, but the net held him fast.

"Too bad you can't find your way," said Mini, spinning Dee Dee so that a shimmering illusion wrapped around the rakshasa.

"Too bad about that freak wind," said Brynne, waving her mace so a cold gust blew against him.

Aiden leaped forward and tossed a glowing scimitar across the cement. "Too bad about that fall," he said, grinning.

The blade tripped the rakshasa. He let out a terrifying roar right before he knocked his head on a telephone pole and promptly passed out.

Aiden, Brynne, and Mini dropped their weapons and surrounded their unconscious foe. Vajra the net gave the demon one last squeeze before boomeranging back to Aru's wrist as a bracelet.

"That. Was. *Amazing*," said Mini.

"Correction," said Brynne, pocketing her mace. "*We* are amazing." She nodded toward three other rakshasas that she and Aiden had knocked out and dragged to the side of the road.

"That too," said Aru.

"Aren't we forgetting someone important...?" said Aiden. "The *clairvoyant*? The ginormous prophecy?"

Mini pointed to a booth three spots up from the sizzling ground-level compartment. Brynne summoned a new wind that turned the Ferris wheel gently. Once it stopped, Mini waved Dee Dee and the air in front of one booth rippled and twisted, as if someone were tearing down a curtain to reveal a compartment wrapped in black vines. From within, a green light pulsed faintly.

"You guys can come out now," called Aru.

The light cut off abruptly, and the vines started to retract with a wet, suctiony sound, like tentacles letting go. Aru lifted her chin proudly. They'd *done* it. They'd rescued the twins and beaten back the rakshasas and kept the prophecy out of the Sleeper's clutches. Aru grinned, thinking of how the Council would react once they got back.

Two days before the assignment, Aru had overheard Boo loudly defending them: *The Pandavas are ready for anything! I'd stake my feathers on it!*

Don't worry, Boo, Aru thought now. *Your feathers are safe and sound.*

And when Aru caught sight of herself in a rain puddle, she thought her hair looked pretty good. So that was a plus.

Aiden moved beside her. As usual, he was reaching for his camera, Shadowfax. But this time... this time he was aiming it at... her? Aru felt like a bunch of hot needles were drifting down her skin—which sounded awful, but in reality was strangely pleasant. She tucked her hair behind her ear, adjusting her posture so that Vajra got a bit more of the spotlight, and moved in front of him.

Aiden looked up at her. "Aru?"

She ignored him.

Indifference, the *apsara* Urvashi had told her, was the key to success in all things *boy*.

"Aru," said Aiden once more.

"Hmm?" she said.

"Could you move? You're blocking my shot of the Ferris wheel."

Aru deflated instantly. Just as she slunk back, the compartment door swung open. Nikita, the stylishly dressed twin, took a dainty step forward. Sheela staggered out next, her face pale and sweaty.

"Careful, careful," said Mini. "There was a lot of swinging around.... You might feel dizzy. Or even nauseous."

Mini offered Sheela a hand, only for Nikita to step in front of her sister, swatting Mini away like a fly.

"No touchie," Nikita snapped.

Brynne's eyebrows shot up her forehead. "Uh, excuse *you*? Where's the thanks?"

Sheela groaned and clutched her stomach, swaying to a stop in front of Brynne.

"The prophecy!" said Brynne. "Is it coming now?"

"Uh, Bee, you might wanna—" started Aiden.

BLERGH! Sheela vommed all over Brynne's shoes.

Aru winced. "Aaand... too late."

Aiden snapped a picture. Brynne looked like she was going to toss the Ferris wheel into oncoming traffic.

"I *cannot* believe you just did that," Brynne said to Sheela. "Don't you know who we *are*?"

"Pandavas," said Nikita. The little girl lifted her chin and grabbed her sister's shaking hand. "And so are we."

THREE

No New Friends

Aru stared at the twins.

More Pandavas? Of course she knew two more existed. But did they have to show up *right now*?

Aru could just picture Boo fainting from dealing with all five of them at once. He'd already been complaining recently that he'd had to start taking pinion supplements because the Pandava sisters were making his feathers go gray. And he hadn't appreciated Aru pointing out that he was already gray... because he was a pigeon.

"You haven't been Claimed already, have you?" Mini asked the twins.

"Obviously not," said Brynne, blowing her shoes clean with her wind mace. "If they had, they would've been acknowledged with a physical object." She raised her weapon as an example and then turned to the twins. "Has your soul father ever made himself known to you in some way?"

Nikita and Sheela shook their heads.

Brynne lifted an eyebrow. "Then what makes you think you're Pandavas? You might just be gifted. Besides, you're *way* too young, and there's no such thing as a Pandava who can tell the future."

Nikita glowered. "There was no such thing as a *girl* Pandava, either."

Aru couldn't help herself. Under her breath she muttered, *"Zing!"*

Brynne rolled her eyes. "Honestly, Aru, they're, like . . . eight."

"Ten!" retorted Nikita.

"Gasp," said Brynne drily.

A crown of bloodred roses wove around Nikita's tiara, sprouting thorns aimed in Brynne's direction.

"Okay, okay," said Aru, stepping between them. "Let's put the spiky flowers away—"

"*Poisonous* flowers," corrected Sheela, patting the air above the blossoms' heads.

"And you're letting them get *that* close to your skin?" said Mini. "But you could—"

"At this point we could *all* die," interrupted Aiden. "Maybe they're Pandavas, maybe they're not—the Council will reveal the truth. The big question is: What are we going to do about these guys?" He swung his scimitar to indicate the four rakshasas passed out around them.

Aru felt a knot form in her heart. Rakshasas could absorb experiences even while in an unconscious state. If these were allowed to go free, important information could get back to the Sleeper. The last thing Aru wanted was for their enemy to find out that two potential new Pandavas had joined their team. Especially since one of them knew a prophecy about him.

Another cold wind brushed against her skin, and Aru shivered as she looked around. It was fully dark now. If the Sleeper was expecting his soldiers back, he would've noticed they'd been gone too long.

He might even send more.

They had to move. And *fast.*

"We should bring the rakshasas to the Court of the Sky," said Aru. "Let the Council deal with them."

"Bring enemies into our territory?" said Brynne. "No way, Shah!"

"But they know too much," said Mini, chewing her lip.

Brynne grumbled. Which was Brynne for *All right, fine.*

"True," said Aiden. "But even if we want to bring them back, how do we do that? The Night Bazaar has serious safety restrictions. The twins are under twelve, so they can't legally travel through a portal without clearance from the Council. Which leaves a magical dead zone as our only option to access the Otherworld. And who knows how far away one of those is—"

"One point one five kilometers," said Brynne, holding up two fingers. Being the daughter of the god of the wind meant that she could always call up exact coordinates when they needed them. "Which is easily a ten-minute walk."

"Magical *dead zone,*" repeated Aiden, massaging his temples. "That means Vajra won't work there. Neither will Dee Dee or Gogo. Brynne is strong, but it's not like she can carry four fully grown rakshasas by herself."

"Challenge accepted," said Brynne, rolling up her sleeves.

"Challenge *not* accepted!" said Mini. "You could strain yourself, and there's no way to secure them."

They stared at the rakshasas for a moment, and then Sheela cleared her throat and poked her twin in the arm.

"*Fine,*" said Nikita dramatically. "I guess."

Sheela beamed.

"I'll take it from here," said Nikita, stepping forward.

She stretched out her hand and green light radiated from her fingertips. The sidewalk trembled as weeds between the cracks grew taller, multiplied, and spread outward until they had formed four rectangular cushions on the ground. Fluffy silver dandelions—or "wishing weeds," as Aru liked to call them—sprang free from the dirt, quadrupled in size, and rolled under the cushions to form wheels. Vines snaked out from Nikita's tiara and grew several feet long before they snapped off and wound around each of the rakshasas, binding them tight. Then the vines dragged the unconscious bodies onto the trolleys. Lastly, all four of Nikita's trolleys grew sturdy pulling-ropes that bloomed with small pink and white flowers.

"Voilà," said Nikita smugly. "Transportation, protection, and, naturally, a touch of beauty."

Ten minutes later, Aru found herself deeply concerned for the citizens of Atlanta. Not one person seemed to bat an eyelash at the four kids lugging masses of human-shaped vines through the streets of downtown.

"Is anyone else alarmed that *no one* is alarmed?" asked Aru.

Brynne scoffed. "I live in New York. Trust me, this is nothing."

"Maybe they can't see us?" asked Mini. "It *is* nighttime."

"Or they're choosing not to," said Aiden. "It would mess up their idea of reality, so they just ignore it."

As they crossed a street corner where a bunch of bikers revved their engines, Aru decided to test Mini's theory. She called out, "Nice ride! I've got a demon!"

"Don't we all!" hollered one guy with an impressive neon-green mustache. "Have a good one!" And he zoomed off.

Aru turned, ready to make a joke, when she saw the twins huddled together.

"Honestly, Nikki, it's fine," whispered Sheela.

"No, it's *not* fine!" said Nikita. "We've wanted this for so long, and it just—"

Abruptly, she got quiet. When Nikita raised her voice, the red roses of her crown curled into tight buds, the way someone presses their mouth closed when they've said something they didn't want to.

Aru looked from Brynne to Mini and Aiden. For a moment they all stopped hauling the rakshasas.

"Sheela, are you still feeling sick?" asked Mini gently, holding out her hand.

Sheela looked up at Mini, shock giving way to a surprised smile. Cautiously, Sheela raised her own hand, but Nikita stepped in front of her twin.

"I can take care of her," snapped Nikita.

"But, Nikki—" Sheela started.

"No!" said her twin.

"You know, I get the whole *no new friends* policy, but we're actually on your side," said Aru.

Sheela smiled up at her, but Nikita scowled.

"I've heard that before," she said.

Walking a few paces ahead of them, Brynne pointed across the street to a large concrete overpass. "The entrance to the dead zone is over there, in the shadows."

Aru eyed the dark area beneath the bridge. In the glare of a nearby streetlight, she could see that discarded blue plastic containers and torn sleeping bags littered the ground in front of it.

"Um, has anyone ever *been* to a magical dead zone before?" asked Mini.

"I have," said Aiden. "Once."

"I saw the dead zone in your dream," said Sheela quietly.

"You've seen our dreams?" asked Aru, panicking.

For a moment, she wondered if the twins knew about her constant nightmare . . . the one where she betrayed everyone she loved, just as the Sleeper had predicted.

But Sheela shook her head. "Don't worry, we won't tell anyone about how, in your dreams, Aiden—"

NOPE! blared an alarm in Aru's head. *NOPE, NOPE, NOPE!*

"Didn't your parents teach you better manners?" demanded Brynne. "That's *so* rude."

Sheela clammed up. Her chin fell. "Our parents are—"

But Nikita shot her a silencing look, and before Aru could ask, Aiden gestured them forward.

"Let's cross now, while we can."

Pulling the rakshasa wagons behind them, they jogged across the road and stopped in a patch of yellow light cast by the streetlamp. The light ended abruptly five feet away from the shadow of the overpass, as if someone had cut it with a knife. Overhead, the concrete bridge trembled from the rush of cars. The humid air smelled . . . unstirred, as if it had been left alone too long. Usually, the air near a magic portal was warped in a certain way, or there was a thrumming sensation, as if someone had plucked a violin string and the ripples of sound never quite died. Aru detected none of that.

Vajra wriggled uncomfortably on her wrist.

"We'll be in the Otherworld soon," Aru assured her lightning bolt.

Nikita pointed at the garland rope Brynne was pulling. "Don't break it, 'cause I won't be able to fix it once we go through."

Aru looked over her shoulder at the vine-wrapped conked-out demon on her trolley. A tendril of fear wound through her. How much longer would the rakshasas stay unconscious?

As the group walked forward, the long shadow of the overpass transformed. It scrunched up, turned into a square, and then peeled itself off the ground and became a sharply defined door.

Beside Aru, Sheela's eyes gave off a faint, icy glow. "We should go through," the twin said. Her voice sounded funny, as if a second voice had been layered on top of it. *"Now."*

FOUR

Magical Dead Zone

The magical dead zone was not what Aru expected.

"It looks kinda like the Night Bazaar," said Brynne.

Aru saw what she meant. Once they walked through the shadow door beneath the underpass, they stepped into a strange parallel-universe version of the Otherworld... but only if that parallel universe was like one of those depressing postapocalyptic movies where everything was awful. Aru glanced up, half expecting to see the Night Bazaar's split sky showing both the sun and the moon. Instead, there stretched only gray twilight that promised neither stars nor the blush rays of dawn. It made Aru feel cold.

People in drab clothing milled about the dead-zone market. Aru saw a few with feathers showing at their collars, and others with sawed-down horns on their head, as if they were trying to hide their true identities. They all had an air of unmistakable sadness about them.

Ash-colored stalls offering expired magical fruit hobbled feebly through the crowd, while merchants wound their way in between, hawking wares like cloudy vials of discount dreams.

In the walls surrounding the market were dozens of doors, all squat and shabby-looking except for one: at the far end of the courtyard loomed a steel exit fifty feet high. At least a hundred people were queued up before it.

"That's the door to the Otherworld," said Aiden. "It recognizes who can access the other side."

The Pandavas made their way closer. In front of the door was a low glass platform roughly the size of a dining room table. One by one, the people seeking to go through the door would step onto the rectangle. It would glow red, and the person would walk off, looking more dejected than before.

Aiden frowned. "The door knows they're exiles."

Off to the side of the platform, a light-skinned man dressed in a bone-white suit held up a roll of parchment and shouted to the crowd: "Step right up, hopefuls, and add your name to the contract! You've heard the rumors—war is coming! The devas need *you!*" He made a sweeping gesture at the line of people standing in front of the door. "Just one year of your life! Think about it! Fight for the devas and we may all earn the chance to return *home!*"

Beside Aru, Aiden scowled. "What a scam," he muttered. "These people don't need false promises."

"You can get kicked out of the Otherworld?" asked Nikita, alarmed. "For what?"

"Some break the laws of secrecy. Some get involved with the wrong crowd." Aiden took a breath, glancing down at his feet for a moment. "Some just fall in love with the wrong people."

Aru looked at him sharply. He was talking about his mom, Malini. Once, she'd been a famous apsara, but when she chose to marry a mortal, she was forced to give up any claim to the magical world. Last year, she and Aiden's dad had gotten divorced, and Aru remembered how he hated that his mom had been forced to sacrifice everything for a love that hadn't lasted.

Beside him, Brynne wrapped her arm around his shoulder and squeezed so tight that Aiden wheezed a little. "C'mon," she said, firm but gentle. "We gotta go back and get in line."

Aru hesitated a moment, staring at the growing number of people waiting for their turn. "If they know they can't get in," she asked, "why do they bother trying?"

A corner of Aiden's mouth lifted in a half smile. "Everyone needs hope."

They scooted back across the market as quickly as they could with the conked-out rakshasas in tow. It wasn't easy to lug them over the uneven dirt floor, especially among so many people. At least no one was paying attention to their strange parade. Everybody had their own baggage—physical and psychological—to deal with.

At last the five Pandava sisters and Aiden reached the end of the line. As they stood there, Sheela swayed nervously, her irises flickering from ice blue to the color of frost. The back of Aru's neck prickled as she sensed a sudden rush of magic coiling through the air around them. How could that be, in a magical dead zone? She knew the prophecy inside Sheela was powerful, but this felt like something else—like standing beside a pent-up tempest.

"Sheela!" cried Nikita, shaking her sister.

The powerful draft of magic disappeared, as if someone had stuffed it in a jar and shoved a lid on top. Aru looked around nervously. The once-empty eyes of the exiled Otherworld members were now alert, turned on Sheela and narrowing in suspicion.

"We need to get out of here soon," hissed Aru. The line was moving quickly, but definitely not fast enough for her taste.

Mini checked her rakshasa's pulse. "Still out cold, but not dead," she announced.

What if the demons wake up before the door opens? Aru wondered, panicking.

While they waited, Aiden snapped photos of the people in line and the dead zone around them.

"Do you *mind*?" asked an annoyed couple a few paces ahead. "What're you doing?"

Aiden lowered his camera, fiddling with the settings. "I'm working on a portrait series capturing universal injustice."

The couple stared at him, then adjusted their posture.

"Well, in that case . . ."

"I'm definitely injusticed!" shouted another person in line. "Take my picture!"

Someone else hollered: "Will this go on Instagram?"

As Aiden quickly managed his small crowd, Sheela slumped against her twin.

"Hold on. We're almost there . . ." Nikita coaxed her.

Soon, there was only one person ahead of them. Like all who had gone before him, he too was denied entry.

Now it was the Pandavas' turn. Aru yanked on her pull rope only to hear a *rrrrip*. She looked back to see that the vine binding the rakshasa had gone slack.

"The plants are losing their magic!" said Mini.

At once, all the dandelion wheels went flat. Brynne gave up

on her cart and started rolling her unconscious rakshasa's body forward.

"We just have to get them onto the platform," urged Aiden.

"All of them at once?" asked Aru. "They won't fit!"

Brynne pushed her prisoner over and lifted him onto the low surface. "I'll . . . pretend . . . they're . . . demon . . . pancakes!" she said between heaves.

She and Aiden managed to stack the other three rakshasas on top of the first and wrap them all with the strongest remaining vines. They looked like the most terrible Christmas present ever.

"We'll have to be careful when we pull them through the door, but the vines should hold," said Brynne. Then she climbed the demon pile and put her hands on her hips.

Aru really wished she'd yell out *ARE YOU NOT ENTERTAINED?*

Alas, not the time.

The other Pandavas and Aiden moved back, and a yellow glow lit up the glass beneath the demons. A golden walkway shot out from the platform to the steel door not twenty feet away. Then a green light started to blink over the entrance to the Otherworld, inviting them to open the door and go through.

"Us next!" yelled Aiden. "Hurry!"

Brynne jumped off and hauled the vines, inching the pile of demons down the path while the rest of the crew hopped onto the platform. The dais glowed yellow again, granting them entrance. They leaped onto the walkway. Mini, Aru, and Aiden grabbed one vine while Brynne took hold of the other. The twins followed, Nikita propping up her nearly catatonic sister.

"Pull!" said Aiden, tugging with all his might.

Aru saw that their vine was starting to fray. She thought that maybe, if they just moved faster, they'd be safe.

A loud shout from behind caught her attention.

"The door!" yelled someone in the crowd. "It's going to open!"

A knot of exiles, their eyes huge, rushed toward the Pandavas. The desperate hopefuls tried to step onto the walkway; electric shocks burst from its sides, keeping the trespassers at bay.

But that didn't stop the crowd from grabbing at whatever they could. Aru was yanked back as someone caught hold of her shirtsleeve. She jerked up her elbow, throwing off the stranger, only for the movement to snap the vine she was holding in half.

Aiden dropped his own plant and ran behind the demons to push them instead. "The door isn't going to let you in!" Brynne shouted to the crowd. "Stay back!"

"How do you know?" demanded a pale-skinned woman with catlike eyes. "Don't we deserve a chance to return home?"

Another exile snatched at Aru's pant leg, sending her sprawling onto the ground. Aru's head thudded on the path. She turned to the right and came face-to-face with an unconscious rakshasa.

Only... he wasn't unconscious anymore.

An angry orange eye blinked open and narrowed at her.

The stack of demons began to stir. Magical vines might have been enough to bind them... but ordinary ones? They wouldn't hold for long. Instinctively, Aru called for Vajra, but the bolt didn't respond. It lay curled around her wrist as a dull bracelet, as if it had fallen asleep and couldn't hear her.

The door handle was now within grasping distance. All the Pandavas had to do was get inside and their powers would be restored and the prophecy would be safe.

But the moment Aru lunged for it, an ear-piercing scream stayed her hand.

"Demons!" cried someone in the crowd.

With a loud roar, two of the rakshasas sprang free of their bindings.

The mob scattered.

"Did you really think you could capture us, little ones?" snarled the first rakshasa. He pulled a blade from his wrist cuff and spun it in his hand. He glowered at the Otherworld entrance. "And drag us into that hateful place?"

"Hand over the girl with the prophecy," said the second.

"Never!" growled Brynne.

Aru shoved Nikita—who was still clutching her sister—behind her, toward the door. *"Go through as fast as you can!"* she yelled.

Nikita nodded and Aiden extended a hand to the twins so he could pull them through. Nikita tried to grab hold, but Sheela started to shake, and then she crumpled to the ground, her eyes burning bright. In an oddly layered voice, as if at once terribly old and incredibly young, she began to speak:

"THE SCORNED POWERS ARE ON THE RISE,
TO CLAIM THEIR STOLEN IMMORTAL PRIZE—"

The back of Aru's neck prickled again.

"She's speaking! Get her!" hollered the first rakshasa.

Aru took a few steps forward, ready to charge headfirst at the demons, but Brynne caught her wrist. Brynne's gaze fell to the broken vines on the ground. Aru didn't have to read her mind to know what to do. She and Mini picked up one end of a vine, Brynne grabbed the other end, and they rushed the demons, tripping them.

As the rakshasas scrambled to their feet, Mini whipped out her danda compact. Its magic was inactive, but it was still a mirror. She angled it so light reflected straight into the demons' eyes.

"Now!" yelled Aiden.

He took Nikita in one arm and grasped the door handle. Brynne scooped Sheela off the ground, and Aru grabbed Mini's hand. They raced to the door, the earth vibrating beneath their shoes.

Just outside the door, Sheela let out a huge gasp. Beams of light erupted around her, lifting her out of Brynne's arms.

"I'm losing her!" cried Brynne.

Sheela hovered in the air before the entrance to the Otherworld, while the demons pressed as close as they could.

"Speak, child!" demanded the rakshasas. *"Speak the future!"*

Sheela's head lolled back:

"THE SCORNED POWERS ARE ON THE RISE,
TO CLAIM THEIR STOLEN IMMORTAL PRIZE. . . ."

"We've got to pull her inside!" said Aru.

Aiden and Nikita held the door open while Brynne, Mini, and Aru formed a chain. Aru reached up and grabbed hold of Sheela's foot, bringing her down until Mini's arms could wrap around her waist. Then Brynne heaved, tugging the four of them into the Night Bazaar. . . .

The rakshasas tried to follow, but Aiden started pushing the heavy door closed from the other side while Mini, with magic once again at her disposal, cast a force field to block the remaining open space. Vajra flickered into action and Mini lowered the shield just enough for Aru to throw her bolt like a spear. It hit one of the demons squarely in the chest and knocked him backward.

But it wasn't enough.

In a voice that sent shivers down Aru's spine, Sheela belted out the whole of her prophecy:

"THE SCORNED POWERS ARE ON THE RISE,
TO CLAIM THEIR STOLEN IMMORTAL PRIZE.
ONE SISTER SHALL TURN OUT NOT TO BE TRUE.
WITH A SINGLE CHOICE,
THE WORLD SHALL RECEIVE ITS DUE.
ONE TREASURE IS FALSE, AND ONE TREASURE IS LOST,
BUT THE TREE AT THE HEART IS THE ONLY TRUE COST.
NO WAR CAN BE WON WITHOUT FINDING THAT ROOT;
NO VICTORY HAD WITHOUT THE YIELD OF ITS FRUIT.
IN FIVE DAYS THE TREASURE WILL BLOOM AND FADE,
AND ALL THAT WAS WON COULD SOON BE UNMADE."

Vajra bounded into Aru's outstretched hand. The steel door shut heavily. . . .

But not quite fast enough.

The last thing she saw was the wide smile of the rakshasa as he sneered, "Thank you, Pandavas," and leaped into the air.

FIVE

Worse Than Being Sent to the Principal's Office

Aru felt time slow around her.

They'd failed.

The Council of Guardians had been clear about the power of the prophecy. The Pandavas' only job had been to make sure the Sleeper's soldiers didn't hear it, and they'd failed. Aru felt like someone had taken a bite out of her soul.

Something bright glinted from the corner of her vision, and she noticed the shoelaces of her customized sneakers sparkling. Great. The Council had tracked them, and now someone was on their way to meet them.

"What are we going to do?" moaned Mini, pacing in a tight circle.

"This isn't totally our fault," said Brynne, pointing at Sheela. "Why couldn't you just *hold it in*?"

Sheela had fallen to the floor once she'd delivered the prophecy. Nikita propped her up, asking, "Are you okay?"

Sheela looked dazed for a moment before yawning loudly and beaming at everyone. "I feel much better!"

"Better?" Brynne exploded. "Do you know what's just happened?"

"Easy, Brynne," said Aiden, laying a hand on her arm.

Sheela blinked, tilting her head. "No?"

"The *prophecy*?" ground out Brynne.

"Oh, right!" said Sheela, smiling. "I displaced cosmic energy from within myself and now it's balanced again! Sometimes knowing the future is like eating way too much food—it gives you a stomachache and you need to lie down. Good job, me."

"No," said Brynne. "*Bad* job—"

Sheela looked confused.

"She couldn't help it!" snapped Nikita, rushing to help her sister stand. "Her prophecies are always like that."

"As a Pandava, you should be able to control yourself," said Brynne, crossing her arms. "Or maybe you're not one."

Nikita narrowed her eyes. "What did you say?"

"Seemed kinda loud to me," said Sheela, shrugging. But if she was as offended as her sister, it didn't show.

"Welp," said Aiden, pinching the bridge of his nose. "She went there."

Mini edged closer to Aru. "Aru . . . *do* something."

Nikita extended her wrist. Inky vines shot out, wrapping around Brynne's ankles and pulling her to the ground.

"You little—" Brynne swung her mace and a gust of wind sent Nikita flying backward.

"Yeah, no," said Aru, stepping away.

Nikita ran back and got too close to Brynne. Maybe she was trying to reach for the mace, or maybe she just tripped. But their fingers touched, and Aru felt a change in the air—a crackling like radio static deep within her bones. The skies parted above them. Two beams of light—one green and one silver—shot down from the skies . . . and lifted the twins off the ground.

Far above, Aru caught the silhouette of two horse-faced gods leaning out of the clouds as if they were looking down on the Pandavas from behind a huge bowl of sunshine. Nikita, in the beam of green light, floated toward the god on the left, who was surrounded by the glow of sunrise: rose-quartz pinks and dewy cream, and all the glittering potential of a new day. Sheela, in the beam of silver light, rose toward the god on the right, who was surrounded by the fire of sunset: scarlet and ruby-dark, and just beneath all that red . . . the mysterious promises of stars and nighttime.

Their soul fathers were none other than the Ashvin twins. Which could only mean that they were the reincarnations of Nakula and Sahadeva, the brothers famous for their beauty, archery and equestrian skills, and wisdom.

Aru had heard that the Ashvin twins were the physicians of the gods. Hanuman, who was a demigod and a patron of wrestling, often stopped by the Ashvins' medical offices to get treatment for his lower-back pain.

You only get one body, he would say solemnly. *You must take care of it.*

Do you really only get the one? Aru once asked him. *I mean, honestly, how many times has Arjuna been reincarnated now? That's at least, like, five bodies.*

Hanuman had not been amused.

Slowly, the twins drifted back to the ground. Unlike Mini, Brynne, and Aru, neither had been gifted with a weapon. But something small and penny-size glowed at the base of their throats. On Nikita, the object now embedded in her skin was a green heart. On Sheela, it was a silver star.

Nikita walked—no, *strutted*—toward Brynne.

"I forgive you," she said.

"I didn't apologize," growled Brynne.

"Must've been hard to recognize me as another Pandava, considering my uniform," said Nikita.

She touched her dress. Flowering jasmine branches wrapped their way around the cloth, creating a kind of hoop skirt before extending down into a glamorous train. A high collar made of frothy-looking pink azaleas grew around her neck. She cast a withering look at Aru, Mini, and Brynne.

Aru gazed down at her own outfit: dark jeans and a long-sleeved green tee with the word NOPE stamped across it. Mini was dressed in an all-black getup ("It hides dirt better!" Mini had said) and Brynne wore a blue romper that kinda looked like an apron, with the word HANGRY stitched across it.

"I'm sure your clothes repel enemies," said Sheela kindly.

"Thanks," said Aru drily. "If only that didn't include the entire male population."

Sheela lightly touched the star at her neck. She seemed completely unfazed by her Claiming, which made sense. She must have already known, Aru guessed. Sheela *was* able to tell the future, after all.

Did the clairvoyant understand the words she'd uttered? The Pandavas might have failed at preventing the Sleeper's soldiers from hearing the prophecy, but if Aru and her friends could decipher all its mumbo jumbo, they would totally have an advantage over the Sleeper.

And yet, one part of the prophecy pricked at Aru's brain like a thorn.

One sister shall turn out not to be true.

With a single choice the world shall receive its due.

Which sister? What did it mean? And how come, when Sheela had said it, her eyes hadn't left Aru's face... as if she'd seen something inside her? Something dangerous.

"Sheela, do you remember what you said?" asked Aru.

"Of course I do," said Sheela dreamily.

"You mentioned something about a sister who wouldn't be true," said Aru. "What... what was that about?"

Sheela sighed, looking up at the sky, and in her faraway voice said, "I don't know?" She twirled a little on the spot. "That's just how the future is. It has a funny way of making itself true. I see stuff that other people can't see yet."

"Like what?" asked Mini.

"Well, right now I see an angry pigeon?"

"Boo!" shouted Aiden, waving his arms.

"I don't think that will scare him off," said Sheela solemnly. "Pigeons are kinda fearless."

"That's his name," said Aiden.

"Fearless the Pigeon?" asked Sheela.

Nikita shuddered. "Pigeons are repulsive."

From the folds of twilight-colored clouds, Boo dove toward them, squawking loudly before alighting on his favorite perch: Aru's head.

"You're late!" he squawked, and pecked her ear. "Look at all the feathers I lost waiting for you!"

"Are you taking your supplements?" asked Mini, concerned.

"Honestly, I think it's all in your imagination," said Brynne.

"One, yes. Two, no. Also, *rude.* And three—" Boo stopped mid-rant.

Aru couldn't see what he was looking at, but she felt his clawed feet reposition in the direction of the twins.

"Oh gods . . . The targets were *Pandavas*? Am I to have *no* rest?"

As Aru had predicted, Boo tumbled over in a faint. She only just managed to catch him before he hit the ground. He stirred weakly in her hands, moaning something about "the cruel ineffable twists of fate" and "three was bad enough."

"Can I pet him?" asked Sheela.

"I am not a *pet*!" squawked Boo.

"Nice birdie . . ." cooed Sheela, reaching out.

Boo snapped at her fingers, then righted himself. "Despite this latest *development*," he said, eyeing the twins, "I'm glad you're here." He puffed up his feathers. "I trust your mission went exactly as planned, which is what I told the rest of the Council—"

"Actually, um, Boo . . ." started Aru.

"We're definitely in for it now." Brynne groaned and crossed her arms. "But it's not our fault!"

"Well, I don't know about that," hedged Mini. "But we really did try."

"In for what? Whose fault?" asked Boo, alarmed. "You *did* get the prophecy, didn't you?"

Aru winced. "Yes, but—"

A thundering voice crackled through the heavens like the loudspeakers at school:

"ATTENTION, ATTENTION. URGENT INSTRUCTION FOR THE PANDAVAS: REPORT TO THE GATE OF AMARAVATI IMMEDIATELY."

"Amaravati?" echoed Aiden, looking stricken.

"Who's that?" asked Nikita.

"It's not a person," said Mini, her face paling. "It's a city."

Vajra buzzed excitedly against Aru's wrist. No doubt the lightning bolt missed its home. The famous heavenly city was the court of the apsaras and, of course, Indra, the god of thunder and lightning and Aru's soul dad.

But none of the Pandavas' soul fathers were allowed to interfere in their lives, so what did it mean that they were being called to Indra's court? There were only two things that would draw the attention of the heavens—either something truly wonderful, or something downright awful.

And Aru had a sinking feeling she knew which it was.

SIX

Password! But Make It Fash-un

You *WHAT?!* Boo had shrieked.

Aru winced at the memory as she sat on the outskirts of the Night Bazaar. She was reliving the terrible conversation they'd just had with their mentor twenty minutes ago. The moment they told him they'd failed to prevent the Sleeper from learning the prophecy, Boo had taken this information back to the Council to "triage."

Whatever that meant.

In Aru's head, it sounded like adult-speak for *You really screwed up.*

She sank a little lower in her seat. The five Pandava sisters and Aiden were squished on a bench atop a grassy hill that looked over the glittering gem of the Night Bazaar. To the right of the market was a wall of entrance portals. To its left loomed the moonlit arches of the *chakora* forest. Boo had flown through one of those arches to get to the heavens.

Aru could barely bring herself to look at the Otherworld. Guilt weighed heavily on her, and she knew she wasn't the only one feeling that way. Brynne was tight-lipped and stony-faced.

Mini looked close to weeping. And Aiden was so out of it he wasn't even fiddling with his camera.

Aru sighed. Almost two years ago, the Sleeper had gotten away because of her, and now, after their latest fiasco, the Otherworld was even more at risk.

Aru felt the threat of war all around them like the atmosphere before a thunderstorm. Which only made her feel guiltier because, despite everything, she still felt a rebellious streak of *doubt*. It had started gnawing at her after they defeated Lady M in the Ocean of Milk not more than a year ago. Lady M had stolen the god of love's bow and arrow as part of a wicked plan to turn people into Heartless zombies, but she'd done it because the devas had disgraced her. Lady M had told Aru that to many people the Sleeper wasn't a monster—he was a hero.

The whole ordeal had jumbled everything Aru thought she knew about good and evil. Sometimes it kept her up at night, wondering about whether she was doing the right thing by fighting on behalf of the devas. Were they really the "good side"?

Ugh. She needed a nap.

You don't deserve a nap! hissed a corner of her brain.

Aru was on the verge of putting her head in her hands when she heard someone softly ask, "Does the Otherworld always look like this?"

Aru turned sharply to her left. She'd been so lost in her thoughts, she'd almost forgotten that the twins were sitting next to her. Sheela stared out at the great expanse of tents that had been magically decorated for the holiday of Holi. Clusters of marigolds spangled the air. Fireflies darted among the floating orange blossoms like little living stars. In the market proper, the tents' usual colorful ribbons had been replaced with a mirrorlike silk that reflected the rainbow-painted floor, the garlands of spring flowers, and strings of twinkling lights, turning the whole bazaar into a dizzying array of sunny yellows, fiery reds, and sapphire blues.

The sight of it made her heart ache.

All this . . . All of it could be destroyed because they'd failed.

"Kinda?" Aru said. "But right now it's decorated extra special for Holi."

Her mention of Holi momentarily perked up the others.

Holi was Aru's favorite Hindu holiday. Depending on who you asked in India, the festival was about love or springtime . . . or both. But the best part about it? *COLOR PARTY!* Every year, the Night Bazaar went *wild*. Everybody showed up wearing white and threw fistfuls of different-colored powders at one another while the apsaras danced overhead and the *gandharva* musicians played a hundred songs on their enchanted instruments.

But because of the war threat, this year the celebrations would be different.

They might even be cancelled entirely.

"Holi is the best. Holiday. Ever. *Period,*" said Brynne. "Last year, I was so covered in color that I sneezed blue for, like, a week. That's got to be a world record."

"Well, I looked like a tie-dyed Oompa-Loompa for ten days," said Aru smugly.

Mini shuddered. "*I* almost got stampeded."

"It's not a competition." Aiden sighed.

"Don't be jealous, Wifey," said Aru.

Nikita frowned. *"Wifey?"*

"You can call him that too, you know," said Aru, glad to be distracted from her thoughts.

"Please don't," said Aiden.

"Or Ammamma," added Brynne with an almost smile. "Aiden is a serious grandma. Always has candies in his purse—"

"Satchel!" corrected Aiden.

"Complains about 'kids these days'—"

Aiden grumbled. "I just think it's kinda sad how our generation—"

"And he gets tired at, like, seven o'clock."

"That was *one* time!" protested Aiden. "And you were tired, too!"

"But why *Wifey*?" asked Nikita.

Aru was about to answer when Sheela spoke up.

"Once upon a time," she said, in her singsong voice, "Aiden's soul lived within a beautiful and powerful princess who married all five Pandava brothers—which was sometimes strange, but mostly okay, because she got five times the presents on her birthday and anniversary. The only sad thing was that she loved one brother more than all the rest."

Sheela didn't bother to look at them until she finished, and when she did, her gaze went straight to Aiden. Her eyes flashed silver for a moment, like someone had flipped a quarter in a beam of light. And then she tilted her head. "Even lifetimes later?" she asked, as if to herself.

Aiden frowned. "What are you talking about?"

But Sheela ignored the question, turning her attention instead to the leaves on the moonlit branches.

Boo came soaring out of the trees. Normally, he would've alighted on Aru's head. Or Mini's shoulder. But this time, he just hovered in the air.

"Come along, children," he intoned. "We have an appointment."

Mini piped up first. "With Hanuman and Urvashi?"

"No," said Boo in a clipped voice. "They've left."

"What? Why?" asked Brynne.

Boo quoted the last lines of the prophecy: *"But the tree at the heart is the only true cost. No war can be won without finding that root; no victory had without the yield of its fruit. In five days the treasure will bloom and fade, and all that was won could soon be unmade."*

Aru was glad he left out the part about the untrue sister and the whole world receiving "its due" from a single choice.

"The Council believes the prophecy means that the nectar of immortality is at risk, and so they have left for Lanka—"

"The city of gold?" asked Aiden, awed.

"The very same," said Boo. "Deep in the city lies the labyrinth containing the nectar of immortality. The rest of the Council is conferring with Lord Kubera to make sure it is well protected, especially over the next five days."

"Are the Guardians mad at us?" asked Mini, in a small voice.

At this, Boo finally relented. With a sigh, he swooped down and alighted on Mini's head.

"No one is mad at you," he said.

Mini sniffed. "You're just..."

Oh no, thought Aru. *Mini's least favorite word.*

"Disappointed?" Brynne guessed.

Boo looked at all of them and then shook his head. "Scared," he said. "We are too close to war.... We cannot make such mistakes. And you... You should have been able to handle this. That you couldn't is not your fault, but ours. Now come. We have a meeting with a crisis manager to figure out what must be done about you."

"All of us?" asked Nikita.

It was the first time she'd spoken up. She stood slightly in front of Sheela, as if ready to shield her at any moment.

"Yes," said Boo, a touch more gently. "All of you."

For the first time, Aru saw fear flash over Nikita's face.

"It'll be fine," said Mini. "Trust us."

Nikita's expression hardened into a scowl. "No chance of that."

Boo flew into the chakora forest, urging the Pandavas to follow. Aru trudged behind the others. *Crisis manager?* That sounded... awful. And Hanuman and Urvashi had flat-out left? Shame roiled through Aru's belly, and she kicked at the moonlit ground. Usually, walking through the chakora forest relaxed her. It was the home of the magical birds who fed on moonlight. But now even the moonbeams seemed harsh, casting a silvery glow that seemed to illuminate Aru's every thought about all the ways they'd failed.

Boo led them through a tunnel that carved through a hill and opened up into a chamber that looked like a fancy hotel lobby with marble floors and warm lighting. Except instead of an elevator bank there was an intricate golden gate, the top of which seemed to disappear into a ceiling of low-hanging clouds. Its metal railings were bent into what resembled a grinning mouth.

"Password?" it prompted.

The gate's voice reminded Aru of her school's guidance counselor. A weird note of sweetness that *never* changed. Seriously. That lady could be politely delighted about the apocalypse.

"Why does it need a password when we were asked to show up here?" demanded Brynne. "Shouldn't it just *know* who we are?"

"You can never be too careful," said Boo.

Mini checked her pockets. "Are we supposed to have a password? I don't have one! Did I miss a handout? Or a homework assignment—?"

Aru gripped her sister's shoulders. *"Breathe, Mini."*

Boo circled overhead. "Now, what was it again...? Something about the heavens' current fascination... Oh yes!"

"That's not the password," said the gate smugly.

"I know that—"

"That's not it, either," sang the gate.

"I will melt you into a thumbtack!" threatened the pigeon.

"Still not *iiiiit,*" crowed the gate.

"Boo, just say it!" cried Aru.

"ATHLEISURE!"

The gate parted, and bright sunlight spilled out.

SEVEN

Bro, Do You Even Lift?

Aru held her breath as that familiar weightless sensation of the portals swept through her. Bright light washed over her face, and when it finally cleared, Aru stumbled forward, still determined to keep her eyes shut. They were going to *Amaravati,* the capital of the heavens! It was going to be drenched in terrible divine light, and what if Aru found herself standing in a beautiful arena surrounded by huge, angry gods and—?

"Gross!" said Nikita.

Wait, what?

Aru opened her eyes.

Her first glimpse of heaven wasn't the awe-inspiring, *fall-to-your-knees-puny-mortal* landscape at all... but the inside of an office. She blinked, staring around her. It looked like an administrative building. No windows, just thick walls made of graying storm clouds, and fifty or so desks scattered about. Down one of the halls, Aru could hear raucous shouting.

"This can't be Amaravati!" said Aru.

Aiden coughed, pointing up at the sign splayed on a wall right above them.

MARUTS OFFICES
PROTECTIVE SERVICES AND
STORM POLICE OF AMARAVATI

"Police?" squeaked Mini. "They brought us straight to the *police station*? Do we need a lawyer? Are we going to be allowed a phone call? Should I call my mom?"

Aru patted her pocket reassuringly. Vajra had dived inside to hide and was currently a trembling ball of lightning. Beside her, Brynne had started to pace, and Aiden kept twisting the lens off Shadowfax.

"Now, children," said Boo, even as he fluttered anxiously above their heads. "I know that meeting with the crisis manager might be stressful, but— Hey! Come back here!"

Sheela and Nikita had started backing toward the portal, their hands tightly entwined. Sheela's normally serene—if not a little out-of-it—disposition had been replaced with fear. And Nikita seemed no better. Her flower crown looked ten times sharper, with an added layer of wicked black thorns, and her eyes kept darting around the room.

"Whoa, what's wrong?" asked Aru.

"Protective services?" said Nikita. "We don't need them! We don't want to go back—"

"Go back where?" asked Mini.

"We're Pandavas now," said Nikita sharply. "You can't just send us back!"

"No one's sending you anywhere," said Aiden gently. "Why don't you explain what you're talking about . . . ?"

Just then, on one of the desks, a voice crackled from a little monitor that was shaped like a storm cloud.

Scrrritch. "Uh, hey, this is Seven paging Forty-Two. Yeah, we got a report about two missing kids from the Otherworld Foster Care System? You hear anything about that?"

Two missing kids? Aru looked over at the twins. Sheela hid her face against Nikita's shoulder, and Nikita's flower crown was now a weapon of war.

"We're looking for a pair of twins, dark-skinned, speak English and Guyanese Creole, surname self-reported as 'Jagan,' but possibly inaccurate—"

Nikita snapped her fingers, and a thick snakelike vine shot toward the desk, toppling the monitor to the floor. The audio cut in and out, but Aru still caught most of it:

"Parents . . . unable to be contacted . . . Our records show . . . deported to Guyana three years ago—" Scrrritch! "Covering east and west perimeters now . . ."

Boo alighted on Aru's head. Aru, Brynne, Mini, and Aiden stared at the twins, not sure what to say. No wonder the girls were on edge and didn't want to answer questions about their parents.

"You can't report us!" yelled Nikita. "We're Pandavas, too, and we have a right—"

"No one is going to report you," said Brynne.

Nikita looked up at her, shocked. "You're not?"

"You're with us now," said Mini.

Boo hopped angrily around Aru's scalp. "What a preposterous notion that you would be taken from my care! You're mine now. Do you understand?"

"Welcome to the brood," said Aru, grumpily smoothing down her hair.

"We're not hens!" cried Nikita.

"You must have been manifesting powers since the beginning," said Boo to the twins. "And no one thought to inform anyone?"

"We tried, and so did our foster parents.... They were really nice, but they had a lot of kids to look after," said Sheela, lifting her head from Nikita's shoulder. "Anyway, the OFCS thought they were lying, and so when I saw you guys in my vision, we... we ran away. We thought once we joined the Pandavas, things would be different." Her face fell. "We thought maybe we'd be able to talk to our real parents again."

A loud crash echoed from a hallway to the left.

"The police are coming to get us, aren't they?" asked Sheela softly.

Aiden moved in front of the twins. He turned his wrist, and Aru saw the sharp gleam of his scimitars poking out from the ends of his sleeves. "I don't think so," he said.

Aru, Brynne, and Mini joined him to form a protective wall. Aru snuck a glance behind her. Nikita and Sheela were huddled together, but for the first time, the thorns spiking out of Nikita's crown looked smaller, and when she met Aru's gaze she didn't look haughty or furious... but shocked.

"I've never heard of Maruts," whispered Mini.

Aru turned her attention back to the hallway.

"They're minor storm deities tasked with keeping rabble rousers out of the heavens," said Boo, from the top of her head.

Mini bit her lip. "I hear they're super-violent and aggressive—"

The floor began to tremble. The shouts grew louder.

"Yeah, they're the *worst*," whispered Brynne. "Gunky and Funky can't stand being around them."

Aru winced. Gunky and Funky were Brynne's uncles and literally the friendliest couple in the world. If *they* didn't like the Maruts, then the storm deities had to be seriously awful.

Just then, a stream of hulking warriors wearing gold-plated armor and pointed helmets marched into the room, their daggers sparking with electricity. One by one, they lined up against the walls, only their grim mouths showing under their visors. On each of their golden breastplates was a number from two to forty-nine. The last Marut to enter wore number one. He strode toward the group, even as Brynne, Mini, Aiden, and Aru closed ranks in front of the twins.

"What's the meaning of this?" Boo demanded from the top of Aru's head. "I'll have you know that I am a member of the Council of Guardians, and we have been summoned for an appointment!"

Number One clicked his heels together. "Due to the circumstances, the crisis manager requested that you be held here until she is ready to see you, for she has *much* to discuss."

Aru's stomach sank even lower. Behind her, she sensed that the twins were on edge. They hadn't yet used their telepathic Pandava link with Aru, but she could feel their anxiety like a candle flame held too close to her skin.

"While we wait," said Number One, "my men and I have a question." His head turned as he regarded the line of them. "Which one of you is the daughter of Indra, king of the gods and Lord of the Heavens?"

Aru held her breath. Had they pegged her as the sister that would ruin everything?

"Why do you wanna know?" demanded Brynne.

"It's a simple question," said Number One gruffly.

Aru imagined saying *ME!* with the same force as Lady Éowyn in that scene from *Lord of The Rings: The Two Towers* when she flung back her helmet and shouted, "I AM NO MAN!"

Instead, she sounded like a hamster choking on air. "Me!"

Beside her, Brynne cringed. Even Mini, who could usually fake a smile, looked like she wanted to sink into the ground.

"We have something to ask you," said Number One.

Aru waited.

A second later, the Marut pushed up his visor to reveal eyes sparkling with excitement. "Can I fight on your side in the war?"

"*I* was gonna ask that!" said one of the other Maruts.

"Too slow, bro," said Number One.

In a rush, all the Maruts started lifting their visors and breaking ranks.

"Pandavas! *Real* Pandavas!" shouted Number Forty-Three. "Yo, this is so sick—"

"Dude, I'm so hyped for war," said Number Thirty-One. "Like, *so* hyped. This place is way too peaceful and harmonious. Ugh."

Someone else hollered, "Yeah! This party sucks!"

A sword was thrown to the floor, where it sparked loudly. The Maruts went silent, stared at the sword, and then started cheering.

"YAY! WAR!"

Brynne leaned over and whispered, "I think I know why Gunky and Funky said they were the worst. . . ."

Behind Aru, the twins relaxed. Boo flew to Aru's shoulder, clucking in disdain. "I despise *young deities,*" he muttered darkly.

"I am going to go look for the crisis manager and try to preserve what few brain cells I have after listening to them for two seconds."

And with that, he flew off.

"Who's the Daughter of Death?" asked another Marut.

Mini, confused, raised her hand slowly. Instantly, a knot of fans swarmed her.

"Can I fight with you?" asked one of them. "I'm super-tough. Check out my tattoos!"

"Uh, okay?" said Mini.

One Marut approached Aiden and flexed his bicep, where the words LEDGENDS ONLY appeared wrapped in inked barbed wire.

Aiden sucked in his breath sharply.

"It has that effect on people," said the Marut. "Wait till you see this one." He lifted his other arm, where the words YOUR A BEAST stretched across his forearm.

Aru wasn't quite sure how much time they wasted—sorry, *spent*—with the Maruts. It seemed the police didn't have much work to do, and so their days were consumed with spontaneous push-up contests (Brynne won today's), eating contests (Brynne also won), and secretly watching reruns of *The Great British Bake Off* (which Brynne insisted she could win).

While everyone else mixed with the Maruts—Mini offering medical advice, Aiden explaining how there was more to photography than selfies, Nikita fixing their outfits, and Sheela reading palms—Aru walked to the single window that looked out over Amaravati. It afforded a perfect view of the celestial city hundreds of feet below. The metropolis was divided into cloud islands connected by sky bridges. On one island, Aru saw an expanse of bright greenery that had to be Nandana, the sacred grove of the heavens. A bridge bearing the sign I-85N CONSTELLATION BLVD/LUNAR MANSIONS disappeared into a shimmering fog.

Amaravati was a place rich with splendor. But it wouldn't be there at all if the devas hadn't won back their immortality by churning the Ocean of Milk. They couldn't do it alone, so they'd asked the asuras for help, promising to share eternal life. But in the end, they'd broken their promise, and people got hurt. People like Lady M, who had just wanted to be remembered for her true self. And even Takshaka, the serpent king who hated the Pandavas because in another life they'd set fire to his forest home and killed his wife.

Those two hadn't been wrong in their anger. They just hadn't been right in how they dealt with it.

All of it made Aru uneasy.

She was still looking out the window when Boo flew through the doorway.

"She's coming!" he squawked.

Instantly, the Maruts scrambled. Sleeves were rolled down, conversations abandoned, helmets shoved into place. Within seconds, all forty-nine were flattened against the wall, serious and silent once more.

Aru wasn't sure what to expect of a "crisis manager," but it certainly wasn't what stepped across the threshold: an apsara with slender, dark limbs, wearing a jumpsuit made out of starry fabric.

She flung up her hands, one of which held a blinged-out tablet. "Helloooo, Pandavaaaas! I'm Opal. You're welcome in advance. Before we get started, let's snap a quick BTS, shall we?"

"What's that? A disease?" asked Mini.

"It means *behind the scenes,*" said the apsara, swiveling around to take a selfie with the Pandavas.

She caught Aru in the middle of saying, "HUH?" which probably made for an awful picture.

Opal quickly edited the photo. "Adorbs. We can use that for a little *day in the life* promo. Just think of what we're doing as *curating reality.*"

"Then it's not reality," said Aiden flatly.

Opal looked up, catching sight of the camera on his hip, and smiled. It was a beautiful but weirdly hollow expression.

"Well, if you'd prefer reality, how's this? You've landed the heavens in a serious crisis, and you do *not* want to face the wrath of angry gods, trust me. Right now, half the Council of Guardians is on an off-the-grid mission to Lanka, where they're trying to decipher the prophecy before the five days are up. The other half is here, trying to keep everything from becoming a marketing nightmare. A lot of people heard about the commotion in the magical dead zone, and now they want to know what this prophecy is about, so we're spreading word that it was nothing more than a false alarm."

"We can help!" cut in Brynne. "Just tell us how to fix it—"

"Oh no, no, no," said Opal with a laugh. "Sweet, but *no.* As if *anyone* would trust you with a mission after that last botched plan. *You* have to keep training and stay out of sight. So leave it to me to salvage the only thing you've got left."

Opal's teeth were so bright, Aru caught a rainbow sheen at the edge of her wide smile when she said, "Your *image.*"

EIGHT

That's So On-Brand

Before anyone could ask Opal a question or even say a quick good-bye to the Maruts, the crisis manager whispered something into the air and the Pandava crew was whisked into a cloud conference room. It was bright and airy, but completely without windows. A wide white oval table appeared in the middle of the space, encircled by seven cloud armchairs and a cushioned perch for Boo.

He fluttered over to it and, once settled there, grumbled, "I can't believe Hanuman and Urvashi left without me."

Opal didn't bother to look at him as she took a seat and motioned for the others to follow suit. "What would they need you for?" she asked dismissively.

Aru almost stood up in anger, but Brynne and Mini caught her eye.

We can't risk it, Mini said telepathically.

Aru hated that her sisters were right. They had messed up, and they had no choice but to wait and hear what Opal would say.

The crisis manager scanned their faces for the first time and stopped on the twins. "I'm not sure this conversation will be appropriate for infants to hear—"

"We're *ten,*" protested Nikita, narrowing her eyes. "And we can help."

Opal didn't look convinced. "I'll be the judge of that."

Bright calligraphy stretched across the air, spelling out the phrases Sheela had uttered less than an hour ago:

The scorned powers are on the rise,
To claim their stolen immortal prize.
One sister shall turn out not to be true.
With a single choice, the world shall receive its due.
One treasure is false, and one treasure is lost,
But the tree at the heart is the only true cost.
No war can be won without finding that root;
No victory had without the yield of its fruit.
In five days, the treasure will bloom and fade,
And all that was won could soon be unmade.

"We know the first two lines refer to the Sleeper and his army," said Opal. "The third is a little alarming. . . . An untrue sister?" She whistled. "Not the best image."

Aru's stomach twisted. The words felt like a taunt, and for a moment, all she saw was the Sleeper's vision in which she turned her back on her family. She pushed the memory aside.

"As for the treasure part, Hanuman and Urvashi are investigating that with Kubera, the Lord of Wealth," said Opal. "We think it's a hint that something among his collection is false or missing. A powerful weapon, probably, that could alter the course of the war." Opal leaned forward. "But do you know anything about this 'tree at the heart'?"

All eyes went to Sheela, who blinked and shrugged.

"Maybe it's a friendly tree?" she said, smiling. "That would be nice."

No one else made a peep.

"Aaand that settles it," Opal said to Sheela. "Thanks for your contribution, but I can't imagine what more you have to offer. Time to go."

Opal snapped her fingers, and the twins' cloud chairs peeled of the ground and floated in the air.

"Ooh!" said Sheela. "Flying!"

"You can't get rid of us!" said Nikita. "I'm not taking orders from someone in a glittering *jumpsuit*! It's the most atrocious mix of sartorial nineties and an overpriced bath bomb."

"Surely that's too hasty, Opal!" wheedled Boo. "They've only just arrived! And they're *my* charges—"

Brynne, Aru, Mini, and Aiden jumped to their feet, ready to grab the twins, but Opal's magic was too quick. Two little seat belts unfolded from the sides of the twins' cloud armchairs and buckled across their laps. Then a hole opened in the ground underneath them and their seats plummeted through.

"Don't worry—you'll be in good hands!" said Opal. Her gaze drifted to Aiden. "In fact... why don't I send a babysitter, too? You can tell your mother all the things you saw, Aiden. It's not like she can see it for herself."

Aiden's eyes widened. "Whoa, wait a second—"

Brynne snapped up her wind mace as Aiden's chair rose.

She whipped up a cyclone, blocking the chair from dropping through the hole. For a moment, Opal's magic struggled against Brynne's. But then Opal unzipped a portal in the wall, sucking in Aiden's chair like a giant vacuum so that he zoomed backward and disappeared.

Brynne whirled on the apsara. Mini swung out her Death Danda, and the moment Aru opened her palm, Vajra lengthened to a glittering spear.

"Shall we add turning on the representative of the heavens to your growing list of mistakes?" said Opal with a smile.

Brynne, Mini, and Aru faltered at the same time.

Boo paced on his perch, flapping angrily. "You may be sure that, crisis managing or not, I *shall* be reporting your impulsive behavior to the others, Opal! They would not stand for such misguided treatment!"

"The little darlings are now on a tour of the Nandana Gardens, which are lovely and bright and safe," said Opal breezily. "Don't fret so much."

Boo alighted on Mini's shoulder, his feathers furiously tufted.

Opal snapped her fingers, and once more everyone was sitting. The words vanished from the air. "Prophecies are inexact things. People don't need inexactitude in their lives—it just causes panic. What the Otherworld needs is to believe that the devas and Pandavas will win the war."

"But we don't know if we can," said Mini, frowning. "Are you... Are you asking us to lie?"

"I'm asking you to—at the very least—give people *hope,*" said Opal. "This is a *prime* branding opportunity. If you can't do the actual heroic thing, let's at least make it *look* like you could while the devas and the Council scramble to fix your mistakes. I trust you can manage a few questions from me."

Aru felt like someone had let loose a thunderstorm inside her skull. Everything roiled together—the prophecy, the twins' and Aiden's disappearance, the barely disguised venom in Opal's voice. But there was no time for it to settle. The cloud floors beneath the Pandavas disappeared, replaced with shiny mirror panels that showed different sketches of them in color-coordinated outfits and new hairstyles. In yet another mirror panel, there were sketched Instagram photos and quotes, sample tweets, and pre-written interview answers.

"Think of your brand as a *promise,*" said Opal. "Let's start with aesthetics."

She got up, walked to Mini, and passed a hand over her face. Mini's chin-length hair instantly looked glossier and straighter, and there was a purple stripe down the middle. Her glasses were gone, and her eyes . . . Were they *violet*?

"A little goth chic," said Opal. "That could work. We have to play to your image—"

Mini shook her head, and the illusion vanished. "I like how I look."

"Aww, that's the spirit!" said Opal, patting the top of her head.

Rude! thought Aru.

"And we need some personal stories." Opal continued moving around the table. "A little vulnerability is great for publicity. Makes you accessible, aspirational, *and* authentic!" She leaned over Brynne's shoulder. "Maybe a background piece about how your mother abandoned you?"

Brynne appeared ready to send Opal into the stratosphere.

But the crisis manager just kept going. "The fifth day of the prophecy will coincide with the Otherworld's Holi party. Perfect timing. When you show up in all your glory, people will be focused on *you,* not the Council. After I'm done tweaking your image, they won't be thinking about your botched missions or wondering which one of you is the 'untrue' Pandava." Opal stopped and looked directly at Aru.

Aru felt punched.

Boo swooped in front of Opal, wings flapping.

"How *dare* you insult my girls?!" he spat. "Their reputations are *spotless*! None of this is necessary—I can vouch for them myself!"

"What do I care about what *you* can vouch for?" asked Opal. "The Otherworld hasn't forgotten that you were once called the Great Deceiver. And now you're training this generation's Pandavas? Some might find that a trifle *curious,* to say the least."

"His name has been cleared," said Mini angrily. "If he vouches for us, people will listen."

Opal flashed a thin smile. "Is that so? Well. Let's review my notes, Subala."

She sat back down and a sheaf of papers magically unfurled in front of her. Boo returned to his stand, where he perched stiffly.

"By my count you're at, what, two hundred visits to Kalpavriksha?"

"Th-that's PRIVATE!" he spluttered.

Aru frowned. What was she talking about?

"Your little teacher is under quite the nasty curse," Opal explained to the Pandavas. "What were the exact conditions again? Oh yes. *'Pay your dues and show your worth; a wish will free you from this earth.'* And you've flown countless times to the Nandana Gardens to visit the wish-granting tree, but it never works, so you're reduced to this rather pathetic hobby."

Opal waved her hand, and across the table sprawled a vision of Boo soaring above the sidewalk when the sun was at its highest.

Aru had seen him do that plenty of times on his days off. Brynne had assumed it was to clear his head. Mini had insisted he wanted vitamin D from the sunshine. But Aru had noticed that Boo never looked up—only *down,* where his shadow sprawled huge and epic.

"Trying to trick yourself into remembering your glory days?" taunted Opal. "Because trust me when I say that all anyone sees when they look at you is a disgraced sorcerer and bedraggled pigeon. No one will care that you've vouched for your poorly trained students."

Boo was so stunned he swung backward on his perch, forcing Aru to catch him before he fell.

"Boo?" asked Aru softly.

He trembled in her grip, utterly silent. Aru glared up at Opal, shaking with anger, but the crisis manager didn't even notice.

Opal stood up and walked in another slow circle around the room.

"You need *me* now, Pandavas, not this old professor," said Opal. "Only *I* will tell you the truth about how all this looks on the outside. The 'untrue' sister? Everyone will be wondering who it is." She grinned, then pointed to Mini. "Maybe the little timid one...probably easy to manipulate into working for the enemies." She gestured to Brynne. "Or the strong, shape-shifting, belligerent one with"—she dropped her voice to a whisper—"*asura blood,* which is never a good look." Next, she swiveled to Aru. "Or you! The flesh-and-blood daughter of the Sleeper. Almost two years ago, you failed to destroy him.... Why *was* that, exactly? Did you suddenly feel sorry for dear old Dad? Surely by now you're used to life without him. At any rate, it doesn't sound like something a *true* sister would have allowed to happen...."

Aru shot an agonized look at Mini and Brynne, but they were both gazing down at their laps.

"As for the twins"—Opal shrugged—"not much to be done about them, frankly. But I will say that a clairvoyant who can't control her powers is *very* dangerous. Henceforth, they shall be kept in Amaravati until they are deemed less volatile."

Mini stood up. "You can't do that! What about their family?"

Opal snorted. "*What* family? They have no family here."

"They have *us,*" said Aru.

Opal ignored her. Instead, she clapped once. The mirror floor instantly brightened, and a diamond-encrusted door appeared in the wall. "Trust me on this, children. I'm on your side. I'm fighting for the heavens just as much as you and the devas are."

She took her seat at the table again. "Come back here in five days' time so I can get you ready for the Holi festivities. In the meantime, I'll start spreading the word about your good deeds to polish the reputations you tarnished with that failed mission." She straightened her papers and cast the Pandavas one last dismissive look. "The best thing you can do for now is just *keep out of sight.*"

She pointed to the door. "Go. I've got a lot of work to do."

When they stepped into the portal, Boo pecked around until he hit the green button for the Nandana Gardens, where they could collect Aiden and the twins. He didn't say anything. Maybe he felt sad having to return to the place of so many unfulfilled wishes, Aru thought.

They were all reeling from Opal's words. Mini seemed close to tears. Brynne looked like she wanted to smash something.

Aru's mind kept churning, and when they arrived at the gardens, she only dimly registered the beautiful greenery flanking the marble walkway.

They crossed several courtyards, climbed up and down terraces, and eventually came to a small bower. In the middle stood a huge golden tree.

The sight of it stopped Aru's breath. When she'd heard stories about the legendary tree as a kid, she'd never thought she'd get to see it in person. She felt lucky enough that she'd seen a few branches from it on the floor of the Ocean of Milk last year.

It towered over their heads like a skyscraper, the top disappearing into veils of mist. Glowing jewel-like fruit of many different colors hung from its branches, perfuming the air with the smell of ambrosia. The ground around the tree was cold and damp, dotted with magical flowering bushes. Nestled between two massive roots was a sign that read:

KALPAVRIKSHA, THE TREE OF WISHES

PROPERTY OF ARANYANI, GODDESS OF THE FORESTS

They found their friends on the other side of the trunk. Aiden was busy taking pictures. Sheela appeared to be talking to a bush while Nikita crouched over the ground, her hands thrust into the dirt and her eyes closed. Her veins glowed a pale green, and when she opened her eyes, the crown of flowers on her head gleamed even brighter.

The moment she saw the other Pandavas, Nikita pointed at the tree.

"*That,*" she said dramatically. "Is a *fake.*"

NINE

Goal: Don't End Up a Dragon Snack

Aru stared at Kalpavriksha soaring above them. It didn't seem fake to her. Fake things should be obvious! Like a bootlegged movie that was recorded by someone who got up and left the theater in the middle.

Nikita lifted her palm off the dirt, her ice-blue eyes sheening bright green for a moment. "I'm an expert on what's designer and what's a dud, and *this thing*? This is a dud. I read its roots," she said. "Its earliest memory is of being carried in a dark pot and placed here. And it definitely can't grant wishes."

"We tested it," added Sheela mournfully.

Nikita clapped once, and the dirt vanished from her hands. She placed them on her hips.

"The tree *can't* be a fake," said Boo. "That would mean… all this time I…"

He trailed off, stunned. But the longer Aru looked at the tree, the more an urgency grew inside her.

"The prophecy," she said. "It mentioned a false treasure."

"One treasure is false, and one treasure is lost, but the tree at the heart is the only true cost," sang Sheela.

Aru said, "If this tree is false—"

"The real one is lost?" finished Mini.

"No war can be won without finding that root . . . no victory had without the yield of its fruit," said Aiden, putting his camera away.

"What if that means winning the war depends on finding it?" suggested Brynne. "And the part about victory—I mean, it's a wish-granting tree. A person could just *wish* to win!"

"But what about 'the tree at the heart'?" asked Mini. "How is that the 'true cost'?"

"Maybe that's a hint about where the real Kalpavriksha is?" tried Aru.

"Maybe . . ." said Mini, but she didn't sound too convinced.

"Well, then we have to find it!" said Aru, growing more excited. "I mean, we've only got five days, right? We have to go right now and tell the Council—"

"You can't."

All six of them turned to face Boo, who was staring up at the tree. He'd never looked so small to Aru. She thought of him searching for his own shadow and felt a pang in her heart.

"It would be impossible to reach Hanuman and Urvashi in Lanka," he said. "The location of their audience with Kubera is wrapped in secrecy. No one would be able to get word to them before Holi. Not even me."

"What about Opal?" asked Mini.

Aru and Brynne scowled at the same time.

"As if she'd believe us," said Brynne. "She told us to stay out of the way. And, according to her, *no one* is going to trust our word right now. . . . If we're going to find the tree, we'll have to do it ourselves."

"I'm in," said Mini.

"Me too," said Aiden.

Once again, the whole fate of the Otherworld depended on them, Aru thought. And it wasn't just the Otherworld's fate... it was theirs, too. She couldn't shake off Opal's nasty words about her being the Sleeper's daughter. If they brought back the Tree of Wishes, no one would ever doubt them again.

"Three," said Aru firmly.

Even the twins raised their hands.

But when they looked at Boo, he was horrified. Aru had learned to pick up on his physical cues: feathers sticking out at all angles, round eyes wider, beak ajar.

"What is it, Boo?" asked Aru. "I thought you'd be happy. If we find the real tree, you can wish on it and... be free."

Their mentor turned his head and shuffled slightly farther away.

"Boo?" pressed Aiden, gently.

The pigeon sighed. "There's something you need to know."

Aru felt the hairs on the back of her neck prickle. "What?"

"I've been coming here for years. I don't know when she put this decoy here, but Aranyani must have had a good reason for hiding the real tree. She must have been afraid the wrong person would try to wish on it...."

"The wrong person... Like... the Sleeper?" Aru guessed.

"If it was, it would've been before he was the Sleeper," said Boo. "He couldn't have gained entrance to Amaravati after."

But what about before, when he was just a man? Aru wondered. *What would he have wished for back then?*

Boo took a deep breath. "If you start looking for the real

Kalpavriksha, the Sleeper might figure out that this one is a fake. Then he could track you to get to the real tree," he said. "That would be a disaster."

"We can keep it secret," said Aru. "We've—"

"This mission is far too risky," butted in Boo. "I can't let you go. And I can't come with you. I'm sure Opal's team is watching my every move."

"Boo, we *have* to," said Aru. "We only have five days! The Sleeper's army could already be on its way, and the Otherworld could be attacked! We can't let that happen!"

"Even if I let you go, what will you do *if* and *when* you find the real tree?" asked Boo.

Aru eyed the redwood-size tree. "Uh . . . I guess we'll just dig it up by the roots, stop by Home Depot, and stick it in a planter on the way back here?" she suggested pathetically.

"Rein in the optimism, Shah, it's too much," said Aiden.

"I don't really trust shapes and sizes," said Sheela, gently stroking the leaves of a brightly colored shrub that seemed to sway even though there was no breeze. "You never know how something could be hidden with just a little bit of"—Sheela poked the leaf—"magic."

The leaf peeled in half, revealing that it was really the bright green wings of a butterfly, and the insect took flight.

Sheela had a point, thought Aru. If there was enough magic to hide a tree that size, then there had to be enough magic to bring it back to the heavens, where it belonged. They'd figure it out.

"Where could the real Kalpavriksha even be hidden, though?" asked Boo.

Nikita cleared her throat. "When I was reading the roots... I saw something."

She placed her hands against the tree trunk. Once more, her veins glowed green. Slowly, a palm-size area of bark peeled back. The branches under the Ocean of Milk had been solid gold through and through. Layers of gold covered the duplicate tree, which Nikita easily rolled up to reveal wooden bark engraved with a snake-dragon-thingy biting its tail:

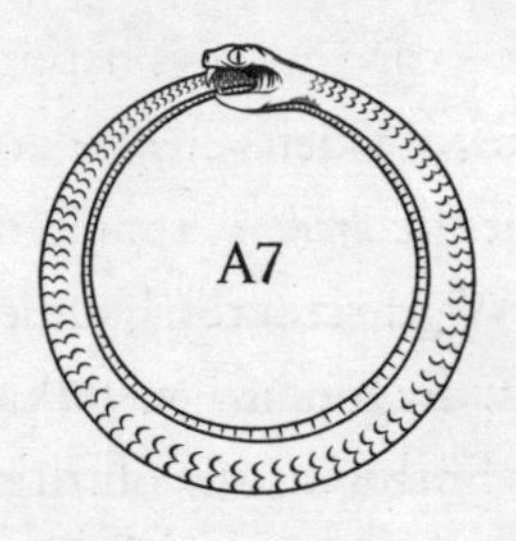

"I know that snake symbol! That belongs to the Crypt of Eclipses," said Brynne.

"Sounds like something Indiana Jones would break into," said Aru.

"Indiana Jones?" demanded Boo. "How dare he?! Where does he reside?"

"Hollywood?"

Boo seethed. "He will pay for the presumption...."

"What's in this crypt?" asked Aru.

"Everyone's secrets," said Boo. "That A7 must be a locker or chamber within. Membership to the crypt is by invitation only, and reserved for the aristocrats, deities, and demons of the Otherworld. Aranyani must have hidden a clue to Kalpavriksha's location in her vault. It would be safe there. After all, the whole place is said to be guarded by a dragon."

"I'm sorry, did you say *dragon*?" asked Mini.

"Could we just save ourselves some trouble and talk to Aranyani?" asked Aru. "We could explain what's happening, somehow convince her to tell us the location. . . . We could bribe her! What's her favorite ice cream flavor?"

Boo shook his beak. "Aranyani is famously elusive. I've only glimpsed her twice in three centuries. She doesn't like the heavens very much."

"Wonder why," said Aiden.

"Um, what about the *dragon*?" repeated Mini.

Brynne flexed. "We can totally handle a dragon."

"Uh, what kinda dragon are we talking about here?" said Aru nervously. "Like Smaug sitting on all his gold, or like a cute friendly little baby Norbert hanging out in Hagrid's cauldron?"

"Probably the first," said Aiden.

Mini whimpered.

"Before we worry about that, let's assume that we somehow manage to get into this 'invitation only' crypt thing," said Aru. "What about the vault? How are we going to open it?"

Brynne touched Gogo, her wind mace, which had taken the form of a choker at her throat. "*I* might have a plan. It's said that the architect of the gods can make anything. I bet he could easily make a key that opens any lock. And guess whose uncle works for him?" She pointed her thumbs at herself.

At this, the look of skepticism on Boo's face melted into something else: *hope*.

"C'mon, Boo," Aru pressed. "We can do this. What

happened with the twins and the prophecy was a fluke. You've got to let us fix this."

"The devas don't want you leaving Amaravati," said Boo cagily.

Aru kept her expression blank. He hadn't said no. That was a good sign. They just had to play this carefully.

"Then we'll do it undercover," said Aru.

"With coordinated outfits?" asked Nikita brightly.

"No," Aru, Brynne, and Mini said simultaneously.

"Though we will need different sneakers," said Mini, pointing at hers. "With no tracking devices."

"Yeah. We'll leave our sneakers here so everyone will think we stayed put," said Aru. "No one will be looking for us for the next few days anyway. Everyone will be too preoccupied with the prophecy and Holi preparations."

Brynne put in, "No one but *us* even knows that the tree is a fake."

"And the Sleeper's army is probably distracted by Hanuman and Urvashi's mission," added Aiden.

Boo swayed back and forth, tossing his beak one way and then the next. Finally, he grumbled. "*No* dawdling at any point in time and throwing off the mission timing," he said, pointing his wing at Aru.

"*No* lecturing about all the opportunities for fatality and thus ruining group morale," he said to Mini.

"*No* picking fights with things that randomly offend you," he said to Brynne.

Boo turned to Aiden. "Keep up the good work."

Aiden beamed, and all three girls glared at him.

"You understand that this can't be a sanctioned quest," said Boo. "Stay completely off the grid. If you run into any problems with anyone from the Otherworld, you won't be able to prove that you're working on behalf of the devas. *And* you'll have to be done in time for the Holi celebrations in five days so you don't raise any suspicion!"

Aru nodded so fast she thought her head would fall off.

"Now, what is your mission?" Boo quizzed them.

"Get a key to unlock the vault in the Crypt of Eclipses," said Brynne.

"Get *inside* the crypt and hopefully find a clue about the real tree's location," said Aiden.

"Stay undercover," said Mini.

Boo turned to Aru, who said, "Um . . . don't end up a dragon snack?"

Boo sighed. "I'm still worried."

"We've got celestial weapons!" said Aru. "Don't worry so much."

Boo looked at them, warmth shining in his round eyes. "Pandavas, you are far more than the things you fight with."

"Sure, but also *celestial weapons,*" emphasized Aru.

Just when it looked as though Boo was going to yell at her, the twins piped up.

"What about us?" demanded Nikita, crossing her arms.

"Until the age of twelve, you're considered underage," said Boo. "And if you leave the heavens, the devas will know, thanks to those gifts from your soul fathers." He pointed his beak at the glowing shapes embedded in their skin. "These symbols not only indicate that your powers haven't fully manifested, but they also work as tracking devices."

"So we can't go?" asked Sheela quietly.

Aru's heart twisted sharply. The twins had been separated from their parents... and who knows what else they'd gone through. No wonder they wanted that wish.

She wanted to tell the twins they'd have their chance. They just needed to give them some time. But the moment she opened her mouth to explain, Nikita stepped in front of her twin and glowered at them.

"Just because we can't go with you in person doesn't mean you're getting rid of us. We can dream-travel. We'll find you."

"And help!" said Sheela. "I like helping."

"You'll need it," said Nikita haughtily. "We're not going to let you screw this one up."

"Remember this, Aru," said Sheela, her eyes clouding over and her voice deepening. "There's lots more to find."

TEN

Knock-Knock, Who's There?

When Aru arrived back home to get ready, Atlanta's Museum of Ancient Indian Art and Culture was already closed for the evening. She glanced at the giant clock positioned over the entrance to the Hall of the Gods. How was it already nine o'clock? She stifled a yawn, patted the stone trunk of Greg the elephant statue, and trudged into the main atrium, pausing only to launch herself over the turnstile.

"Aru?"

She looked up to see her mom walking down the staircase from their apartment.

"It's late. I was getting worried," her mom said.

"I have a note for you from Boo," Aru said, digging it out of her pants pocket and handing it over. "I have to go on another mission, but you can't tell anyone."

Her mom read the message, frowned, and sighed in resignation. Then she opened her arms for a hug, and Aru fell into them, inhaling deeply. No matter how many miraculous fragrances filled the Night Bazaar, this was her favorite scent: her mother's jasmine shampoo combined with the trace smells of paper and straw from her work as an archaeologist and historian.

"This 'vital sacred object' you're trying to find," said her mom quietly. "I think I may know what it is."

"Don't say it out loud!" said Aru, eyeing the shadows.

"Someone else went looking for it long ago..." her mom continued.

Aru drew back and saw that there were tears in her mom's eyes.

"Your f—" Her mom stopped herself and took a deep breath.

So I guessed right, thought Aru. Her dad *had* been the "wrong person" who tried wishing on the tree.

"There's something I've been meaning to show you," her mom said. "I've been carrying it around with me for a while, not knowing when would be the right time, but now seems as good as any."

She stepped back, and from her jacket pocket she pulled out a delicately folded paper bird no bigger than Aru's thumb. It woke in her mom's hand, shook its parchment feathers, cocked its head to one side, and warbled a charming tune. The edges of its beak and tail were worn, as if it had been held many times.

"Your father made this for me," she said, not looking at Aru. "He was of partial gandharva descent, and he loved music. I was so nervous when I found out I was going to have you, Aru. He told me to write each fear on a piece of paper. Then he turned them into songbirds, to remind me that the things that scare us can also give us joy. We just have to learn how to see them in a different light." She paused, smiling to herself. "Once, he was wise and funny, thoughtful and determined. We knew the prophecy about him... that somehow he would become a force of destruction, the terror of the gods. More than anything, he wanted to change his future. And so he went looking for Kalpavriksha."

Dr. K. P. Shah took a deep breath, then tucked the bird back into her jacket pocket. "He came home an entirely different person, like something was missing from him. I never knew if he found the tree. He refused to speak about it, and by that time, I had other things to worry about." Her hand moved to her belly.

Aru remembered the image she'd seen of her father in the Pool of the Past, back when she and Mini had ventured into the Kingdom of Death. In the vision he was cradling a baby in his arms, looking down at her with such joy it had made Aru's heart hurt in the present.

"When I saw how much he had changed, I didn't know what to do," said her mom. "I had to protect you, no matter what. I trapped him in the lamp, thinking I'd find a solution one day, but I—" Her words choked off and Aru grasped her hands, holding tight.

Aru couldn't imagine what her mom must have felt. All that panic and love fusing into the impossible choice to trap the man she loved for eleven years . . . all for Aru's sake.

"I don't know what happened when he went looking for Kalpavriksha," her mom went on. "Whatever it was, it made him lose himself. I don't want that to happen to you, my Aru."

As her mother kissed the top of her head, Aru felt something slide around her neck. It was the necklace her mom always wore: a small sapphire pendant hanging from a delicate silver chain. Aru loved the sapphire, which was set above a row of three small holes. She'd never seen a jewel quite the same color—as if it weren't just the blue of a stone, but the blue of oceans and horizons.

"Mom, what's this for?" asked Aru, touching the jewel lightly.

"Protection," said her mom. "Years ago, a *yaksha* gave this to me. He promised me it was for guardianship and for finding lost things. I hope this will protect you from whatever danger Suyodhana found on his journey. Be safe, okay, my Aru? I love you."

A nameless fear flew into her chest. What had happened to her father? And would it happen to her, too? Would something she encountered in this quest change her so much that she'd end up becoming the "untrue" sister from the prophecy? *No,* she told herself. She couldn't start thinking that way or she'd never leave. Besides, her father had traveled alone.

Aru wasn't alone.

The pendant felt cold against Aru's skin. Even though it was small, it seemed heavy. But it wasn't uncomfortable. Instead, it felt like a talisman. Aru touched it once more and felt a little braver.

"I love you, too, Mom," she said.

Before dawn the next morning, the clock in the museum's lobby chimed five times. Mini, Brynne, and Aiden would be arriving soon, and Aru hadn't quite finished packing. Vajra, who was supposed to be acting like a flashlight, kept bouncing around the walls.

"Could you be a *little* helpful?" asked Aru.

Vajra paused, as if considering this.

Then the lightning bolt continued to bounce around.

Aru rolled her eyes. She was in the middle of deciding which shoes to wear when a strange shadow rose on the walls. It stretched itself huge, the head bizarre and misshapen.... Was that a *tail*? A cold wind drifted through the atrium.

Had she left the front door unlocked and someone had opened it without her noticing?

"Psssst—"

DEMON! thought Aru.

"Vajra!" she called, holding out her hand.

The lightning bolt flew into her grasp, and Aru spun on her heel and flung Vajra like a javelin. It glowed brightly, drenching the demon in light and almost blinding Aru. When the light faded, Aru blinked to see Vajra splayed on the wall as a net, the demon pinned underneath.

Only...

It wasn't a demon.

"Well," said the not-demon, grinning, "you're definitely not boring."

ELEVEN

Get In, Heroes, We're Going Questing

The not-demon was a boy her age, who had a pair of sunglasses perched on his head even though the sun wasn't up yet. He wore a bright eyesore of a tie-dyed denim jacket over dark jeans. It wasn't until he smiled that Aru recognized him.

"You," she said.

"Moi," agreed the boy.

It was the *naga* boy who had freed them last year from Takshaka, his own grandfather, by playing loud music. Although he didn't look part snake right this second. Now he looked thoroughly human, except for the strange scale-like pattern across his right temple, though to someone else it might just appear to be a birthmark. Aru glared at him. The way he managed to stay smug even while being pinned to the wall by a lightning net was almost impressive.

"Told you I'd call in that favor someday, Aru Shah."

"How did you get into my house?" demanded Aru.

"Can I ask my question first?"

"No."

"Figures," the boy said. "Girls have trouble organizing their thoughts after they meet me."

"I will *literally* electrocute you," said Aru. "What are you doing in my house?"

"First, it's a museum—"

"Vajra," commanded Aru.

Electricity prickled over the net.

"Ow! Ow!" said the boy. "All right, all right! Call off your demented rope!"

Vajra, highly affronted by this description, shocked him again.

And then the front door slammed shut. Aru turned to see Aiden standing in the threshold, his camera slung over one shoulder and his backpack hanging from the other. Just then, Greg the stone elephant (Mini had named him after reading about gangrene infections, which apparently turned dead tissue gray as stone) lifted his trunk and dropped his jaw to the floor, allowing Brynne and Mini to climb out of the portal.

Aiden looked at the boy trapped by the lightning net and sighed. "I see you've met my cousin Rudy."

"It's actually *Prince* Rudy. Just saying."

ZAP!

After Aru gave him another shock, Rudy tumbled to the floor, and Vajra zoomed back into her hand. Not as a ball this time, but an imperious spear crackling with electricity. Aru even felt her hair lift from her scalp and wave around, which she suspected made her look ridiculously epic.

Aru mentally checked in with Brynne and Mini, who were making their way toward her. *On a scale of one to Galadriel, how awesome does my hair look?*

Mini: *Well, uhh...*

Brynne immediately responded with *I love you, but you look like you got in a fight with Pikachu.*

Aru scowled.

And lost, added Brynne.

The lightning bolt's electrical charge abruptly shut off. Aiden, Brynne, and Mini drew closer, and the three of them watched as Rudy wobbled to his feet and...grinned?

"Did you get a shot of that, cuz?" he asked Aiden.

"Don't call me that," said Aiden.

Aru couldn't help herself. "Around here, he's called Wifey."

Aiden sighed. "Thanks, Shah."

Rudy frowned. "Someone's going to have to explain that one to me later."

"No one here owes you any explanations," said Aru.

"Let me start over," said Rudy. He took a deep breath, then bowed. "I, Prince Rudra of Naga-Loka and descendant of Queen Uloopi, am here to offer my services to the Pandavas."

Aru frowned. What was the protocol here? Was he going to give them a fruit basket or something?

"I'm sorry, who *asked* for your services?" demanded Brynne. She elbowed Mini. "Right, Mini? Tell him we don't need him."

Behind Brynne, Mini looked suddenly wide-eyed, and Aru remembered the first (and last) time Mini had seen Rudy. He had winked at her. And Mini?

Well, she had walked into a telephone pole.

Mini hadn't yet mastered the art of boy. At the Otherworld Halloween dance, she had spent so much time talking to a guy about the different germs on people's hands that he'd excused himself to grab some punch and never returned. Then there was the time when Mini wanted to tell a boy that he had nice eyelashes but instead told him about eyelash trichomegaly and pulled up some truly disturbing photos on Google.

Looking at Rudy, Mini opened her mouth, closed it, opened it again and said, "*Need* is a weird word. I guess it depends on the circumstances, right? Like, I wouldn't want my internal gut flora lying around on a table, but I sure *need* it in my intestinal lining!"

Then she started laughing hysterically.

Rudy frowned. "What?"

"Aiden, why did you bring this snake here?" asked Brynne, slowly shielding a still-cackling Mini.

He sighed, scrubbing at his dark curls. "Mom only keeps in touch with one *nagini* princess cousin—"

"My mom," cut in Rudy, "thought it was best for me to get some mortal cultural exposure. So she sent me to *his* mom's! And I overheard Aiden talking about the quest you guys are going on—"

"You read my texts."

"Details, cuz, details," said Rudy dismissively. "Basically, I *heard* that you need to get inside the Crypt of Eclipses, but you can't do that without a member. I just so happen to *be* a member. So, you know, you're welcome and all. Just let me know when we're leaving."

Rudy walked off, leaving the three girls to glance at each other with shared *What just happened?* looks. Aiden shrugged helplessly. Rudy proceeded to cruise around the museum and poke at the statues.

"Do these things come alive and eat thieves?" he asked.

"Uh, no?" said Aru.

"Huh," said Rudy, shaking his head. "The mortal world is *so* weird."

"Why do you even want to join in on this quest, *Prince*?" demanded Aru. "You're not going to be waited on by us."

Brynne flicked her wrist and her wind mace zoomed into her palm. "And don't even dream about asking," she said threateningly.

Rudy didn't seem perturbed. "I've got my reasons, Shah. You owe me a favor. I'm calling it in." He winked at her.

Aru rolled her eyes, but even as she did, she felt a little thrill. No boy had ever winked at her before. Well, except for that one time she thought David Kyrre was incessantly winking at her on a school trip to the zoo, but it turned out he'd just had an eyelash in his eye. Almost as soon as the thought crossed her mind, Aru caught Mini's expression. Her eyebrows were scrunched up—not in envy, but in sadness, which was way worse. Aru's tiny thrill vanished.

Brynne cast a withering glare at Rudy and said to Aiden, "*Your* cousin, *your* responsibility."

They waited for their ride, which Brynne had arranged, outside the museum. Rudy kept asking Aiden to snap dramatic shots of him in various poses against the lightening sky, and Aiden kept refusing. Brynne busily assembled whatever she'd raided from the fridge, while Mini practiced her transformation skills, her small frame practically drowning in her huge gray sweatshirt as she changed Dee Dee into random objects: a backlit skull and a jar of teeth, a pair of violet wings, and a black lacquered apple. Daughter of Death indeed.

"You know, you're probably the only person here who isn't wishing they were still in bed," said Aru.

Mini sighed. "I can't help it. I get anxious before I travel. What's the point in sleeping?" She looked over at the boys, now sitting about twenty feet away, and groaned. "Aru, how weird was I with Rudy?"

"Not that—"

"Be honest."

"Okay, awful."

Mini whimpered.

"But no worse or better than usual when you meet someone you think is cute."

Mini slumped to the ground.

Oops, thought Aru. Even Vajra in bracelet form scolded her with a sharp electrical shock. *Ouch! Message received!*

"First impressions aren't everything," said Aru. "Think of how many weird things I end up saying."

Mini sniffed. "That's true."

"Do you even like him?"

Mini's cheeks flamed red. "He probably thinks I'm a freak."

"Daughter. Of. The. God. Of. Death," enunciated Aru slowly. "Say it with me! You're inherently cooler than ninety-nine point nine percent of the population—"

A loud honking sound interrupted Aru. It seemed to be coming from above. A huge flying car came into view. It looked like a super-fancy taxi, but with massive white wings that beat gracefully as it descended to the street. The words VIMANA EXPRESS flashed across its side.

"Get in, heroes!" shouted Brynne. "We're going questing!"

TWELVE

A Wild Goose Chase

Aru and Mini clambered into the *vimana,* which was a lot bigger on the inside than it looked on the outside. The backseat was a generous seven-seater, with each chair fashioned like a small velvet throne, so the effect was more like sitting in a fancy lobby than in a car. Large windows flanked the thrones. A pair of speakers hung from the corners of the vimana, and tiny shelves jutted out from the partition between the backseats and the front ones, along with glass goblets in cup holders and little jars of hoof-socks, horn polish, fang floss, talon trimmers . . . and an iPhone charger. Aiden, Rudy, and Brynne already had their seats. Rudy's obnoxious jacket stood in stark contrast to Aiden's usual somber getup of a dark long-sleeved shirt and darker pants.

The cousins were engaged in an argument.

"The whole point is to be *subtle,*" said Aiden. "It's an undercover mission."

"I was born to stand out," said Rudy.

"Well, you're going to die that way too, apparently."

Rudy shrugged. "Haters gonna hate."

Aiden grumbled to himself and reached for his camera.

Brynne dug through her backpack, handing out food wrapped in aluminum.

"I got breakfast covered," she said. "Berries reduced in sugar and acid, fused with a blended nut butter and spread on toasted wheat."

"So... a PB and J?" asked Aiden.

"Yup!" said Brynne. She rapped on the ceiling of the car. "Drive on!"

The flying chariot yelped, then zoomed into the air so fast that Aru got flattened against her seat. When she looked up, she noticed a screen on the ceiling. Someone had muted the Otherworld television, but the headlines still flashed by:

BREAKING NEWS: SECURITY CONCERNS FOR THIS YEAR'S HOLI CELEBRATION! IS WAR COMING?

ARE THE DEVAS COVERING UP A PANDAVA PROPHECY?

AND NEXT UP...

ARE SOME OF YOUR LIMBS TURNING RANDOMLY TO STONE? YOU MIGHT BE CURSED! OUR EXPERTS WEIGH IN!

Aru tried to push all thoughts of the prophecy from her mind as she righted herself in the chair.

"Please tell me this isn't a stolen flying car..." said Mini nervously.

"Of course not!" said Brynne. "And this isn't a flying car.

It's a vimana—more like a flying chariot. This model is actually based on the super-luxurious version that Ravana used to ride in back in the day."

"Ravana?" asked Mini. "As in . . . the *demon king* Ravana?"

Brynne nodded. "Gunky's the head architect at VPD, so he gets flying-chariot service from our apartment to work every day."

"VPD?" asked Aru.

"Vishwakarma, Prajapati, and Daksha," said Brynne. "It's one of the best celestial architecture firms."

"So, what's the plan here?" Aiden asked. "We're going to show up at this firm, say 'Make me a key!' and that's it?"

Brynne nodded. "I mean . . . yeah? Vishwakarma is literally the god of architects. But he only works on projects he likes, so we'll have to pitch it to him."

Aru raised her eyebrows. "With what, a PowerPoint presentation?"

"Ew, no," said Brynne. "We just have to tell him who we are, and that'll be enough."

Mini cleared her throat. "But . . . according to Boo, we're supposed to do this whole thing undercover."

Brynne's face fell. "I forgot about that."

"Shouldn't be a problem," said Rudy.

He was tinkering with the sound system, holding real gemstones up to the speakers.

"Sound modifiers," he explained. "Can't go questing without a proper playlist."

He picked up another gem from the orange messenger bag at his feet and rotated the tuning dial below the speakers. The music skipped from nineties hip-hop to Latin pop before he finally settled on a song Aru had never heard before. With its strong beat, it sounded like a fight song. When Rudy placed the gemstone by the speaker, the sound didn't just get louder—it felt *alive.* The music seemed to sink through Aru's skin and make her very soul bristle. She had the weirdest urge to throw a pair of boxing gloves dramatically on the ground.

"Music makes all the difference," said Rudy.

Brynne crossed her arms. "Neat trick," she said grudgingly. "But can we talk about VPD?"

Rudy bobbed his head to the rhythm. "I'm a prince, remember? You guys can pose as my lackeys while I ask Vishwakarma to make me a key," he said. "Boom."

"Boom?" repeated Aiden, rolling his eyes.

"Lackeys?" echoed Brynne angrily.

Suddenly, the chariot tipped forward, and the five passengers slammed against the partition. For the first time, Rudy's calm splintered a bit.

"What's going on with this thing?" he asked, panicked. "I thought it was safe!"

"It *is* safe!" retorted Brynne. "Well, mostly safe, as long as the chariot doesn't see any birds. It can get jealous of them. Or want to eat them . . . Gunky's not really sure which. But don't worry, it's too early in spring for many birds to—"

"Brynne . . ." said Aiden, his voice full of warning.

He was sitting closest to the window and had been leaning out to snap photos, as usual, but now he pressed himself hard against the seat. "I'm really hoping I'm wrong, but I just saw—"

HONK!

"Oh no," whimpered Mini. "Not—"

As if in response, the chariot stopped short and hovered in the air. A ripple went through its velvet cushions, like the muscles of a cat on the verge of getting deeply annoyed.

HONK!!!

A swarm of at least a dozen geese zoomed through the air around them. The vimana started to buck violently, and the small glass cups trembled in their holders.

"Bad car!" said Brynne. "Very bad car!"

"Who's driving this thing?" demanded Mini, gripping her armrest.

"It's self-driving!" said Brynne.

Aiden reached forward, slid open the partition, and clambered through to the driver's seat. "I'll get us back en route!"

"You can't drive!" said Brynne.

"I've handled a go-kart!"

"That's not the same thing!"

But Aiden had already slid into the driver's chair. Rudy, however, sat on the floor, clutching his seat, all suaveness totally gone.

Outside, the geese started to batter the chariot. It tilted right and left. Aru fell back against the window and got a horrible view: The vimana had climbed through the sky, and they were above the patchy clouds. Pieces of downtown Atlanta loomed hundreds of feet below.

"I *really* do not like heights," whimpered Rudy.

"At least the windows aren't—" started Brynne.

The windows dropped down, opening and closing like gnashing teeth. Mini held tight to one of the overhead handholds. "I think the vimana's trying to bite the birds!"

A goose poked its head inside the window, squawked, and grabbed Brynne's sandwich.

"I think *NOT!*" yelled Brynne.

She aimed Gogo and blasted the goose with a wind vortex. It got flung out of the car, spiraling into the sky. The geese paused for a moment. And then, as one, they barreled toward the vimana.

"Can't you do something to make the car ignore the birds?" asked Aru.

"I'm trying!" hollered Aiden.

And he was. His hands gripped the wheel, turning it this way and that, but the chariot continued to swerve in circles like a dog chasing its tail. Or, in this case, a goose. The car lurched again. This time, Aru didn't fall against the window . . . she went *through* it! Wind tossed her hair as she gripped the edge of the door, her feet dangling in the air.

"Vajra!" she screamed.

Her lightning bolt crackled to life, and Aru caught hold of it with one hand. She aimed Vajra, and electricity spangled the air. The geese drew back. . . .

But the sound must've frightened the vimana. It veered sharply, and Aru's one-handed grip loosened.

Don't look down don't look down. . . .

She looked at the ground hundreds of feet below, and a wave of nausea hit her. Vajra zoomed beneath her feet as a hoverboard and hurtled her back through the window.

"You made it worse!" said Rudy, now flat on the floor of the chariot.

Brynne couldn't get a good hold on her wind mace in the

commotion. There was no way Aru was going to use Vajra on the geese again. But then Mini stepped up. She didn't love heights, either, but she staggered to her feet and pointed her Death Danda out the window. With one muttered word she made a huge mirror appear on the back side of the vimana.

"Nothing to see here," she said quietly. "Just clouds. Only clouds."

It must have looked that way to the geese. The mirror reflected the sky and disguised the vehicle. The birds fell back. The seesawing motion of the vimana slowed, and Brynne was finally able to use her wind mace. She whisked it through the air to create a cyclone that blocked out the honking of the geese.

Aiden swerved the vimana higher into the clouds, quickly adjusting the autopilot setting so it rode smoothly. And then he promptly collapsed in the backseat.

As they left the birds behind and Mini withdrew the mirror, Aru peered out the window at one last fowl straggler.

"*Never* feeding you again," she said darkly.

"There it is," called Brynne. "VPD headquarters!"

When Aru had heard that VPD had its own skyscraper, she assumed it would look like any of the other tall buildings that made up the New York City skyline. It did not. It was wedged between two huge buildings and seemed, for all intents and purposes, completely invisible to ordinary humans. And it was literally a skyscraper. The building looked like a giant arm made of molten gold, and on top it had fingers that held clouds and swayed back and forth as if it were scratching at an itchy spot on the sky.

The vimana flew toward the slanted golden palm, which had a large dark hole in its center. Brynne explained that it was the opening to a chute that went directly down into the building.

Rudy swallowed hard, clutching the outer edge of the chariot. "Can we take the stairs?"

Beside him, Mini beamed, which made Rudy recoil a bit.

"What is it?" he asked.

"I like that you get scared."

"That makes you happy?" asked Rudy, inching farther away.

"So, what happens now?" cut in Aru.

"We jump," confirmed Brynne. "Gunky says all the employees at VPD enter this way. It's supposed to signify a leap of faith and inspiration or something. I dunno. Architects can be a little weird."

Brynne pulled Gunky's employee-ID card out of the front pocket of her backpack. She waved it over the dark opening and a faint light beamed from inside. "Let's link hands and go."

She took Aiden's hand, and he offered his other one to Aru. She hesitated, then started reaching toward him. She knew it was just for the jump, but time seemed to slow as she thought of a thousand terrible scenarios: What if her palm was sweaty? If it was, Aiden could slip out of her grip and tumble to the ground. What if it wasn't sweaty but weirdly callus-y and he was so grossed out he let go and fell to the sidewalk?

Oh my gods, I'm turning into Mini.

Aiden grabbed her hand.

"Sorry if I'm sweaty and callus-y?" blurted out Aru.

Aiden looked deeply confused. "Good to know?"

With her other hand, Aru grabbed Mini, who was linked

to Rudy. Aru noticed that Mini was smiling, but Rudy looked downright terrified. Rudy was linked to Brynne.

"On the count of three," Brynne said. "One, two—"

Brynne leaped out, and as they tumbled through the dark, Mini hollered, *"WHAT ABOUT THREEEEE?"*

THIRTEEN

Begone, Discount Artichokes!

In theory, getting to work by going down a giant slide sounded great to Aru. In practice, though, it was downright terrifying. Wind howled against her face as she zoomed down what felt like the dark throat of a giant monster. Their hand link had totally broken in the fall, and Aru started flailing. She summoned Vajra in ball form, but it was as if the slide were enchanted against any light. Maybe it wouldn't have been so bad if she could've heard her friends, but an intercom system started blasting through the tunnel, and a voice that she could only assume belonged to the great Vishwakarma—or Mr. V, as Brynne called him—thundered:

"TODAY'S CREATIVE THEME IS *MINDFULNESS*! WHICH IS TO SAY...I'VE GOT A MIND THAT'S FULL. DO NOT APPROACH MY OFFICE WITH WORTHLESS DESIGN IDEAS LIKE TRANSLUCENT STAPLERS. YES, THAT IS A DIRECT REFERENCE TO YOUR BUFFOONERY, CASEY LIEU. WE NEED TO DO BETTER. DAZZLE ME, PEONS! I'M OUT!"

The voice paused, and then said ominously:

"AND REMEMBER... EVERYTHING IS BY DESIGN."

At last Aru tumbled out of the chute, landing facedown on shiny blue tiles. Her first thought was *Poor Casey*. Her second thought was *Where the heck* am *I?* She stuffed Vajra in her pocket, pushed herself up on her elbows, and turned her head to look around.

They were beneath a giant stained-glass dome designed to represent a magnified butterfly's wing, each segment of color outlined in white. The walls loomed sleek and pale, with one of them covered in a display of polished mirrors that bore reflections of different settings: seashores and desert dunes, cloud-wrapped cliff tops and steaming green jungles.

Aru got to her feet and read a little glass plaque on the wall:

THIS BUILDING IS CELESTIAL LEED CERTIFIED. ALL MATERIALS USED HERE ARE 100 PERCENT RECYCLED! THE RECLAIMED WOOD IS FROM THE LOST CIVILIZATION OF KUMARI KANDAM; THE STAINED-GLASS PANES WERE PRESSED FROM THE FORAGED TEARS OF DESPAIRING PRINCESSES; AND ALL THE BORDERS WERE MADE FROM THE DISCARDED BABY TEETH OF LEVIATHANS FROM OFF THE INDIAN COAST. REDUCE YOUR CARBON FOOTPRINT/HOOFPRINT/PAWPRINT BY INQUIRING HOW OUR ARCHITECTS CAN ASSIST WITH YOUR BUILDING NEEDS.

Along one of the pale walls was a glass bubble with a receptionist standing inside. He was dark-skinned and handsome. He wore an oversize white tee full of holes, a ginormous pair of bright-red framed glasses, and jeans with so many rips it looked like he'd somehow wrested them from the jaws of a shark.

"Namaste," he greeted the group, pressing his palms together. "How can we redirect the energy of the universe to"—he hesitated, looking them up and down—"better serve your needs?" His voice tipped up a bit at *needs.*

Aru looked down at her outfit. Okay... so, it wasn't exactly couture or anything, but it wasn't that awful. Or maybe it was, judging from the receptionist's curling lip. Mini ducked behind Aiden, who defiantly shoved his hands in his pockets. Rudy, who was the only one who didn't earn a sneer from the receptionist, adjusted his collar. Brynne took the lead and approached the desk.

"We're here to see Mr. V," she said.

The receptionist peered over his glasses at her. "Do you have an appointment?"

"Well, no, but you see, we're..."

Brynne paused. She couldn't say *Pandavas.*

"You're... what?" repeated the receptionist. "Lost, perhaps?"

A cold draft swept through the lobby, indicating that Brynne was *not* pleased.

Rudy stepped toward the desk and cleared his throat. "Sorry about my assistant," he said smoothly. "She must've hit her head on the fall down the slide. We don't have an appointment, but Mr. V is expecting me. I'm Prince Rudra of Naga-Loka, and I've come to solicit his services. These are my"—he gestured at the others—"entourage. Photographer, cook, assistant, healer. Traveling with a skeleton staff today."

The receptionist's eyes widened a bit, and he rose to his feet, quickly bowing. "Oh!" he said. "Excuse me, Your Highness!"

"Please, call me Rudy."

A hallway materialized in a formerly blank wall.

"I'll let him know you're here," he said. "But I have to warn you, Mr. V is not in the best of moods today." He motioned to the corridor. "Go right ahead... if you dare."

The hallway to Mr. V's office was lined with blueprints revealing all the great cities he had designed, like Dwarka, where the god Krishna once ruled and lived, or the mythical golden city of Lanka, ruled over by Kubera, the god of riches.

"So what's this Mr. V like?" Rudy asked Brynne in a whisper. "Gotta adjust my attitude, you know? Am I going for charming? Rich? Rich *and* charming? Kinda weird? But, like, intellectually weird? Or—"

"Silent?" suggested Aiden.

Rudy paused, then tapped his own chin. "*Yeahhh.* Silent and brooding, like you! Okay, so give me some tips. Do you hate everyone, or is it more like an inward, self-loathing thing?"

Aiden glowered. "I don't hate anyone, but you're proving to be the exception."

"Okay, so not an inward, self-loathing thing..."

Aru couldn't help herself. A terrible snort-laugh escaped her lips. Rudy caught her eye, and the corner of his mouth lifted.

"Gunky says that Vishwakarma is really creative," said Brynne. "But that sometimes he can be a little unpredictable—"

At the end of the corridor, a wastebasket flew out of an office, followed by a howl of curses. The five of them flattened themselves against the wall as the trash can rolled to a stop in front of them and caught fire.

"WHY ARE PEOPLE OBSESSED WITH YOU?" yelled Mr. V to someone in his office. "I don't understand your appeal! *Give* me some inspiration! None of you are inspiring—"

A loud clattering sound echoed around them. Mr. V must have knocked a bunch of stuff off his desk.

"That's it!" he yelled. "GET OUT, YOU FLATTENED DISCOUNT ARTICHOKES!"

Aru raised her eyebrows.

What a weird insult.

And then dozens of succulents emerged from the office doorway and rolled down the hall. Some of them looked slightly charred. One of them quivered as it sped faster and faster away from Mr. V.

"Huh," said Aru, staring at the little plants. "They *do* kinda look like discount artichokes. . . ."

Rudy took a few tentative steps toward the office door, and all of a sudden the marble floor under his feet lit up, veins of gold brightening and casting light onto the walls.

"WHAT IS IT?" screamed Mr. V. *"COME IN HERE WHERE I CAN SEE YOU!"*

"Maybe we should send our proposal by email instead?" asked Rudy, inching backward.

Brynne shoved him forward. "It was your idea to be the front, and we *need* that key!"

Aru cast an eye toward the door, her heart beating loudly in her ears. What if Vishwakarma refused to make the key? They'd have no way of opening vault A7 in the crypt and hopefully learning the whereabouts of the wish-granting tree. Then again, if Mr. V decided he hated them, they might never even make it to the crypt.

"I need a second!" said Rudy. He breathed in through his nose and out through his mouth. "Happy thoughts, people. Tell me some happy things."

"I perfected my macaron recipe," offered Brynne.

"Cool, I'll take it." Rudy looked at Aiden, who glared at him in return. "Okay, I'll skip you."

He turned to Mini. "Got anything?"

"I, um, well . . ." Mini turned red. "There's about forty thousand bacteria in the human mouth? And the human intestine is twenty feet long, and—"

Rudy wrinkled his nose. "All right, let's stop there. I'm going in."

Inside the office, floor-to-ceiling windows let in the sunlight and looked out on skyscrapers in different cities: Mumbai and New Delhi, New York City and London. In the corner of the room, next to a golden potted plant, sat a pure-white goose. It honked when they entered and Rudy reared back, probably still traumatized from their earlier encounter in the vimana. But the bird didn't leave its nest.

At the center of the room, seated behind a huge mahogany desk with a single sheet of paper on it, was the god of architects and craftsmen, in a charcoal-gray suit. Mr. V had four heads, each one sporting a neat white beard, black hair with silver stripes at the temples, and rimless half-moon glasses perched on the tip of the nose. His skin looked like bronze, and his four arms swiveled around him in an agitated manner. In one hand, he wielded a fountain pen. In another, a highlighter. In the third, a golden hammer, and in the fourth, a slim black ruler.

"I understand you have a proposition for me, Princeling," he spat, fixing the eyes of Head Two on Rudy.

The other heads didn't follow suit. One stared at the paper. The third gazed out the window, sighing. And the fourth narrowed his eyes at Aiden, Brynne, Aru, and Mini. Aru shrank back. The last thing she wanted was Vishwakarma figuring out that they were Pandavas.

"Yes, I do," answered Rudy, pitching his voice lower.

An immediate change took place in the snake boy. His grin didn't waver, but he stood up straighter and arched his eyebrows as if he'd just heard something supremely unimpressive. "My father's kingdom has long loved your exquisite designs, and he—"

Vishwakarma leaned back, plunking his feet up on his desk. "Let me guess . . . wants a golden kingdom?" he said with a sneer. "Because *I'M ALL OUT.*"

"No—"

"A flying swan chariot with gilded wings and eyes of jet?"

"No—"

"Then *what*? Spit it out! You're wasting my invaluable brain energy on guesswork!"

"A *key*," Rudy sputtered.

Vishwakarma stared at him for what seemed like ages. At last he blinked, then threw his head back and laughed.

"A *key*?" he howled. "What am I to make next? *Roombas?*" Mr. V paused. "You know, that might not be a bad idea. They're strangely charming. . . . Perhaps they could be a sort of hybrid pet-device. It would need some improvements, of course. It has no capacity to defend itself, so fangs are critical. A tail could also serve as a mop. And then—"

"We need a key that can unlock all doors," cut in Aru. "Including magical and enchanted ones."

Mr. V paused and turned to scrutinize them a little more closely. "Who did you say your companions were?" he asked Rudy.

"I didn't," said Rudy casually. "They hardly matter. My entourage changes daily."

Vishwakarma's fourth head craned its neck toward Aru. "That one looks familiar."

"She gets that a lot," said Brynne. "Very, uh, generic face."

Aru cut her eyes at Brynne, who gave her a grin and a tiny wave.

"Oh, come now, Four," Head One said. "It's just a little girl."

The fourth head scowled. "I don't trust little girls."

"Well, now you just sound like a curmudgeon," said Head One. "What do you think, Two and Three?"

"Fanged roombas..." the third head said dreamily.

"We've lost Number Three," Head One said with a sigh. "I, for one, am thinking about the utility of such a key. Would it be used to free imprisoned maidens? Steal treasure? Hide cookies? I do like cookies...."

"I'm known for building cities, Princeling," thundered Head Four. "Palaces! Things of beauty! Not hardware! What does a naga prince want with such a key, anyway? It would be a hungry, curious thing indeed."

Rudy cleared his throat and crossed his arms. "In the realm of Naga-Loka, we have an extensive underground tunnel system where we store our jewels and treasures. We've had these for at *least*"—he flipped his hand dramatically—"four millennia. Sadly, we sometimes find ourselves locked out of our own vaults or forgetting the passwords. A key like yours would solve the problem."

For the first time, Vishwakarma looked troubled. He stroked his four chins with his four hands. Then his third head ducked so that one of the hands could scratch the tip of his nose.

"I have not taken such a commission in some time," said Head One. "I suppose it's not an outrageous request, given your status as a naga prince. And it *would* be within my power to grant. . . ."

Mr. V raised his four hands. When he twisted them, the room went completely dark. A glowing orb appeared in the air, rotating slowly before darting around like a laser pointer and shifting into different forms—from orb to shovel to key and back to a ball of light.

It was unlike any key Aru had ever seen. Vajra bobbed up from her pocket, as if curiously inspecting this new magic. Vishwakarma's fourth head stared hard at the glowing ball, and Aru quickly shoved Vajra out of sight. Her lightning bolt shot her with a quick, disgruntled *zap!*

"Using a key like this will not be easy," mused Mr. V. He reached up, caught the ball of light, and spun it on his palm. It shifted into a slithering snake, and then a fish with rainbow scales. "A key that unlocks all things has to be able to see what it's doing. It is, in a sense, *alive,* and it might demand something in return for its services."

Mr. V glared at them with all four pairs of eyes when he said, "Are you willing to pay the price?"

FOURTEEN

In Which A Giant Nose Spells (Smells!) Trouble

Are you willing to pay the price?

As if that were a real question. With each passing minute the Sleeper grew more powerful. And if they didn't find the real Kalpavriksha, he could win the war. Aru only had to shut her eyes for her mind to conjure images of the Otherworld laid to waste. The beautiful tents of the Night Bazaar ripped open like sacks of grain. The heavens on fire. Her friends and family . . . *gone.*

"Yes," she said.

Vishwakarma bowed his heads, and the walls of the office drew closer together.

"Very well," he said from all four mouths. "In this part of the world, payment must be made in advance. If you can capture the key, it is yours."

The walls shimmered, so bright they were almost impossible to look at. Aru shielded her eyes, blinking rapidly. When she could open them again, she was in an entirely different room.

The god had vanished, and so had the walls and the windows with their views of distant cities.

Aru looked down to see cold rock beneath her feet.

The five of them had been plunged into an area that resembled a crypt. It was lit by a handful of candles mounted in niches of the rock wall, and slick, leafy vines netted nearly everything. When the candlelight flickered across them, it almost looked as if the plants were moving.

Aru detected a slight flutter in the corner of her vision. Was that a moth? No, she realized as she looked closer. It was a small white flower hopping along a vine.

At the very center of the room stood a glass column. And within it hovered the shimmering orb containing the golden key.

Brynne took one look at the column and raised her mace. "We just have to break it and—"

"No!" cried Mini, grabbing hold of Brynne's arm. "If we do that, Mr. V will know we're Pandavas."

Brynne frowned momentarily before flashing a grin. "Then we'll try brute force."

She walked over, revved up her arm, and punched the glass. Inside, the key trembled but didn't move. Something else did.

From overhead came a terrible creaking sound.

"You broke the room!" exclaimed Rudy.

Aru looked up. The ceiling bore the likenesses of Vishwakarma's four faces, all of them carved from stone and fixed with identical stern expressions.

"Can I be excused?" called Rudy loudly. "I'm not the one paying for the key—*they* are!"

"You're the one who wanted to be part of this quest," said Aiden.

"Yeah, *quest*, not fatal shopping experience!"

"I've seen the Kingdom of Death," said Mini. "It's not that bad."

Rudy whimpered, calling out, *"Helloooo?!"*

Something broke off from the ceiling, clinking on the ground like a pebble. Aru crouched to pick it up.... It *was* a pebble. More and more pelted down on them, accompanied by an eerie groaning sound, like someone was moving a heavy boulder into place.

"Guys..." said Aiden. "Is the ceiling collapsing?"

Sure enough, the four faces of Vishwakarma had slowly begun to descend. The glass column holding the golden key shrank little by little, and Aru realized what Mr. V had planned for them:

Death by architecture. He was going to squish them.

"Better he finds out who we are when we're alive and not dead," said Brynne, raising her mace once more. She looked up at Aru and Mini. "Any other ideas?"

"I just..." Aru started, then paused.

Something struck her, and it wasn't a rock. The key in the center of the room... The falling ceiling... The way Vishwakarma's voice had twisted when he spoke of the key as *alive*...

"What?" yelled Aiden, but then the ceiling groaned once more and Aru lost her train of thought.

"We don't have time to talk! Let's break the glass!" said Brynne, baring her teeth.

Mini nodded, sweeping Dee Dee to the right. Her Death Danda turned into a long, blunt hammer. Aru flexed her fingers, and Vajra shot into her hand as a lightning bolt. Aiden pushed a button on Shadowfax, and the camera folded up and disappeared as two long, shining scimitars grew from the bands around his wrists.

Beside them, Rudy's eyes widened. He awkwardly patted the front of his jacket. "Huh," he said. "I think I missed the memo about carrying a concealed weapon. Can I borrow one?"

"Can you even fight?" demanded Brynne.

"Um, *yes,*" said Rudy, holding his hand to his heart. "I am a trained prince of my realm, after all."

Aiden pulled a short dagger from his satchel. He tossed it to Rudy, who reached out, failed to catch it, and scrambled to pick it up off the floor.

"How do I—?"

"Pointy end out!" yelled Brynne.

Brynne waved her wind mace overhead, creating a funnel of air, and volleyed it at the column of glass. The wind bounced back, swiping her feet out from under her and sending her sprawling against Aiden. He caught her right before she hit the floor.

Above them, the ceiling loomed closer. Close enough that Aru could see the details in the stone faces and *smell* the rock, which had an iron tang like dried blood. Terror shot through her veins, but Aru pushed it down.

Not today, Shah, she told herself. *You are not going to be squished like a bug by a giant NOSE.*

She aimed her lightning bolt at the crystalline column and let Vajra loose. With a loud crackle, the bolt sparked against the glass. Prickles of light shot up only to spin outward. The column was unscathed.

Aiden frowned, then charged the column himself, his

scimitars flashing. His blades landed with an empty thud. *Nothing.* Mini slammed Dee Dee against the pillar. Violet light burst through the room, but still the enchanted cylinder wouldn't break.

The stones from above fell faster. Now the ceiling was hardly five feet above their heads. Rudy held his hand over his perfectly coiffed hair and measured the distance between it and the descending ceiling. "Shouldn't you guys be *doing* something?!"

Brynne growled and whirled on him. "We're trying to break this thing! If you have any smart ideas, feel free to chime in!"

She charged the column once more with Aiden and Mini right beside her, but Aru hung back. "Shah!" called Brynne. "Get over here!"

But Aru knew that column wasn't going to budge. Against all their powers, it remained as pristine as ever. And yet... off to the side that small white flower danced and hopped, skipping from vine to vine as if it were...

Alive.

"Forget about breaking the glass!" hollered Aru. "It's not the real key!"

"What are you talking about? It's right *there,*" insisted Brynne.

"It's a trick," said Aru.

She ran over to the small white blossom, which had jumped to a leaf at Aru's shoulder level. She reached out and gently cupped the flower in her hands. It lay still in her palms for a moment before a flare of light shot through the petals. Luminescence skittered up the vine, moving from the top all the way down and disappearing into the ground....

"The roots," said Aru. "The key is in the roots!"

The ceiling kept descending. Brynne glared at it. "You work on the roots, I'll take care of the ceiling," she said.

In a flash of blue light, she transformed into a sapphire-colored elephant kneeling on the floor. Her broad back held up the ceiling.

"Can't—do this—forever," she managed.

Aru gripped the plant tightly. She felt a sudden pressure around her waist and looked down to see Brynne's trunk was wrapped around her.

I've got you, Shah.

Aru smiled. "I know," she said aloud. "Mini, Aiden, stay alert. Whatever's at the base can change and come alive, so you guys have to be ready. On my count... One, two—"

On *three,* Aru and Brynne yanked out the vine. The root ball emerged from the dirt, glowing intensely, and on the bottom of it, something thrashed and twisted. The light was so bright, Aru almost couldn't see it, but eventually she caught fluctuating shapes—a silver fish turned into a silver bird turned into a silver key. An impossible key that fluttered like a heartbeat.

The vine wrestled with Aru, flapping like a possessed octopus.

"Grab the key!" she called to the others.

Mini lunged for it, but the tiny thing wriggled out of her reach. She dove again, trying to pluck it off the roots, but the key was too tricky.

A clang sounded, and out of the corner of her eye, Aru saw Aiden leap forward, his scimitars blazing. He sliced off the root ball with one sharp move. The strange plant howled and flopped to the floor.

Aru reached forward and snatched the key off the ground just before Brynne collapsed with a groan, changing back to human form, and the rock ceiling finally gave way.

There was a flash of violet and a yelp of surprise from Rudy as a translucent dome covered the group, protecting them from the falling rubble. Mini stood with her Death Danda pointed upward, a triumphant look on her face. An expanse of afternoon sky stretched above her.

Rudy turned his face to the light, gazing up at Mini in shock. "You made this shield?" he asked. "If you hadn't, I could've *died* in, like, a second."

Mini lowered Dee Dee, her smile spreading wider. "I don't think it would've happened that fast," she said. "Eventually you might have suffered from asphyxiation—that's when you suffocate."

"Um, thanks?"

"You're welcome!" said Mini brightly, before adding, "Brynne protected us, too."

Aiden crawled over to make sure Brynne was okay. She gave him a thumbs-up. "Cleverness saves the day again," said Brynne, nodding with genuine appreciation.

Aru closed her fingers around the cool silver object in her palm. As she did so, she felt as if she were seeing the past few months in a new light. Something had begun to shift among the group. She felt the weight of her friends' reliance on her, as if she were supposed to *know* what to do when she was just trying to figure it out like the rest of them. Brynne was right that Aru usually came up with the plan, but that didn't mean she wanted to be *in charge* of what they did. That much trust...

it felt like a burden. What if she let them down? Aru thought of Opal's words: *Or you! The flesh-and-blood daughter of the Sleeper . . .*

Aru wanted to respond, but just then a voice thundered above them:

"YOU'RE PANDAVAS?"

FIFTEEN

No One Signed Up for a Horcrux Hunt

The five of them were transported back to Mr. V's office in the blink of an eye. The god of architects was standing behind his mahogany desk, his four hands splayed on the surface, his four heads craned forward, and his four sets of eyes wide open.

Aru held the key close to her chest, and as she did, it seemed to squirm not just in her hands, but also in her heart. A long-buried memory wormed through her thoughts, conjuring her sixth-grade semiformal dance. It was a big deal at her school. She'd been so excited to go, and her mom had even let her borrow one of her real gold bangles. But it had opened with a father-daughter dance, and Aru had panicked. She couldn't stand the idea of leaning against the wall, clutching her cup of fruit punch, while her lack of a father shone on her like a spotlight. The moment the dance started, she pretended to slip and sprain her ankle. One of the teachers had driven her home in silence while Aru fought back tears the whole way. If she'd had a dad, would he have danced with her? Or at least driven her there and back, lecturing about boys the way dads did in movies?

You do *have a father,* whispered a voice in her head.

And he'd gone looking for the Tree of Wishes, just like she was about to do.

Aru abruptly dropped the key. Instantly, all those thoughts and feelings were sucked back into their usual hiding places, and her pulse slowed to normal. She made no move to pick it back up.

The sound of the key hitting the floor seemed to bring Vishwakarma back to himself. His eight eyes roved from the key to the Pandavas' faces, and he crossed his four arms, a shrewdness sneaking into his gaze.

"What do you want with such a key, Pandavas?" asked Head One.

All five of them burst out at the same time.

Rudy pointed at his own face and said, "*Prince,* not *Pandava.*"

Brynne said, "I invoke architect-client confidentiality before I say anything to you!"

Aiden grumbled, "Technically, I'm not a Pandava—"

Mini cautiously said, "I'm not sure we should disclose that information. Sorry..."

But the key had unlocked something new and terrible within Aru: honesty.

"To save the Otherworld," she said. "We only have five days."

The rest of them fell silent as Vishwakarma's eyes snapped to her. He seemed to look both past her and *into* her.

"The key is a very dangerous thing to use for that purpose," said Head One.

"I think we know how to open a door," retorted Brynne, but she cowered when the four heads swiveled in her direction.

"This is a living key, child," said Head One. "Living things cannot help but be curious, to demand answers. There is a cost to opening doors that are meant to stay closed. Some have paid the price quite dearly."

Aru shivered, remembering the key sparking her thoughts and feelings like someone had flashed a light into her brain's dark corners.

"Are you going to tell the devas that we came here?" asked Brynne.

Mr. V regarded them silently for a moment before Head Three finally said, "No. I am a builder of grandeur, not an agent of destruction—"

"Well, then maybe you could build something grand for us—" started Aru.

"Do you think you are so clever?" asked Head Four in a rasping voice. "Perhaps you believe you are the only ones who've ever sought to change their fate? Foolish children! I've made this commission before. . . ."

He waved his four hands and his view of the city skylines disappeared, replaced with a murky image of a young man victoriously holding up a golden key. Its glow illuminated his unusually colored eyes—one blue and one brown.

Aru's heart twisted in recognition. It was *him.*

When Mr. V's window returned to normal, Aru realized that Brynne and Mini had drawn closer to her. Mini's shoulder touched hers; Brynne laid a hand on her arm. But as much as Aru wanted to draw strength from them, she couldn't. At her throat, her mother's pendant felt ice-cold against her skin.

"The Sleeper was here," said Aru.

"He used the key, child," said Head One.

"What did it unlock in him?" she forced herself to ask.

Head One hesitated before answering. His gaze became distant then, and a strange pearlescent sheen covered his eyes. "You shall find out, Pandavas. He unlocked as much of himself as he dared to in his pursuit, and the pieces still remain."

Pieces? Aru felt her stomach churn uncomfortably. What did that mean? It reminded her of what her mother had said in the museum. . . .

He came home an entirely different person, like something was missing from him.

"Are you saying the Sleeper left behind Horcruxes?" Aru demanded.

"Yeah, I didn't sign up for a Horcrux hunt," said Rudy, looking around for the exit.

Mini held out Dee Dee, blocking his way.

"I am merely saying there are pieces to find should you follow this path," said Mr. V.

The key floated off the floor and transformed into a snake that coiled around Aru's wrist, resting its silver head against her pulse. She couldn't shake it off, even though she tried.

"It's taken a liking to you, Aru Shah," said Head One. "And that means that for its first use, only you may wield it."

"But I—"

Mr. V slid a blue velvet pouch across the desk. "This will keep it from moving around. Now go. You've earned the key, but it may not bring what you desire."

Aru took the bag and loosened its drawstring. Immediately, the key slid off her arm and toppled into the pouch. Aru hastily balled the whole thing up and shoved it into the bottom of her backpack. She felt the key's phantom presence and imagined she could hear it purring contentedly. She wanted to feel a rush of accomplishment, of *excitement,* but all she felt was fear.

That *thing* had read little bits and pieces of her. What else would this quest demand? Would it cut slices from her, return her home an entirely different person? And what did it mean that the Sleeper had lost pieces of himself on his search for the wish-granting tree?

Sheela's voice rose from beneath all those thoughts.

There's lots more to find.

SIXTEEN

Florals for Spring? Groundbreaking.

The vimana took them to Brynne's penthouse, where she lived with her uncles, to have a home-cooked meal and get some sleep before the next day's journey.

Rudy trailed Gunky and Funky around the apartment, asking them important questions like:

"What's a microwave? Is it like a bottled-up part of the ocean?"

"Does this remote open a portal?"

"Could you make me some lasagna?"

After a dinner of awkward small talk with the uncles, because the Pandavas couldn't reveal anything about their mission, Aru wanted nothing more than to crash in Brynne's room. The pullout bed was already made up, and luckily she didn't have to share it with Mini, who had promptly passed out on the living room couch after lamenting that she'd forgotten to pack floss. Aiden had made a beeline to the guest bedroom.

Rudy paused outside Brynne's room, leaning against the doorway like he owned it.

"First thing in the morning, we're heading to the Crypt

of Eclipses," he said excitedly. "But that's inside the House of Months, and there's no *way* I can be seen with you guys there if you don't level-up your outfits. I'm thinking you could—"

Brynne slammed the door in his face, growling, "*Good NIGHT*, Rudy."

Moments later, Aru was fast asleep.

This wasn't one of Aru's usual dreams.

She knew that because her dreams typically started with her wandering through Home Depot only for the aisle to end up looking like her math classroom. This time she was in a fashion designer's studio. One wall had panels of different color swatches. Another wall was covered with racks holding bolts of fabric. A third was all windows, and the last wall was a giant chalkboard with sketches of fashionably dressed women. The drawings magically peeled themselves off the black surface and sauntered down the middle of the room as if it were a runway.

Sheela and Nikita sat across from Aru at a worktable. Nikita was sitting in a bizarre flower throne, and Sheela perched on a high stool covered with star stickers. Sheela waved happily, then went back to tracing letters in the air. At every gesture of her hand, a trail of tiny stars lit up the space and hovered there.

"Told ya we'd see you in your dreams!" said Sheela.

Aru blinked, and Brynne and Mini were standing beside her wearing identical expressions of confusion.

Brynne looked at Aru, shocked. "I was literally just in the middle of winning a cooking competition! Why am I now in your dream?"

"If you were in Aru's dream, we'd be in Home Depot," said Mini.

"It's a great place!" said Aru a little defensively. "You can—"

Nikita clapped twice, and the three girls snapped to attention. She was dressed, as usual, in a completely new outfit: white pants, white blazer, white scarf to pull the braids back from her face, and a delicate choker of vines.

"Nice outfit?" tried Aru.

"Obviously!" snapped Nikita. "It's my spring ensemble."

"Doesn't really look spring-y to me. Don't you need flowers or something?"

Nikita's eyes narrowed. "Florals? For spring? Groundbreaking."

Rude! thought Aru.

Aru couldn't decide if she was annoyed or impressed. Was this common little-sister behavior? If so, they were the worst.

"Boo told us the Crypt of Eclipses is inside a super-swanky place," said Nikita. "To get into the House of Months, you guys'll need a change of clothes."

Aru crossed her arms. "Between now and dawn—not a whole lot of time to go shopping."

"And that's where I come in," said Nikita. "I'll whip something up. We've got access to all the plants in the heavens, which can easily become outfits with a bit of magic. Boo said he could arrange for a celestial messenger to get them to you by tomorrow morning."

"His exact words were 'I'll do anything if you stop treating me like an avian mannequin—get that silk hat off my head this instant, you abominable child!'" quoted Sheela.

Nikita snapped her fingers and a yellow tape measure ribbon appeared in the air. It snaked around, then darted toward Mini, its metal tip quivering as if it were a predator snuffling out prey. The next few minutes were a chaotic blur as Nikita sent an army of measuring tapes after them. The tapes wriggled like eels, circling the Pandavas' waists and legs. Brynne tried to rip them off, but they held fast. Aru found herself floating as several different pairs of shoes took turns wedging themselves onto her feet before scuttling off like angry mice. All the while, Nikita was shouting random fashion remarks like: "A-line cuts are too boring!" and "MORE DANDELION FAUX FUR!" and the occasional "I'm thinking *rich,* luxe tones. A color that screams *WATCH OUT, DEMONS!* Maybe aubergine..."

Eventually, Aru was released from the tiny cyclone of measuring ribbons, and she stumbled toward Sheela, who was still perched on the same stool, quietly staring at a picture in her lap. The small stars still drifted around her, and Aru caught one in her hand.

"Nikita really likes clothes, huh?" said Aru.

"They're hers," said Sheela simply. She didn't look up. "When you move a lot, you don't get to keep many things. So she learned to make her own outfits. Nikki calls them armor. She thinks there's no reason armor shouldn't be pretty, too."

Aru's lungs felt squeezed. She moved closer and saw that Sheela was staring at a picture of two people who could only be the twins' mom and dad. The woman, who had large brown eyes and a gap-toothed smile, had her arms wrapped around a large black-skinned man who was laughing so hard that his eyes were shut.

Aru had no idea what she'd do if she couldn't see her mom, but she knew every family was different. Brynne, for example, was used to it. Then again, her mother, Anila, wasn't really interested in being around in the first place.

"How long has it been since you've seen your parents?" asked Aru gently.

"One thousand one hundred and seventeen days," said Sheela, her voice tight. "I thought we'd be able to see them in our dreams, but every time we try to get to them, the nightmares come. . . . I can't stop them. Because of the Otherworld's rules, our parents won't be able to find us until we turn thirteen. We thought getting Claimed would change things, but it hasn't. And the wishing tree was a fake. What if nothing works?" The room began to darken. Sheela's eyes started to go unfocused. "What if—?"

"Sheela!" barked Nikita.

Her design studio began to warp and shift.

A black sinkhole opened in the middle of the floor. It started sucking in the sketches that had come to life, the bolts of fabric, even the dream stars that swirled around Sheela.

"What's happening?" asked Brynne.

"The nightmare!" choked out Nikita. "Sheela, wake up! Wake up! It's okay!"

Mini ran over and to pull Sheela off the stool and away from danger, but the girl wouldn't move. Maybe she couldn't, thought Aru, as she too tugged uselessly on an arm.

"I miss them," sobbed Sheela. "I miss them so much."

This is a dream, Aru told herself. She tried to will things to change—to stop the sinkhole from spreading, to silence the sudden growl of thunder.

But it wasn't her dream. It was Sheela and Nikita's.

She balled her hands into fists and the tiny star she'd caught moments ago pricked her skin.

"Leave!" shouted Nikita. "Get out! You're not supposed to be in our dream anymore!"

Aru looked at her. Now Nikita's pantsuit was way too big on her, if she'd been playing dress-up with her mother's clothes. She was just a kid stuck in a nightmare with everything unraveling around her.

Aru reached out, and Nikita stared at her outstretched hand.

"We're not leaving you," said Brynne fiercely.

"But—" started Nikita.

Sheela began to sob. Mini wrapped her arms around her, soothing and shushing, but it was as if Sheela couldn't hear her anymore.

"Nikita, what do we do?" asked Aru.

But when she turned around, the dream changed. The twins, now three years younger, were crouched on the floor of a bedroom while Aru, Brynne, and Mini hovered above the room like ghosts. The twins' mother stood at the closed door, holding a finger to her lips in a *Shh* gesture.

"Open up!" called a man's voice. *"We know you're in there!"*

The voice thundered through the house, shaking the photos off the wall.

"Mommy!" cried Nikita, stretching out her arms.

"No!" said their mom in a whisper-shout, her eyes wide and frantic. "Stay there, and stay quiet. Someone from the Otherworld will come and get you. Don't try to follow us. I love you, my precious girls. We'll find you again, I promise."

"Don't go!" shouted Sheela. "Please—"

Tears streamed down their mother's face.

"I would do anything not to leave you," she whispered. "I'll see you in your dreams. Don't worry, my babies. There is so much more to you than you know. I—"

The dream began to shift and twist again. One moment, the twins' mother stood at the door. The next, the door stretched sideways and turned into a wave that crashed over her.

Aru, Brynne, and Mini were swept up in a dark flood that churned and swirled around the twins. Sheela and Nikita remained rooted to the spot, their arms wrapped around each other, and Aru knew they'd forgotten they were in a dream. The older Pandavas tried to swim toward the girls, but the nightmare held them back.

"Wake up!" screamed Brynne.

"Don't yell!" said Mini. "They need comfort."

Aru's heart ached. She looked down at her hands and realized the tiny star was still in her grip, glowing brightly. An idea came to her.

"They need light," she whispered.

Slowly, she opened her hand, and the wisp traveled outward.

"Wake up," said Brynne, more gently now.

"We've got you," said Mini softly.

Aru wished she could reach them, give them both a hug. She didn't care if Nikita was snobby and cold. She understood what it meant to wake up from a nightmare only to find you were still caught in a real-life one. And so she reached for the words her mother always said when Aru had a bad dream.

"If you're scared . . . just turn on the light."

SEVENTEEN

Never Trust a Hot Dog Stand

Aru woke up to Brynne dangling a package over her head. Mini stood behind her, shoulders bent and face clouded over with worry.

"We got a delivery from the heavens," said Brynne stonily.

The girls untied the brown silk ribbon and tore open the gold wrapping paper to find a carved white soapstone box. As they looked for a way to open it, Mini asked the question that weighed on all of their minds: "What are we going to do about the twins? They can't even talk to their parents, and now they're being held in Amaravati, and they can't…" Mini trailed off, sniffing loudly.

Fury rushed through Aru. No wonder Nikita acted the way she did. She would've been the same way if everything had been taken from her.

"Once we have the tree, we can fix everything," said Brynne. "No more war. No more doubt—"

"No more nightmares," finished Aru.

The box sprang open, revealing three gleaming outfits, and a letter tucked inside a fold. Brynne pulled it out, and a slow smile spread across her face as she showed it to Aru and Mini. It looked like instructions, and right on top, in neat black script, was a single line:

Thanks for turning on the light.

Aru grinned.

Fine, she thought. Maybe little sisters weren't so bad after all.

"We. Look. *Awesome,*" said Aru, inspecting her enchanted pants.

They were bright-yellow silk with glittery white swirls sewn on the hem. According to Nikita's notes, the embroidery was made out of sticky threads that could detach and form a nearly unbreakable rope.

Brynne had on a fuzzy sky-blue jacket designed to act as a parachute—while also keeping her comfortable in any temperature. Mini wore a plum-colored sweater and skirt that not only could serve as armor but also coordinated perfectly with Dee Dee.

"*Now* can we go?" shouted Aiden.

He and Rudy had been forced to wait for them in the hallway.

"Yes, yes," said Aru.

The boys trudged into the living room. Rudy stepped back. For today's ridiculous outfit, he was wearing a white denim jacket, a white tee, white jeans, and blindingly white high-tops. Beside him, Aiden looked like an elegant shadow.

Rudy looked them over. "You guys almost look as good as me."

"Thanks!" said Mini brightly, but then she frowned once she caught on that it was a typical Rudy compliment. Which is to say, it wasn't one.

Aiden, for his part, didn't say anything. He just looked from Brynne to Mini and, finally, Aru. His gaze seemed to linger on her a fraction too long. Long enough that Aru wondered if maybe she should've put up her hair or borrowed Mini's eyeliner or—

"Aren't you going to agree we look awesome?" she blurted out, lifting her chin.

On one level, Aiden's opinion didn't matter. Aru thought she looked awesome and her sisters thought the same, and that was enough. But another part of her wanted him to notice that she wasn't just some kid scuttling around with a lightning bolt and making Sméagol sounds. That she was a demigod and looked the part.

"You look . . ." he started to say, before suddenly glancing away.

Aru leaned forward, her skin prickling, but she knew it wasn't Vajra this time.

"Yeah?"

"Fine," said Aiden flatly.

Fine. Something behind Aru's chest sagged a little with hurt, but she shrugged it off. *Well, okay, then,* she thought, and marshaled everyone to the door.

"Time to make like a tree and—"

"Oh, Aru, please don't," groaned Mini.

"I can't take it," said Brynne with a sigh.

"LEAVE!" Aru cackled.

Using her ability to conjure exact coordinates, Brynne led them to a busy crosswalk. Around them, bright-yellow taxis honked and scooted their way down the streets. Tall trees swayed beside glossy, luxurious storefronts showing mannequins draped in jewels and silks and lots of other stuff Aru couldn't imagine actually wearing because it looked super itchy. Across the street lay the alley they were looking for, only it was blocked by a hot dog stand whose owner was fast asleep.

Brynne rubbed her stomach and sniffed the air hungrily. "I could really go for a hot dog."

"How can you be hungry when we *just* ate breakfast?" asked Mini.

"I'm a growing girl," said Brynne daintily.

Aiden rummaged through his camera bag and tossed Brynne a protein bar.

"Woot!" She grinned. "Thanks, Ammamma."

Rudy looked deeply horrified. "Hot *dogs*?" asked Rudy. "That's messed up."

"They're not actual *dogs*," said Brynne.

"Oh, so they're like mutant chimera creatures that you just call *dogs*," said Rudy, nodding as if this were completely sensible.

"No," said Brynne.

"Now I'm confused," said Rudy, shaking his head.

They ventured into the alley, which was crammed with trash and (at least) two dead rats. Aru wasn't usually squeamish, but *hello?* Her new yellow pants had not been made for this.

"*This* is the entrance to the super-fabulous House of Months?" asked Aru.

"Trust me," said Rudy.

Mini turned to face the opening of the alley. The hot dog owner was still asleep. A couple of people walked by toting their small dogs in huge purses or staring down at their phones.

"Adrishya," said Mini.

She swiped Dee Dee through the air as if she were drawing a curtain, and a veil of violet light shimmered down between them and the street. When Aru looked through the force field, it was like glimpsing the city beneath water. The images wavered and seemed far away—even the sound had dulled.

Rudy slowly rolled up his sleeves. Aru noticed, for the first time, a pattern of scales around his left wrist. He waved his hand in a complicated gesture.

"I, Prince Rudra of Naga-Loka and *frequent* visitor to the House of Months"—he mumbled something under his breath that sounded a lot like *with my mom*—"hereby request passage to see the guardian of a day."

Guardian of a day sounded pretty epic. Yesterday, Rudy had told them that the being who allowed or denied visits to the House of Months was the embodiment of a particular day, though not necessarily the current date. This struck Aru as rather strange. What would a day guardian even look like? Would Friday the thirteenth of October be really creepy? And what about National Cat Day?

Suddenly, the air right in front of Rudy shimmered and rippled.

A large silver door materialized before him. It was engraved with the words FEBRUARY 3 and the notation: THE DAY UPON WHICH RESENTMENT OF THE NEW YEAR SETS IN, AND ALL THOUGHTS OF PERSONAL IMPROVEMENT SLOWLY LEACH FROM ONE'S BRAIN.

Well, thought Aru, *that's cheerful.*

In the center of the door appeared a gigantic knocker in the shape of a lion, his mouth pulled back in a gruesome snarl. From his teeth hung a slender iron ring that Rudy lifted and dropped with a bang. At his knock, the lion blinked awake. He worked his jaw back and forth and then spat out the iron circle with a decisive *Plah!* The circle clattered to the ground, and the lion smacked his lips and glared at them with bleary silver eyes.

"Infants summoned me?" huffed the door lion, before shutting his eyes. "You're not our clientele. Please go."

"Excuse me, but I'm a *prince,*" said Rudy.

The door lion cracked open one eye. "What a novelty."

"I demand that you let me and my entourage in."

"I demand meh, meh, meh," mocked the lion. "No! Now go away!"

"All righty, let's have some words," said Brynne, and she pushed up the sleeves of her jacket.

"Ooh, a threat!" said the lion. "What are you going to do, *jamb* me? Attempt to make me *board* out of my mind so I let you through? Let me remind you that your entry *hinges* on my decision."

Brynne shouldered past Rudy, her hand going to the blue choker at her neck that could immediately turn into her wind mace. Aru grabbed her arm and sent a mind message: *If our cover is blown, so is this mission.*

Brynne grumbled, but she held still.

The door lion gloated. "See? You can't get a *handle* on me."

Aru was about to steamroll into the door when something happened....

Mini giggled, a smile breaking over her face.

The lion paused, his silver eyes going wide. If he could have tilted its head curiously to the side, he probably would have.

"I made you laugh," said the knocker, astonished.

Mini looked at her companions somewhat guiltily. "What? It was funny."

"I'm *funny*?" echoed the lion. He looked off to the side, as if scanning through all his past interactions. "Nobody's ever said that to me before. It's always *Open up!* Or *Shut up!* Do you know someone once used my snout as a coat hanger? A *coat hanger!*"

Aiden crossed his arms, his hand on his camera. "Was it a nice coat, at least?"

The lion considered this. "It was fine, I suppose."

If this door didn't like them, Aru realized, they'd never get to the Crypt of Eclipses. An idea came together in her head.

"Wait a minute," she said loudly. "You're *the* door lion of February third?" She took a step back, as if rereading the engraved sign.

The lion's whiskers twitched. "You've heard of me?"

"Of course we've heard of you!" said Aru, turning to her friends. "*Right?* Weren't we all just talking about how we wished *we* had a door like you?"

Aiden blinked, then said, "Yeah! We...uh, we totally said that."

Mini nodded eagerly. Brynne continued to glare.

"I've always been sad that my front door doesn't have a face," said Aru.

The lion gasped. "*No!* The *indignity*! Poor door. How does it bite intruders?"

"It, um, closes really hard on their fingers?"

The lion nodded. "Very sensible."

"You know, you're kinda famous, door," said Aru, shooting a pointed look at Rudy.

Rudy cleared his throat. "It's true, O benevolent... door."

The cheeks of the silver lion darkened, as if he was blushing. "Well, I—"

"In fact," said Aiden, lifting his camera, "could I take your picture?"

"Mine?" asked the door. "I... I... Why, yes! Yes, you may!"

Aiden counted down from three, and a bright flash went off. "Thanks!" he said. "It's too bad we can't do some shopping at the House of Months. Maybe we could've found at least *something* that reminds us of you."

The door lion's whiskers drooped. "Well, I mean, I suppose I could grant you *one* peek...."

"That would be very generous of you," said Mini sincerely.

The lion preened a bit and then the door swung open. As they filed inside, Aru paused to bow at the knocker, who faked a huge yawn.

"It's really nothing," he said loftily, but he could not help but grin back at Aru.

The passageway beyond the door was lit with constellation chandeliers. The walls on either side appeared like sheets of pristine ocean dotted with moon jellyfish, their delicate frost-colored tendrils trailing behind them. The floor felt like a lush carpet but was actually packed moss striped with bright wildflowers.

"Where the sky, sea, and stars meet," explained Rudy,

gesturing around him. "Oh, and by the way, you're welcome for me getting us in here."

Aru rolled her eyes, trying to ignore him as she gazed up at the world they'd entered. Magic still sometimes caught Aru by surprise. She loved how it made her feel *small.* Not like she was insignificant, but like the world was so much vaster and more colorful than she could ever imagine. Like she belonged to something greater than herself.

And yet, all that beauty could be so easily destroyed.

In five days, the treasure will bloom and fade,
And all that was won could soon be unmade.

They only had four days left. If the Sleeper won, it wasn't just the Otherworld that would be destroyed. It was families, too.

Aru stuffed her hands in her pants pockets, thinking of the twins and their mother's face when she had said *I would do anything not to leave you.* She felt a sharp wrench behind her ribs, as if the key from Mr. V were back in her hands. Aru's mother loved her, but she'd never said anything like that to her. And as for her dad... Well, he'd had no problem leaving her behind and didn't care that she was his kid. The Sleeper was a monster, she knew that—so then why did she want so badly to know if there had ever been a moment where he would've fought to keep her safe the way the twins' mother had?

Aru pushed the thought away as she walked on the path of wildflowers. A few paces down, the floor transformed into glass and the hall divided into two forks. On the left was a tunnel with a sign over it that read STAFF AND MAINTENANCE ONLY. Through the floor on that side, Aru could make out the dark, rushing waters of the Yamuna River. The passage looked too narrow for more than one person to fit through at a time.

On the right side was an ornate, gaping archway, and beyond it . . . the House of Months.

Aru had never seen anything like it.

It looked more like a mall-meets-a-skyscraper than a house. It was clearly divided into twelve layers, with one floor dedicated to each month. The bottom level was December, and through the windows, Aru could see racks of gowns crafted from gleaming ice and delicate silver. Stacked atop it was November, with drapes made of autumn leaves the color of old gold. Then October, piled with pumpkins, and September, sporting trees heavy with apples. Beyond that, Aru couldn't see. The building was too high, and she'd have to go through the archway get a better view. Rudy seemed to guess her thoughts. He stepped in front of her, shaking his head.

"That archway documents *every* person and creature that walks through," he said.

"And we've got to stay undercover," added Brynne grimly.

Aiden kept staring at the House of Months, his camera already in hand. "But where's the Crypt of Eclipses?"

"In an eclipse?" answered Rudy in a tone that clearly meant *duh*.

"How do you . . . hide a place . . . in an eclipse?" asked Aru.

"It travels around," explained Rudy. "Each of those floors includes all the days in a month. Whichever day held the last total lunar eclipse, *that's* where the Crypt is. Simple."

Sure, thought Aru, *simple*.

"When was the last lunar eclipse?" asked Aiden.

"January twentieth and twenty-first," said Mini. "It was a super-blood-wolf moon."

"January twentieth and twenty-first," said Rudy at the same time. "I think the mortals called it a werewolf's doom or something weird."

"Super-blood—" tried Mini halfheartedly before she gave up.

"Mini just said that," pointed out Aru.

"Oh," said Rudy. "Didn't hear."

"Or didn't listen," said Mini sadly.

Brynne reached out and squeezed Mini's shoulder as she walked toward the cramped service-and-maintenance entrance. "So we have to go through here?" she asked.

Rudy nodded. "It's the only way to get into the House undetected. It'll take us to December twenty-first, I think."

"And they leave it unguarded like this?" asked Aru.

"I think they just assume nobody would ever want to go through the river tunnel."

Aru looked at the dark, narrow entrance. This close, she thought she could hear the Yamuna River beneath them, cool and secretive. It raised the hairs on her arm.

"C'mon!" said Rudy.

Aiden looked to Aru. "Do you really think this is going to work?"

Aru almost reached for something silly to say, to make it less serious . . . less scary. But Aiden wasn't the only one focused on her. Rudy's eyes were full of hope. Mini's gaze was nervous, but unwavering. Even Brynne, who normally wanted to lead the way, was waiting expectantly for Aru's answer.

Aru squared her shoulders. "Of course the plan is going to work."

EIGHTEEN

The Plan Does Not Work

The maintenance entrance was no more than three feet wide and five feet high. Next to the tunnel opening, a little yellow sign read DO NOT DRINK THE WATER, which struck Aru as kinda weird. Who would want to drink river water anyway? Gross.

At first the group thought about entering in a single-file line, but that would be too risky if something went wrong and only *one* person could see ahead. So the plan became to send in a scout who could check things out and report back.

Rudy didn't seem to have a clue about how long the passage was. Aru didn't know much about the river herself other than it was named for a river goddess who once parted her waves to allow a baby god, Krishna, to escape when his evil uncle wanted to kill him. That sounded pretty dramatic, but Aru had learned that having one of your relatives want to put your head on a stake was par for the course in mythology.

"It must be short," said Rudy, trying to feign casualness. "The House of Months isn't far from here. Maybe it opens into a bridge—"

"Or maybe the tunnel ends suddenly," cut in Aiden, "and you have to swim the rest of the way. Could be they only hire people from the aquatic parts of the Otherworld."

Mini whimpered, and honestly, Aru wasn't exactly thrilled at the idea of swimming through those dark waters either.

"Come on, guys," said Brynne, rolling her eyes. "It probably just stretches over a stream."

Aiden coughed lightly, which he'd started doing after Aru once threatened to electrocute him for beginning a sentence with *Well, actually*...

"What is it, Ammamma?" asked Brynne.

"The Yamuna River is the second-largest tributary that connects to the Ganges."

"Meaning?" prompted Aru.

"Meaning it's huge."

"Well, one of us has to go in first to make sure it's safe," said Brynne.

"I agree completely," said Rudy, taking a step back. "Be my guest—"

"Rudy," said Brynne. "Since you're the only one of us who actually has permission to be inside the House of Months, *you* have to go first. That way, if you get caught and sent back, we can troubleshoot what to do next."

Rudy looked like he'd swallowed a bug. "But—"

"You're a prince," said Aiden. "I'm sure no one will mess with you."

"Yeah, you're right. I'm... a prince," echoed Rudy sadly.

He looked from them to the entrance, then steeled himself. "Fine."

He drew a gemstone out of his messenger bag. It looked like

a chunk of quartz, but when Rudy held it tightly, it released the sound of raindrops gently hitting a windowpane. The white noise sanded down the sharp edges of Aru's anxiety and slowed her shallow breathing. Without another glance, Rudy walked into the entrance, disappearing into the dark and humming to himself as he went.

Eventually, the sound of Rudy's singing vanished, replaced with the rush of water.

"Rudy?" called Aiden.

No response.

The four of them exchanged worried glances.

"He should've been able to call back," said Aiden nervously. "My mom is going to kill me if anything happens to him."

"He'll be fine," said Brynne, crossing her arms.

But two minutes turned into three... then seven.

"I'm going in after him," said Aiden finally. He touched the ends of his sleeves and his scimitars shot out. "Shah?"

Aru flicked her wrist and Vajra crackled to life. She brought it to Aiden's weapons and electricity ribboned down his blades.

"You've got two minutes, then we're going in after you," said Brynne.

"I'm sure he just got distracted looking at his reflection," said Aiden.

And in he went.

Once more they waited, and once more... nothing.

"I really don't like this," said Mini, holding Dee Dee close.

"I bet it's a magical barrier, and they're waiting for us on the other side," said Brynne, but for the first time she didn't sound so convinced. She looked at Aru and Mini. "I don't want to leave you guys alone."

"We'll be fine," said Aru even as Mini began to shake her head. "If anything happens, at least the two of us can go in together."

Brynne sighed, still uncertain. "If I don't come out in two minutes, come after me. Got it?"

"You got this," said Aru, clapping her on the back.

"Brynne, be careful," said Mini, holding her hand tightly for a moment. "Do you know what could be in the water? *Huge* fish. And riptides. Even a shark—"

"You really need to work on your pep talks," said Aru.

But Brynne was the bravest out of all of them, and at first Aru really wasn't worried when she entered the narrow passage.

At first.

The seconds trickled by, and Mini began to sing softly to herself. Then she stopped. "Something's gone terribly wrong, I can feel it," she insisted.

"We don't know that," said Aru. "It hasn't been two minutes—"

Ding!

The timer on Mini's watch went off, and the two girls stared at it. Aru felt a pressure building in her heart. They couldn't ignore the dark waters of the river any longer.

"What happened to them?" asked Mini.

"I'm sure it's nothing to worry about," assured Aru, but she could taste the lie on her tongue.

Rudy might've gotten distracted or lost or something, but Aiden and Brynne? They wouldn't have gotten turned around that easily.

"All right. Let's go," said Mini.

That was Mini. She had a list of unpronounceable phobias,

but still she somehow managed to be fearless when it mattered most.

Squeezing into the passage together wasn't that hard. As the smallest of their group of four, Aru and Mini usually had to take turns being squished in the middle of the backseat whenever Aru's or Mini's mom drove them to the movies. Luckily for Aru, Mini was pretty slow at Nose Goes! and ended up in the middle seat way more often.

The moment after they stepped into the tunnel, shadows rushed in and sealed up the space behind them, hardening into a solid black wall. Darkness swallowed them, and all Aru could hear was the river roaring in her ears.

She looked down, holding Vajra in ball form for light. Rudy's guess had been right. Instead of a glass floor, they were now standing on a slender bridge made out of iron grating. About a foot or so beneath them, the river flowed quickly. There weren't any railings on the sides to keep them from falling in, so they clutched each other for dear life.

A sharp pang of thirst hit Aru in the back of her throat. She swallowed impulsively, hating how dry her mouth felt. She reached for her backpack, then let her hand drop. Aiden had all the water bottles, and who knew where he was? Aru would just have to wait. As soon as they got out of here, she could have all the ice-cold water in the world.

Her gaze traveled back to the rushing water below. It looked as dark as poured ink, but Aru found herself fantasizing about how the water would taste. Like bottled-up winter. Like her whole soul had shriveled up and a single drop would be enough to plump it once more. Like—

"What's that above us?" asked Mini.

She pointed to the ceiling, and Aru became aware of her surroundings. In the air above the water shimmered a hundred reflections. The wavering images of temples and cities, grassy reeds and muddy banks, were all crammed together and reminded Aru of a collage of holograms.

"It must be every shore that the river touches," said Mini, staring up in awe.

"Must be," said Aru. She felt a little guilty about it, but she wasn't really listening. All she could think about was how parched her throat felt, how the inside of her mouth kept sticking to her teeth. She needed to get them out of here. The faster she could do that, the sooner they could join the others and get a drink. Aru cast Vajra's light farther out and saw an answering gleam from a small lantern not thirty feet away. It was affixed atop a little metal door.

"That has to be the exit," said Aru. "But that means they didn't even have to walk very far...."

Chills ran down her spine.

Mini looked to her left and right. "They're not here. They must have gone through...."

Aru didn't bother answering. She was too busy thinking about the water beneath them. Gods, she was thirsty. All she wanted was a glass of water. But not just any water. The rushing current of the Yamuna River called to her like a lullaby. It would be so easy to sink into it, let it soak through her clothes and drag her down to the bottom, and then she could gulp all the water she wanted—

"ARU!"

Aru felt Mini's hands on her shoulders. She blinked. Vajra shimmered right before her eyes, as if the lightning bolt had been zigzagging frantically to get her attention. Aru looked down and her heart slammed into her throat. *What was she doing?* She was crouching on the bridge, her hands gripping the edge, her knees not far behind, and her whole upper body leaning toward the night-dark water.

"What's gotten into you?" yelled Mini, pulling her backward. "I kept saying your name and you didn't even hear me!"

Aru scrambled back from the edge of the bridge, then sat with her arms wrapped around her knees.

"I don't know what's going on with me," she said, panicked. "I really want to drink the river water."

"Ew!" said Mini. "I'm thirsty, too, but you saw the sign, and there's *no way* I'm breaking that rule. The water could be contaminated! You could get some serious infectious diseases from river water, like shigellosis, norovirus, or even cryptosporidosis! And you know what happens if you—"

"Mini, I legit feel like I'm dying already, so please don't remind me," grumbled Aru. "I just want a *little* water."

"No!" said Mini, stamping her foot. "Let me run the symptoms past you, because they're truly horrific, and maybe then you won't want *dirty* river water. First of all, every time you go to the bathroom—"

But whatever horrific factoid Mini wanted to spout was interrupted by a smooth feminine voice. Just the sound of it quickened Aru's intense craving.

"Child, aren't you thirsty?"

"Y-yes," Aru croaked.

"Then drink your fill and be sated like the rest of your companions."

The ceiling disappeared, revealing a steel-gray sky. Below

them the Yamuna River churned, then parted in the middle. Mini screamed, pointing wildly into the deep. There, curled up on the riverbed with their eyes closed and their lips a dangerous shade of blue were Aiden, Brynne, and Rudy.

NINETEEN

Isn't This . . . a Bit Much?

Waves crashed over their friends and rose to form a shape like an inverted hurricane that towered nearly fifty feet above the bridge. Aru and Mini didn't even feel a drop fall as they strained desperately to catch a glimpse of the others. The water was murky, but little things breached the surface of the vortex: a fish spine here, an uncapped water bottle there. At one point, Aru saw the tail of a crocodile whip through the frothing water. Everywhere she looked there were far too many plastic bags.

At last Aiden, Brynne, and Rudy reemerged, swirling in a tight knot, their heads dipping in and out of the water. Mini gave a terrible shriek, but the trio seemed completely oblivious. In fact, they seemed, well . . . dead. Fear ripped through Aru's heart. This couldn't be real.

Could it?

The churning stopped. The riverbed beneath the bridge was sucked dry. Now Aru did feel a few drops fall on her arms, and she looked up, her pulse skyrocketing. Looming above them, draped in the river as if it were an elegant sari, was Yamuna, the goddess of the river. Aru recognized her from artifacts back home at the museum.

Her long black hair was pinned back with fish teeth and dotted with pearls. Around her neck and wrists she wore writhing snakes brighter than any jewels. Her skin was night-dark and gleaming. She was stunning to look at, but there was an unsettling quality to her beauty. It was like staring at a vast, thundering waterfall—one you didn't want to get too close to. Brynne, Aiden, and Rudy were caught in the hem of her huge flowing gown like fish in a net.

Yamuna's gaze darted between Mini and Aru but came to rest on Mini.

"Please," begged Mini. "Let them go! They could die!"

Aru opened her mouth, wanting to chime in, but... she couldn't speak. Her voice had been snatched away from her.

Aru glared at Yamuna. *You did this! Why?*

The water goddess had stolen her voice, and not even in a remotely stylish way, like how Ursula trapped Ariel's voice in a pretty glowing shell. Nope. One moment it was there, the next—gone.

The river goddess tilted her head. "*I* shall ask the questions."

Mini gulped audibly. She looked to Aru, who pointed helplessly at her throat.

She took my voice, Aru tried to express through their Pandava mind link, but even that seemed blocked in the presence of the goddess.

"You did not wish to drink my waters, little one?" asked Yamuna.

As the goddess's cool voice washed over her, Aru's desperate thirst finally vanished. Aru breathed a sigh of relief and shakily rose to stand. Just because she couldn't speak didn't mean she couldn't support Mini.

"Um, no thank you?" squeaked Mini. "There's a lot of bacteria that... Wait! I mean, I'm sure it's not your fault and all, and I'm sorry I called you dirty—"

"The pollution that accumulates upon my surface has no bearing on my soul."

Aru nodded to herself. Nice one. Maybe she'd use that excuse next time she didn't feel like showering.

"I..." Mini clenched her hands into fists by her sides. "I think your soul would be a little polluted if you let our friends drown."

BOLD, MINI! MAYBE TOO BOLD!

Aru tried to direct this thought at her sister as hard as she could, but it only resulted in a headache.

"You are the only one who was not tempted to break the rule," said Yamuna. "Why is that?"

Mini blinked, shuffling a little in place. "The sign says not to? And I don't want to die of an uncontrollable infectious disease?"

The river goddess paused to consider this, and then she bent closer, the rushing current of her sari slowing a little.

"I will ask you three questions, Daughter of Death," said Yamuna. "Answer them to my satisfaction, and perhaps we might arrange the resurrection of your friends."

"How 'bout asking Aru?" suggested Mini. "She's a lot better at answering stuff than I am."

The goddess shook her head. "I am asking *you*, child. Should you succeed, she may live, but she cannot speak for you."

Aru was liking this less and less by the moment. Granted,

Aru had almost broken the rule about drinking the river water, but how was that her fault if an enchantment had made her extra thirsty? Yeah, there'd been a sign, but who was going to follow—?

MINI, answered her brain.

Okay, fair, allowed Aru.

"I'll answer your questions," said Mini, lifting her chin.

"Very well, child. Here is my first query.... What is the heaviest weight to carry?"

What kind of question is that? thought Aru. First, it was super subjective. For example, Aru would say *An elephant.* But Brynne, who could turn into an elephant, might say *A skyscraper.* Second, how exactly would answering this question convince a goddess to bring their friends back? Maybe she was looking for summer interns to pluck all the plastic bags and water bottles out of her water....

Mini seemed to turn the question over in her head. She looked between Aru and the goddess, then said, "Guilt."

Her answer coiled heavily inside Aru. How many times had her own shoulders felt bowed by the weight of knowing she'd let the Sleeper escape? It explained her fear, too, of carrying the living key. Aru didn't like what it made her think, or rather, what it *let* her think. The key didn't put those thoughts and doubts in her head. It had only brought out what was already there.

"What do you think is the greatest wonder, child?" Yamuna asked next.

Mini creased her brows in thought, skimming her fingers along her father's Death Danda, which she clutched tightly in one hand.

"I know a thousand ways a person can die, but that doesn't

make me want to live any less," she said quietly. "I think other people feel the same way...otherwise, how do we get through the day? That, I think, is a huge wonder."

Again, Aru was shocked by her answer. If she had pompoms, she'd *cheer*! Mini was wrong if she thought Aru was the only one good at answering stuff. Aru might find an answer *quickly*, but Mini spoke from the heart.

"Your answers please me, Daughter of Death. I have only one thing left to ask...."

Yamuna stepped back, and a wave pressed forward the limp bodies of Brynne, Aiden, and Rudy. They rotated slowly in the hem of her gown, dark water lapping at their noses, hair matted to their heads.

"Not all may leave my domain. You may only choose one. Who do you pick?"

Aru's heart slammed into her throat.

Choose *one*?

But that meant...that meant they were—

"Only one can come back to life?" asked Mini, staring at her three friends.

The goddess nodded.

"Who among them deserves another chance at life? You are the daughter of the Dharma Raja—surely you can choose fairly?"

Their three friends floated, completely oblivious to the decision placed before Mini.

"Will it be the naga prince whose quick smile and musical talents have captured, perhaps, a little more than your eyes and ears?"

When Yamuna said this, a slender ribbon of water dangled

Rudy right before Mini's face. Aru jumped back. The snake prince's head lolled to one side, and water ran down his neck. Mini bit back a sob, and her lip trembled, but she didn't weep. Instead, she reached out and grabbed Aru's hand tightly.

"Or the boy who has come to be another brother to you? The one who always listens?"

A strip of Yamuna's dress bore up Aiden like a wave. Aru turned her face. It wasn't that she didn't want to see him like that.

She *couldn't.*

Something in her soul recoiled at the thought.

"Or your sister...?"

There was nothing else Yamuna needed to say as her sari drew out the third Pandava sister. Brynne, who would probably try to wrestle the river if she thought it was insulting her. Brynne, who would protect the rest of them no matter the cost to herself.

Tears stung Aru's eyes. If she'd known the dangers of this river ahead of time, she would've figured out some other way into the House of Months. She couldn't bring herself to think of losing any of them—

"Rudy," said Mini.

Aru stood there, stunned.

What?!

Aru looked between Mini and Yamuna and—Brynne! Their Pandava sister, who was slowly melting back into the folds of the goddess's gown...

"Why?" asked the river goddess.

Yeah, Aru wanted to scream. *Why?* Why him and not their sister? What would happen to Aiden?

Mini lifted her chin and spoke in a clear voice: "You asked

me to think like my soul father, the Dharma Raja," she said. "He would look at who had already lived... and, judging by that, me, Aru, Brynne, and Aiden have had more lives than most people. We've been reincarnated a lot... but not Rudy. Therefore, he would be the most deserving of another chance at life."

There was a cold, almost godly logic to it, which struck Aru like an arrow. And yet, all she could think when she looked at her sister was *How could you?*

Yamuna considered Mini for a moment, and then...

Burst into laughter?

The liquid dress trembled with the force of her laughter and the goddess raised her hands and clapped. Instantly, water crashed down, filling the riverbed beneath the bridge once more.

Aru felt warmth spread through her throat, and she clutched her neck, gasping. "What the—?"

Hey! She could speak! That would've been awesome if not for the fact that Mini had just let Brynne and Aiden *die*. Aru whirled on Mini, only to see something land on the far side of the bridge.

Brynne, Aiden, and Rudy lay on the metal rails.

They were unconscious, but color had returned to their cheeks and lips, and their facial muscles twitched faintly, as if they were stuck in a long dream. The water dripped off them quickly, and their clothes gradually lightened as they magically dried.

Behind them stood Yamuna, no longer an embodiment of the river, but a young woman with dark skin, a pearl clip in her hair, and a long blue maxi dress.

"You did better than I expected, niece," said Yamuna.

Mini looked shocked. "Wait... *niece*?"

The goddess grinned. "I guess you didn't know that your soul father, Yama, had a twin—*me!* It was truly awful growing up with him. He could never take a joke and haaaated it whenever I flooded his bedroom. Oh well."

"So I . . . I passed your test?" asked Mini.

"Oh, completely," said Yamuna, waving her hand. "You were coolheaded when others usually aren't. You followed the rules when most people can't control their impulses. And you had the empathy to put yourself in someone else's place and set aside your feelings. That is a rare quality, my niece. And for that, I will spare your friends."

"All of them? Really?" asked Mini, bright spots of color touching her cheeks. "I'm never the one who, you know, saves stuff."

Relief flooded Aru. "Wait till we tell them what you did!" she said. "They're gonna lose it! You were amazing!"

Mini grinned. "I was?"

"Completely."

Yamuna smiled, but her expression turned regretful. "I'm afraid there's one last condition I must make," she said, "though it pains me to do it, for you are my own family."

Aru clutched her throat. "No take-back on the speaking. Please?"

Yamuna gestured at their three unconscious friends. "Before I wake them, you must promise to forever remain silent about this episode. They can never know that you saved them."

Aru was just about to ask why when the goddess continued. "As for you, daughter of the god of thunderstorms, I must take this memory from you."

Wait . . . what?

Aru felt crushed. Mini was usually in the shadows. She was always watching, always analytical... but hardly ever the star. Aru wanted to remember this, to celebrate it when Mini sometimes forgot.

Mini stared at her friends, then glanced at Aru with a sad smile on her face before she turned to her aunt. She squared her shoulders.

"It doesn't really matter if they know I saved them, does it?" Mini asked. "I mean, they still got rescued in the end."

Yamuna smiled. "Spoken with true wisdom, little Pandava."

"At least I'll always know what I did," said Mini quietly.

The river goddess turned to Aru. A cool mist enveloped her body, and Aru's mind went blank.

Aru, Mini, Rudy, Brynne, and Aiden stepped off the end of the bridge and onto the pathway to December, the ground level of the House of Months. Crisp snow crunched underfoot. The silver trees were strung with lit candles that cast a warm glow over everything.

Rudy turned and looked at them triumphantly, both hands on his hips. "You're welcome," he said smugly. "Told you I could get us to the other side."

"Yeah, well, you needed my help," said Aiden.

"And mine," added Brynne, crossing her arms.

Aru shook herself. She had the weirdest sensation of having just woken up from a dream she didn't remember. The others looked a little dazed, too... except for Mini, who smiled to herself.

Aru had a weird flash-forward, if that's what it could be called. For a moment, it was as if she were seeing Mini not as she was, but as she *would be.* A young woman with chin-length cropped hair and a serene gaze. Someone totally comfortable with letting another person drive the car because she had picked the destination. It made Aru proud of her friend, even though she couldn't say why.

"Thought you'd be a little nervous in there," said Aru.

Mini twirled Dee Dee on her finger and shrugged.

"Nope, I'm good," she said, grinning.

TWENTY

At Least There's Not a Dragon

No one tells you what to expect when you walk into a month. Would there be ugly souvenir key chains? Commemorative plates? It took a moment for Aru's eyes to adjust to the brightness of December when they went inside.

Lengths of shadow hung from the ceiling beams, with placards beneath each proclaiming things like:

SOURCED FROM THE FINEST CAVES AND TREES

FREE OF HUMAN LIGHT POLLUTION

IDEAL FOR EVENING GOWNS,
OR DRAPES FOR A MONSTROUS LAIR

The carved walls radiated cold and shimmered like freshly fallen snow. Aru peered closer. It *was* snow. A small sign nestled in it declared: FORAGED FROM THE PEAKS OF THE HIMALAYAS!

AN ORGANIC, BREATHABLE MATERIAL DESIGNED TO KEEP THE BODY COOL.

"There!" said Rudy, pointing to a low platform of carved ice in the middle of the room. "We need to take the elevator up to January. The Crypt of Eclipses should be located just inside January Twentieth."

The group watched as a crystal elevator just big enough to fit all five of them descended to the platform. The doors slid open, and out stepped a beautiful *kinnara* couple. The man's skin was the color of strong tea, and the woman's skin reminded Aru of a shiny new penny. Delicate wings swept down from their shoulders and across the floor.

The woman smiled at Aiden. "Love your outfit."

Aiden turned red. "Thanks."

As the couple walked away, Aru wanted to riot. *HELLO. What about us?*

Rudy threw up his hands. "*Seriously?* My jacket is from the fall collection, which hasn't even been released yet! And she compliments *you*? Where's that sweatshirt even from?"

Aiden shrugged with just the hint of a smile. "The back of my closet?"

"Ugh. Let's just go," said Rudy.

They headed to the elevator.

"Are you strutting, Wifey?" asked Mini.

Aiden suddenly slowed. Brynne looked him over and snorted.

"Yup, he's definitely strutting."

"Am not," said Aiden.

"Yeah you are!" said Aru, laughing.

"Am *not.*"

"R-2—"

"D-2," said Aiden before giving up and shaking his head. "Why are you guys like this?"

"Boredom," said Mini.

"Belligerence," said Brynne.

"Brilliance," said Aru.

The three of them grinned at each other.

The elevator featured twelve differently colored buttons, one for each month. January's was a shiny gold that looked brand-new.

"Ready?" asked Rudy.

They nodded.

"It can be a bit bumpy—"

"We can handle it," said Aru, rolling her eyes.

Rudy pressed the topmost button. The elevator jerked to life, shooting upward with such force that they fell to the floor.

"Is this elevator *possessed*?" said Aru, gripping the railing.

"Nope, just covering a lot of ground!" Rudy shouted over the clatter the elevator made as it rocketed higher and higher. "The House of Months is huge!"

Aru's ears popped and she scooted closer to the middle, linking arms with Brynne and Mini. Aiden seemed perfectly content standing by the railing and staring out the clear doors. Rudy, utterly used to the ride, just fidgeted with one of his jacket buttons.

After they passed through December and November, Aru adjusted to the speed and started to appreciate the view. They were now entering October. Even through the elevator doors she could feel the month's crisp air, smell the toasted cloves and rolled cinnamon bark in steaming cider, and see the sunlight spangling through red leaves.

In what seemed like a blink, the elevator flashed past September and through summer, rising to April, where it stopped. The doors opened, and a burst of botanical scents rushed in.

"Ugh!" said Mini, burying her face in her elbow. "Allergies!"

Aru peered out to see clouds of white flowers drifting across a ceiling of blue roses and sapphire lilies. The room was crowded with huge bouquets in crystal vases, and there were bright signs that said things like:

BUY ONE SNAPPING VIOLET, GET ONE FANGED DAISY FREE!

FOR A LIMITED TIME, NIGHT-BLOOMING CORPSE FLOWERS—
GUARANTEED TO MAKE YOUR DEN REEK OF THE DEAD!

A gigantic light-skinned asura in a glamorous suit made of scales stood before them with an armful of flowers. He took one look at the crowded elevator and sighed.

"I'll wait for the next one," he said before mumbling to himself, "Why are florals so expensive? I hate anniversaries."

The doors closed and up they went, climbing through windy March, then February. Aru asked to get out for a minute at her birthday month, curious to know what kind of wares were sold there.

Turns out, it was a famous *parfumerie*. Aru poked her head out, peering into the sea of aisles carrying fragrances that ranged from "the scent of middle school love, with notes of Burt's Bees Lip Balm and AXE Body Spray" and "the aroma of breakfast, with a maple syrup base" to "a freshly opened new book blended with ink and hot cocoa."

Brynne cleared her throat impatiently, and Aru retreated back onto the elevator. It took off and, at last, they reached January.

Abruptly, the doors slid open and Aru and her friends stumbled into the bleary light of a new year. Unlike the other months, January *spun*. They stepped onto a revolving floor where numbered chambers starting with January 1 sped around them, each one displaying a different scene: a loud holiday party, a lazy Sunday by the fire, a snowball fight. Aru felt like she was on one of those spinning theme park rides that always got shut down because someone vomited.

"The eclipse fell on January twenty-first," said Mini, her eyes darting down the line of days coming their way.

Once they hit January 10, the festive cheer and tinsel of the previous scenes vanished, replaced with a series of empty gray rooms marked STORAGE. It was as if these days served no purpose but to account for the passage of time.

"Ready?"

Rudy jumped into one of the scenes. A wave of magical energy crested over the Pandavas and Aiden, and they were swept in after him. Aru braced herself, shutting her eyes and raising her arm as a shield....

When she blinked her eyes open again, they were standing in another space entirely, on a marble walkway that stretched about twenty feet before it ended under a huge silvery arch, with the words CRYPT OF ECLIPSES printed across it in neat black letters.

"We made it!" Rudy said, flashing them a grin. "Don't everyone thank me at once."

No one said anything.

Rudy shrugged and turned to walk toward the arch.

"Why hide stuff in an eclipse?" wondered Mini as they followed him.

"Well, an eclipse is when one celestial body obscures another and a source of illumination is cut off," said Aiden. "So, if there's no light, it sounds like a good time to hide something."

"One celestial body what?" repeated Rudy, shaking his head. "Everyone knows eclipses are just when Rahu or Ketu get mad and swallow the sun or moon."

"Rahu or Ketu?" asked Aru. "Who are they?"

"Technically, they're the custodians of the crypt, but they leave it to the *yalis* to handle security," asked Rudy. "Don't worry, it's not like R and K come here. At least, *I've* never seen them."

"Is this the entrance?" asked Brynne.

They had made it to two pillars that looked like they were made of wet shadows. Where the thin January light hit them, Aru could see shapes in the damp black stone. They flickered strangely, as if they were *alive*. She shuddered, the hairs on the back of her neck prickling. She tightened her grip on her backpack, which held the living key in its velvet pouch. All they had to do was get to the A7 vault, use the key to open it, and find the clue to the tree's whereabouts. *Easy enough,* thought Aru.

"Not like I'm scared or anything, but this place is kinda creepy," said Brynne.

Mini took a deep breath, steadying herself. "Well, at least there's not a dragon?"

Aru, Mini, and Brynne passed between the pillars together. Aru closed her eyes against a fine mist of rain that drifted across her face. No sooner had she opened her eyes when a siren blared.

"I DETECT THE PRESENCE OF GODS! I DETECT THE PRESENCE OF GODS!"

Vajra sprang into the air, on the verge of transforming, but Aru quickly caught it and shoved it back onto her wrist.

"We can't give away who we are!" she hissed at it.

Beside her, Brynne and Mini were trapped in similar struggles with their own weapons. The alarm shouted louder. Bright lights flashed on, blinding Aru. She could just make out the shape of a huge door ahead when plumes of steam shot toward them.

The smoke parted, revealing a huge reptilian face. It had cat-like yellow eyes with black slits, and its nostrils were smoldering. The creature's scaly head was the size of a dining table, with slender horns protruding above its eyebrow ridges. Aru didn't even want to imagine what the rest of it looked like.

The monster's gaze lingered on them one by one, and then it croaked out, *"Gods?"*

TWENTY-ONE

Well, Never Mind, Then

Aru had only just processed that there was an actual *dragon* staring at them when the sound of something lumbering echoed through the antechamber. The only thing worse than one dragon was... two.

Aru braced herself and drew closer to her sisters. There was no way they could take down two dragons without using their Pandava weapons. Their clothes might be enchanted, thanks to Nikita, but Aru doubted that her pants, Brynne's jacket, and Mini's skirt and sweater would do much for them in this situation.

Beside them, Aiden had his hands in his sleeves, ready to summon his scimitars. Rudy was trying to hide behind Aiden with little success due to his blindingly white jacket.

A new form manifested before them... but it wasn't exactly a dragon. Rather, it was *part* of a dragon. Specifically, its tail, four taloned feet, and a torso that looked as if it had sprouted flames at the top. The other creature turned its head, and Aru bit back a gasp. That's all it was—a head! A head glancing at the rest of its body.

"You're late, Ketu!" said the dragon head. "I *despise* it when you're late—"

"You despise most things, Rahu," said Ketu calmly.

Aru's eyes widened.

Um... did the headless dragon torso just talk? she asked her sisters.

Their incredulous stares were answer enough.

Ketu sighed and the flame atop the torso wavered. Aru realized that the fire functioned as his head.

"We've been through this before, and there's simply no point in getting worked up over it again," said Ketu. He plopped onto his tail, pressing his taloned front feet together like he was praying. "You must free yourself from attachments."

"Easy for you to say! You *are* unattached!"

"And that is by the will of the universe—"

"Oh, don't give me that. The universe didn't throw a spinning chakra at *our* neck—a god did, you blithering trunk!" spat Rahu.

"Anger," said the torso serenely, "makes one blind to happiness. Again, free yourself from useless attachments."

"And how does that fit with your collection of scented candles? That's definitely a useless attachment, if you ask me. What's the point when you don't even have a nose?"

Ketu rolled off his tail and planted his feet on the ground. The flame rippled across his back. "They were on sale!"

Aru was watching all this, utterly spellbound, when she felt a sharp jab in her side. She looked over to see Brynne pointing with her chin. About fifty feet beyond the two pillars where the dragon halves bickered was the door to the crypt—solid black with shadows and mist curling out from its gap. All they had to do was get to it.

Maybe they could sneak past while the head and the torso argued.

Brynne took a step forward, and Rahu swung to face them.

"You," he said.

"Oh, right—them," said Ketu, waving his tail. "How do you do?"

Aiden shoved Rudy forward. The naga boy trembled for a moment, then took a deep breath, fixing the dragon parts with an imperious stare. He raised his hand, and the scales on his wrist shimmered.

"I am Prince Rudra of Naga-Loka, and this is my entourage," he said, his voice wavering only a little. "I'm here to enter the crypt, which I've visited many times with my parents. My father has a chamber here, and—"

Rahu sniffed the air, moving closer.

"We are requesting entry," Rudy finished quickly.

Aru had to hand it to Rudy. She didn't think she'd be able to keep her cool if a disembodied dragon head struck up a conversation with her.

"The presence of gods was detected," said Rahu. "We do not *allow* gods into this crypt. They may send an attendant, but they themselves are not welcome here."

"Do we look like gods to you?" asked Aiden. "I mean, seriously. Maybe your alarm system is faulty."

"Maybe a god snuck past?" tried Brynne. "We'll go inside with you to check—"

"Ha!" Rahu snorted. "Even *we* are not permitted past the Door of Shadows." His eyes rolled in its direction.

"We only guard its entrance," added Ketu. "Which is preferable, really. I don't like the crypt—it's very drafty in there."

A spark of hope shot through Aru. If the dragons couldn't go in, all the Pandavas had to do was figure out how to get through the door without the guardians noticing... which meant they needed a distraction.

"We'll have to see some identification," growled Rahu.

"Please," added Ketu.

Aru glanced at the hem of her pants, where the coiled-up sticky threads were disguised as embroidery. A plan formed in her head. Through their mind link, she quickly shared it with her sisters.

Aru took a step forward. "We need some ID from *you*, too. How do we know you really are Rahu and Ketu?"

"You want *us* to prove *our* identities?" Rahu was so insulted his nostrils started smoking again.

While Mini whispered the plan to Aiden and Rudy, Brynne started to pace.

Rudy said, "You've never been here when I've come with my mother or father. We always head straight to the door and trust the yalis inside to act as security guards."

"Yeah," said Brynne. "I mean, why would the *great* and *fearsome* Rahu and Ketu be protecting the entrance to their own crypt?"

"I *am* great," said Ketu delightedly. "I think I shall add that to my list of morning affirmations, right after 'Though I am a half, I am whole.'"

Aru bent down and pretended to adjust her shoelaces. Her fingers brushed the enchanted swirl designs on her pant legs. At her touch the threads separated from the fabric, entwined, and elongated to form a sticky translucent rope. Aru quickly balled it up and tossed it to Aiden.

He caught it with a sharp clap.

Rahu swiveled to face him.

"Couldn't agree more," Aiden said, his hands clasped in front of him like he had just finished applauding. "Give it up for the yalis."

Mini quickly changed the subject. "You don't seem to like gods very much," she said to the dragon body.

Rahu snorted. "The gods are liars! Despicable! Tricksy!"

Aru couldn't help herself. "Hobbitses?"

"Hobbitses?" Rahu blinked. "Is that a profanity of the human realm?"

"Sure," said Aru.

Aiden cast her a look that clearly said *Why are you like this, Shah?*

Rahu grumbled, "Then they're all tricksy hobbitses, and we hate them."

By now, Aiden had tossed the sticky ball to Mini.

"Hatred solves nothing," said Ketu peaceably. "Hey—what are you doing there? I hear footsteps."

Mini, who was sneaking behind the dragon head while trying to unwind the rope, froze. In the firelight from Ketu's torso, the cord was slightly visible. Aru hoped his vision was weak... given that he didn't have any eyes.

"Just trying to appreciate, um—"

"All angles of the situation," finished Aru loudly.

Ketu turned back toward Aru.

"Are there other split dragons like you?" she asked.

Rahu huffed. "It is impossible to be like us! We were created by the gods!"

"By accident, perhaps," mused Ketu. "But Rahu is correct. We're unique, because nobody could've been made like us...."

"Made?" prompted Brynne, while Mini looped the middle of the cord around a pillar. It stuck fast.

The fire atop Ketu's back roared as it climbed higher. "It was a *terrible* day," he moaned. "So much walking. My legs and feet and tail ached horribly...."

Images formed in his wall of flames, showing the devas and asuras churning the Ocean of Milk. In the long line of asuras tugging the snake-rope with all their might, Aru recognized Rahuketu, a dragon with a slick head and wingless serpent body.

"I was so thirsty," said Ketu with a sigh.

"We were in an ocean of *milk!*" said Rahu. "You could've just had me lap some up!"

"And pollute my body? My temple? With *milk* that people had sweated into and stepped in?"

"Get on with it, Ketu," grumbled Rahu.

The flashback in Ketu's flames changed, showing the devas and asuras separated into two lines. When it came time to divvy up the nectar of immortality, the god of preservation, Vishnu, took on a new avatar and transformed into the beautiful enchantress Mohini. She was so enchantingly lovely that everyone agreed to let her pour out the nectar. Mohini walked to the devas first, but she kept her head turned toward the asuras... smiling all the while so that none of the asuras even noticed she was giving away all their nectar.

None except Rahuketu.

In the scene playing out in the flames, Rahuketu disguised himself as a deva and switched sides, quietly slipping in between Surya and Chandra, the gods of the sun and the moon. Mohini stopped in front of Rahuketu, not looking at him, just tipping a bright gold jar of what looked like liquid sunshine toward his mouth. Rahuketu closed his eyes, parted his lips, and *drank*. A glow radiated from within him, bursting through the pores of his skin, and then…

Thwhip-thwhip-thwhip-thwhip-thwhip!

A razor-sharp silver disc spun straight toward him and chopped off his head.

"That was so *rude*!" said Ketu.

Rahu closed his eyes, shaking his head at the memory. That gave Rudy and Aiden a chance to slip Aru the two ends of the magic rope, which she quickly tied together.

Aru *tsk*ed sympathetically, and Rahu opened his eyes again. By now, she and her friends had formed a circle around the head and torso, holding the cord behind their backs. Following Brynne's lead, they all took tiny steps forward, gradually herding the celestials closer to the column.

"But we'd swallowed the nectar of immortality," said Ketu, "so we became separate entities with separate responsibilities as the ascending and descending lunar nodes, and we take that responsibility very seriously—"

"Except when one of us gets mad and tries to devour the moon," added Rahu.

"To be fair, it does look like a cookie," said Ketu defensively.

"See?" said Rahu. "You're not so high and mighty after all!"

Rahu and Ketu launched into a new argument, this time over which was the more popular eclipse: Solar? Lunar? The third *Twilight* book? They were close enough to each other that Rahu could've poked Ketu with his nose.

It was time.

Aru nodded to her friends and they let go of the rope. She held on to it and walked slowly backward until it was stretched taut. One by one, the others ducked under it and stepped away.

When Aru lifted the cord over her head so she could hold it out in front of her, Rahu turned toward her, his eyes narrowing with suspicion. "What are you doing?"

"Sorry about this!" she yelled.

Aru let go of the sticky line. *Snap!* It contracted like a rubber band, binding Rahu and Ketu to the pillar.

Rahu roared. Steam hissed out of his nostrils, clouding the chamber.

"I can't see!" yelled Ketu.

"When can you *ever* see?" snapped Rahu.

Aru swiveled around, lost in the mist, until she felt Brynne's hand around her wrist.

"Run for it!" yelled Brynne.

Together the group raced to the Door of Shadows.

"Come back here, children," bellowed Rahu, "and let me eat you!"

TWENTY-TWO

That's a Nice, Creepy, Destructive God You've Got There

Rahu's screams chased them through the Door of Shadows, but the moment they tumbled into the crypt, there was only silence.

Aru shook herself. She was sprawled on the ground, and it took a moment for her eyes to adjust to the dark. Overhead, the ceiling seemed to be wreathed in a thin, hazy light. It reminded her of how the last eclipse had looked through the special sunglasses her mom had ordered: a black blot radiating wispy rays. The crypt's floor was cold and hard-packed, but with an odd texture. Like scales. Specifically, Rahu and Ketu's scales. *Gross,* thought Aru. It was like they had said, *Nah, who needs a carpet when I've got dead skin!*

"Those must be the vaults over there!" whispered Brynne.

Aru looked to where her sister was pointing. After a while, she could recognize doors along both sides of the space. They weren't ordinary doors with locks or knobs or handles. Instead they looked like faint shadows, discernible only by the thin outline of light around their edges. Like in an eclipse.

The faint illumination allowed Aru to see some detail in

the stone columns that supported the ceiling. Like on the pillars outside, the black rock *rippled* slightly, as if it were breathing.

"Okay," said Rudy in a low voice. "The moment I announce my intentions, the yalis will wake up.... They're creepy as anything." He shuddered a bit.

"Worse than a bisected dragon?" whispered Mini.

"Rahu and Ketu are bizarre, but they're not creepy," said Rudy.

Mini stared at him. "In what world is a bisected dragon *not* creepy?"

Rudy was on the verge of answering when Brynne interrupted.

"Just tell us what will happen next," said Brynne.

"Right, so, after they greet us, the yalis will lead us to the vault, where Shah takes over."

"I use the key," said Aru, softly patting her backpack, secretly loath to wake the living thing.

"Wait a second," said Rudy. He paused. Then shut his eyes tight and winced. "I... may have forgotten about something."

"*Seriously*, Rudy?" growled Brynne, not bothering to whisper anymore. "Why are you even on this quest, anyway?"

He looked stung but quickly masked it with a hapless grin. "C'mon, you guys are Pandavas. Surely you can handle any—"

"Spill it, Rudy," said Aiden, crossing his arms.

"Okay, one tiny hiccup. I forgot that the yalis can see *inside* the vaults."

"So they're going to know what we're up to!" said Aru angrily.

"Not if we camouflage it," said Aiden, touching his camera. "With Mini's help, we can make a pretty convincing illusion in the doorway."

"Yeah, but first Aru has to open it with the key," said Rudy. "If they see that..." His face grew pale. "In fact, if they figure out that you're demigods..." He groaned and slumped against a column.

"WHAT?" asked the others simultaneously.

"I didn't think this through," whined Rudy, his head in his hands. "We should just turn around and—"

"Maybe they don't have to know we're here at all," said Mini quietly. "I could do that. I can—"

Rudy scoffed. "I don't think one of your shields is going to help in this—"

"And *I* don't think you should interrupt me," said Mini, drawing herself up. "You've got no idea what I'm capable of."

Aiden looked surprised, and Rudy actually flinched. Brynne, biting back a grin, caught Aru's eye. This was probably a bad time to yell *SHE IS THE DAUGHTER OF DEATH, LOOK UPON HER AND DESPAIR*, but Aru really wanted to.

Mini pointed her Death Danda at Aru and whispered, "Adrishya."

Cold violet light shot out from Dee Dee and crept over Aru's skin, clothing, and backpack. Aru looked down at her disappearing feet, then legs, and finally, her hands. She did a little dance. It was a horrible dance. Luckily, no one saw it, because she... was... *INVISIBLE*!

"This is amazing!" said Aru. She spun in place. "How come you've never done this to yourself, Mini?"

"It feels... sneaky," said Mini uncomfortably. "And what would I do with it, anyway?"

"You'd always have an advantage over your enemies," said Brynne.

"You could capture some great candid shots," mused Aiden.

"Or you could randomly move things around without anyone knowing," said Aru. "You know that ficus plant Mom keeps in the museum lobby? You could tell someone it's haunted and then carry it around so it's following them."

Everyone fell silent.

"Plant-stalking?" said Aiden. "*That's* what you'd do with powers of invisibility?"

"Duh," said Aru. "With great power comes great opportunity to annoy."

"All right, all right. Fine, that's a pretty cool trick, Mini," allowed Rudy.

Mini rolled her eyes.

"Now do it to Brynne and yourself," he said. "Aiden can be my servant."

"I'll serve you up to the yalis," Aiden muttered through gritted teeth.

As the invisibility spell washed over Brynne, she said, "So Aru uses the key, Mini and Aiden create an illusion in the front of the vault, we get whatever is inside, and we leave immediately."

Everyone nodded. Then Aru remembered she couldn't be seen and said, "Yes."

"The vault may have some booby traps in it, though," said Rudy. "We won't know until..." He hesitated, a look of pain crossing his face. "Until we see it."

Before anyone could ask him about that, Rudy quickly swiveled around and announced to the darkness:

"I, Prince Rudra of Naga-Loka, am here to make a withdrawal."

A handful of bright lights flickered against the walls and then went out. Vajra sparked nervously on Aru's wrist, but remained invisible. Aru crossed her arms, trying to hug her lightning bolt reassuringly even as a chill crept up her spine.

"A withdrawal?" asked a voice in the dark.

On the three closest support columns, more lights flashed, then started traveling downward as if they were... Aru froze. They weren't lights at all, but three pairs of *eyes*. Long shapes twisted sinuously before sliding onto the scale-covered floor. The eyes belonged to the yalis, living temple carvings in the shape of three hybrid animals that slithered toward them. In the half-light, Aru just could make out their bodies: crocodile-shaped but with huge dragon-like spikes knifing out of their spines. They seemed to be one with the rock, occasionally sinking into the floor and then half emerging to stare up at the visitors.

"How strange to see the princeling without his family," said a second voice, scratchier and higher-pitched than the first.

"Has your father decided to trust your judgment after all, little snake?" asked the third voice, as cruel and sharp as a blade. "Has your vision improved? Or is the family simply blind to your weakness?"

The first yali whipped its head back and forth, as if scenting the air. "I smell sacred objects," it said.

The second groaned hungrily. "It smells so much like freedom. Is that what you've come to do, sweet prince? Break us from our bonds of servitude? How grateful we would be...."

"No..." said the third. "It is not just objects, but *beings*."

The blinking eyes circled Aru, and she had the distinct

memory of watching one of those nature documentaries where a crocodile lies like a log in the water, barely visible... before it rushes its prey, jaws open wide.

"Enough of this," said Rudy imperiously. "Take us to chamber A-Seven."

The yalis stilled.

"No one has entered that particular crypt in some time.... What do you want with it?"

"As if that's any of your business," said Rudy haughtily. "Lead on."

The yalis slunk ahead, and without another word, Rudy strolled after them with Aiden in tow. Aru fell in line behind them, and she assumed Brynne and Mini did, too. *Invisibility is awesome but kinda awkward,* she thought, hoping she wouldn't bump into or trip either of her sisters.

The crypt was longer than it had looked at first. It stretched out before them like a never-ending grocery-store aisle. On the floor, images skipped and hopped, as if the whole thing were a ginormous screen....

Aru didn't like the story it told. One scene showed a cracked and weathered pillar in a courtyard under a sky between day and night. Dusk? Dawn? The pillar split down the middle to reveal a deity who was a lion on top and a man on the bottom. Aru knew he was a god by the divine glow that clung to him, but it was a terrible light—like a wall of fire. The god let loose a silent roar, and his red eyes narrowed as he clawed himself out of the rubble.

"Admiring our little warning, sweet prince?" hissed the first yali.

Rudy stumbled a little but quickly regained his footing. "Who is that?"

The image of the lion-man-god was familiar, but Aru couldn't place a name to the face.

"Narasimha," whispered the second yali, as it scuttled up a nearby column.

Aru felt his breath on the back of her neck and fought the urge to whimper.

"One of Lord Vishnu's most vicious manifestations... The gods allowed us to us bottle up Narasimha's divine wrath, and now it sleeps beneath the Crypt of Eclipses, waking up only when it's time to devour little thieves...."

Rudy gulped audibly. "Charming."

"Surely you know the tale, little princeling?" asked the first yali. "Once upon a time, a demon king got a little too power-hungry. He asked the gods to make it impossible for him to be killed by man or beast, during daytime or nighttime, indoors or outdoors, or by any weapon."

Aru glanced at the images again, seeing how they pieced together. Narasimha had arrived not indoors or outdoors, but in a courtyard, which was both. And not in daytime or nighttime, but at dawn or dusk—both. And not as a man or a beast... but as both.

After seeing those sharp claws, she could guess how he'd killed the demon king.

"No other way around those conditions," said Rudy, shuddering.

Actually, Aru had noticed a pretty large loophole. But Brynne beat her to the punch.

They could've just sent a girl, said Brynne through their mind link. *Satisfies all the conditions.*

Specifically, you*—there's no way* I'd *go,* said Aru.

Mini laughed, and the yalis froze in their tracks. Three pairs of glowing eyes turned in her direction. For a terrifying moment, Aru thought the yalis were going to sniff them out. But instead they swiftly melted back into the floor, emerging partway to lead them the rest of the way to the chamber marked A7.

When they arrived, Rudy asked, "May we have a moment of privacy, please?"

"We always bear witness..." said the first yali. "'Tis our curse to guard."

"To see," added the second.

"To know," said the third.

"Until the instruments of gods free us from our bondage," said the three of them at the same time.

"You have always turned your backs when my parents unlocked the doors of this vault," said Rudy, "and I demand the same treatment. You may look *after* the door is open."

Aru saw one of the yalis' heads rear back, its skin rippling angrily before it sank back into the floor as if it were water.

"Very well, princeling."

"But remember that we—"

"Are always watching."

With that, the yalis vanished, leaving the five of them alone before a smooth metal panel. Aru brought the velvet pouch out of her backpack, her nerves on fire. No one could see it but her.

Mr. V's warning about the key rang out in Aru's head: *It might demand something in return for its services.*

The last thing Aru wanted to do was touch the key. It was

too alive. And she hadn't liked the feeling of it rummaging around in her soul. But they had to do this. The fate of the Otherworld hung in the balance. If the Sleeper won, everything would be lost. Aru blinked and saw the twins clinging to each other in a nightmare; Boo staring at his huge shadow; Opal taunting her about failure.

Aru grabbed the key, pressed it to the metal, and gasped. It was as if a safe she'd tried to keep locked inside her was suddenly flung open. She was flooded with a bone-deep aching, an overwhelming sense of loss. She saw every time she had made a card on Father's Day only to end up throwing it in the trash. She saw every moment her mother's face had shuttered with grief, every nightmare in which Aru had pressed her hand to her heart and known without a shadow of a doubt that she was missing something.

She pulled back the key, and the panel shivered before them. A slit appeared down its center and the two halves slowly retracted into the wall. Bright golden light began to spill out of the opening. It was too bright to see the interior of the vault clearly, but its magic felt powerful, like a hurricane crammed into a closet.

The key in Aru's hand turned warm and purred like a cat that had eaten its fill. She quickly dropped it back into the velvet pouch, which she closed and stuffed into her backpack. Then she sighed with relief.

"Shah... are you okay?" asked Aiden.

She was still invisible, but somehow Aiden was looking straight at her. Aru caught her breath, trying to bury the empty feeling the key had left behind.

"Duh," she managed to whisper.

"Quick! Get inside!" hissed Rudy. "Aiden, the entrance!"

Once Aiden knew—from their pats on his shoulder—that all three Pandavas had stepped across the threshold, he lifted his camera and snapped a photo of Rudy entering. A moment later, Aiden touched the view screen and then literally peeled off the image. He walked into the vault, turned, and flung the small rectangle at the opening, where it expanded into a semi-transparent banner that filled the space. Mini projected a force field with Dee Dee, solidifying the illusion.

Now if the yalis peeked inside, all they'd see was Rudy.

Okay, then, said Aru, speaking to her sisters through their Pandava mind link. *Let's go steal a wishing tree.*

TWENTY-THREE

The Bird of Mass Destruction. Maybe.

Brynne groaned.

"You've *got* to be kidding me," she said flatly.

Aru turned in a circle, expecting to see a magical tree or, honestly, just *magic*. But the room was empty. There was nothing! Not even a leaf. Or a note that said *At least you were on the right path!*

The invisibility glamour had melted off all three Pandava sisters, revealing an angry-looking Brynne and a confused Aru. As for Mini, she seemed... proud.

"Nice work, Mini," said Brynne, impressed.

Aru gave her a thumbs-up before looking around the room. "You sure it's okay for us to ditch the invisibility?"

"Yeah, but maybe not talk so loud?" whispered Mini, holding a finger to her lips.

"Oops." Brynne spun Gogo over her head, creating a wind cyclone that would allow them to speak without being overheard.

Aru was on the verge of walking farther into the room when Rudy lunged forward and grabbed her arm.

"The floor!" said Rudy.

The ground was crisscrossed with yellow and green tiles. The yellow tiles glowed warmly. But the neon green struck Aru as a warning.

"It's the yalis' alarm system," Rudy said. "My father always said to step carefully—the colors tell you where it is safe."

"I'm guessing we should avoid the green tiles?" said Aru.

"Green?" asked Rudy, frowning. "What green tiles?"

"The ones all around us?" said Aiden, pointing at the floor.

A fleeting look of panic crossed Rudy's face before he laughed it off and ran his hand through his hair. "Oh, duh. Yeah, no green."

Aru tracked Rudy's eyes. He didn't seem to be looking in the right place.

"What's the point of an alarm when there's nothing here to steal?" asked Brynne. *"Where's the tree?"*

A soft caw sounded above, and the five of them went silent. Aru glanced up. At first, she didn't see anything, but then there was a darting movement above her head. She spotted a small creature flitting around the ceiling—a bird no bigger than her palm, circling around and around in the same corner.

"Why would the goddess of the forests hide a bird in here?" asked Aiden.

"Maybe it's secretly a bird of mass destruction?" ventured Mini, shrinking away from it.

"Or it's a clue," said Aru. "Aranyani could've hidden a long trail of clues to the tree's actual hiding place . . . especially if she thought someone could break into the crypt."

"Only one way to find out," said Brynne, turning to Aru.

With Brynne still making sure no one could hear them with

her wind cyclone, and Mini keeping up the illusion at the door with Dee Dee, it was up to Aru to retrieve the bird.

"On it," said Aru.

She tapped Vajra on her wrist, and the lightning bolt sprang out and immediately flattened to form a hoverboard. Aru jumped onto it and arced upward. On the floor below, she saw the bright green tiles still flashing their warning. If she fell, the yalis would come into the vault. Aru didn't want to imagine those three sets of black jaws stretching wide. . . .

She urged Vajra higher, toward the bird flying in its relentless circle. The closer Aru got, the easier it was to hear the bird's strange, rough call, which sounded like its syrinx had been ripped out. The noise reminded her of a broken machine. When she saw the thin clear string affixed to the bird's back and attached to a circular gear on the ceiling, she realized the bird itself *was* a machine.

The bird was made of pale wood and must have had some kind of mechanism inside that enabled it to squawk and pump its wings. Its beak held a small sapphire, the color of which Aru had only seen in one other object.

Her mother's necklace.

Aru's hand automatically flew to the pendant as Dr. K. P. Shah's words floated through her head. *Years ago, a yaksha gave this to me. He promised me it was for guardianship and for finding lost things. I hope this will protect you from whatever danger Suyodhana found on his journey.*

"Mom," whispered Aru.

It was too much of a coincidence not to mean something. As her fingers worked over the three depressions in the necklace, Aru realized that the stone inside the bird's beak would fit perfectly within one of those hollows. She remembered what

Mr. V had said about the Sleeper having lost parts of himself along the way. Her throat tightened with sudden longing… and then misgiving. Whatever that bird was carrying…could it possibly be one of those pieces?

"Speed it up, Aru!" called Brynne from below.

Aru's pulse raced. She stretched out her arm as far as it would go, the tips of her fingers reaching for the bird. After a few misses, her hand finally closed around it, and she yanked it from the string. Its wooden body felt warm, and its exquisitely carved feathers fluttered as if it were alive.

"Got it…" she started to say, before faltering.

The moment she tightened her grip, images flashed through her mind. She saw a young man pleading, *Please! You don't understand—I have a daughter on the way. I can't let her inherit a world I am destined to destroy. Tell me what I must do. Please, tell me—*

It ended there, but Aru knew there was more to the flashback, which must have been unlocked by the living key. She'd gotten a glimpse of truth—a truth she had wanted so desperately to know.

Her dad *had* made a wish—for *her*. And, in the process, he'd somehow lost pieces of himself. Then he'd returned home… only to be trapped in a lamp.

Aru still couldn't believe her mom could do such a thing.

Neither of her parents were who she thought they were.

In her shock, Aru lost her balance and nearly slipped off the hoverboard. She fumbled with her footing, frantically trying to right herself, when she lost hold of the mechanical bird.

"ARU!"

"Don't let the bird hit the ground!" she called down.

Time seemed to slow down and speed up all at once. Brynne

lunged forward, careful not to touch the green tiles that would summon the yalis. She angled her wind mace upward, directing a stream of air at the wooden bird and steering it toward the others. Aiden and Mini were focused on protecting the threshold, but without Brynne's silencing wind, the yalis would be able to hear *everything.*

"Rudy!" ordered Brynne. "Grab it!"

The naga boy hesitated, glancing down at the ground and then up at the wooden bird coming right at him. Just as his hand snatched it, his foot crossed the boundary of light, slamming onto a green tile.

A loud blaring echoed throughout the chamber, ringing in Aru's ears. Reflexively, she turned Vajra back into a bolt, falling the rest of the way.

She crashed down next to Brynne and Aiden, only for the floor beneath all five of them to give way, plunging them into darkness.

TWENTY-FOUR

You Poor, Unfortunate Souls

What most people don't realize about plummeting headfirst toward impending death is that it's kind of hard to yell at the same time. Air is rushing down your throat, and everything is literally the worst, and when you try to holler, you sound like a cat with laryngitis. Aru had this particular thought as she fell, choking on a scream while she tried to see out of the corners of her eyes. She could just barely make out the four fuzzy shapes of her companions falling alongside her. Every time Aru reached for her lightning bolt, the wind ripped it away from her.

"Light up!" commanded Aru.

Vajra responded, flickering brightly. For the first time, Aru could see the ground....

Just as it rose to meet her.

"No-no-no-no-no-no-no-no!" she cried, her arms pinwheeling wildly.

She was all set to become Aru pâté when another gust of air caught her tight in a wind funnel. Aru froze, blinking slowly.

The ground was a good four inches away from her nose, and her hair trailed on the paved floor of what looked like a giant courtyard.

"I've got you, Shah," called Brynne, parachuting down in the fluffy jacket Nikita had enchanted. "Ready, everyone?"

Aru turned her head a fraction to see that Brynne's wind had managed to catch not only her, but also Aiden, Rudy, and Mini right before they would've cracked open their skulls.

Aru tried to curl into a ball. "Give me a second, I—"

Fwomp. She was dumped on the ground.

"OW!" she yelled, rolling over and clutching her face. "My nose!"

Mini ran over and examined her.

Aru whimpered, and Vajra curled protectively around her wrist.

Mini prodded at Aru's nose. "Does this hurt?"

"WHAT THE—?"

"Going to take that as a yes," said Mini in her calmest *trust-me-I'm-a-medical-professional* voice. "So, there's good news and bad news."

"Good news," moaned Aru.

"It's not broken!"

"Yay."

"But it is bruised... and swelling up..." said Mini.

"So basically my face looks like it's trying to become a melon."

"I mean..."

Aru wished Mini could lie sometimes. Brynne marched over, hauled Aru to her feet, and inspected her nose.

"Looks the same to me?" said Brynne.

"Spectacular."

"We can ice it as soon as we get out of here," said Mini. "That'll bring down the swelling."

"We don't even know *how* to get out!" said Brynne. "We're stuck in this... whatever this is. Thanks a lot, Rudy."

"I didn't mean to trip the alarm," he protested. "I..."

Aiden drew his thumb and index finger over his closed lips in a *zip-it* gesture.

Aru held Vajra aloft, but the air was so murky not even her celestial weapon could provide enough light to illuminate their surroundings fully. Aiden held out his scimitars, Aru electrified them, and together they raised their weapons high like torches. Then they could see that walls of smooth rock stretched nearly three hundred feet above them toward a slice of silver-purple twilit sky that was just barely visible. The ground beneath them was gray marble. It would've been kind of pretty if it hadn't been for one detail.

The bones.

Broken skulls and jumbled skeletons dotted the courtyard in haphazard piles. Here and there treasure glinted in the heaps: bright coins or gems. A handful of charred swords lay still, many of them bearing a final dusty handprint.

Aru shuddered. *What* had happened to these people? She turned around the space, but the only thing she saw was a huge pillar in the middle of the courtyard bearing a single fracture. Why did she feel as if she'd seen it before?

Brynne whirled around to face Rudy.

"You had one job," she scolded. "*Don't* step on the stupid green tiles! It was so easy anyone could have done it!"

Rudy stood there, his eyes wide with panic, his hands

clutching the mechanical bird that—upon third glance—looked like a tiny eagle.

A rush of fury swept over Aru. All that trouble, all that effort they'd gone through to get to the vault... and for what? A wooden toy with a broken voice?

"Brynne," said Mini firmly. "Stop."

Brynne fell silent, anger bright on her face, and Aru shook herself. It was her fault, too, she acknowledged with a stab of guilt. She'd been thrown off by the vision of the man who had been her father. She hadn't expected to see him. Worse, she hadn't realized how much she'd *wanted* to see him.

"Rudy... are you okay?" asked Aiden.

The naga boy's hands trembled. A look of understanding passed over Aiden's face. He put away his scimitars and stepped toward his cousin, placing a hand on his arm. "What happened back there?"

For a long minute, Rudy stared at the ground. Finally, he raised his chin.

"I have trouble seeing certain colors," he said softly. "Yellow and green look kinda reddish to me, and I can't tell the difference between blue and purple." He took a deep breath, one corner of his mouth twitching like a snarl. "I wish that wasn't the case."

All of them were quiet for a moment until Mini piped up.

"It's a lot more common than you think," she said gently. "In fact, deuteranomaly, the most common form of color blindness, affects, like, five percent of the human male population."

Rudy laughed, but it was a hollow sound. "*Human* population, sure. But nagas? You know what it means to be a colorblind naga prince?"

Aru thought of all those jewels and riches deep in the naga palaces.... Things that Rudy wouldn't be able to distinguish.

"Color and magic are basically the same thing for my family," said Rudy, his words coming out in a rush. "If I had to make a crown that warded off curses, I'd need to cut emeralds and rubies a certain way, arrange them in a pattern.... I can't do that. Instead, I *listen* to the sounds inside a stone and make magic that way. But if I had to go by color, I'd put a bunch of topazes and tourmalines in a clump, and probably get someone's head turned into a jellyfish. Or turn *myself* into a jellyfish. At least, that's what my parents think, and that's why they never let me do anything. They don't really understand the kind of enchantments I work, and they're always worried I'm going to mess something up. I know it's for my own good and all that, but I *can* do magic. It's just... *different.* Anyway, I'm... I'm sorry. I really am."

Aru remembered when Rudy had rescued them from the naga treasury by playing all that music. His grandfather Takshaka had called him a disgrace. The insult wasn't because his own grandson was getting in his way, as Aru had thought at the time. It was because of who Rudy *was.* And Aru finally understood why the naga prince had wanted to join them.

"I know how that feels," said Mini.

Rudy looked up at her and smiled sadly. "You don't have to say that, Mini. You guys are *Pandavas* and"—he nodded at Aiden—"Pandava adjacent. It's different. Everyone is proud of you."

"Yeah... not really. People tell us all the time how much we've messed up," said Mini.

"Or that we're doomed to mess up before we even start," added Aru.

"Or that we can't change anything," said Aiden, quietly running his thumb along the top of his camera.

The anger vanished from Brynne's face, replaced with frustration. "Truth."

Aru's hand went to her mother's necklace. She couldn't let Rudy take the fall for everything.

"Listen," she said. "It's not Rudy's fault. I saw something, and—"

Creeeeak.

The five of them froze.

"What was that?" asked Mini, her voice going high.

The stone walls around them rippled as if they were made of cloth and someone on the other side had started to run their fingers across it.

"Silly..."

"Little..."

"Pandava thieves..."

The hairs on the back of Aru's neck prickled. The yalis bubbled up and disappeared again as they ran just beneath the surface of the stone. Out the corner of her eye, Aru caught sight of a spiked spine and the powerful whip of a crocodile tail.

"You are now in one of our favorite stories...."

Aru really wanted it to be the kind with a happily-ever-after ending, but judging by the pile of skeletons, she didn't think that was likely.

"We do enjoy what little entertainment we are granted...."

Aru swallowed hard and placed her hand on Vajra.

"Entertainment?" she echoed, turning slowly in the same spot. "Have you tried streaming instead? Tons of options."

"We prefer something . . . messier."

"There's always cable?" tried Aru.

"Get in formation!" yelled Brynne.

At once, the yalis vanished. The ground undulated beneath Aru's feet.

"Where's the attack coming from?" asked Mini. "I don't see anything!"

"Stories . . ." said Aiden. "Why did they mention stories? Is that a clue, or . . . Wait."

Aru craned her neck, squinting. Where had that grate up top come from? She wanted to call out to her soul father, Indra, for help, but the sky beyond the bars looked frozen, still stuck in that moment of purple twilight. She checked behind her.

She knew this courtyard. She knew this exact *sky*. And, unfortunately, she knew what came next.

"The reflection on the floors of the crypt," Aru whispered, looking at the others.

The story of Narasimha. The bottled-up wrath that the yalis unleash on thieves.

"Have you ever wondered what a god's wrath looks like?" whispered a yali.

Out the corner of her eye, Aru saw a pair of glowing eyes melt into the gray marble.

"We can show you," said another yali.

A dark and scaly tail whipped out of a wall and slammed the pillar that had once held the fearsome lion-headed god.

The column began to crack.

TWENTY-FIVE

This Is Not Fine

Within moments, everyone had formed a tight semicircle around the pillar (Rudy mostly cowered behind it). If they could beat back the yalis, maybe Narasimha's anger wouldn't be awakened. And then they could figure out how to get out of here.

"On the count of three," said Brynne. "One . . . two . . ."

"Three!" yelled Aru as a yali sprang toward them, jaws snapping and spines waving.

"Shields up," said Mini. Dee Dee lengthened in her hand, and a blast of violet light shot forward, forcing the creature back.

Aru didn't even wait for Aiden to say his usual *Light it up, Shah.* She whipped Vajra to the right and electricity crackled up Aiden's scimitars so fast he nearly jumped backward.

Aru heard the three yalis, somewhere unseen, hissing and whispering:

"It cannot be. . . . Freedom! Ah, sweet freedom . . . Close enough to taste . . ."

"It is, it is!" said the second yali hungrily. "Instruments of the divine."

"I knew I smelled godhood. . . ."

The second yali lunged at them, trying to reach the pillar. Deftly, Mini raised her force field, allowing just enough space for Brynne to blast him backward with Gogo. Wind roared through the air, and the creature hit a pile of stones with a hard thud. Brynne whooped triumphantly, but a moment later, the first yali jumped out of the ground a few feet away. The second yali got up and shook rubble from its scales as it zigzagged toward them.

"Camouflage o'clock," said Mini.

She whirled Dee Dee around her, rendering herself invisible. A moment later, Mini suddenly appeared between Brynne and Aru, standing directly in front of Aiden, who had his sparking scimitars raised to eye level.

"Over here!" Aiden taunted the yali.

The second beast loped toward the pillar. Mini stood her ground. The monster leaped, its huge claws swiping at her body. . . .

Which disappeared immediately.

On the other side of the pillar, the *real* Mini had turned off her projected illusion. The yali fell onto its belly.

Aiden dashed forward, brandishing his scimitars, and brought them down on the creature's thick skull. The steel didn't make a scratch.

The yali hissed as it slunk a few feet away.

Rudy ran to the front side of the pillar, holding out a gemstone that screeched horribly. The first yali flinched but stood its ground.

The third yali emerged from the marble floor. "You cannot hurt us, little demigods," it scoffed. "Our skin is impenetrable. Now we shall awaken the god's wrath, and you shall be finished."

"But our freedom..." said the first yali. The third one hissed at it.

The five kids drew closer to the pillar. By now, another, larger crack had appeared.

Aru spun Vajra in front of her, and the lightning bolt changed from a spear into a glowing lasso. She swung it around her head—briefly imagining she was Wonder Woman minus the cool outfit, great hair, and, well, never mind—and threw it at the third yali. But the creature was too fast. It loped up a wall, out of reach.

Brynne directed all her powerful gusts at the second yali, but the moment it was blown back, the first one returned.

"Come now, surely you must be tired of this game..." said the first yali.

"Let us do our job..." said the second.

Too late, Aru realized they didn't have visuals on the third yali—it had disappeared into the wall.

On her right, the missing yali zoomed up from the ground, arced across the pillar, and smashed its huge tail against the stone. A huge fissure spiderwebbed down the column. Aru heard the scritching and scratching of claws on rock, and a new odor invaded the air. It was the old-penny smell of blood.

"He is hungry..." said the first yali.

"His bloodthirst must be slaked...."

"And thieves make such sweet morsels...."

The yalis slunk into the marble—in anticipation of Narasimha's arrival, Aru guessed.

She and her friends were trapped.

If they backed away from the pillar, the yalis could pick them off one by one. If they stayed close to the column, Narasimha would finish them in five quick bites as soon as he broke out. Aru tossed Vajra between her hands as she tried to come up with a solution.

"We're going to die here, aren't we?" asked Rudy, collapsing against Aiden. "I can't die like this! There's things I haven't seen! Music I haven't listened to! *I still don't know what a microwave does!*"

Aiden smacked him upside the head. "Rudy. Shut. Up."

The naga prince whimpered.

"Well, Shah?" asked Aiden.

"The yalis' skin is impenetrable," she mused. "If we can't hurt them on the outside . . . we need to go *inside.*"

"What, like prop open their jaws and toss in a grenade?" asked Brynne sullenly.

Mini looked at Aru, then looked down at her plum sweater and skirt, which were secretly armored. "I think I know what you're going to ask me to do," she said with a sigh. "And I don't like that I'm going to agree."

Aru called to the yalis, "All right! Kill us! This is boring anyway, and I could use some reincarnation!"

A chasm opened in the floor not ten feet from her. The first yali emerged from it and fixed its glowing eyes on Aru.

"Is that so?"

Aru nodded. Behind the yali, the floor rippled as the other two rose to gaze at her.

"Then allow me to honor your request," said the first yali.

Aru adjusted her grip on Vajra. Behind her, Brynne stood at the ready. Aiden slashed the air with his scimitars, startling the second yali, who had gotten way too close. Rudy gathered up stones and flung them at the third yali, who laughed and laughed.

The first yali dove toward Aru, its huge jaws unhinged.

"Now!" commanded Aru.

Brynne directed strong winds at something right in front of Aru. Mini's invisibility glamour melted off as she was lifted and thrown sideways right into the yali's maw.

"I—HATE—THIS!" yelled Mini. She summoned Dee Dee in stick form.

The yali, confused, fell to the floor. It tried to shut its mouth, to shake Mini out of its teeth, but she didn't budge. It growled and clamped down harder, but Mini's armored clothes protected her. She thrust up the Death Danda and wedged the stick between the yali's jaws, opening them further. Then she slid out of the mouth.

"Do it, Aru!" she yelled.

"Sorry, Vajra," said Aru, hurling the lightning bolt deep into the yali's throat.

The monster thrashed angrily as its insides lit up.

The other two wriggled backward, alarmed. The second one said, *"How dare you try to kill us?"*

"I can show you if you'd like," said Aru coldly. "All I'd have to do is explode my lightning bolt."

All three yalis growled.

"But I won't turn your friend into monster sushi . . . as long as you play by my rules."

Behind her, more and more chunks of rock rolled off the shattering pillar as sharp talons tore at it from the inside. In just a few more minutes, Narasimha would be free.

And they'd be goners.

"Get us out of here," she commanded the yalis.

"We are but humble prisoners," said the third yali. "Cursed to stay within these walls...."

"Didn't I hear one of you say something about freedom?" asked Aru.

The first yali grunted twice, as if saying *Me! Me!*

"Yes!" the second said hurriedly. "It has been foretold. Godly beings will free us...."

"It is only a rumor," said the third yali. "The curse cannot be broken."

Aru wondered if the monsters were trying to trick her somehow. But they were nearly out of time—the pillar was breaking. Mini blasted a force field above them, and rocks bounced off the violet shield.

"Maybe we shouldn't mess with a curse?" said Mini.

"I don't plan to die here!" said Brynne.

Rudy raised his hand. "Make that two!"

"It's your call, Shah," said Aiden.

Aru turned to him. Dirt smudged his face and his clothes were torn. Exhaustion shot through her. They couldn't win this battle. And they couldn't save the Otherworld if they ended up dead.

Aru faced the yalis once more. "We'll free you from this place. In return, you get us out of here *safely*—or I'll blow you up."

The first yali grunted three times, which Aru took to mean *You have a deal, puny demigod* rather than *Come closer so I can eat you.*

The second yali took a step forward and said, "We promise to deliver you and your friends from this courtyard."

"And we always keep our promises," said the third, bowing its head.

Aru raised her hand, and Vajra zoomed from the first yali's mouth, hooking Dee Dee along the way. Mini caught her danda in midair and immediately spritzed it with hand sanitizer.

After shaking monster saliva from her own weapon, Aru said, "I release you," in as authoritative a tone as she could muster.

For the first time, a ghostly collar could be seen around each of the three yalis' throats, connected to chains that snaked down their backs and wrapped around their torsos.

Aru used Vajra to zap the collar and chain off the monster she'd nearly roasted.

The other two yalis waited expectantly before Mini and Brynne. The glare never left Brynne's face as she aimed her mace at the second yali's collar. One blast and the restraints shattered off its hide. The other yali hissed in Mini's direction. With pursed lips, Mini jabbed her Death Danda at the chain around the monster's rib cage.

Once freed, the three yalis rose before them, as tall as bears standing on their hind legs. They stared with grateful glowing eyes and panted, showing teeth that were yellow and pocked.

Behind the Pandavas, the pillar finally cracked all the way open. A deafening roar shook the courtyard.

"Climb onto our backs or die," said the first yali.

"Well, when you put it like that..." said Aru, hurriedly grabbing some spikes on the creature's back for handles and swinging her leg over its wide body.

Brynne and Rudy took the second yali, while Mini and Aiden clambered onto the third.

Giant feet stomped toward them, shaking the marble floor. The yalis reared back, and Aru held on tight as her beast launched itself upward and wriggled through the air toward the grate covering the twilight courtyard. She flattened herself against its scales as it snaked through the iron bars. Behind them, Narasimha howled, swiping at them with huge bloodied claws....

Aru squeezed her eyes shut as they broke past the clouds, climbing steadily higher and higher. The yali's hide was uncomfortably hot; it felt like sitting on the hood of a car in summertime. Every now and then it whipped its head around, jaws wide and tongue lolling, as if reconsidering what it had done to gain its freedom.

Where should we ask them to take us? asked Mini.

My place? offered Brynne.

Aru nodded and said, in her most imperious voice, "Yali, we wish you to return us to New York City. The address is—"

As one, the three yalis dived toward the earth.

"Whoa! Hold up!" said Aru. "What are you doing?"

"Keeping..."

"Our..."

"Promise..."

The yalis zoomed down so fast, Aru couldn't catch enough breath to speak. They burst through the clouds again, and the air turned from cool to humid and heavy. Aru spotted a mountain range—beautiful rolling greenery ribboned with silvery mists. But it was coming up at her way too fast.

"AHHHH!" she screamed.

Because of the wind, it was a lot more like:

"Ahhh"—*spits out bug... gasps for air... chokes a bit*—"ahhhhh!"

She reached for Vajra. Maybe she could manage to turn her lightning bolt into a hoverboard and dive off in time. But what about the others? Aru tried to sneak a glance back at them, but clouds obscured her view. The only thing she could hear was Rudy yelling, "BUT I'M A *PRINCE!*"

Aru's stomach swooped as they descended altogether too fast and finally came to a bumpy landing on a grassy patch on the top of a hill. She tumbled off her yali, and probably would've kept rolling down the hill if a huge log hadn't stopped her. The others dropped to the ground moments later. Brynne and Aiden dismounted immediately, their weapons blazing. Mini took a minute longer to get up, her face looking kind of green. Rudy stayed sprawled on the ground, his hands still clutching the wooden bird they'd found in the vault.

The yalis turned away from them and bent their short legs, preparing to spring into the air.

"Wait a minute!" said Aru, her lightning bolt falling to her side. "You're not leaving us here, are you? You said you'd bring us to safety!"

The third yali looked back at her. "We promised to deliver you from the courtyard," the creature said, its lips curling in a snarl. "And we did."

"Why would we want you to know our whereabouts?" said the second yali. "This is far safer."

And then, as one, they flew off, disappearing into the clouds.

"Well," huffed Aru. She opened her mouth, closed it. Then she crossed her arms. "That's just *rude.*"

TWENTY-SIX

Is a Platypus a Bird?

Aru stared around at the soft, rolling mountains cloaked in gray.

"Okay, where the heck *are* we?" she asked.

Brynne raised a finger to the air. "We're 35.6532 degrees north and 83.5070 degrees west."

Rudy stared at her. "What?"

"We're in Tennessee," said Brynne. "Or more precisely, Great Smoky Mountains National Park."

Aiden plopped down on a fallen tree branch. "At least the lighting is great." He took out his camera and snapped some photos.

"Aren't there bears in Tennessee?" asked Mini, holding Dee Dee close.

"Of course not," said Aru. *There definitely are,* she thought privately.

Aiden caught her eye, raising an eyebrow, and Aru made a *shh*-ing gesture.

"Okay, good," said Mini. "My inhaler is almost out of juice," this mountain air is really thin, and I could become acutely hypoxic and—"

"Die?" asked Brynne, Aiden, and Aru at the same time.

Mini looked highly affronted. "It's not a joke! I could *lose consciousness,* which is really serious!"

"The big thing we're losing is time," said Brynne. "We're down to *three* days to find Kalpavriksha, the vault was a bust, and we're trapped in the mountains with no camping supplies—"

Aiden reached into his backpack and pulled out a coin. He flipped it onto the ground, and three tents sprouted up immediately.

Brynne scowled. "Okay, well, definitely no food—"

Aiden dug out five protein bars and tossed them in front of the tents.

Rudy stared at him. "Dude, *what* is in that bag?"

"Precautionary stuff," said Aiden simply. "And an ice pack for your nose."

Aru gratefully placed the cold bag on her nose and then shivered. "Any chance there's a campfire in one of those pockets?"

"Allow me," said Brynne. She whispered something to her mace, and warm flames flickered out from the top. "Courtesy of Uncle Agni."

Last year, Agni, the god of fire, had given each of them a present after they'd cured his awful stomachache. Except for Aru. She got an "IO(F)U" and the promise that when she needed it, he'd have weapons ready for her.

"The whole crypt mission was totally pointless," groaned Brynne. "All we got was that bird thing. Where'd the wishing tree go?"

Rudy pulled out the wooden eagle, and its soft, broken tune floated through the air. Aru saw the bright bead caught in its beak. The longer she stared at it, the more she remembered the ache that had taken root in her heart the moment she'd placed the key in the vault door. Her father's voice rang in her ears: *You don't understand—I have a daughter on the way. . . .*

Aru turned to Rudy and held out her hand. "Can I see that?"

The bird was the size of a tennis ball, and it struggled in her grasp like a living thing. Whoever had crafted it had done a beautiful job. The pale wood feathered out like real wings, and its lacquered eyes gleamed. Its small chest rose and fell as it chirped out the same hoarse tune.

"Sounds broken," said Rudy.

Aru agreed that something about the tune seemed off. "What if it's trying to say something, though? Like a message, or a riddle," she said. "There has to be a reason the fake tree in Nandana sent us to that crypt."

Plus, she still wondered whether the jewel in its beak held a part of her father. How else could she have seen one of his memories? She gripped the bird tightly, but no vision came forth. She couldn't decide if she was relieved or disappointed.

"Sadly, none of us speak bird," said Brynne.

"I hate birds," said Rudy. "Smell weird. Beady eyes. And they *hate* snakes. In fact—"

But Mini cut him off. "Hey, Brynne, would you be able to understand it if you turned into a bird?"

"Whenever I've shape-shifted, I've never understood the animal's language," said Brynne.

"But did you ever try?" asked Aru.

"Well, no, not exactly . . ."

"Shah has a point," said Aiden. "Give it a try, Bee."

"Ooh, can you turn yourself into something extinct?" asked Aru. "Like a dodo bird?"

"Or an emu!" said Mini.

"Emus aren't extinct," said Brynne.

"Platypus?" asked Aru.

"Is a platypus even a bird?" asked Brynne.

"Actually, it's a semiaquatic egg-laying mammal that's similar to the echidna," said Aiden, fussing with his camera. "They've got venomous ankle spurs."

Rudy wrinkled his nose. "What kind of terrible animals exist in the human world?"

The girls ignored him and stared at Aiden.

"What?" Aiden asked. "I like nature documentaries. The cinematography is unparalleled."

"Snob," said Aru.

"Troll," said Aiden, not even bothering to look up at her. But Aru noticed that a corner of his mouth lifted. Almost like a smile.

Brynne sighed. With a snap of her fingers, she transformed into a scowling swan with cobalt-blue feathers. Rudy held up the bird to her, and Swan-Brynne craned her neck around it. A second later, she changed back.

"Still can't speak bird," she declared.

Just then, an idea struck Aru.

"But Boo does!" she said. "I once saw him arguing with a falcon in Atlanta! I think it was during the Super Bowl. . . ."

"If he's with the twins, maybe they can bring him a message? We could send it in a dream," Mini suggested.

Aru nodded, then ran her thumb along the bird's wing. *What are you trying to tell us?* she wondered. Her thumb brushed aside one of its wooden plumes, and underneath, a dark curly symbol caught her eye.

"There's a weird marking on this bird," she said. "It looks like the letter *G*."

"G?" repeated Rudy. He sat up straight, panic in his eyes. "Is he around?"

"Who is *he*?"

"Uh, the *king* of the birds? Sworn enemy of all snakes?" he said, swiveling his head. *"Garuda?"*

"You think *he* knows where the wish-granting tree went?" asked Aru.

"He might, but I'm not sticking around to find out. That guy hates my whole family."

"I'm sure you did nothing to deserve it," said Brynne drily. "And speaking of *deserve,* once we figure out where we're going next, I'm not so sure you should come with us."

Rudy's expression crumpled. "Look, I'm sorry. But I can help—"

Brynne's voice was gentle but firm. "I know it's not your fault, but you still landed us in that yali pit."

In the bird's beak, the small gemstone glimmered, calling to Aru once more. With a pang, she remembered that she'd never explained her role in how they'd fallen into the pit. She couldn't let Rudy take all the blame.

"He didn't," said Aru quietly.

The others turned to look at her.

Aru took a deep breath. "I saw something when I was trying to get the bird. A vision of the Sleeper. I think it came from the gem thing in its beak—I don't know. I got startled, and I lost my grip."

Rudy took the bird from her and gently pulled open the bird's beak. It paused in its tune to squawk indignantly as Rudy plucked the jewel from its mouth.

"This isn't an ordinary jewel," he said. "It's a receptacle for thoughts, emotions, memories. . . . I've seen stuff like this before, in my dad's collection. This must've been what Mr. V was talking about! He said so himself, remember? That the Sleeper lost pieces of his soul or something when he went looking for the tree? In fact, I think if I—" Rudy pressed down hard on the jewel.

"NO!" yelled Aru.

But it was too late.

Something like a hologram emerged from the jewel, rendering an eerie sequence of scenes in front of them.

They saw a young boy in a market, his face turned away as he stared after a young child walking off hand in hand with her two parents laughing and smiling beside her. Someone grabbed the boy's arm impatiently. "There you are! Come. It's time to return home."

The boy responded in a small voice: "The orphanage isn't home. Homes have families."

Whoever stood beside him laughed. "It's the only home *you'll* ever have."

The vision jumped ahead, showing the young boy studying hard, building inventions, reading books. In every image, his face was hidden.

And then the projection changed to show the boy grown up—a man in his early twenties standing before a council of five elder Otherworld Council members. His dark hair flopped in front of his face, and when he pushed it back, Aru could see his eyes: one blue, one brown. It was *him*. The Sleeper. Only he was so young. He wore a dark polo with four red letters embroidered on the chest: OFCS. Aru recognized that acronym. It stood for the Otherworld Foster Care System, the same system that had taken in Sheela and Nikita.

"Ah, Suyodhana," said a dark-skinned man, who leaned forward, steepling his taloned fingers. "You are perhaps the youngest and most accomplished member ever to seek permission to pursue a higher education in the magical arts. It's tradition that every student wishing to pursue such studies takes on the burden of a quest. Yours was simple: show us the strongest substance in the world. And yet you have arrived empty-handed."

The elders looked at each other, exchanging smirks.

Suyodhana smiled. "I have certainly fulfilled my quest, but before I show you the results, perhaps we can share a toast? I am honored to have even been given this opportunity to prove myself."

He snapped his fingers and five golden goblets floated before the elders. The drink must've smelled delicious, because all five Council members sighed deeply.

"To our dreams," said Suyodhana, lifting his own goblet. "May they never turn to nightmares."

The members drank, and then the eldest one wiped his mouth and said, "And as for your quest?"

Suyodhana pointed at each of the goblets. "Every single

one of those was filled with a rare poison for which there is no antidote."

At once, the members paled. They scrambled to their feet, clutching their throats. One of them fell to the floor with a loud crash and started thrashing about and yelling, "I can't breathe! I can't breathe!" Another fainted dead away. All the while Suyodhana watched without emotion.

"What's the meaning of this?" gasped the elder. "How dare you!"

"How dare I what?" asked Suyodhana. "How dare I lie?"

They all paused.

The person who had been yelling about how he couldn't breathe suddenly sat up. He pointed a shaky finger at Suyodhana. "So you poisoned us and then magically administered an antidote?"

"No."

"Then explain why I am suddenly able to breathe!" said the man.

Suyodhana shrugged. "Because I never poisoned you. But you believed I did. And that, dear members, is the strongest substance in the world: *belief*."

The vision jumped ahead once more.

The Sleeper was older, with faint lines framing his eyes. When he pushed the hair away from his face, Aru saw a wedding band. In his other hand, he held a wriggling key that looked just like the one Mr. V had given them. Aru recognized the floor covered with scales, the dimly lit hall. The Sleeper was in the Crypt of Eclipses.

He closed his eyes and twisted the ring around his finger. "I know the prophecy concerning me," he said in a choked voice. "I wish to avoid it completely. Please! You don't understand—I have a daughter on the way. I can't let her inherit a world I am destined to destroy. Tell me what I must do. Please, tell me—I'll pay any price."

Tendrils of shadow appeared and wrapped around his hand; then they wound up his arm and plunged into his chest. He gasped in pain as the shadows seemed to tug something out.

"Childhood memories? Is that all?" he asked weakly. "I can bear it."

And with that, the vault door opened before him and light spilled onto the floor.

The vision faded. And once it was gone, Aru realized there were tears streaming down her cheeks. When Mr. V had said that the key had unlocked pieces of the Sleeper, she didn't think she'd actually have to see it happen.

"Does this mean I can stay?" asked Rudy, holding up the little blue jewel. But then he must have noticed that Aru was crying. "What's the big deal, Shah? I mean, it's kinda sad and all for the Sleeper, but imagine being his daughter. That would—"

Aiden elbowed Rudy in the ribs, and a look of understanding crossed the naga's face. "Oh . . ." he muttered.

"Gimme a sec," said Aru, walking down the hill to be alone.

She didn't know what to think or how to feel after seeing the vision.

I'll do anything.

Dimly, she remembered the twins' nightmares. The way their mother had screamed at them not to follow her, the tears in her eyes as she choked out, *I would do anything not to leave you.*

Aru felt a flash of fury. The twins had gotten to experience that love, at least for a little while. They'd gotten to see it in action. But not Aru.

If her father had never become the Sleeper, her life would have been so different. Full of smiles and laughter. And love.

What had happened? Why had he failed at changing his fate? And how could her mother have locked him away when all he'd done was try to fix things?

What if the same thing happened to her? The prophecy mentioned an untrue sister.... Could it be her, even though she had no intention of betraying anyone? All Aru wanted to do was save the Otherworld, save her friends and family.... But what if she still somehow ended up the villain? Opal's taunting words flew back to her: *The flesh-and-blood daughter of the Sleeper.*

Maybe evil ran in her blood.... Like father, like daughter...

"Aru?"

She spun around and saw Brynne, Mini, and Aiden walking toward her.

"Talk to us," said Mini.

"I'm fine—" started Aru, but her voice cracked, and she stood there shaking.

Mini went to her first, wrapping her arms around Aru in a tight hug before stepping away to search her face.

"I get it, you know," said Brynne softly.

Aru looked up. Brynne's arms were crossed and she was staring at the ground.

"It's really tough to see the mom or dad you *should've* had," she said. "Gunky and Funky used to tell me how nice Anila once was. I don't know why she couldn't be that way for me." Brynne fiddled with her stack of melted-down-trophy bracelets, her mouth a grim line. "For a while, I thought it was because I wasn't good enough, or that it was somehow my fault... but now I know that's not it."

A lump rose in Aru's throat. That was exactly how she'd felt. As if the mere act of being born had somehow caused all this to happen.

"This isn't about you, Shah," said Aiden firmly. "And maybe you thought you lost someone great, but you don't know how he would've been as a dad. People change. Trust me."

Aru forced herself to nod. Maybe he was right. She'd never know.

"But the prophecy..." she said. "And Opal—"

"Forget Opal," said Mini, throwing up her hands. "She doesn't know everything! And just because what you saw back there made you upset, that doesn't mean you're sympathizing with the enemy and going to go rogue on us."

Aru gaped at her. "How'd you know—?"

"Because we're sisters," said Mini, squeezing her arm.

Brynne looped her arm through Aru's. "Now c'mon. We've got a tree to find and some sleep to catch, and I found everything we need for making s'mores in Aiden's bag."

"Good job, Wifey," said Aru.

Aiden rolled his eyes.

But he still smiled.

In her dreams that night, Aru found that she, Brynne, and Mini were once more in the twins' astral realm. It wasn't a nightmare like last time. But it wasn't exactly happy, either. The twins stood on a worn stage inside an abandoned theater. Glittering cobwebs hung from chandeliers made of hard candy. It was a dream, and so things were just standard weird—ten jellyfish bobbed in the air, patterned in purple polka dots. A stingray moved overhead, the underside of its wings plastered with sheet music.

Sheela ran to greet them, throwing her arms around Mini, who had clearly become her favorite.

Brynne awkwardly patted Sheela on the head, whispering to Aru, "Is this what you do with children?"

"She's a *human,* not a *puppy,*" said Mini.

Nikita stood off to the side, wearing a silk turban and a velvet dress on which clouds slowly gusted across the fabric.

Aru walked over to her.

"How'd you like the outfits?" asked Nikita brusquely.

Aru grinned. "They were—"

"Fabulous? I know," said Nikita, waving a hand. "Don't tell me more. I don't need to be bored with the details of my genius."

Aru smirked. Before, she would've found Nikita rude and annoying, but she understood her a little better now.

Nikita must've found Aru's silence unnerving, because she crossed her arms, pouting. "Don't think just because you saw our nightmare that we're going to be close or something," she said. "We can take care of ourselves."

"I know."

"We're used to people leaving," said Nikita.

Aru's voice softened. "I know."

"Good," added the scowling ten-year-old.

Aru nodded, then looked up at the dream chandeliers. "Trust me, I'd love to be rid of you, but you're pretty useful. The outfits were amazing and probably saved our lives. Plus, I kinda like the novelty of having baby sisters."

"I'm not a baby!"

"That's what babies say."

Nikita scowled. "I don't like you, Shah."

"Now you sound like family!"

A smile pulled at Nikita's face, but then Sheela suddenly screamed.

"No!"

Aru and Nikita whirled around to find Sheela sitting on the floor, rocking back and forth. Her eyes glowed, and tears streamed down her face. Mini grabbed her shoulders, trying to help her up, but Sheela wouldn't move.

"He's making a terrible mistake. . . ." Sheela turned her unfocused gaze on Aru. *"And you will hate him for his love."*

Aru jolted awake to sounds of commotion outside the tent, which was suddenly empty. She pulled on a sweater and trudged into the cold night. Rudy, Aiden, Brynne, and Mini already stood in their campsite, looking up at the sky. And they weren't alone. *Thousands* of birds filled the trees around them.

The wooden eagle, lying on its side between the two tents, called out its strange riddling tune.

"Remember how the eagle has the letter *G* on it?" Aiden asked her.

"Yeah..."

"It *does* stand for Garuda."

The king of the birds? Aru frowned. "How do you know?"

Aiden pointed up at the stars, and Vajra sparkled with panic.

"Because," said Aiden, "he's decided to pay us a visit."

TWENTY-SEVEN

Quoth the Raven...

Garuda, king of the birds, flew toward them. Aru hadn't met very many kings. She had, however, seen advertisements for pro wrestling matches, and this was starting to look like one. She and her friends might have been standing in the middle of a ring for all that was happening around them.

The surrounding trees bent and groaned under the weight of thousands of birds cawing and screeching from the branches like an audience thirsting for a fight. Maybe it had something to do with being in Garuda's vicinity, but Aru found she could *understand* everything the birds were saying... and it wasn't exactly polite.

"Eat them, my king!" shouted a jackdaw in the branches.

A blue jay with a southern accent hollered, "I brought some Tabasco sauce to share with y'all!"

A small chickadee the length of Aru's pinky chirped in a sweet, high-pitched voice, "SHOW THEM A FRESHLY WASHED WINDOW AND HAVE *THEM* RUN INTO IT A HUNDRED TIMES." Then it cackled hysterically.

Aru was starting to regret every time she'd filled up the bird feeder.

Something sailed out of the trees toward them. Brynne held out her mace. Mini cast a shield. Aiden pulled out his scimitars. And Rudy . . . well, at least he had the mechanized eagle between his hands. Aru aimed Vajra as a spear, on the verge of letting it loose. . . .

Bam!

An object fell to the ground, tendrils of smoke writhing from it.

It was . . .

"Toast?" asked Aru.

Aiden inspected the smoldering loaf of bread. "Well, it is now."

"How would *you* like empty carbs thrown at your head?!" shouted a duck. "Some of us don't like that processed nonsense!"

"Some of us are gluten intolerant!" honked a goose.

"Why don't you featherless noodles ever give us things that don't taste like cardboard?" huffed an owl.

From the trees, the birds began to chant:

"NO MORE BREAD!"

"NO MORE BREAD!"

"NO MORE BREAD!"

Aru turned to her friends, but they were just as bewildered as she was.

A gust whooshed past them. Aru shielded her eyes with the inside of her elbow, squinting as dirt and twigs rose in a tiny storm. She had never stood next to a helicopter, but she imagined it was kind of like this. In the midst of that powerful wind, a figure landed in front of them. The force of his touchdown sent a tremor through the earth.

Aru lowered her arm when the gust died down. She knew Garuda from the statues her mom had on display in the museum. Aside from the fact that he wasn't made of sandstone, the real king looked a lot like those sculptures. His eyes were a handsome shade of amber, and human-shaped, but his face was covered in brilliant green feathers, and he had a sharp golden beak instead of a nose. Bronze wings nearly seven feet long lay folded behind his shoulders; their tips brushed the grass. From the neck down, he looked like a strong man with tanned skin, except that his hands and feet ended in sharp bird-of-prey talons. Garuda had a wide-brimmed solid-gold baseball cap over his dark curly hair, and wore long silk shorts covered in trophy badges. On his shoulder, a shiny black raven cawed loudly, and the bird chant stopped.

"You know him as Khagesvara!" shouted the raven. "*King* of the birds!"

The birds cheered. The Pandavas drew a little closer. Rudy tugged his hood over his face.

"You know him as Suparna!" squawked the raven. "He who has *beeeeee-ooootiful* feathers!"

At this, Garuda nodded, acknowledging the crowd for the first time. He shook out his wings, vast enough that Aru and her friends ducked instinctively to avoid getting thwacked in the face. His feathers shone brightly, Aru thought, like the glint of a knife's blade.

"You know him as Nagantaka!" said the raven. "THE DEVOURER! It's the one, the only . . . GAAAARUDA!"

The king turned in a slow circle, arms up and muscles flexed. The birds cheered so hard, a fine layer of feathers drifted down to cover the forest floor.

"And what do we have here?" asked the raven, its beady eyes fixed on Rudy.

"Can I leave?" he mumbled to the Pandava crew. "This is *not* going to end well for me."

"Is that a . . . ? No!" said the raven, hopping onto Garuda's head. It cocked its head to the side. "It's a *snake!*"

The birds honked and screeched in displeasure.

"I'm not a snake!" said Rudy, puffing out his chest. "I'm a—"

Aiden smacked his palm over his cousin's mouth. "Not the time, dude."

"*Ooh,* I know I see me a snake!" the raven hooted with delight. "We *hate* snakes!"

Garuda nodded, scowling.

"Leathery ropes with faces," the raven said with a shudder, before turning its attention to the Pandavas. "And some demigods. Aww, that's cute. Folks, let's give 'em a round of indifferent applause. Congrats, kids! You've got some shiny weapons! I like shiny. But none of those can even *scratch* our king! Ask Indra. He tried with that same lightning bolt."

In response, Vajra gave an electrical shiver of displeasure.

"We have no desire to scratch Garuda—" started Mini.

"Who put glasses on top of this pair of living toothpicks?" cackled the raven.

Mini flushed, pushing her glasses up the bridge of her nose. At the same time, Aru and Brynne lifted their weapons.

"I'm surprised you've got so much to say," said Aru. "Shouldn't you be squawking from some old guy's fireplace?"

"Yeah. Come back when it's Halloween!" chimed in Brynne.

The raven froze. The birds fell silent. Slowly, the raven turned to her. "What did you say to me?"

"Go haunt a poet!" snapped Aru.

"Or do you not do that anymore?" asked Brynne.

"I think you mean *nevermore,*" said Aiden.

"THAT'S IT!" screeched the raven.

It launched itself off Garuda's head, but the king of the birds caught him one-handed. He narrowed his amber eyes at the bird before putting it on his shoulder. The raven huffed, its feathers settling. Silent as ever, Garuda crossed his arms, his gaze falling to the mechanized eagle in Rudy's grip.

The raven sighed and declared, "You are hereby charged with the theft of a precious object on loan from King Garuda to the goddess Aranyani. Following a thorough investigation of the crypt, it was found that four to five persons escaped after freeing the bound yalis. His Majesty, King Garuda, was able to track the stolen object to the whereabouts of the thieves." The raven coughed, then leaned forward. "That means *you.*"

"You don't understand—" started Brynne, but Aiden held her back.

"Furthermore, the fact that said stolen property was found in the hands of none other than a descendant of Garuda's most vile aunt, Kadru—"

From the branches, the birds hissed. Garuda's scowl merely deepened.

Aru swiveled around to face Rudy. "Garuda's *aunt?*" she asked. "You guys are related?"

"I mean, yeah, but she's literally my least-favorite relative," mumbled Rudy. "She pinches my cheeks all the time—I hate it."

"Confirms the treachery and wrongdoing of all persons present," concluded the raven. "And *finally*, not only did you steal the property of Garuda, you *broke* it. You robbed it of its voice."

"We didn't know it belonged to anyone!" protested Aru. "And it was broken already!"

"Pah!" spat the raven. "You broke it because you *knew* it could tell the truth!"

Tell the truth? So it *was* a clue, Aru thought.

Rudy turned the bird over in his hands, understanding dawning on his face.

Aru felt frantic. The one thing that could save them was broken, and they had no idea how to fix it.

"Therefore, you shall be ..."

The raven flailed his wing at the branches, and hundreds of birds hollered, "EXECUTED!"

They cheered and whooped, and Garuda himself clapped and nodded. Aru took a step back. Vajra began to shift and spark with electricity.

"That's not fair!" Mini said. She stepped forward, holding up Dee Dee like a scepter. Behind her, Rudy's eyebrows shot up. "You can't just execute us because Rudy is a naga—"

"Prince," whispered Rudy. Then he looked at them innocently. "What? It's the truth."

"He's never done anything to you," Mini said to Garuda.

"It's true." Rudy nodded.

"He can barely defend himself," continued Mini.

"*Very* true," said Brynne.

Rudy opened his mouth to protest. Aiden reached over and closed it.

"How could this boy threaten the king of the birds?"

finished Mini. "We had no intention of stealing anything from you—we didn't even know it was yours. We were looking for something else, found this, and thought it would lead us in the right direction."

Aru had to hand it to Mini—she was becoming a smooth talker. And she'd kept everything vague. No reason for the whole world to know that they were searching for the wish-granting tree.

Garuda regarded them. Then his gaze slid to the raven.

"You want an explanation, little demigod?" demanded the raven. "Observe."

The raven cawed three times, and the birds dove from the trees, all of them converging and flying in a circle around the accused. In the middle of the vortex they created, images appeared in the air. Aru saw a younger Garuda covered in writhing snakes as he walked down a huge white hallway in what looked like a palace. There was a look of anguish on his face as the snakes twined around him and flicked his ear with their tongues. Garuda glanced behind himself, and the view shifted to show two older women standing at the entrance of a large door. Their similar eyes and chins told Aru they were related.

One of them, draped in a sari made of glimmering scales, smiled slyly at Garuda. "Go on, then," she said. "Take your cousins out to play, and do not let any harm befall them."

"Please, sister, let my son rest," said the other woman. "You have no quarrel with him." She wore a simple outfit of spun cotton, and her hair was pulled back. Her face was sad and gaunt, whereas her sister's was round and shining.

"*You* are the one who lost the bet, Vinata," said the fancier woman. "How is it *my* fault that you agreed to be my servant?

I can command you to do anything I please. I may not be able to control your son, but he will listen to you. And right now, my sweet children desire fresh air. I do not wish their poor, soft bellies to be torn up by the ground, so Garuda will carry them."

"When Kashyapa returns, he will be displeased at how you've come to treat me, Kadru," said Vinata.

Aru recognized the name Kashyapa. He was a powerful sage.

"*When* our husband returns. He'll be meditating for a thousand more years, I imagine!" scoffed Kadru. "Which means I can enjoy a thousand more years of *your* servitude. Leave us, Garuda. My hair needs to be braided, and if your mother is distracted, she'll do it sloppily."

Garuda looked at both women with barely restrained rage. His mother merely nodded.

The image in front of Aru faded as the birds broke out of their circle and hovered in the air.

"Our king spent *years* in the service of his aunt, the mother of all snakes," declared the raven. "It was only through hard work and nobility that he managed to free both himself and Vinata. And that is why birds and snakes do not trust one another to this day."

Aru had no idea there was a mother of snakes.... Now she kind of wondered whether the whole "mother of dragons" thing from *Game of Thrones* was actually real, but it didn't seem the right time to ask.

"The naga boy before you is a direct descendant of Kadru and her slimy spawn!" said the raven. "He's the grandson of the naga king Takshaka, after all!"

"Yeah, well, he and I are not on great terms, trust me," said Rudy.

"Trust you?" the raven squawked. "I think not."

"But—" started Rudy.

With a flash, a ring of magical torches instantly illuminated the night sky. Aru blinked against the sudden light while the birds flapped in place before them. She glimpsed thousands of shining black eyes and sharp beaks and had the uncomfortable realization that they looked a lot like missiles.

Garuda raised his arm, then brought it down. As one, they struck.

TWENTY-EIGHT

Surprise Ostrich!

"Incoming!" hollered Brynne.

The girls moved immediately into defense mode.

Aru cast Vajra, and the lightning bolt transformed into a net. A swath of birds was caught in mid-flight. They squawked as they dropped to the forest floor, squirming beneath the mesh.

"Knock 'em out," Aru commanded Vajra.

With one pulse of the lightning net, the birds fell unconscious. Vajra zipped back to Aru's side, electrifying Aiden's scimitars on its way.

Brynne tossed her mace between her hands, looking hungrily at the birds. "Braised, roasted, shredded...I like fowl," she said.

At that, some of the birds veered away, swooping close enough that Aru felt a breeze on her face.

Aiden leaped in front of Brynne, swirling his scimitars to amplify her wind vortex. It blew through the birds and they cartwheeled away, cawing angrily.

"Adrishya," said Mini.

Violet light swept up the Pandavas, Aiden, and Rudy, instantly rendering them invisible.

They ducked, weaved, and sidestepped to avoid attack, and the birds whooped and cawed in frustration.

"Now!" said Brynne.

Aru, Brynne, and Aiden channeled everything they could at the flock—concentrated tornadoes, winnowing electrified blades, and bolts of lightning. When a large percentage of the birds had fallen away, Mini replaced the veil of invisibility with a violet shield. The birds that had somehow managed to slip through the cracks were rewarded with a powerful conk to the head when they hit the force field.

The Pandavas regrouped, quickly catching their breath. Aru glanced over at Rudy to see that he was kneeling on the ground, rummaging around in his messenger bag.

"Rudy, what are you doing?" demanded Aiden. "Go hide!"

"No," he said. The wooden eagle lay before him on the grass. He pulled out glowing stones with a glimmering mesh overlay—something that looked like the heart of the moon, and a chunk of quartz that wriggled as if it were alive. "Garuda thinks it's broken, but I can fix it."

"Are you sure you know what you're doing?" asked Aiden.

"Of course not!" said Rudy cheerfully.

"Then why—?"

"Because I'm the only chance you've got."

Aiden spun as a furious albatross dove toward him, nearly taking out his eye with its vast wings. Mini's force fields were getting better with practice, but they could still just barely cover the five of them. A flock of sparrows dove repeatedly at the violet shield until small cracks appeared in it, like ice breaking on a puddle. At one point, a horde of parakeets flew at Brynne, spurring her to leap into the air and shape-shift into a huge blue bird with skinny legs, and squawk, "SURPRISE OSTRICH!"

The parakeets screamed as Ostrich-Brynne kicked them out of the air and plopped back to the ground.

"Surprise ostrich?!" yelled Aru. "That's the best, most random thing you've ever—" She dove behind Mini's shield as a flock of hummingbirds with needle-sharp beaks zigzagged toward her.

While Aru was on the ground trying to get her bearings, she noticed that only one figure remained silent and still in all the chaos:

Garuda.

He never moved, never flinched, and *never* took his eyes off the Pandavas. She bet that even when they were invisible, the king of the birds could see them just fine. The fact that he refused to fight sent a chill through Aru.

He didn't fight because he didn't need to.

Garuda was invincible . . . and he was biding his time until he was needed to close the deal. Which meant Rudy had to fix that broken eagle, *stat.* Aru didn't think Garuda was the type to make small talk. Or, actually, *any* kind of talk.

Aru looked over at the naga, who was nodding and . . . *humming along with the jewels.*

"This isn't rearrange-your-playlist time, Rudy!" shouted Aru. "Can't you go any faster?"

Gogo had just blown away another group of birds, but the sky buzzed with new attackers.

Rudy sat with his knees pulled to his chest while the mechanical eagle perched on his shoulder and croaked its hoarse tune into his ear. He closed his eyes as he worked, rearranging jewels by touch until he'd shaped what looked like a lopsided star. "Just a little more time!" he said. "Keep doing what you're doing."

He shoved a sapphire into place, then set the eagle in the middle of the jewels. A wild look of joy spread across his face. "There! Listen! Don't you hear it?"

Aru tilted her head, expecting something grand. But she didn't hear anything except the powerful beat of wings just outside Mini's force field.

She stood up. *This is it,* thought Aru. *A parakeet is going to be the death of me.*

"I hear it..." said Mini, a look of awe blooming across her face. She lowered her hand for an instant, and the violet shield flickered out.

"Watch out, Shah!" yelled Aiden.

Holding up a sparking Vajra just in time, Aru repelled a flock of cackling chickadees. At the same instant, she heard something, too. It was a sound that made the whole world seem like poured honey—slow and thick and golden. She glanced at Brynne and Aiden as they spun in perfect tandem. Pollen from the springtime trees dusted them like stars. Even the chickadees didn't look so awful now.

The eagle was singing a new song. It made Aru think of the slow shift of something vast and celestial, like the rotation of a planet, or the sound constellations made when they settled into the sky at night.

All at once, the birds stopped attacking.

Mini's force field vanished. Brynne and Aiden lowered their weapons, and Vajra snapped back into a bracelet on Aru's wrist.

A shadow fell over them, and Aru looked up just in time to see Garuda hovering above them. The shiny raven on his shoulder cawed once, then flew off to join the other birds, shouting, "False alarm! False alarm! If we want a fight, let's watch *The Bachelor*!"

And with a vast *whump!* of wings, all the birds vanished into the air. Only Garuda remained. He landed, his eyes pinned to the repaired eagle on the ground. Rudy swayed as its haunting melody washed over him.

"How did you do that?" asked Garuda. His voice was raspy, like he'd yelled too much in battle. It wouldn't be great for karaoke, but everyone would probably be too scared to tell him so.

"I...I have a good ear," said Rudy finally.

Garuda cocked his head, as if he weren't just looking at Rudy but weighing his whole life.

"Do not forget it, little prince," said Garuda. "May I have that?"

Rudy picked up the bird and handed it to Garuda, his face shining with pride. Rudy had said his family thought he couldn't do anything important. They were wrong.

At Garuda's touch, the bird warbled another tune. Aru could only describe it as moonlight melted into song. It wasn't of this world, and she knew she'd never forget it for as long as she lived.

Then the bird fell silent. As they watched, its segments rearranged themselves until the eagle had transformed into a flat translucent rectangle with a silver streak in the middle, like a moonbeam pressed between glass. Indecipherable writing was scribbled across it.

Garuda's face grew thoughtful. "I see now," he said. "You did not break the bird."

DUH! Aru wanted to yell.

Beside her, Brynne glowered, and even though she remained silent, Aru 100 percent imagined her saying, *Oh,* now *you see?!*

"You're welcome, dude," said Rudy happily.

Mini elbowed him sharply.

"But you entered the crypt under false pretenses," said Garuda. "Why were you there?"

"That's our business," said Aru quickly.

"It is my business too," said Garuda. "After all, I am one of the protectors of the treasures that arose from the churning of the Ocean of Milk. And one of those treasures is the Tree of Wishes." The king glared around at them meaningfully.

Busted, thought Aru.

"Why you?" asked Brynne. Then she promptly added, "Um, no offense, of course. Your Highness."

The king of the birds took a step back. He extended both arms, held up two talons on his left, and made a wide circle in the air with his right. A couple of moments passed with the five of them standing around and wondering what was happening.

In the space where the king had been waving his arm, an image popped up. A young Garuda flew through the skies, carrying a heavy golden pot. He dove through a dense jungle and then alighted in a shady grove full of huge dark snakes that reminded Aru of those climbing ropes that gym teachers brought out just to torture her.

"I have brought the nectar of immortality as you commanded," the Garuda in the vision said, eyeing the snakes warily. "Now you must free me and my mother from your servitude."

The snakes' soft hissing sounded like laughter.

"Very well, giant bird," they mocked. "You are free. But

perhaps you shall not stay that way. Who knows what power we might wield once we taste the nectar of the gods?"

Garuda hesitated at that, and he held the pot of amrita closer to his body. "It is, as you said, the nectar of the gods. You cannot approach it in an unclean state. Go bathe yourselves, and I will wait here."

The snakes murmured in agreement, then slithered away toward the river.

Once they were gone, Garuda's head dropped to his chest. "You are free, Mother," he said aloud, thrusting the pot into the air. "O Lord of Preservation, I have no intention of sharing this nectar with my brethren, and I have no wish to ingest it myself. What must I do?"

A bright orange light filled the air and the vision faded. Garuda clasped his talons. "That is how I entered the service of Lord Vishnu," he said. "He rewarded me for resisting temptation when power was within my grasp, and then he took the amrita and buried it in a labyrinth beneath the Ocean of Milk."

"That's also how half my family ended up with forked tongues," muttered Rudy. "Some of the amrita spilled on the grass, and they got super excited, licked it up, and cut their tongues."

He stuck out his, tapping the end of it. "But not me!"

Although it sounded more like: *Bah nah nee!*

"Because of how I protected the amrita, Aranyani, goddess of the forests, entrusted me with the task of helping to hide Kalpavriksha," said Garuda. He lifted the panel of moonlight. "This sacred object can reveal its whereabouts. But that secret is not meant for your eyes. The tree demands too great a sacrifice—it may only be used at the will of the gods."

"There was a prophecy..." said Mini. "We think it's about us and the tree. If we don't find the real Kalpavriksha within two days, the Sleeper's army could destroy the Otherworld."

Garuda took his time responding. "If you could use the tree, what would you wish?" he asked quietly. "To win at war? You know nothing of what victory looks like. I regret what I must do, but I cannot let you continue."

He stretched out his wings, snuffing out the torches and letting the night's darkness crash around them. Aru was going for her lightning bolt when she heard a loud squawk. There was a flash of tufted gray and an indignant caw that could only belong to one bird.

Boo soared toward them, screeching at Garuda: "NOT MY PANDAVAS, YOU BIRDBRAIN!"

TWENTY-NINE

We Are All Potatoes

Boo alighted on his favorite spot in the world....

The top of Aru's head.

He pecked her affectionately, then hopped about. Even though Aru couldn't see him, she assumed he was making sure Brynne and Mini were fine, too.

Their pigeon guardian made a strange hissing sound at Garuda, who looked more bewildered than terrified out of his wits, but perhaps that's to be expected when a pigeon starts insulting you out of nowhere.

"Subala," said Garuda in his gravelly voice. "You are much changed."

"He's been taking new feather supplements," said Mini defensively.

Boo puffed out his chest. "I am here to tell you that the Pandavas' mission was sanctioned by me, a member of the Council of Guardians, and therefore you cannot punish them."

Garuda's wings lowered, and he looked down at the pane of moonlight in his talons. Aru's hands twitched to take it. Once they had it, they could finally find the Tree of Wishes.

"You allowed them to go on this quest?" asked Garuda quietly.

Aru frowned. Why did it sound like he was insulting Boo?

Garuda did not take his eyes off Boo. "You should know better. You know the cost. Or perhaps you were blinded by the hope of gaining a new form for your soul. You should have protected your charges."

The pigeon seemed to wilt.

"Boo *does* protect us!" said Mini angrily. "He always has!"

"I care very deeply for my girls," said Boo, a barely restrained fury in his voice.

Garuda regarded him steadily. "And yet even the ones who love us and have our best interests at heart make mistakes. My mother enslaved herself to my aunt by impulsively accepting a bet. Maybe it was her pride. Or maybe she hoped it would put an end to my aunt's bullying of me. Instead, my mother and I both suffered more. I do not trust any instant fix, be it a bet... or a wish."

After a moment of consideration, Garuda laid the pane of moonlight on the ground. "As this journey has been sanctioned by a member of the Council, I cannot stand in your way. Though I wish you would let me."

He pointed to the moonlit square. "Only chakora birds can decipher what is written here. It will reveal where Kalpavriksha has been hidden. But know this: the birds are gossipy things, and they honor no currency except secrets."

"How do we find them?" asked Aru.

"Follow the path through the moonlight," said Garuda. He lifted his chin. "I pray you know what you are doing."

And with that, he unfurled his giant wings and took off.

Aru stared after Garuda as his silhouette shrank into the

clouds. She thought she would feel victorious, but instead she felt hollow. Maybe the others felt the same way too, because only Brynne bent to retrieve the moonlit pane.

"Well," said Boo, almost awkwardly.

He hopped down into Mini's outstretched palms, tilting his head from one side to the next as he gazed at the unreadable message, and then at Aru, Brynne, Mini, Aiden, and Rudy.

"I must return to the heavens soon," he said. "I've been watching the twins, and—"

"Wait a sec, Boo," said Aiden. "How'd you know where we were?"

"And that we needed help?" added Brynne.

Boo's feathers stiffened for a moment, as if he'd been caught off guard. "The Maruts," he said breezily. "They're keeping me updated."

Aru frowned. He'd answered too quickly. Also, the Maruts didn't know about their mission, did they? As a kinda-sorta-reformed liar, Aru was pretty good at recognizing when someone wasn't telling the truth.

"Now, please tell me you've each brought a change of clothes and you're not questing *in your pajamas*," he said, before leveling a glare at Aru. *"Again."*

"Again?" echoed Rudy and Aiden.

"HA," said Aru a touch too loudly. "Let's move."

She had only just noticed everyone's sleepwear choices. Aiden wore flannel pants and his dad's old law-school sweatshirt. Rudy was wearing a shimmering snakeskin, patterned with music notes. Brynne looked a bit like an angry armadillo in her silver reflective-armor set. Mini was practically drowning in a long black T-shirt.

And Aru? Well, her old Spider-Man pajamas got incinerated after their first quest.

So she'd switched it up to Iron Man.

"We've got stuff to change into," said Brynne.

"So do I," said Rudy shyly. "If . . . you know. If I can go, too." His cheeks turned red.

The others paused, looking at each other.

Aiden was the first to relent. "I guess we *could* use a playlist guy."

Rudy beamed.

"BUT YOU HAVE TO LEARN HOW TO USE A SWORD!" said Brynne.

"I'm sorry. *Who in the world are you?*" demanded Boo.

"I'm Prince—"

"My cousin, Rudy," explained Aiden. "He's adjacent to me, a Pandava adjacent."

"Pandava adjacent-adjacent," said Boo, clearly unimpressed.

"Well, if we can't call all of us Pandavas, then what *do* we say?" asked Aru. "We need a secret code name—something that sounds *strong* and *capable.*"

"How about the Masseters?" offered Mini. "It's the strongest muscle group in the body based on its weight!"

They stared at her, and Mini clarified: "Your jaw muscles? Duh. It can put two hundred pounds of force on the molars."

Aiden rubbed his temples, and Boo seemed to wither a little on the spot.

Aru folded her arms across her chest. "What about the Pandava Avengers?"

"I'm thinking . . . potatoes," said Brynne.

"The vengeful potatoes?" asked Rudy.

"No," said Aiden. "*Avengers* Potatoes."

"No!" said Brynne. "Just. Potatoes."

"That's the most depressing group name ever," said Aru. "What if we have to explain ourselves? We can't just be like 'Look, it's us! The Potatoes! AKA the Pandavas!' "

"Potatoes are strong, hearty, starchy, and versatile," said Brynne. "You can do all kinds of things with them: grate, bake, boil, broil, roast, dice, slice, scallop, steam—"

"Please stop," said Aru.

"—grill, flambé—"

"That does it! You're officially the Potatoes!" squawked Boo. "Now I must be going. The twins were en route to the House of the Moon when I left and—"

A radio-crackle sound emanated from a small gadget affixed to Boo's ankle. A deep voice crackled out over the night air:

"Emergency alert! All guardians return to base! The clairvoyant has been abducted. Return immediately!"

THIRTY

But Soft, What Light Through Yonder Window Breaks?

Mini gasped, covering her mouth with her hands. "Sheela must be terrified!" she said. "We have to go right now—"

On Aru's wrist, Vajra blew off sparks of angry electricity. "I bet it was the Sleeper."

"No *way* we're letting that fly," said Brynne rolling up her sleeves.

Boo hovered before them. "I know you want to go after her, but you can't stray from your mission," he said sternly. "You have only two days left to find the tree. No doubt the Sleeper's army took Sheela to locate it because of her ability with plants—"

"Oh gods," said Aru. A cold pit opened in her stomach. "They took the *wrong* twin! They meant to take Nikita, but they took Sheela!"

At this, Boo paused. Something flashed in his eyes, like irritation, and Aru couldn't understand that. Why wasn't he angry? Or worried? Or flapping about and shedding feathers?

"Where was she last seen?" asked Aiden.

Rudy held up his messenger bag. "I think I've got a gemstone here that helps locate—"

"*No,*" said Boo again. "If they get to the Tree of Wishes before you, then everything is lost, including Sheela. The best way you can help her is to find Kalpavriksha before they do."

Aru set her jaw. She hated how coldly he'd said it, but Boo was right. Maybe the moment they found the tree, they could wish Sheela back to their side. And Nikita, too. Aru couldn't imagine how she must be feeling now, with no parents, no Pandavas, and no *sister.*

"I'm going to coordinate with the Maruts right now. We'll start the search for her," said Boo, rising in the air. "Stay safe! I don't want to lose any more feathers!"

And with that, he took off.

Aru watched him go, unease coiling at the back of her brain, though she couldn't pinpoint why.

"We need to talk to the twins," said Mini.

"You're right," said Aru.

But the only way to do that was through their dreams.

"I don't think I can fall asleep after all this."

"I can help with that," said Rudy, pulling out something that looked like a moonstone wrapped with strings. It made a soft jingling sound.

"Maybe Sheela will tell us where she is," tried Brynne hopefully.

"Maybe..." said Aru, but she didn't think it would be that easy.

The three Pandavas headed back to their tent as Rudy

released a song like snow falling lightly on the ground just before bedtime.

"You've got fifteen minutes," said Aiden. "Then we're waking you guys up."

Aru, Mini, and Brynne got into their sleeping bags and linked hands.

"We'll fix this," Aru muttered sleepily as she immediately drifted off.

When Aru opened her eyes, she was in the dream studio where Nikita had previously made their outfits for the Crypt of Eclipses. Only now the walls and worktable were empty.

Nikita stood before them in a plain white robe.

"Where's Sheela?" asked Brynne, turning around in a circle.

"Gone," said Nikita, her eyes dull.

"What happened?" asked Brynne. "Have you heard from her at all?"

Nikita wouldn't look at them. Aru noticed that her flowery tiara was missing, and there were scratches on her forehead, as if she'd torn it off.

"The Maruts were taking us to the House of the Moon by cloud carriage," said Nikita, rubbing her arms.

Aru felt a new stab of fear. The storm deities—the defense guard of the entire heavens—had been protecting the twins, and still it hadn't been enough.

"One moment Sheela was looking out the window, and the next, the door was ripped open and this . . . this . . . *demon* just plucked her out! It said she would lead them to victory." Nikita shuddered at the memory. "The Maruts went after the demon, but it vanished. They don't even know how it got into the heavens."

"Did she get hurt?" asked Mini, her face paling.

Nikita screamed, "I DON'T KNOW!"

Oily vines—dark as shadows, and with thorns sharp as blades—emerged from the dream ground.

"I don't know where my sister is! I saw them do something to her tracking symbol.... I don't know if she can reach me in her dreams." Nikita sobbed. "You have to go after her! Promise me you will!"

Nikita looked at all three of them as she said this, but her gaze lingered on Aru.

Aru faltered, Boo's words zipping through her skull. "The best thing we can do right now is find the tree, and then we'll find Sheela—"

"Liar!" hissed Nikita. "You don't care about her at all!"

"That's not true!" said Brynne. "Of course we do!"

"I thought you'd be different," said Nikita. "I thought you'd be like..."

She clammed up, but Aru knew the word she wouldn't say. *Sisters.* Even though it was just a dream, Aru felt the air squeezed out of her lungs.

"We're doing everything we can," said Aru. "We've already got the next clue to the wishing tree—we just have to take it to the chakora birds. If the Sleeper is looking for the tree, too, he'll bring Sheela with him as he searches! I know it. Trust me—"

"NO," said Nikita. "I'm done with that." She turned on her heel.

"Wait!" yelled Brynne. "We can help!"

"Leave. Me. *Alone.*"

Nikita snapped her fingers, and Aru jolted up in her sleeping bag, gasping for breath and clutching her chest. Guilt racked her. But she had to believe they were doing the right thing. They could fix this. Nikita would see, and then she'd forgive them.

Would you *forgive you?* asked a nasty voice in Aru's thoughts.

Mini looked over at her. "I'm sure she didn't mean it," she said quietly. "She's grieving."

Aru nodded, still feeling a little numb over the whole thing.

Brynne jumped to her feet, hauling up Aru and Mini. "No more clues," she said, practically growling. "We're getting to that tree. It's the only way to find Sheela."

For all the bravery Mini had been displaying ever since the House of Months, she could still be pretty jumpy. The Potatoes had been walking for nearly an hour in the forest when Mini hollered, "SPIDER!"

It turned out to be a bunch of twigs on the ground.

"Did you know there's like forty thousand venomous spiders in the world?" said Aiden.

Mini whimpered.

Aru heard a sharp "Ow!" from Aiden. Brynne must've elbowed him in the ribs.

"She likes facts. I thought it would help!" he muttered.

At least they hadn't encountered any bears. Aru suspected that was because Brynne was too scary and Mini too annoying.

As the five of them wandered, Aru noticed that the stars overhead were starting to fade. Still, they hadn't yet found a chakora forest. In one of their lessons, Boo had told them that, in the old days, chakora forests were places where humans sometimes accidentally stumbled into the Otherworld at night.

They'd see a ton of strange things, and then, as soon as the sun came up, be tossed out.

The Irish loved their Otherworld experiences so much, they made a habit of getting lost in the forests just for the stories, Boo had said.

In the distance, finally, she saw it: a shaft of moonlight breaking through the trees, spreading into a puddle of molten silver on the ground. The hairs on Aru's arm prickled, and she recognized something familiar in the air.

Magic.

"That has to be it!" said Brynne excitedly.

Aru tapped her Vajra bracelet, and the lightning bolt zoomed into her hand. Now they could see that they were entering a grove of birch trees. In the glow, the bark looked like it was covered in frost. The sky was still dark overhead, and there was no sign of wildlife anywhere. Aru raised Vajra and then heard a high-pitched *gasp*.

"What was that?" asked Aru, swiveling around.

Brynne, Aiden, and Rudy pointed at Mini, who stared back at them, her brown eyes huge behind her glasses.

"That was *not* me!" she said.

One of the branches beside them bounced, and the five of them jumped back and turned toward the sound.

It was a chakora bird.

Aru had never seen one up close. It was lovely—the size and shape of a dove, with a faint glimmer to its feathers as if someone had outlined each of them with a trail of glitter. Its crest ruffled up, each plume as long as Aru's hand and white as snow.

"But soft, what light through yonder window breaks?" it declared.

That was . . . a strange thing to hear from a bird. Aru remembered the line from her Shakespeare unit in English class.

"You," it said with a sigh, its black eyes fixed on Aru. "You're the most wondrous thing I've ever beheld! Refulgence incarnate! What is your name, fair bird? For I must declare that you, and only you, possess *my heart.*"

THIRTY-ONE

It's Not You, It's Me. All Right, Fine, It's Also You.

Aru was *mortified*.

Brynne burst out laughing. Aiden and Mini looked at the chakora bird with pity.

Rudy just shrugged. "You know, I had an aunt who married a bird. *Huge* family drama, actually. At the wedding—"

"But we just met?" blurted out Aru.

This was, probably, the least of her concerns about a bird professing its undying love to her.

"I know," said the bird, shaking its head. "But *you*, O glowing one, complete me."

"Or maybe you're just missing a lot," whispered Brynne, tapping her temple.

"I've never seen lights as electrifying as you!" declared the chakora.

"Uh, thanks?" said Aru, taking a step backward.

"The world is dimmed in your presence!"

"I—"

"You've shocked me!"

"You're welcome?"

The bird flew toward Aru, and she instinctively raised her arms to shield herself. It alighted on her arm, and Aru was plagued with the thousand things she didn't know about birds. First, did birds try to kiss people? Was that a thing? She really hoped not.

The bird bumped its forehead against her lightning bolt. Bird eyes are fairly dark and round in the first place, but if it were possible, this bird's eyes got even rounder.

"Wrought from the heavens themselves," whispered the bird adoringly.

Vajra shocked it, and a sheen of neon blue shirred over the bird's feathers.

"Ah!" it declared. "A feisty thing, you are!"

Okay. So, the bird was not in love with her.

The bird was in love with her lightning bolt.

Aru was both relieved and, if she was being honest, a little insulted.

Vajra turned from a towering lightning bolt to a bracelet trying to inch its way up Aru's sleeve and hide from the moon bird's affections.

"I've been too forward," mourned the chakora.

"A bit," said Aru. "Listen, now that I've got your attention—"

The bird finally glanced at Aru. It hopped up her arm, looked her up and down, and declared, "Ew!"

"Thanks a lot," said Aru.

"A mortal!"

Aru did jazz hands. *"Surprise!"*

"What are you doing here, frightful being?"

"I really don't think adjectives are necessary—"

"Perhaps it's a boon that the fair lightning bolt has dimmed so I might bear your visage."

Mini frowned, then leaned over to Aru and whispered, "I think it's calling you ugly...."

"Yes, okay, *noted!*" grumbled Aru. She gestured to Rudy to hold up the rectangle of moonlight. "We need you to decipher this."

The bird hopped down her arm, tilting its head. "Ah! The Council will be able to read that. I am not yet permitted to learn the vernacular of moonlight, though I recently taught myself English."

"How'd you do that?" asked Mini.

The bird turned to her, startled all over again as it looked between Mini and the others. "*More* frightful mortals?"

"I think it's calling you guys hideous," muttered Aru, smug.

"I learned English by chancing upon a wondrous collection of documents on the camping grounds. I believe it was called *No Fear Shakespeare*. Who is Shakespeare? Why did he feel compelled to shake a spear? I may never find out...." The bird sighed wistfully. "The world is full of enigmas."

"So can you help us, or not?" asked Aiden.

The bird shivered, all its silvery feathers sparkling. "It is forbidden to bring mortals before our Council."

Brynne swung her mace. "Are you sure about that, bird? Because I've never made rotisserie chakora, but I'm prepared to try."

The faint gleam of Vajra caught Aru's eye, and an idea took root in her mind. She murmured a silent apology to her lightning bolt who—as if it could read her mind—at first stung her reproachfully, and afterward grudgingly sent a warm prickle of electricity over her skin.

"Then I guess we'll just have to leave," Aru said, waving her hand very deliberately.

The bird honed in on her wrist and squawked with alarm. "No! Do not steal the luminous one from me!"

"Then take us *reprehensible mortals* to the Council," said Aru.

The bird hemmed and hawed, then flew to a nearby tree branch.

"I shall," it said, reluctantly. "But only for the sake of my beloved."

"Good!" said Brynne, taking a step forward.

"Swear it," said Aru.

She might love the Otherworld, but that didn't mean she trusted it.

The bird glared at them, then sighed. "I swear on a heart that I'll lead you to the brightest moonbeam of them all!" declared the bird. "I shall take you to none other than the entrance to the House of the Moon, where all of my kind roost and hold council. We watch over the elevator that belongs to Chandra, god of the moon himself, and the twenty-seven *nakshatra* constellations who are his wives and queens!"

Twenty-seven wives? thought Aru. And she'd thought poor Draupadi ending up with five husbands was bad.

In her head, she felt Mini's message, soft and cool as velvet: *House of the Moon? Isn't that where the twins were headed? Maybe Nikita is still there. . . .*

"Uh, excuse me . . . moon bird. . . . Why did you swear on *a* heart?" asked Aiden. "Why not *your* heart?"

"Well, there are plenty of hearts lying around the world—I'll just use one of those. Besides"—the bird looked at Aru's bracelet and sighed dramatically—"from the moment I laid eyes upon you, I decided that *my* heart belongs to you, O illuminating, resplendent, lambent creature."

Vajra cringed, which registered as a high-voltage electric shock through Aru's skin.

"Easy, Vajra!" she said.

"Vajra!" cried the bird. "What a lovely name! I am called"—it bowed its white head—"Sohail."

"Well, Sohail," said Aru, pointing ahead and making sure Vajra was visible on her wrist, "lead the way."

THIRTY-TWO

A Parliament of Foul Fowls

Sohail took them to a sloping amphitheater set in a low valley. The meeting place looked as if it had been cobbled together from the ruins of old temples. Each chakora bird lorded over its own boulder, and each stone anchored a slanting moonbeam. Aru had never known that a shaft of moonlight could be a tangible thing, but the chakora birds roosted on them as if they were heavy branches. At the center of the space stood a thick pillar of moonlight that stretched in an unbroken line toward the sky and disappeared in the clouds. There was a red button on the rock beside it, and Aru wondered if perhaps this was the elevator Sohail had mentioned.

Sohail alighted on a moonbeam not far from the three largest boulders, where a trio of chakora birds perched on their glowing moon boughs. They looked older than Sohail—their cheek feathers drooped, and there was something faded and ragged about their tail feathers. Sohail chattered to them in the language of birds, and then the elder chakoras turned to face the Potatoes, regarding them haughtily.

"Why have you brought these creatures to us, Sohail?" demanded the bird sitting on the highest moonbeam. "You know mortals have no business in these parts. What could they possibly want?"

Sohail bowed, then looked mournfully at Vajra. "I have come at the behest of my beloved, who requires that we translate a piece of preserved moonlight for them. Therefore, *I* vouch for the mortals' presence and hope you might grant them an audience."

"Lovestruck *again*?" spat another bird. "What is it this time? A lantern?"

"A flashlight left behind in a campsite?" teased another.

"A car's headlights?"

The rest of the birds laughed, and Sohail hung his head in shame. "A car, 'tis a fearsome thing. And it is true, I have been lured by false lights before. But what I feel now . . . it is like realizing my whole life has been lived in shadow."

Brynne rolled her eyes and muttered, "What do you think this bird would do if it saw a glow stick?"

Aru stifled a giggle, then glanced over at Mini, Rudy, and Aiden. They weren't laughing. Mini's eyes were shining. Aiden looked stony-faced, but there was something wistful in his gaze. Rudy's lip trembled . . . and he started slow-clapping in genuine appreciation.

"Yes, all right, fine," grumbled the highest bird. "So you wish us to *translate* something for the reprehensible mortals. Where is this fair love of yours? Is it being held captive by the odious children?"

"Hey!" said Brynne.

"No!" said Aru vehemently. She raised her arm, where Vajra sparkled. "*It* is a fearsome weapon."

The birds took one look at Vajra in bracelet form and burst out in raucous hoots and caws.

"Oh, Sohail has really fallen this time!" said one, choking with laughter. "What do you think he'll do when the battery runs out?"

Sohail could not blush, but Aru noticed that the delicate feathers around his cheeks fluffed out in shame.

"Perhaps I see what you do not," he said quietly.

A prickle of energy wound through Vajra. Without even a command from Aru, the lightning bolt shot up to its true, staggering size of at least six feet. Even Aru had never seen Vajra so big. Usually, her lightning bolt preferred to be compact, subtle.

Now Vajra looked like all the crackling heavens wrought into a single zigzagging shape.

The laughter quickly died. The silence was only broken by the sudden *click!* of Aiden's camera.

Sohail looked proudly at the rest of the birds. "*There* shines my beloved."

Vajra sparked one last time and elegantly folded itself back into a bracelet on Aru's wrist, reminding her of a queen who has deigned to sit at a table with commoners.

"Ahem," said the highest bird. "Well. I, uh... As you can see... Well—"

The second-highest bird piped up: "We don't work for free! Man or monster or god, we don't care. We demand fair compensation in the form of secrets."

"What do you need secrets for?" asked Aiden.

"They draw the moonlight closer," said Sohail. "And we can bask in the light."

"We don't have any secrets," said Aiden quickly. *Too* quickly.

Aru winced. It was like he had thrown chum toward sharks.

The second-highest chakora bird flew toward them. "No secrets, eh?" it said, leering. "Well, why don't we just see about that?"

At least a hundred chakora birds rose into the sky.

"Oh, is that quite necessary?" asked Sohail gently. "Is it not best to coax out the secrets of those around us through mutual trust and respect?"

The flock ignored him. They beat their wings and a glittering dust fell upon Aru and her friends.

"What *is* this?" demanded Brynne.

Mini pinched her nose. "What if I'm allergic?"

Rudy furiously tried to brush the stuff off him.

"Is this... Is this *moon-bird dandruff*?" asked Aru. "Because that"—*shake*—"is"—*shake*—"unacceptable!"

Aiden stared at his sleeves with growing horror. "It forces out secrets," he said, his voice tinged with fear. "Keep your mouths closed—"

"Perhaps we might start with what currency *you* have available," said the head chakora bird, staring directly at him.

Aiden clamped his hands over his lips, then lurched forward as if someone had lassoed him with a rope and *tugged*—

"I always volunteer to be the official photographer at school dances because I don't want anyone to find out that I'm a good dancer," he said in a rush, his eyes wide. "And for six months,

I practiced the poker-chip trick that Le Chiffre did in *Casino Royale*. But I don't know how to play poker, so I don't know when I'm ever going to use the trick."

About two feet away, a small pile of silver dust gathered on the floor—the equivalent weight of Aiden's secrets. He slumped to the ground, clutching his stomach, mortification written all over him.

Rudy was next. He backed away, but the birds' magic worked on him all the same:

"I'VE NEVER KISSED A GIRL. ONCE I PRACTICED ON A GEM, BUT I CHOKED ON IT!" he yelled.

Aru plugged her ears with her fingers. *"Do you have to shout?!"*

Rudy sank onto the rubble, blushing deeply.

Brynne looked wild-eyed. "Oh wait, no, no-no-no—"

"Ah, but we demand a secret for our work," said the bird. "And *all must pay!*"

Brynne went blue in the face trying to hold herself back, but she too lost the battle. Aru thought she was going to yell, but her secret came out in a whisper. "I stole from Anila so she'd have to visit me again just to get her stuff back."

Aru felt a burst of sympathy for her sister. Aiden grabbed Brynne's hand and held it tight.

Mini turned bright red and blurted out, "When I didn't think anyone was watching, I practiced using my dad's stethoscope on my teddy bear. My brother saw it and laughed, so I put him in a force field bubble and recorded him running in it like a hamster."

She sniffed loudly, tears glossing her eyes while everyone else broke into laughter. Even Brynne cracked a smile.

"How is that a secret?" said Brynne. "You should've told us ages ago!"

"It was so *mean,*" said Mini pitifully. "The guilt still makes my stomach ache."

"Does it feel like a hamster is running around inside it?" asked Aru.

Mini glared at her.

The birds turned their beady eyes on Aru. Panic swept through her. After using the living key and having her whole soul unlocked, there was far too much of her that could be exposed. The others had funny stories or understandable pain. *Normal* secrets. Not her. What would they think if she ended up saying her deepest, darkest secret—that she didn't know if she was fighting for the right side?

Not that the Sleeper was "right" by any stretch of the imagination... but the devas weren't, either.

If she uttered something like that, her friends wouldn't trust her anymore.

Or what if she said something horrifically mortifying? Like how she sometimes practiced make-believe conversations with Aiden?! Aru would rather set herself on fire.

Her mother's necklace pulsed around her neck. And she remembered the three hollows in it, each one the perfect size to hold the bead containing a piece of the Sleeper.

A secret. That was all that the birds wanted. *A* secret. Not necessarily hers.

"Now your turn..." she heard the head bird start to say.

Aru looked at Rudy. "Give me the jewel you took from the eagle's beak."

"What?" he asked.

"Now," said Aru.

She must've said it with enough force, because the snake boy rummaged through his messenger bag right away and pulled out the tiny blue stone. As soon as he handed it to Aru, she tossed it in front of the chakora elders. The moment the jewel hit the ground, the Sleeper's secret blasted across the grove.

As the visions played, Aru kept her face turned away and tried to shut out the sound of his voice. It was too painful to see how he'd once been. She felt a flash of anger whenever she thought about his memories. Maybe he would've been a great dad. But that whole future had been stolen from her... all because of a stupid prophecy. Who was to blame for how things worked out? Him, for failing to prevent it? Her mom? *Herself*, just for being born?

She watched a pile of sparkling silver grow until the Sleeper's story ended. It had to be enough payment, thought Aru. The blue jewel floated back to her, and she popped it into one of the depressions in the pendant.

"Sneaky," said Aiden.

"You know me," said Aru.

But her voice sounded flat in her ears.

"Surely we've paid for the translation by now," said Mini.

"I have no idea who Shirley is," sniffed one of the elder birds, "but I assure you I am not her."

"And yes," said another bird slowly. "Your secret was sufficient."

"Then tell us the clue," said Aru.

But the birds didn't look done with them just yet. There was a greedy sheen in the beady black eyes of the highest chakora. Its feathers fanned out, and it hopped down from its moonbeam.

"I find it very curious," said the bird, walking a circle around Aru, "that you are the secret another mortal used before."

"What are you talking about?" asked Aru.

"I think you know well, Arundhati."

THIRTY-THREE

What's in a Name?

Aru stared at the bird. How did it know her full name?

The head chakora must have guessed her question, because it hopped over to its boulder and began pecking something on the ground in front of it.

For the first time, Aru noticed a nest there, full of shiny objects.

"Arundhati, Arundhati," it sang. "Ah, yes! Here we are!"

It picked up a bright pebble with its beak, flung it out of the nest, and a new vision leaped up before her.

Aru held her breath as the Sleeper once more flickered to life, walking through the chakora forest. He looked the same age he had been when he visited the crypt, but there was something different about him. His shoulders were hunched as if carrying a heavy weight, and his mismatched eyes looked haunted.

"If you wish to pass through our lands and continue your search, you must give us a secret," chanted the birds in the vision.

"I've given enough," said the Sleeper hoarsely.

Aru felt a chill race across her arms. In the crypt he had sacrificed all his memories of childhood. And it showed. His clothes looked a little frayed, and his wedding band fit looser around his finger, as if he'd lost weight.

"But you've given nothing to us," said the birds.

The Sleeper inhaled deeply, seemingly to gather his strength. "A secret..." He placed his hand over his heart and said, "My wife said I could pick our daughter's name, and I've found something that I hope will suit her," he said. "I will name her Arundhati. For the morning star. So that my daughter will always be a light in the dark."

The vision faded.

"This secret belongs more to you than us, Arundhati."

The head chakora nudged the pebble into a splinter of moonlight, which lifted it from the ground and floated it over to Aru. Before she could grab it, the bright stone lodged itself into the second hollow on her pendant.

Two lost memories of the Sleeper now dangled from her neck.

Aru stood there, numb. She wondered how many times the Sleeper had said her name before her mother trapped him in the *diya*. Just that once? Twice? Ten times? Had he thought of the name when he was stuck in that lamp for all those years and come to hate it—and her? Or had he given up so much of himself by the end that it didn't bother him at all? Aru wasn't sure which thought made her sadder.

In all these years, Aru had never thought to ask her mom about the origin of her name. She wished she had, if only so it wouldn't feel like such a horrible surprise to know this connection to the Sleeper. He'd named her. Out of love. With the hope that she'd be full of light.

And yet, when he'd first spoken to her, there'd been no

love or light in his voice, just something cold and alien as he'd taunted, *Oh, Aru, Aru, Aru . . . what have you done?*

Aru squeezed her eyes shut.

What had *she* done? She could have asked him the same thing: What had *he* done? What had been done to both of them?

And what did it mean that he'd named her? What if she was more like him than she'd thought?

"It's just a name, Shah," said Aiden.

Aru jerked and opened her eyes to find him standing beside her.

"I was named Aiden because my parents couldn't decide and picked something from the Internet," he said.

"I got mine from my grandmother," said Mini.

"Mine was chosen for its auspiciousness," said Rudy loftily.

Brynne grunted. "Well, my name literally means *hill,* and my mom chose it because I turned out to be a girl and she couldn't use the name Brian."

That made Aru look up sharply. "*Brian?* You would've been *Brian?*"

"Yep," said Brynne, grinning. "Watch out, world."

Aru laughed, feeling somewhat better.

"It's just a name," she said, mostly to herself.

But in her heart, she knew it was more than that. It was a promise that had been ripped from her. A treasure she hadn't even realized she'd lost. Before he came to be the Sleeper, Suyodhana was just someone who wanted to be her dad. Maybe he would've been the one who nicknamed her Aru first, howling it like a wolf: *Arooooo!* Maybe it would've started out a joke between them instead of something she'd done to make fun of herself before anybody else could.

A terrible ache of loss settled in her chest, and Aru tried to hide it. She didn't want to feel this confusing mix of anger and pity and pain, much less show it. It would make people believe all the more that she was destined to turn on them. To become the "untrue" sister.

Aiden faced the chakora birds. "We've done our part and spoken our secrets. Now it's your turn. Read the piece of moonlight for us so we know where to go."

"Are you sure you don't want to stay longer?" asked Sohail plaintively.

Aru hadn't noticed until now that he'd hopped closer to Vajra... and that her lightning bolt didn't seem to mind.

The elder birds nodded and lifted off their moon branches, circling over Rudy, who held out the thin pane. The moonbeams traveled with them, trailing silvery threads that landed on the mysterious message and scanned it like lasers.

A woman's voice echoed through the forest as the words appeared in English:

All growing things know where the tree can be found,
But it takes the right ear to hear the right sound.
All growing things know, but not all wish to talk.
The youngest of roots are the best to unlock.

When the voice faded, Aru saw that each of her friends wore a matching expression of confusion.

Sohail piped up from his branch. "I like trees," he said. "And I'm excellent with growing things."

"The right sound..." said Rudy, staring at the now blank message. "Maybe it's talking about me."

"I think it means Nikita," said Mini. "Sorry."

Sohail puffed out his chest. "Show me this Nikita, and I shall vanquish him for the heart of my true love!"

The group ignored the bird.

"All the more reason to get to her," said Brynne, eyeing the elevator to the House of the Moon's palace. "If only we knew how to operate the elevator." She said this last part in a stage voice, glaring meaningfully at Sohail.

Sohail immediately flew over to the pillar of moonlight and landed next to its control button. "I do!"

On the horizon, they could see a faint seam of red. Dawn was coming, and the pillar began dissolving like sugar in tea. The other chakora birds squawked and cawed as their moonbeams began to fade.

"Come, Sohail!" they yelled. "Let us go to another moonlit grove!"

But Sohail only had eyes for Vajra. He hung his head. "I know you have to go. I just wish I could come too," he said sorrowfully. "But I will still help you, my beloved. You and your companions may board, and I shall ensure you arrive safely. But hurry before the night disappears."

They raced toward the elevator. At Sohail's soft caw, the pillar of moonlight expanded and two silver doors slid open to reveal a moonlit lounge with plush chairs, chrome and glass tables, and glittering portraits lining the walls. Even though the sunrise was beginning to lighten the world outside, the tall and narrow windows in the elevator looked out onto eternal night.

"Never fear," explained Sohail as the Potatoes stepped inside, "it is a long but pleasant ride."

Aru was the last to board. Vajra leaped off her wrist,

transforming itself into a bird with electric wings. It flapped its wings twice and a gentle shower of sparks cascaded onto Sohail. The chakora rolled over, basking in it, and then Vajra turned back into a bracelet at Aru's wrist. A slight sensation of warmth infused Aru's skin, as if her lightning bolt were letting out a sigh.

"Farewell, my love!" said Sohail mournfully.

Just before the elevator doors closed all the way, the bird called out, "Maybe we can try long distance?"

THIRTY-FOUR

What's a Publix?

Brynne immediately made a beeline to the elevator's snack table. "DIBS ON THE SANDWICHES!" she hollered.

"Be careful, Brynne," warned Mini, walking after her. "You devour food like you're conquering it, and honestly, if you eat too fast, you could choke! Or perforate your stomach! And then you'd get peritonitis, become septic, and *die.*"

Aru laughed to herself, and then went back to examining the rest of the space. About ten feet up from the white marble floor hung several gilded portraits of someone who could only be Chandra, the god of the moon.

"Someone clearly likes himself," Rudy said as he stepped up beside her.

Chandra was startlingly handsome....

And it looked like he knew it.

The god had pale, glowing skin, perfectly arched eyebrows over sparkling dark eyes, and a slim nose perched over perpetually smirking lips. His shiny black hair was streaked with silver.

In the first portrait, he was wearing a tuxedo covered in stardust and holding a glass of something sparkling as he stood on a balcony overlooking the night sky.

In another painting, he was surrounded by beautiful women, whom Aru recognized as the twenty-seven *nakshatras,* or constellations. He'd married all of them.

"Valentine's Day must be a nightmare for him," she said.

"Nah," said Rudy. "From what I hear, he's got a favorite: Rohini. She gets most of his attention."

Aiden, who'd been staring out a window, looked over at them, his expression darkening. "So then what? The other wives get a box of chocolates from Publix and a card he couldn't bother signing?"

"That's specific," said Rudy.

"I've seen it before," said Aiden tightly.

From the familiar way Aiden's brows were pulled together and the grim line of his mouth, Aru knew he was talking about his dad.

"What's a Publix?" asked Rudy.

"A supermarket," said Aiden.

"Ah," said Rudy, nodding. Then he added, "What's a supermarket?"

"Where people go to buy food."

"Or eat all the free samples and bounce," said Aru.

Aiden shook his head.

"So people *buy* food..." said Rudy slowly, working out the strange concept. "You don't have servants deliver it? Or do the servants come with the meals you purchase?"

Aiden pinched the bridge of his nose. "When we get back, we're going on a field trip."

"A trip to a field?" said Rudy, repulsed. "No thanks."

"What about Chandra's other wives?" asked Aru. "What do they get?"

Now that she'd noticed them, she couldn't stop staring at their faces in the portrait. All of them were beautiful, yes, but only one of the wives had fully defined features, and her outfit was more glamorous than the others'.

"Revenge," said Rudy.

Brynne wandered over from the buffet table, her cheeks stuffed. "Who said *revenge*?"

"I did," said Rudy, pointing up at the picture of the wives. "Those constellations are the daughters of King Daksha, who got super angry when he found out how Chandra had been treating them. He cursed him. Made it so he'd start withering on the spot. Typical overprotective parent."

Brynne went a bit quiet after that, and Aru wished she could sometimes just make Rudy shut up. Brynne couldn't say *Duh* about how Daksha rushed in to save his daughters. Her mom, Anila, would never do something like that.

Mini pointed at a photograph of a muscle-bound Chandra in a sleeveless tee—he was holding up a planet one-handed. "He doesn't look withered to me."

"Yeah, well, that's because Chandra begged Shiva to save him. Shiva fixed it so Chandra gradually dies each month, but then becomes whole again," said Rudy. "Phases of the moon and all that." He looked up at the portraits of the constellations and shrugged. "Too bad for the other wives."

Brynne's jaw tightened. "Yeah, too bad. Must be a blast walking around your house and wondering why someone who should love you just won't."

Oh, Brynne. Aru wished she could comfort her, but she wasn't sure what to say.

Aiden pushed himself off the wall. "Bee?" he asked softly.

Brynne stomped off then, but not before saying over her shoulder, "Sohail said it's a long ride. Let's get some sleep and see if we can't reach the twins."

Aiden sighed and walked after her, and the two of them stood in a corner and talked in low voices. Rudy seemed confused for a moment, but he obligingly dug around in his bag. After a moment, he pulled out a moonstone wrapped in a silver cord that was strung with little rose-shaped bells. It was the same contraption he'd used to help them fall asleep in the tent.

"Where'd you get that?" asked Aru.

"Nowhere," said Rudy. "Made it myself after my brothers forced me to watch this human movie called *The Grudge*. Couldn't sleep for a week."

Aru shuddered. She *hated* that movie. Which was to say: IT WAS AWESOME! It had this dead lady who made croaking sounds and her hair was all in her face. Part of the reason Aru was keeping her hair long was so she could step out of the shower, do a weird disjointed walk, and scare off intruders.

The five of them settled back into the plushy armchairs. Rudy made some complicated gesture with the moonstone; music lifted out of it, and a wave of calm swept through Aru. She pushed a pillow behind her neck, kicked off her shoes, and propped her feet on one of the white couches. All around her, the stars gleamed brightly, and she thought of her name, Arundhati.

I will name her Arundhati. For the morning star, the Sleeper had said. *So that my daughter will always be a light in the dark.*

Honestly, things would be so much easier if she'd never found out he once cared about her. The fact that he'd tried so hard to fix his own future summoned a pit of cold in Aru's gut.

In all the memories she'd captured so far, there was one answer that danced out of reach.

"If the Sleeper got this far in his search for the tree, why did he stop?" she asked aloud. "What stopped him from finding it and making a wish to change things?"

Aru looked over, but Brynne and Mini were passed out. Aru closed her eyes and tried to focus on Rudy's music, but it didn't work.

Aiden sat on the couch two feet away from her. Moonlight had a tendency to make everything beautiful—not that people like him needed it. Sometimes Aru suspected that the closer Aiden got to the heavens, the more his celestial blood shone, as if declaring that he belonged there. He held up his camera, adjusting the settings.

Rudy had sat next to him, on the far side, despite Aiden pointing to the many *empty* chairs.

"Nah, I'm good," Rudy had declared, scooting closer.

Now Rudy was snoring, his enchanted sleeping jewel in his lap and his cheek on Aiden's shoulder. Aiden was careful not to disturb him as he adjusted Shadowfax.

"Something on my face again, Shah?" he asked, looking over at her.

Aru ignored the sudden warmth in her cheeks. "No," she said, averting her eyes. "I just thought you'd try to fall asleep, too."

He shrugged. "I'm Pandava adjacent, remember? I can't follow you guys into your astral meeting with the twins. Might as well stay awake and grab some shots. I wasn't able to get that many in the chakora forest."

At the mention of the chakora forest, Vajra glowed a little. Maybe it was thinking of Sohail.

"*I* don't miss that place," said Aru grouchily. "If I'd stayed any longer, Sohail might have passed out from having to endure the sight of me."

By now, the music had started to reach her in fits and starts. Her eyelids grew heavier, and she gave in to the lull of sleep.

As Aru slipped away, she could've sworn she heard Aiden say, "Maybe he didn't see you in the right light, Shah."

But she must have been dreaming.

Brynne, Mini, and Aru met inside an ugly dream theme park. It was empty and dingy, and the roller coasters creaked and swayed in the wind. The pale cement beneath their feet was littered with soda cans and fast-food wrappers. All that moved was a Ferris wheel, glossy and bright amidst the dullness. It looked similar to the Ferris wheel they'd rescued the twins from.

"Do you think they're in there?" asked Mini.

"Of course!" said Brynne.

"I dunno," said Aru, glancing around them dubiously. "This place doesn't look right. I don't think Nikita is ready to talk to us yet."

It was hard to forget how viciously Nikita had dropped them out of the last dream.

As they walked toward the Ferris wheel, strange details leaped out at Aru.

She noticed that one of the booths was in the shape of a stingray, and beneath its wings were row upon row of music sheets, only they looked stained and ripped. Frozen soap bubbles with spinning ballerinas trapped inside bobbed silently overhead on a string of dead lights. And although the concrete floor looked pale and dusty, Aru could faintly make out the design of polka dots splashed across it. There were none of the riotous gardens and plants that Nikita usually favored.

"This isn't Nikita's dream," said Aru. "It's Sheela's."

Dream logic doesn't always make sense. One moment Aru was approaching the Ferris wheel, and the next all three of them stood before an open compartment door. Aru's heart leaped in her chest when she saw Sheela sitting inside. Her knees were pulled to her chest, and she was rocking slowly back and forth. Aru, Mini, and Brynne ran to her at once, but Sheela held up a hand.

"I love you, but you have to stay away from me right now," she said in a tiny voice.

She turned to them slowly. Her ice-blue eyes hadn't lost their silvery prophetic sheen. With a shiver, Aru remembered the last words Sheela had said to her.

He's making a terrible mistake. . . .

And you will hate him for his love.

Aru had only a dim idea of what it could mean.

"Oh, Sheela," said Mini, her hands to her heart. "Are you okay? We're so worried. . . . Are you hurt? Are they feeding you?"

The dream began to fade, the floor thinning and dissolving. A loud crackling sound like thunder lashed across the sky and shook the compartment, and Sheela whimpered.

"They meant to take Nikki, but they grabbed me instead. She needs you," Sheela said. "You can find her behind the favorite star of the moon."

The dream quaked again, and Aru held out her hand, as if she could wrench Sheela from this nightmare.

"Where have they taken you?" asked Brynne. "Tell us! Tell us and we'll find you!"

Sheela looked as if she were about to answer when a strange look came over her face, and her voice took on an oddly layered tone. . . .

"He knows," she said. *"He knows what you seek, and he wants it too."*

With a final crack of thunder and lightning, the dream spat them out.

THIRTY-FIVE

Where the Deer and the Cantaloupe Play

A loud banging woke Aru. She sat upright, her mind spinning from that last glimpse of Sheela, lonely and terrified. Aru dropped her head in her hands, wishing more than anything that they had found out her location.

And Aru's ears still rang with Sheela's pronouncement: *He knows.*

"We're here," said Aiden.

Aru looked around, realizing the elevator had come to a stop. She and the others got up and collected their things. Brynne grabbed one last sandwich for the road.

The doors slid open and Aru stepped out, head on a swivel, trying to make sure her jaw didn't totally hit the floor. Which was actually the night sky, stretched out before them like a road. A rotating sign above them in starlit calligraphy declared: WELCOME TO NAVAGRAHA AVENUE, THE PATH TO THE STARS! All the famous planetary mansions stood here on a huge elliptical street that looked like it had been stitched together from a hundred night skies. One looked carved from a massive emerald, another was dappled all over with amethyst, but all were equally extravagant. After the last planet house, there was a glowing door wrapped in a shimmering fog that dissolved into the endless night.

"It's called the Door . . . of New Day?" said Brynne, consulting a small map affixed to a nearby podium.

Navagraha Avenue was stunningly beautiful . . . and weirdly empty.

"Where *is* everyone?" asked Aru.

"The celestials are super into their time away from ordinary people," said Rudy, grumbling. "It's like they think they're so much better than us just because they have a planet. Like, so *what*? *I* could make a planet out of all the jewels we have, but you don't see me running off into space."

Aiden patted his back. "There, there, rich prince. I'm sorry there's other rich people in the world."

Rudy sniffed. "It's really hard."

Up ahead, a different road led to the House of the Moon. The mansion shone bright as a coin, spotlighted by thousands of moonbeams.

"Let's go," said Brynne, leading the charge.

They followed her. The moment they set foot on the lawn in front of the House of the Moon, it seemed to shift and expand, revealing what appeared to be hundreds of acres lined with silver fruit trees and pools reflecting crescent moons. Frost-colored peacocks stalked across lunar-white grass, and a wandering path of pale white pebbles marked the way to the towering front doors.

When the Potatoes reached them, the doors flung themselves

wide open and Brynne strolled right inside, despite Mini's squawk of panic.

"What? No! Stop! Shouldn't we knock or something?"

"If they wanted us to knock, they would've kept the door shut," said Brynne.

In the foyer, Aru turned in a circle, holding Vajra aloft. So far, the interior design of the House of the Moon looked a lot like the inside of the crystal elevator. Lots of portraits of Chandra, and maybe two of Rohini, his favorite wife. A huge glittering staircase spiraled up from the floor and faded into the night sky, which could be seen through the translucent domed ceiling. Several ivory couches with silver feet scuttled off when the Potatoes entered the hall. A couple of armchairs bearing silver-gilded antelope horns made a strange huffing sound and stalked down one of the many intricate mirror-lined hallways. Aru glanced at the floor. Even *that* was mirrored.

"He sure likes to admire himself," said Rudy.

"I don't blame him," said Mini.

The others turned to look at her, and she flushed red.

"What?" she said quietly. "He's not exactly an eyesore."

From the hallway on the left came a sudden *clip-clop* of hooves. The Potatoes tensed, drawing closer to each other, their weapons raised.

A moonlit antelope with a silver hide, large dark eyes, and slender horns stepped into the room. Aru recognized it from a painting in the elevator. It had to be Chandra's *vahana*. The mount was every inch as beautiful as its master.

Aru had never seen a real antelope. Not even at the Atlanta Zoo. For the longest time, she'd thought an antelope was a horned melon, the ugly cousin of a cantaloupe. Which had made the song "Home on the Range" particularly confusing, because every time she heard *where the deer and the antelope play,* she thought a giant melon had gained sentience and escaped from the fruit aisle of the grocery store.

"He's been expecting you," said the antelope haughtily. It sniffed at the air and their weapons, then turned up its nose. "*Those* are useless in this place. Please follow me, and do not *touch* anything. Everything here is an invaluable artifact, and my lord takes especially good care of his treasures."

Aru, having been raised in a museum all her life, scowled and crossed her arms. She hated being treated as if she didn't know what to do around priceless objects. She was well versed in the protocol! Keep hands in pockets, wait till no one's watching, then furtively poke at something with both hands before fleeing.

"Dumb melon," she mumbled as she followed the rest of her friends down the hallway.

The antelope led them into a huge light-filled chamber. The floor was mirrored here, too, and the walls shone with gigantic chunks of incandescent moonstone and milky jade, filigreed with silver. In the center of the room, on a throne made of quartz, sat Chandra himself with his chin on one hand and his other hand lazily twirling an ivory-colored rope. It appeared he had been awaiting their arrival for quite some time.

Flanking the throne were the twenty-seven goddesses of the constellations. Each of them wore a long shimmering silver gown. Their ink-black hair, studded with stars, sheeted down to their waists. Behind each goddess loomed a tall, thin door.

Aru shook her head, squinting. For a moment it seemed as if…

In her head, Aru heard Brynne say, *Is it just me, or do all Chandra's wives look* exactly *the same?*

Chandra rose from his throne, opening his arms like he was greeting long-lost friends.

"Pandavas!" he said brightly. "I've been expecting your visit. On behalf of myself and my lovely wives, welcome to the House of the Moon."

He looked to the twenty-seven goddesses, who clapped haphazardly. Their facial features were identical, but a couple of them seemed angry, most of them were bored, and a handful looked a little nervous.

"I'm assuming you didn't come all this way for an autograph," he said, strolling toward them. Then he paused, lifting an eyebrow. "Or did you?"

His vahana trotted beside him. "They would surely be remiss not to ask for such a gift, my lord."

"Sorry," said Aru loudly. "I'm all out of pen and paper."

"Mmph," said Chandra. "Pity."

"How did you know we were coming?" asked Mini.

Chandra chuckled. "*Please,* child. I see everything. Not that everyone likes that, of course. I remember a particular incident when I saw Ganesh after a party in Lanka—a city which, if you're curious, throws *the best* events. Anyway, on his way home, his silly rat vahana got spooked by a snake, and Ganesh fell off!"

Chandra guffawed himself silly, clutching his sides.

"Ah." He sighed when he had gathered himself. "Anyway, I couldn't help laughing. Apparently, he heard me—which makes sense. I mean, he's literally got the head of an elephant. What *else* are you going to do with ears that big?"

"I know that story," said Aiden quietly. "Didn't he throw his tusk at you?"

Chandra scowled, then rubbed his cheek. "That's not really relevant," he said irritably. "The point is, I knew you'd come. Like I said, I see everything. Granted, I've got a great view."

He gestured at the walls, which shifted to reveal images of the world at nighttime. In one of them, Aru recognized her group standing in the chakora forest. A cold feeling twisted up her spine. If he wanted to, Chandra could tattle on them to the rest of the Council, and they'd never have a chance to find the wishing tree.

He clapped. "I know what the devas are hiding and what they aren't," he said with a sly twist of his mouth. "They thought the littlest Pandavas would be safer here, far in the heavens, and so I agreed to take them. Too bad one was lost along the way."

He didn't seem sorry at all, Aru thought.

"I know you want the other one back," said Chandra. "And I have no need to keep her…"

"Great," said Aru, looking around. "Now, where is—?"

"Still," said Chandra, "there's no reason we can't make the exchange interesting. My wives and I are in need of a bit of entertainment from time to time."

Brynne took a step forward, no doubt getting ready to protest, and Aiden held her back.

"If you win my challenge," said Chanda, "I will grant all of you—including your little sister—passage out of the House of the Moon. Plus, I shall not reveal your whereabouts to the devas. I'll even disable the tracking device in the girl's neck."

"But if we fail?" asked Aru.

"You must cede your weapons to me."

Instinctively, Aru clutched Vajra to her. "You can't take them!" she said. "They're not yours. They belong to—"

"Indra?" drawled Chandra, rolling his eyes. "As if he'd notice anything among his vast collection gone missing. Trust me, child, he gave you a throwaway."

Vajra bristled with indignation, and sparks of electricity shot up and down Aru's arm.

"And that mace is definitely scuffed," said Chandra, pointing at Brynne's weapon.

He moved on to Mini and laughed. "A stick? Cute."

Chandra's gaze roved to Rudy and zeroed in on the orange messenger bag. The moon god snapped his fingers, and the satchel zoomed into his grip. Chandra pawed through it, but the eagerness melted from his face.

"Broken jewels?" he asked. He picked one up, shook it, and a low, mournful tune filled the air. "And you've charmed them with useless *sounds*? Ugh." He threw the bag back at Rudy, who clutched it tightly.

When he got to Aiden, though, Chandra's interest reignited.

"Well, well, well," he said softly. "If it's not the human spawn of Malini herself. How is your mother these days? Single, I hear. Is she seeing anyone?"

Aiden glowered, and his scimitars shot out from beneath his sleeves.

Chandra merely laughed. "You can't protect her, my boy. I mean, look at you. What could *you* possibly do to *me*?"

Brynne interrupted him. "You said we could win back Nikita. How?"

Chandra smiled, then gestured at his twenty-seven wives. "These are my queens, though you may know them best as the nakshatras, the glorious constellations who hold the fate of humans in their every movement," he said proudly. "Now—"

"What are their names?" asked Aiden loudly, his expression fierce.

Chandra blinked. "Names? Well, there's uh . . . um . . . Rohini, of course. Then . . . Hasta, Sravana, Revati, Pushya . . . Ashwini . . . um, anyway! They're goddesses, and they're my wives. Done. And they've"—he paused, frowning a little—"*agreed*"—he nodded—"to wear my beloved Rohini's face for this little game. Behind one of their doors hides the treasure you seek. But which door is it?"

The moon god laughed to himself, then held up a finger.

"You have one chance," he said. "Succeed, and you shall have what you want and be on your way. Fail, and your weapons will join the rest of my dearest treasures."

THIRTY-SIX

Pick a Wife! Any Wife!

Aru paused, her mind running through the different options before them. She weighed Vajra in her hands, wondering if there was some way around the conditions Chandra had set. Could her lightning bolt somehow zap all the doors open at once?

Beside her, Aiden stared at the nakshatras.

"I can't believe he made all of them look like Rohini," he said, disgusted.

Rudy winked at the goddesses. "That one just smiled at me."

Aru followed his line of sight to a goddess whose lips were curled over her teeth, her smile wolflike. "Uh . . . sure."

"Which door do we pick?" asked Mini.

"If we open a bunch of them at once, it won't matter," said Brynne, rolling up her sleeves.

"Whoa, Bee, what are you doing—" started Aiden.

"CHARGE!" she yelled.

In a flash of blue light, Brynne changed into a ram with huge curling horns and hurtled toward one of the doors.

Aru, Aiden, Mini, and Rudy looked at each other for a

moment and then ran forward, too. Aru knew in her bones it wasn't the right move, but she didn't want to just stand there when everyone else was doing something. She flung Vajra toward a door, but the god of the moon was faster. He flicked his wrist, and a silvery rope lashed out like a snake, knocking her lightning bolt to the floor. Aru skidded to a halt, gathering up the weapon in her arms. It was limp and gave a weak shudder.

"Vajra?" croaked Aru.

The bolt buzzed faintly, and Aru pressed it close to her chest.

"BAAAAA-TRAYAL!" hollered Ram-Brynne as she was lassoed by the whip and pulled backward. She changed back into her usual form, stepped out of the loop, and started to swing her mace, only for it to be snapped out of her hands. It skittered across the floor.

When Mini tried to cast a spell with Dee Dee, Chandra's whip struck again. There was a sad violet spark as the danda shrank into compact form in Mini's grasp.

Rudy was holding one of Aiden's scimitars, but it didn't seem like he knew how to wield it. He lowered his arm and the weapon scraped the ground.

Aiden darted out of the way just as the moon god's whip thrashed. Aiden spun, ready to slice it with his scimitar, but the rope swept his feet out from under him and knocked him onto his back.

Chandra's throne broke away from its podium to float far above them.

"Playing dirty, are we?" he called down, making a *tsk* sound. "That seems unwise."

Chandra snapped his fingers. The ground beneath them began to quake and tremble, and the mirror floor shattered, the pieces drifting apart like giant ice floes. A giant fissure opened beneath Aru's feet and she made an awkward hop to the right. Her arms pinwheeled as she fought for balance, and she glimpsed what lay between the cracks in the floor....

Nothing.

Just the night sky and the promise of hard ground thousands of feet below. Her stomach swooped uncomfortably.

"Since you insist on playing unfairly, I shall raise the stakes!" called Chandra.

His twenty-seven wives now stood on a crust of unbroken floor that was so narrow the tips of their toes peeked over the edge and their long flowing gowns hung over the dark abyss below. They weren't bored or annoyed anymore, but *scared.* A couple of them tried to inch back against the wall, but there wasn't space for them to move.

Aru looked around, panic swelling in her chest. Beside her, Aiden and Rudy were huddled precariously on a mirror floe no bigger than a chair seat. On her right, Mini sat clutching the edges of a piece the size of a bedroom pillow, and Brynne balanced one-legged on a shard no larger than a serving platter. Fortunately, she'd been able to retrieve Gogo before it fell.

"This is hopeless!" said Mini.

"Hey! Don't forget about us!" called Rudy frantically from the other side of the room.

Brynne wheeled her mace high above her head. A mini cyclone burst from the tip and traveled downward. She expertly guided the wind around the space, pushing the floor shards closer to one another until some of them came back together like a grand jigsaw puzzle. The kids leaped from one piece to the next until they all met up on the largest one.

"Clever!" said Chandra, clapping. "I'll have to remember that trick when I possess the wind mace."

"We can't plan anything with him listening," said Aru.

Mini nodded. She changed Dee Dee into a danda and raised it. A burst of violet light formed a bubble over them. Chandra scowled and seemed to call out something. . . .

But they couldn't hear a thing.

"Our weapons aren't going to work against him," said Aiden. "Fighting isn't how we're going to win back Nikita."

"So, what do you suggest?" snapped Brynne.

Aru tightened her grip on her lightning bolt and felt its strength course through her. Vajra was still weak, but it was slowly regaining power. In the back of her mind, Aru heard Boo's voice, the words he'd drummed through their skulls in every practice fight:

"We are *more* than the things we fight with," Aru said firmly.

The other four fell silent, and Aru felt that—for once—she'd come up with the 100 percent right thing to say.

"I want to believe that," said Mini. "But say we don't fight and somehow reach the other side—how are we going to know which door to open?"

"Remember what Sheela said?" asked Aru. "*You can find her behind the favorite star of the moon*. That's gotta mean Rohini is guarding Nikita's door!"

"But they all look like Rohini!" said Rudy.

"And yet he only loves one of them," said Aiden.

That, Aru realized, was the answer.

"*We* don't have to figure out which one Rohini is—we just have to make Chandra reveal it by accident," said Aru. "Then we'll know which door to open."

"How're we going to do that?" asked Aiden.

At first no one responded, and then Brynne cleared her throat. "Chandra reminds me of Anila," she said, staring up at the moon god.

Aiden's face darkened. "I can see that."

"Am I supposed to know who that is?" asked Rudy.

"No," said Aiden and Brynne at the same time.

"Someone like that only shows you what they care about when it's in danger," said Brynne.

She rubbed at a spot on her arm neatly covered by the stacks of bracelets she was wearing. Aru saw the shiny patch of scar tissue left there from a nasty kitchen accident. When a boiling pot of water fell off the stove, Anila had been standing right beside Brynne, but instead of pushing her daughter out of the way... Anila had saved her purse instead. The patch on Brynne's skin wasn't the first scar Anila had left, but it was the most visible one.

"So does that mean we have to go after the star goddesses?" asked Rudy, shocked. "That's horrible! Plus, what if they get *mad*? They could curse me!" He paused. "I mean *us*!"

"It'd be horrible if we *actually* went after the goddesses." Mini smiled and twirled Dee Dee. "But we've got illusion on our side. Good thinking, Brynne."

Brynne beamed.

Boo was right—they were more than just the items they fought with. Sometimes a weakness felt like a blade turned inward, but that meant it was sharp enough that when turned around, it could be a weapon. You just had to be willing to face it and adjust your grip. And that made it a magic far more powerful than any celestial weapon.

"So what do we do?" asked Rudy.

"What you do best," said Mini, pointing at his orange messenger bag. "Cause a distraction."

A cautious smile slipped onto his face. "All right. I'm on it."

"We'll play defense," said Aiden, looking at Aru.

She nodded and transformed Vajra into a flashing spear.

Mini said, "Lowering the shield in three..."

Rudy reached inside his messenger bag, his face tight with concentration.

"Two..."

Brynne took a deep breath and closed her eyes. Aru reached for her hand, and Brynne squeezed back so hard that Aru temporarily lost feeling in her fingers.

"One," said Mini.

The force field dropped, and Chandra's voice rushed into the void:

"Given up already?" he asked, sinking into his pale throne. "How utterly boring..."

Aru's hair lifted off her shoulders in the sudden wind. Beside her, there was a burst of violet light. Twenty-seven silver arrows with cruel tips hovered in the air above Mini's hands. Rudy crushed a jewel under his heel, and all the noise in the room got sucked into silence. A beat later, a hypnotic rhythm took over, as lulling as rain on a roof. Even Aru felt the magical music tugging at her senses. On his throne, Chandra reached for his whip, but his gaze became unfocused and he stilled.

"Now, Brynne!" yelled Rudy.

She raised her wind mace high above her head. In a rush of air, she picked up all twenty-seven of Mini's arrows and sent them hurtling toward the constellations. "Run!" Brynne yelled.

The five Potatoes raced across the room, leaping from one piece of the floor to the other as a bottomless abyss yawned beneath them. The arrows sped toward the constellation-wives. Aru looked up and saw their eyes widening, flicking between the weapons and their dazed husband. They tried to get away from their assigned doors, but their feet were stuck fast to the floor. Fury swept over their faces, and a chorus of different voices yelled out "Chandra!" and "This has gone too far!"

The moon god finally snapped to attention. He whirled around in his seat, appraising his wives and then the arrows as they zoomed closer. Twenty feet away, then fifteen . . . now *ten.*

Chandra fused the floor and dove to the fifth door, wrapping himself around the woman in an effort to protect her. *Rohini,* thought Aru.

Mini snapped her fingers, and the arrows vanished.

Chandra looked up, stunned.

Aru and Aiden kept barreling toward him. In Aru's hands, Vajra's weight became more solid. More *powerful.*

"Open up," she commanded, taking aim with her spear and letting go.

Vajra smashed into the fifth door and it swung back, creaking loudly. Mist poured out from the room. Aru's heart beat frantically. Had they made a mistake? Had they somehow gotten everything all wrong?

But when the mist thinned out . . .

There was Nikita, asleep on the ground.

Bent over, with her hands braced on her legs and heaving with every breath, Brynne grinned at Chandra.

"We win," she said.

THIRTY-SEVEN

Gods Don't *Nap*. Ew.

"You won by trickery!" said Chandra. "I do not accept defeat!"

"Then stop us!" yelled Brynne.

Aru looked back to see Chandra take a step toward them and falter. It was as if his own palace knew that the Pandavas had won fair and square and wouldn't let him get any closer. He tried using his whip, but it refused to lift off the mirrored floor.

Aru knelt beside Nikita. She was wearing a dress made of blue flowers, all the blossoms closed up as if they were taking a nap.

"Nikita?" asked Aru, shaking her shoulder.

But she wouldn't move. Mini checked Nikita's temperature, then held her wrist and looked at her watch to take her pulse.

"I don't understand," said Mini. "She seems fine?"

"Let's just get her out of here," said Brynne, scooping up the twin.

Nikita's head drooped, and Aiden rushed to tuck it more securely in the crook of Brynne's elbow.

"Watch her head," he scolded.

Rudy stood guard at the threshold. A couple of Chandra's wives poked their heads in to see before drawing back to let the Pandavas exit.

The rest of the constellations had surrounded Chandra. Their twenty-some-odd faces now looked completely different from one another. Some of them scowled. One of them walked off, throwing up her hands and declaring, "That's it! I need a bubble bath." Still more took one look at the Pandavas, bowed their heads in acknowledgment—or was it apology?—and vanished on the spot.

A handful stayed behind to berate their husband.

"You did not tell us we would be *rooted* to the spot," spat one of the wives.

"We are the constellations, husband," huffed another. "Do you think you can pin down a star goddess just because you married one?"

"Do not forget that your power waxes and wanes because of us," said another.

Chandra wilted a little, and he seemed to shrink—literally—beneath his wives' angry gazes.

"Now, now, my loves," he said. "It was merely a precaution! I didn't actually think—"

"What a novelty," said another wife, yawning.

"And making them all identical to me?" demanded Rohini. "Tacky!"

"If you ever bothered to look at the rest of us, maybe you could've been more creative," added another star goddess, tears shining in her eyes.

"But, my dearest . . ." said Chandra, reaching out to Rohini.

She shushed him and turned to face Aru and the others. "My sisters and I grant you full leave of the House of the Moon, with our blessings," she said, raising her hand.

The green heart in Nikita's neck grew dim. Rohini had fulfilled Chandra's promise to deactivate the tracking device.

"I just wanted *one* of their weapons," grumbled Chandra. "Make them give me one of their toys!"

"Alas, your hour of power is up, my dear," said another star goddess.

All of a sudden, Chandra looked different. He seemed younger and smaller, like a teenager. His once-muscular arms now appeared thin and scrawny. There were even some pimples on his chin and across his forehead, and his voice broke when he complained.

One of his wives laughed and patted his head. "Come now, little husband," she said. "The moon in the sky is no longer full, and you know your strength diminishes with it. It's time for you to get to bed."

Chandra pouted. "I hate bedtime! I am a god."

"Yes, yes," said another wife, holding his hand. "Now, how about some milk and cookies? Or just milk?"

"Milk *and* cookies."

"If you are very good, I will let you sit with me as I review the lunar reports," said another star goddess.

"But I was going to have *all* their weapons," he whined, flailing a hand at Aru, Mini, and Brynne.

Chandra's antelope vahana trotted beside him, occasionally nudging its lord with its muzzle. The moon god did not turn to say good-bye to the Pandavas, which was just as well.

"I must apologize for Chandra," Rohini said when he and

all the other constellation queens were gone. "Our husband is not usually like the person you just encountered. One might even say that our father's curse was the best thing that ever happened to him. It made him kinder. He can be thoughtful and secretive, illuminating and inspiring. But for four days of the month, we must handle him when he's at his worst. The whole house is flipped upside down, all the decor changes, and it can be quite annoying. But we manage."

"You have to deal with *that* four days out of every month?" asked Rudy, shuddering.

"Many women are accustomed to such monthly inconveniences," said Rohini, lifting an eyebrow.

She gestured widely, and the room from which they had retrieved Nikita transformed into a corridor that led them back out to the grand boulevard that linked all the planetary mansions.

"Quickly now," she said. "There's only one day left before the Holi celebrations, and this is the path you must take." She pointed down the avenue.

Aru narrowed her eyes. "Do you know something we don't?" she asked, then immediately regretted how she'd phrased the question.

"Inevitably," said the goddess. "But that is for me and my sisters to know, and for you to discover. Now, to exit this place, you must pass by the House of Saturn. Beware the baleful gaze of the god Shani, or you will never make it to the Door of New Day."

Mini raised her hand shyly. "Um, excuse me... but what's wrong with Nikita? Why won't she wake up?"

Rohini frowned. "My husband might have given her a

draught to lull her to sleep, for she was in such poor spirits about her sister. A couple of loud noises should do the trick, but I wouldn't risk it in this place. Wait till you are in the mortal realm."

The mortal realm? Aru mused. They had to go back there to save the Otherworld? They still had to find the tree, and Nikita was their only hope....

Aru paused on the palace's front steps before following her friends. In many stories she'd read, there were terrible consequences for looking over one's shoulder when you were supposed to move on. Someone's wife would turn into a pillar of salt. Or the wife would become a ghost and float back to the Underworld. Or the wife would—

Why was it always the wives? Rude. Good thing she didn't have a wife. She stole a glance at Aiden just ahead, gilded in moonlight. He turned to her, his lips quirked in a smile, and Aru quickly looked away. Nope. Definitely no wife.

Rohini's eyes met hers. "Yes, daughter of Indra?"

"I was just wondering if... Well... you said all this stuff about the path we must take and all that, and I was hoping you could tell me if... um..."

The star goddess seemed to know the question Aru couldn't bring herself to ask.

"You're wondering, perhaps, if you are on the *right* path?" Rohini guessed.

Aru nodded.

"*Right* is a word invented by humans, little one," said the star goddess. "We are all stitches in a fabric too vast to comprehend. But perhaps that is a good thing, for it means we are always exactly where we need to be."

Rohini stretched her hand over the night-dark Boulevard of Stars. For a moment, the world slipped away and Aru saw only the vast shimmering cosmos, and within it, each object, place, and feeling wrought of the myriad decisions of millions of people. It made her head ache just to look at it. Honestly, she could barely comprehend even a corner of what Rohini showed her.

"No matter what happens to us, we have choices," said Rohini. "We choose how to look at our lives. We choose what we can live with, and what we cannot, and only you can decide."

Rohini snapped her fingers, and the images faded immediately.

"Now go, Arundhati, named for the morning star," she said warmly. "For your father has caught wind of the Pandavas' hunt... and there is much left to be done."

THIRTY-EIGHT

Someone's Got a Burning Gaze. Literally.

Like all the other planetary palaces, the House of Saturn was opulent and grand. This one was crafted from sturdy onyx shot through with veins of silver. But it was oddly dilapidated, like the scene of one of those garage sales where you'd find a broken bathtub next to a collection of drinking glasses featuring obscure Star Wars characters. From where Aru stood, she could spot a blasted television set, a broken pool table with snapped sticks, one half-incinerated Etch A Sketch, and a smoldering BUILD YOUR OWN PLANT TERRARIUM! kit, all of which lay at the base of a great archway, plumes of smoke wafting from it.

At the far end of the lawn loomed the gleaming Door of New Day. As they got closer, Aru saw that it was as big and unadorned as a school cafeteria door, except that it seemed to be made of quicksilver. It quivered and vibrated, as if in a constant state of flux.

"Yeah . . . *none* of this stuff bodes well," said Aru, toeing one of the broken things on the ground.

"Is this what Rohini meant by 'baleful gaze'?" asked Mini. "Does Shani just look at stuff and it breaks?"

Rudy nodded. "That's what I've heard."

"Then we have to move as *quietly* as possible," said Brynne.

Aiden hoisted Nikita higher across his back. "Be careful, Bee."

Earlier, they'd taken some of the camping materials from Aiden's satchel and fashioned a human backpack that strapped Nikita to him. It was probably a good thing Nikita was knocked out. Aru could imagine the fashionista twin *hating* everything about this.

In a flash of light, Brynne transformed into a blue snake, slithering easily and silently over the crowded lawn. Rudy rummaged silently around in his messenger bag, pulling out a violet jewel and whispering to it. At once, a low sound crept over the lawn... the sound of indifferent things, like someone clacking on a keyboard in an office, the occasional thud of a book falling over on a library's bookshelf, cicadas in summer.

Nothing out of the ordinary.

Nothing to notice.

Aiden brought out his scimitars slowly, casting his gaze about, while Aru followed Brynne's footsteps. Even with Rudy's enchanted music, Aru felt a low prickle gathering at the base of her spine. Two minutes passed... then three... and the Door of New Day got closer and larger with every step.

"So far so good," whispered Mini, carefully stepping over what looked to be a smashed xylophone.

"A xylophone?" asked Aru, glancing down. "I bet he owns an electric triangle—"

Brynne the snake turned her head sharply and hissed.

Aru felt a low buzzing in her skull, as if Brynne was trying to get a message to her, but something about the House of Saturn confused it.

"I—I can't send mind messages," said Aru.

She concentrated her energy, trying to push words toward Mini and Brynne, but it was as if something had built a wall between them.

"What's happening?" asked Mini, rubbing at her temples.

Brynne hissed again.

"In snake, that means *Shut up,*" said Rudy helpfully.

Aru rolled her eyes. "We're being quiet!"

Aiden fixed Aru with a pointed look, and she went back to tiptoeing over a pit of broken crochet needles, a candle-making kit, three record players, and a paint-by-numbers set. She hoped the mind-message problem would clear up the moment they got back to the human world.

"What a dump," said Aru, grimacing as she shook a bit of dried paint off her sneakers. "Has he never heard of recycling?"

Just then, a silver beetle scuttled over her foot. "Bug!" she whisper-yelped.

"What'd you expect with this mess?" asked Mini. But she shuddered too when the silver beetle moved closer to her.

By now, the door was within sprinting distance. Brynne slithered faster. Aru felt a reckless hysteria bubbling up inside her chest. This was it. Once they were back in the mortal world, everything would be fixed. Nikita would wake up and help them. Aru cast a sidelong glance at the twin. In sleep, the girl was still frowning, but her crown of flowers had been restored.

A loud *Honk! Honk!* broke the silence of Saturn's realm.

"Someone's here!" said Aiden.

Brynne slithered under a magazine for cover. Mini cast an invisibility shield over the rest of them just as Rudy's song abruptly went quiet.

They held their breath as they looked out over the littered lawn, trying to figure out where their attacker was coming from... but everything remained still. Maybe it had just been a sound from one of the broken instruments? Maybe a battery was dying out?

Mini lowered the shield. Brynne transformed back to normal. Aru's heart pounded in relief.

Rudy sighed. "Well, that was close—"

Ding-dong! Ding-dong! Ding-dong!

To the left of the Door of New Day, at a jet-black gate that marked the edge of Saturn's mansion, a pale-skinned yaksha wearing a bowler hat rang the doorbell three times. He dropped a takeout box and, without bothering to wait, hopped back into his small silver chariot and sped away as fast as he could.

The ground began to shake beneath them. Brynne motioned frantically for them to run toward the Door of New Day, but the ground was bouncing too wildly and it knocked them off their feet. From inside the palace, a friendly voice rang out.

"Wow! I'm amazed! You know, I'd heard you guys were fast, but two seconds is pretty quick even for Uber Eats' Celestial Division."

Shani, Lord of Saturn, chuckled to himself as he emerged from his halls. Aru had never considered what it would be like to meet a planet... and in all her imaginings of Saturn, she'd always thought of it possessing a giant ring like a frozen Hula-Hoop.

Shani did not have a Hula-Hoop.

Instead, he was dressed in a plaid silk nightgown with house slippers shaped like ducks with little mirrors affixed to their foreheads. His skin was a deep violet flecked with stars. But it was his head that threw her off.

Whereas most people would raise their heads to meet you straight in the eye. Shani looked *only* at the ground. He seemed to frown at his feet, and Aru realized he must be looking at their reflections in his duck slippers.

"Wait…you're not the delivery guys, are you?" he asked. He waved a bag of coins. "Otherwise, I don't have enough for the tip."

THIRTY-NINE

And I— Oop!

"We're definitely not the delivery guys," said Aru.

"Good!" said Shani, pocketing the coins. "So what are you doing here? Have you come to fix the sink?"

"What's wrong with it?" asked Mini.

"Well, it's making this strange growling noise—"

"We're *not* here about the sink," cut in Brynne. "We're trying to get to the Door of New Day. We're on urgent business on behalf of the heavens."

"Urgent business?" asked Shani, perking up. "Do tell! I've been a bit out of the loop, unfortunately."

"We're in somewhat of a rush, sorry," said Aru.

Shani paused. "Wait a moment. Young, female, high-pitched voices...access to the Otherworld and the heavens... urgent business...Are you...Are you the Pandavas?"

Brynne lifted her chin. "We are."

"And there's also me?" added Rudy resentfully. "A naga prince."

"And me," said Aiden, raising his hand. "Not a prince. Or a Pandava. Well, kinda, but it's more of an 'adjacent' thing. . . ." He trailed off, his face suddenly red.

Brynne took another step closer to the Door of New Day. "So perhaps you might let us pass?"

"Wow!" said Shani, clapping his hands excitedly and kicking out his duck-slippered feet. "Pandavas! *Real* Pandavas! How thrilling! Tell me, what news is there in the worlds below? I'd take a look myself, but that doesn't tend to go very well." He mournfully patted the top of his head.

"Apologies if this is rude, but . . . why can't you look up?" asked Mini.

Shani's eyebrows furrowed and he shook his head. "I got in a bit of a spat with my wife some time ago. One must never offend one's wife. Especially if one's wife happens to be a goddess of the arts exceptionally skilled in cursing." He sighed. "I was consumed one day with reading a new book. It is, I believe, an ancient human tome called *Twilight.* I liked it very much. Anyway, my lady queen asked if she looked better wearing a gown with roses or a gown with stars, and I replied that I didn't care, because I was learning about vampires. Since I could not take the time to look at her and thus ruined her day, she set a curse upon me that whatsoever I looked at would be blighted by my gaze."

Mini looked appalled. *"Always?"*

Shani rubbed his temples. "Well, no, not *always.* She eventually relented and gave me a pair of glasses that allowed me to look at things, but I had to be very careful not to look outside the periphery of the lenses. One day I was reading in bed, and the glasses slipped down my nose and I incinerated our new duvet! It had a two-thousand-star thread count and was so comfy. Very unfortunate, and I was *right* in the middle of a new romantic thriller, too."

"What happened to your glasses?" asked Brynne, taking another step toward the Door of New Day.

Shani followed. "Well, you might've noticed that there's an awful lot of beetles running about." He scowled. "It's all because of Ratri! She refuses to use pesticides, going on and on about organic dreams in her grove."

As he spoke, Aru noticed another silver beetle scuttling toward them. She elbowed Brynne in the ribs.

"I *hate* those bugs," muttered Shani. "They're *vicious* killers. They caused me to destroy my own purple roses!" He flailed a hand in the direction of an incinerated archway.

Aru elbowed Brynne again, keeping an eye on the silver beetle inching toward them, but Brynne didn't notice. Aru tried to grab Mini's attention next, but she was mournfully listening to Shani's tale. Aru's mind messages were still not working, either.

"They took me completely unawares, and I jumped. My glasses fell off, and then I stepped on them, and ugh." Shani sighed. "Manda left a few days ago to buy me a new pair, but she needed to stop by and visit her sister, too, and these things take time! So now I'm deeply bored, and every time I try to read anything, it either bursts into flames or gives me a headache. And forget movies. I tried to watch *The Avengers* with a mirror and ended up burning my entire entertainment system."

"You could try an audiobook," suggested Aiden.

"Why would I want a book that eavesdrops on my conversations?" demanded Shani.

"No, the book is read to you," said Aiden. "By a narrator."

Shani cocked his head. "Fascinating witchcraft..."

Brynne cleared her throat, tilting her head toward the door. Aru took another step forward. Shani didn't seem to notice. Aru chanced one more step. Just twenty more and they could throw open the Door of New Day and escape into the mortal realm.

"Yup, humanity is wild," said Aru, hoping Shani wouldn't see the bug. "Well, it was great talking to you!"

"Oh, but don't go just yet!" pleaded Shani. "I'm so lonely. How about some tea? I can boil water with a glance, but the sugar will taste burnt, sadly."

"No, but thank you," said Aru. "We really have to be going."

The bug scuttled closer. Aru finally caught Brynne's eye, then made a fist and hit her own palm.

Brynne frowned at her. *You want a mortar and pestle for grinding spices?* she mouthed.

Behind them, Rudy squeaked, "Bug!"

"What?" asked Shani sharply. "Where?"

"He didn't say *bug*!" said Aru.

"Then what'd he say?" demanded Shani.

"He . . . uh, he said . . . um—"

"Hug!" said Aiden brightly. "He wants to give you . . . a *hug*."

"He does?" asked Shani.

"I do?" said Rudy.

Aru threw him a look. Rudy gulped.

"I do!" said Rudy fumbling for something to say. "You know, it's hard not to see stuff clearly. I should know. I'm color-blind. But think of it as just experiencing reality . . . differently."

"Oh, well, that's lovely," said Shani, clasping his hands. "And I do like hugs." The planet extended his arms.

"We'll hold the door for you, Rudy!" called Brynne, taking another step forward.

Meanwhile, the bug kept inching its way toward them. Aru pointed at it wildly. *Finally* Brynne noticed. She aimed her wind mace at it, trying to blast it out of the way. It flipped upside down, then righted itself. It seemed even more determined now. A glinting silver light emanated from its hard shell. It clicked its wings.

Uh-oh.

The bug charged forward. Aru realized it was heading straight for Shani's duck-slippered feet.

Rudy gave Shani a quick and awkward side hug. Shani started talking about how terribly sad it was that no one seemed to read poetry anymore. Aiden darted forward, Nikita bouncing across his back, as he tried to stab at the bug with his scimitars, only for Mini to block him.

"It's a living thing!" she said.

Shani said, "Quite right, child. Literature *is* a living thing, much like myth itself! Fairy tales gain new life with every retelling and such. Very wise of you—"

"That living thing could get us all killed!" shot back Aiden, trying to spear it once more with his blade.

Shani frowned. "*Kill?* Well, people *have* died for the right to make art...."

Time slowed as everything spiraled out of control. Mini tried to trap the bug in a force field, but her aim was off and she only ended up bouncing the beetle into the air. Aru spun Vajra in her hand, thinking she could net it.... Unfortunately, Brynne aimed her wind mace at the same time, which sent the beetle arcing through the air. Too late, Rudy spied it. He leaped up, his palm outstretched....

But instead of batting the beetle out of the air, he sent it flying *right* toward Shani's face.

"I've been meaning to reread *Twilight*. I could never decide if I was on Team Edward or Team Jacob, and I— Oop!"

The beetle smacked into his forehead.

Aru froze.

The beetle froze.

Shani froze.

EVERYTHING FROZE.

Then the beetle scuttled over his nose, and the planet screamed, *"IT'S ON MY FACE! GET IT OFF! GET IT OFF!"*

"Keep your eyes shut!" called Aiden.

Brynne jumped to the side, frantically directing them all toward the Door of New Day. Aru started to run. Twenty steps, now fifteen...

But then the earth trembled. A tendril of ice wound through her heart as Aru realized that Shani had lifted his head.

FORTY

Not the Tiny Legs!

Brynne, as strong and sturdy as ever, didn't even blink.

"Don't look back! Just *go!*" she ordered the Potatoes.

Aiden sprinted ahead, holding on to Nikita's feet as he ran. One jump, then two, and he'd made it to the threshold of the Door of New Day. The door sparkled, and Aru could almost imagine the sensation of its strange, cool metal beneath her palms, like a pond that wasn't frozen but whose surface she couldn't breach.

"Come on, Shah!" called Aiden.

The ground shook under Aru's feet, tripping her forward. Aru risked a glance over her shoulder and saw that Shani had flung the beetle off his forehead and was now scrubbing furiously at his face. He blinked once, and a smoking line of fire shot straight out of his eyes. The glare of it sent spots blinking through her own vision. His burning gaze fell on a birdbath, which, two seconds later, split down the middle like a banana.

"So revolting!" shouted Shani. "Where'd it go? Someone kill it!"

"It's gone!" called Mini. "Just keep your eyes closed!"

But Shani wasn't listening. He kept blinking, searing a new hole in the land each time. Rudy darted past him, clutching his messenger bag to his chest, and caught up with Aru.

"Well, there goes the garage!" howled Shani. "Manda will be *furious* with me!"

Aru could see the Door of New Day shining brightly not ten feet away, along with Aiden's outstretched hand. She tried to take a step forward, but the ground opened right in front of her, plunging into a fifty-foot-long chasm that separated her, Brynne, Mini, and Rudy from the door.

Brynne hollered at them to move, and Shani loudly squealed, "I CAN STILL FEEL ITS TINY LEGS ON MY NOSE!" A burst of fire lit up the air behind Aru, and she felt as if a thin line of flames had started to nip at her heels. Shani was turning his gaze toward her and she needed to jump. *Now.*

Aru squeezed her eyes shut, preparing to leap forward, when someone yanked her sharply to the right.

"He almost looked at you!" said Mini.

Aru blinked. In the spot where she'd stood just seconds ago there were now plumes of smoke and a fathomless hole that promised an infinite drop.

"Over here!" shouted Brynne.

Shani whirled to where Brynne stood, nearly ten feet back. Before his flames could reach her, Brynne transformed into a giant eagle and grasped Rudy in one talon. With her other talon she pushed two huge boulders near Aru and Mini. They hunkered down behind the rocks. If Shani looked in their direction, at least the boulders would take the hit first.

And then they'd be out of places to hide.

Brynne said, "I'll come back for you two!" As she flew Rudy

over the chasm, Aru heard him moaning. "I can't die now! I haven't seen enough of the world! I don't know what Florida is!"

Mini cast a force field around her and Aru, but Shani was a planet, and the cursed power of his vision could likely pierce anything.

"Aru, this would be a good time to come up with something sneaky," said Mini.

Why didn't they teach emergency tactics in Otherworld school? Aru wondered. Hanuman's tutoring was all about thinking like the opponent, but this opponent was only thinking of himself. Urvashi's lessons about etiquette and grace were useless in this situation, too. Boo hadn't ever mentioned what to do in the event a planet with laser vision focused on them. She'd never even heard of something like this outside of *X-Men*. The Cyclops character also had laser vision . . . but when his let loose, there really wasn't much to do except hope he looked somewhere else.

Aru paused.

Look somewhere else.

This whole time, they'd been telling Shani that the bug was gone, but he wasn't listening, convinced it was still somewhere close by. What if this time they agreed with him?

Aru turned to her sister. "Mini, can you make an illusion of a beetle?"

She nodded and set to work fashioning a small light that flickered to life between her two palms. Judging by the sound of more things being incinerated, Shani seemed to be getting closer.

"If I can just find it and be rid of it, then it'll be fine!" said Shani, his voice half-crazed.

Mini whimpered.

"What was that?" shouted Shani.

"The beetle!" called Aru, standing up slowly. "It's right behind your feet!"

Shani whipped around. In the same second, Mini whispered something to her Death Danda and a plume of violet light wound its way toward him, scuttling forward in the shape of a beetle.

"Take my arm!" Aru said to Mini.

Shani swung his head, searching for the beetle. His gaze seemed to be everywhere at once. One glance, and a palm tree hissed as it went up in flames. One blink, and the pit of broken musical instruments burst into flames, filling the air with the twanging of popped guitar strings.

"I'll stomp you out of existence in *every* universe!" roared Shani.

He turned about in wild circles. Aru flicked her wrist and Vajra sprang to life as a hoverboard.

"Children!" he called out. "Children, do you see it?"

"Watch out, Shah!" yelled Brynne from the other side of the chasm.

Aru jumped onto Vajra and pulled up Mini, who clung tightly to her as they soared over the chasm. Aru didn't blame her. It was like staring into the vast abyss of space. There was nothing but endless stars and the light of dying planets, sketches of universes yet to be made....

Deadly heat snaked toward them.

Shani was lifting his gaze....

Up ahead, Aiden raised his camera to his face and yelled, "Close your eyes!"

Aru did as she was told and sensed the flash of Aiden's enchanted camera against her closed eyelids.

Shani yelped. "Ah! Too bright! I can't see!"

Aru and Mini tumbled onto the ground right before the Door of New Day. Quickly, Aru reached out, grabbed hold of the knob, and turned it as hard as she could. When she flung the door open, a cold voice asked, "Where do you wish to go?"

In the reflection in the silver door, Aru watched as Shani's white-hot laser vision burned a thin path from the edge of his property, across the chasm, and... Right. Toward. Them.

"Don't you dare say Home Depot, Shah!" hollered Brynne.

But now it was in her head! And it seemed the door heard, because the light around it rippled. The next instant, they were toppling through the ether with the faint sound of Shani's voice trailing them:

"So sorry about that! Do visit again! Would love to hear more about your adventures!"

FORTY-ONE

You Brought Us to *Home Depot*?

Aru plopped to the ground, feeling warm asphalt beneath her palms and inhaling springtime air full of the familiar scents of wet grass and hay. She lumbered to her feet, blinking away the sudden daylight.

Rudy was lying on the pavement, kissing it and declaring, "Sweet ground! I'll never leave you again!"

Meanwhile, Brynne, Mini, and Aiden were helping Nikita to her feet. Rohini had said a couple of loud sounds would wake her up. Apparently, their escape from an angry planet had done the job.

Nikita rubbed her eyes, and the blossoms on her crown of flowers opened slowly. She looked first at everyone, then stared around at her surroundings, her eyes focusing on something just behind Aru. The corners of her mouth turned down.

"Really, Shah?" she said. "You brought us to *Home Depot*?"

Only now did Aru realize they were standing in an empty parking lot right outside the giant hardware store. She couldn't care less. All that mattered was that Nikita was awake and safe with them.

"Always the rude attitude with you," said Aru.

"Especially after we just pulled off that daring rescue," said Brynne.

"Um, technically, we *won* her," said Mini.

"I mean, I *knew* you would," Nikita said snootily. Then she beamed. "And you're going to save Sheela, too, right?"

Aru forced herself to smile even as she wondered just how exactly they were going to pull that off. She sighed, then looked at the sky. The Door of New Day had spat them out at dawn. Just like Rohini had warned them, they had exactly one more day to find the Tree of Wishes.

"You know me," Aru said. "More saving, more doing. All that."

Brynne checked her watch and grimaced. "It's Holi," she said. "The Otherworld is going to expect us back at Amaravati for the festivities tonight."

Aiden lowered his camera, blinking against the sunrise. "Then that means we've still got twelve hours."

"We can't go back without the tree," pointed out Mini.

For once, Rudy was exceptionally quiet. He kept turning around in the parking lot, looking a little dazed.

"Why are there white marks on the ground? Is this an ancient battlefield?"

"It's a parking lot," said Mini. "We tend to end up in those often."

"And depending on when you're trying to park, it's definitely a battlefield," added Aiden.

As Aru considered next steps, she touched her sapphire pendant. Two of its hollows were now filled—one with the memory of the Sleeper's sacrifice of his own childhood, the other with the memory of when he'd chosen her name. Aru may not have found the tree—yet—but she had made other important discoveries. And she wasn't going to give up. Not when the Sleeper knew what they were after, and definitely not when Sheela was depending on them.

"We have a riddle," she said to Nikita. "And we think you're the answer to it."

"I don't like riddles," said Nikita. "Those're more Sheela's thing."

Rudy reached into his messenger bag, pulling out the little pane of moonlight and reading it aloud:

"All growing things know where the tree can be found,
But it takes the right ear to hear the right sound.
All growing things know, but not all wish to talk.
The youngest of roots are the best to unlock."

"Can you, um, talk to plants?" asked Aru.

Nikita shook her head.

Aru's stomach plummeted. She had been so sure....

"They prefer it when you talk *with* them," said Nikita. "They like conversation."

"Oh," said Mini. "That's good!"

"But only if they're magical," said Nikita. "And from the riddle, it sounds like we need baby ones."

"Where are we going to find magical baby plants?" asked Brynne, peering around the parking lot.

When Aru looked back at the store, she saw the familiar arched awning with bright orange lettering declaring:

PLANT NURSERY

"I know where we could start?" she said.

The five of them walked toward the entrance, dragging Rudy behind them as he swiveled his neck around and frowned. "What's that?" he asked, looking at one of the soda machines outside the store.

"A vending machine," said Aiden.

"What does it . . . 'vend'?" asked Rudy.

"Soda," said Aiden tightly.

"What's soda?"

"A drink."

"Can I try one?" asked Rudy.

Aru had a brief but vivid image of Rudy after he'd downed a can full of sugar syrup, running in circles around the parking lot. Maybe everybody else had the exact same vision, because as one they responded with a resounding *"NO."*

Brynne looked at Aiden. "Can I knock him unconscious?"

When they got to the entrance, everything was locked. According to the hours of operation, the store wouldn't open until six in the morning, and that wasn't for another thirty minutes.

"We could wait?" offered Mini.

"And give the Sleeper an extra half hour to find us and kill us?" asked Brynne. "No thanks." She took one look at the door, then curled her hand into a fist.

"Breaking and entering? That's illegal!" said Mini before pointing to a corner of the building. "And there's a camera!"

Aru summoned Vajra, transforming the bolt into a tiny spear no larger than a Sharpie. She flung it at the security equipment, which sparked once and drooped.

"There *was* a camera," said Aru.

Brynne grinned, raising her fist once more.

Rudy clapped and started chanting, "Heist! Heist! Heist!"

"Just do it already!" said Nikita. "Sheela's waiting for us."

Mini turned her cheek. "I can't be a witness to this."

"Um, guys?" cut in Aiden. "How about using Mr. V's key?"

Brynne scowled, dropping her hand.

"He said that only Aru could use it first. He didn't say that none of us could use it after that."

Aru didn't like this idea. She herself wanted *zero* part of the thing. "You know what it does to people," said Aru. "But if you're willing to take that risk, go wild." She dug the velvet pouch out of her backpack and handed it to him.

Aiden pressed the key to the door and a delicate filigree of golden light spread across the glass. The lock whirred softly as its gears shifted and twisted. Aru watched Aiden's face intently, wondering what exactly was being opened inside him. . . . For her, it had been a bruised ache for the father she'd never had. Aiden paused for a moment, his eyebrows drawn together. His eyes darted in her direction, and for one full second he openly stared at her. His eyebrows quirked up like he was shocked by whatever he'd seen there. But then he quickly shook himself.

"Let's go," he said. The door slid open, and he waited for everyone to go in before him.

"You okay?" asked Aru as she walked past.

"Yeah, um, I'm fine, Shah," he said, hastily shoving the key inside its velvet pouch and returning it to her backpack.

Overhead, harsh fluorescent lights beamed down on them. Bright orange placards denoted aisles for everything from lamp fixtures to doorknobs. The silent cash registers looked like dormant guards stationed at the entrance.

Nikita shivered from the chill of the store's air-conditioning. She snapped her fingers and a new dress swallowed her last outfit. It was made of sky-blue silk and patterned with daisies at the hem. Hope lit up her ice-blue eyes, and she pushed her dozens of tiny braids off her shoulder.

"Much better," she said.

"Nice," said Rudy appreciatively. "Could you make me a blue blazer? I want something with tassels—"

"Nope," said Nikita.

"Why not?" Aru asked.

"'Cause she's a life-ruiner," said Rudy darkly. "She ruins people's lives."

"Because I think red is more your color," said Nikita flatly.

Rudy perked up, then started preening again. "Oh. Well, *obviously*."

Aiden snorted back a laugh, and they walked toward the plant nursery at the end of the huge floor.

"This place is . . . *gross*," said Rudy, flicking an imaginary piece of lint from his shoulder. "Is this the best of human establishments?" He turned to Aiden and sighed. "I thought you said we were going to do fun tours of the human realm. What about Disneyland?"

"We're a little busy with, you know, preventing the destruction of the world," said Aiden.

"All the more reason to take a vacation," said Rudy, rolling his eyes. "You must hate this place, Shah."

The comment dug at Aru in a way she hadn't expected.

She looked down the aisles, feeling a pang of homesickness. She remembered all the times she'd come here with her mom, who was always in need of new storage containers for the museum objects, or different lightbulbs so the lobby looked "warmer," whatever that meant. Aru used to love shopping with her. They'd wander around and talk, and even when Aru got too old for it, her mom never minded when Aru leaped onto the back of the cart and pretended she was sailing through the store.

But they hadn't gone shopping together in a while. These days, if her mom needed something, Aru just picked it up in the Night Bazaar. Magic had replaced a lot of ordinary stuff, and there just wasn't time anymore to lurk in the Home Depot aisle with all the doors and pop out at random strangers. There was a war coming and training to be completed. Not to mention eighth grade to survive.

Aru's throat felt tight, and a moment passed before she realized she'd never answered Rudy.

"I don't hate it," she said.

He wrinkled his nose and said loftily, "Well, if you find this place remotely interesting, wait till you see my father's palaces. You're welcome to visit, you know."

A couple of paces in front of them, Mini slowed. It looked as though she had been about to gaze over her shoulder but changed her mind. Aru felt her face grow hot with guilt. She hadn't asked for Rudy's attention, and she didn't want it if it meant hurting Mini in the slightest.

"I'll ask Brynne and Mini if they wanna go," said Aru, and then she picked up her pace to join her sisters.

As Aru left the boys behind, she heard Rudy say, "I really thought she'd hate this place."

Aru couldn't see Aiden's expression when he answered, but she imagined him shrugging and instinctively fiddling with his camera when he said, "Then you don't really know her."

Nikita stopped in front of the doorway to the nursery, which was strung with thick strips of cloudy plastic. She held open the curtain, and Aru could see familiar rows of black shelving holding budding plants. Ceramic pots were stacked in one corner, and overhead, the lights buzzed on automatically. It smelled like wet dirt, and Aru suspected the humidity was making her hair frizz. But this place didn't have the usual sheen of portals to the Otherworld.

"Do you think any of these plants are magical?" Aru asked Nikita.

Brynne squinted. "They look pretty ordinary to me."

"Yeah," said Mini, with a guilty glance at Nikita. "I don't think this is where we're supposed to be...."

Nikita threw up her hands. "Fine," she said. "Enjoy your lack of faith."

She flicked her braids over her shoulder once again and slipped into the nursery. It took a moment for the curtain to settle behind her, and when it did, Nikita was...gone.

"Where'd she go?" asked Mini.

Aru frowned, then went through the plastic. Again, no sense of magic. Just a mundane plant nursery in a typical Home Depot.

But when Aru took another step forward, she was drenched in a sudden downpour of magic. Like she was on one of those tube rides at a waterpark and had gone through an unexpected waterfall.

She spluttered loudly, shaking her head as if she could rid herself of the sensation.

Aru looked up, and her jaw dropped as she took in the new room. She was in the middle of a huge fancy greenhouse with a wide sign fluttering just above her head.

ARANYANI'S GARDEN SUPPLIES

FOR ALL YOUR MAGICAL LABYRINTH,

CRYPT, AND LAWN NEEDS

Nikita popped up beside her and said, "Told ya so."

FORTY-TWO

Shh! The Baby Is Sleeping!

The magical plant nursery shared *some* traits with the ordinary one. There were still rows of budding plants under fluorescent lights. There was still a concrete floor and the humid smell of piled leaves and muddy rainwater.

But that was where the similarities ended.

Along the shelves, Aru caught sight of a familiar green container of Miracle-Gro. Only this one sparkled, and when she looked closer, she saw that it read GROW MIRACLES! ADD A TOUCH OF WONDER TO YOUR GARDEN. Another one had been overturned and spread a gold puddle on the floor, which was sprouting unnatural objects, such as a small tree with coins for leaves, a weed with butterfly wings, and miniature topiary creatures. A beetle made of flower petals scuttled beneath an overturned ceramic pot.

Flowers of every size and shape grew from the lattice ceiling, crowding out the early-morning light. Aru had never heard growing things make sounds, but in the magical plant nursery there was a kind of music, high and bright, that conjured images of roots pushing through damp ground and newly opened blooms turning their faces to capture the sunshine.

Six towering moss-covered statues lined the back wall. They reminded Aru of mongooses, those weaselly creatures with clever paws and sleek bodies. Except the statues were the Hulked-out versions: their stone muscles bulged, and their jaws opened wide, revealing teeth so sharp Aru wondered if the wind got hurt just blowing past them. Though their stone eyes were unseeing, the statues gave off a sense of *waiting,* like a creature holding itself still while stalking prey.

"Those are forest yalis," said Rudy nervously, glancing up at the statues. "Guardians of whatever belongs to the forest goddess, Aranyani."

"Yalis?" echoed Aru. "Yeah, no thank you."

"They're not whispering to us, at least . . ." said Brynne, but even she looked wary.

Aiden yelped and stomped the floor, which made the rest of them crowd together into a tight knot.

"Is a yali coming out of—?" asked Aru.

"Just a spider," said Aiden, heaving a sigh of relief.

"For *now,*" said Brynne, stomping the floor herself for good measure.

"What's wrong with you guys?" asked Nikita, tossing her hair. "They're just statues."

"Until they come alive and turn into freaking crocodile things that snap at your feet!" said Rudy.

Nikita turned in a circle, then cupped her hands to her mouth. "Helloooo?" she called.

The floor started bubbling. Aru, Mini, Brynne, and Aiden crowded together, and Rudy darted behind them. Aru tried to grab Nikita, but the twin shrugged her off. Rising from the concrete, a life-size holographic image of a *yakshini* with pepper-gray moth wings appeared. She had rich brown skin the color of tree bark, tightly coiled black hair, a small heart-shaped mouth, and wide, friendly eyes. On her bright orange apron was a name tag that read I'M LIZZIE! ASK ME ABOUT TODAY'S GREAT DEALS!

The hologram seemed to be prerecorded. She fixed them with a bright smile, even though her eyes were focused somewhere slightly above their heads, and said, "Welcome to Aranyani's Garden Supplies, perfect for all your botanical needs! We are the world's leading supplier of guard manticores, behemoth-fire-ant pest control, alchemical flowers, and more! Our hours of operation are Monday through Friday, eight a.m. Eastern Standard Time to ten p.m. Otherworld Standard Time."

The holograph paused, its visage shimmering. "If you have arrived outside normal business hours, please record a message and our customer service representative will get back to you as soon as possible. And remember"—the holograph's smile grew even wider and she raised her arms, gesturing to the statues—"we are watching! Do not attempt to steal, incinerate, or otherwise compromise our stock. Have a wonderful day, and thank you for your patronage!"

The holograph disappeared.

"See?" said Nikita, crossing her arms. "Nothing to worry about! We don't steal, the yalis don't wake up. Now let's go."

And with that, she stalked off toward a row of plants.

Brynne beamed proudly. "She's so brave! She's like me when I was ten. Definitely a Pandava."

Mini shook her head. "When I was ten, I hid in the bathtub during thunderstorms."

Aru did not volunteer what she was like at ten years old, mostly because it involved two straws, Pumbaa's iconic line *When I was a young WARTHOG!*, and a very bad recess. Anyway.

"After you, Prince," said Aiden, moving aside to let Rudy break through the pack.

Rudy was still staring up at the yali statues. "I'll guard the exit?"

Brynne shoved him forward. "Nice try."

They followed Nikita to a bed of seedlings. It sprawled the length of a narrow dining table and came up to Aru's hip.

For the first time, Aru realized that what she thought was fluorescent lighting overhead was actually hardened beams of raw sunlight. On the underside of the floating beams, cramped black writing spelled out HARVESTED ON SEPTEMBER 24, 1993/ EXPIRES ON APRIL 7, 2023.

"Light has an expiration date?" asked Aru.

"*We're* going to have an expiration date if the plants get angry," said Rudy, pointing at a sign hanging below the table.

KEEP QUIET! WE'RE GROWING!

Aru risked a glance at the nearest yali. These didn't seem like the ones they'd met at the crypt, alive and slithering and snapping...they seemed like ordinary statues. But she didn't like the dark moss clinging to their faces. Or the sharpness of their teeth.

Then she noticed that a white chalk circle outlined the small nursery.

"That's *definitely* not good," said Rudy, following Aru's gaze. "I've seen enchantments like that in Naga-Loka. If a yali crossed that boundary, their kill mode would be activated."

"Nothing bad is going to happen if you do what I say," whispered Nikita.

She put her hands on top of the dirt, spreading her fingers as if she were pressing her palms into a soft blanket. She closed her eyes, humming, and then pulled her hands back.

"They're fussy," she said, rolling up her sleeves. "And full of magic. Very powerful."

"They don't look very powerful," said Brynne, peering down at the bed.

Aru had to agree. The plants didn't seem special, certainly not like they could reveal where the wish-granting tree was kept. The fifteen baby plants were arranged in three rows of five, their grass-green tops sticking barely three inches out of the dirt. It was only when she examined them close up that she saw some unusual qualities. There was touch of real gold in one plant's leaves. There was a heady scent to another, which seemed to conjure visions. One whiff and Aru saw corpses hanging from trees and a greedy, lengthening shadow. She jerked back, her heart pounding.

"That one is a dream rose," said Nikita, patting the top of its head.

"You mean nightmares?"

"Nightmares are just its defense mechanism," said Nikita.

The plant seemed to snuggle a little deeper into the earth. When Nikita turned her back, Aru stuck her tongue out at the rose.

"I have to talk to all of them," said Nikita. "Interview them one by one . . . But that means taking them out of the soil. Otherwise it's hard to hear through all the dirt and stuff."

Aru glanced again at the statues . . . so still.

Suspiciously still.

Nikita turned to look each of the Potatoes in the eye. "When I take them out, they'll be loud and fussy. You're going to have to keep them quiet, okay?"

"You want us to hush up some plants?" asked Brynne, rolling her eyes. "How hard can that be?"

FORTY-THREE

I'm Not a Regular Mom,
I'm a Cool Mom

One by one, Nikita lifted up the baby plants, whispering to them as a soft green glow enveloped her hands and face. And one by one, she put them back....

Only, the plants weren't asleep anymore.

And they definitely weren't happy.

Ten down, five to go. All ten of the uprooted baby plants threatened to summon the statues. One plant hiccupped loudly, and Aru felt her blood run cold as a mongoose statue started to creak. It wouldn't take much noise for the yali to peel off from the wall and take a step toward them.

"Shh, shh," said Aru to her two plants.

They were the color of dusty roses with chubby roots and squinty eyes beneath a riot of petals on their heads. Aru wasn't sure if plants even made expressions, but these two were definitely glaring at her.

"Be quiet or we'll die!" she said in a singsong voice.

One of the plants burped loudly in response, and dirt sprayed from its roots. The sound of stone grinding on stone echoed behind Aru. She snuck another glance at the yalis. The statues had halfway detached from the walls. It would take them ten steps to cross the room and reach the magical white-chalked boundary.

Once Nikita spoke to a plant, it was up to the Potatoes to shush them. But Aru's plants weren't cooperating. She tried to squish them back into the dirt, but they kept climbing out, making strange gurgling sounds, and sometimes wrapping their roots around her wrist.

"Stop that!" she scolded.

One of them began to cry, then the other. Why did *she* end up with the worst plant babies? Aru glanced around the table to see how everyone else was managing.

Mini was crouched over her pile of plants, diligently tucking them into the soft dirt. The fronded tops of their heads wilted in sleep... or maybe it was boredom. Mini seemed to be muttering something to the plants as she worked.

"What are you doing?" Aru asked.

Mini blinked up at her. "I'm telling them about the human anatomy! They're finding it so fascinating they're keeping quiet."

A low hum broke through the wailing of Aru's plants.

"They're snoring," said Aru.

Mini looked down and sighed. "I really thought they *liked* hearing about the endocrine system...."

Aru gathered her plants back in her arms, shivering when the cold dirt touched her skin. "Be quiet!" she said, trying to clamp a hand over a little plant mouth, which seemed to work until...

"OW!" she yelped, shaking out a bitten finger.

Aru felt the hairs on the back of her neck stand up. A creak sounded behind her. She risked a glance over her shoulder. The yalis were now seven steps away.

"What happened?" asked Brynne from the other side of her.

"It bit me!" hissed Aru in a low voice.

"Then bite back!"

Aru had zero desire to do that.

"Why aren't yours yelling?" Aru demanded.

Brynne dangled a packet of sugar. "Mixed some sugar and water and sprinkled it on them. Bam! Instant sleep."

"Do you have any more?" asked Aru, feeling frazzled. She tried bouncing the plants a little, but that shook some of the petals off their heads and they cried even louder.

"Nope, all out."

Behind her, Aru could hear the groans of the approaching statues. Five steps away.

"Get it together, Shah!" whisper-hissed Brynne.

Aru tried to cover the baby plants with more dirt when they suddenly quieted, their wrinkled faces upturned at the sight of... Vajra? Her lightning bolt shone softly on her wrist, and the plants reached their leaves toward it curiously.

"That's right," crooned Aru, piling dirt onto their roots. "Look at the shiny thing! Shiny, shiny, shiny."

At the front of the table, Nikita continued murmuring to the plants. The one cupped in her hands was now violet, and its ink-black roots waved around like the tentacles of an octopus. Nikita raised her head, grinning.

"This one knows!" she said. "But it has trouble talking... bit of a root lisp, so keep it quiet."

Aru was severely offended.

HELLO, she wanted to say, *did you not see the miraculous feat I just performed?* Well, probably not. Aru continued to move her hand back and forth over the baby plants, who kept turning their heads to watch Vajra, hypnotized by the light. It was now totally silent in the plant nursery. Behind her, the mongoose statues took a step back, and Aru's heart rate slowed. Soon, they'd be against the wall again and—

"WAHHHHH!"

A huge piercing wail rose from Aiden and Rudy's section. Nikita held her plant closer and glared at the boys. "I said quiet! You're scaring this one!"

A squat green potato-plant baby with one orange spike on the top of its head sat between Rudy and Aiden, howling.

Rudy picked it up and bounced it in his hands. "It's *your* fault!" he said to Aiden. "It liked chewing on the jewel, and you took it away!"

"Because it could choke!" said Aiden, tossing one of Rudy's shiny gems over his shoulder.

"They're *plants!*"

"And that jewel could cut its roots!" said Aiden, snatching back the baby and awkwardly patting its spiky head. "Shh . . ."

"You're so controlling!" said Rudy, reaching for the plant baby.

Aiden gripped it harder, giving Rudy his shoulder. "You're reckless!"

"Uh, boys?" tried Aru as the ground began to tremble.

"Well you're *boring!*" said Rudy. "At least I'm *fun*—"

"Fun? Fatal? What's the difference to you?" demanded Aiden.

"AIDEN," shouted Brynne.

He stopped and swiveled around. The statues all took one thunderous step forward. Aru wondered if she could just zap them backward with Vajra, but the moment she moved her wrist away, her baby plants started to wail.

In three more steps the yalis would be at the boundary.

"Stay where you are, Aru," said Mini. "I'll make sure they can't get to us."

She let loose her Death Danda, but the violet glare woke her plants and set them howling.

"Oh no!" said Mini. "Don't be frightened! Remember the cardiovascular system? Wasn't that fun?"

Her plants howled louder, as if saying *It was not fun!*

The yalis were now two steps away. Small pebbles quivered and tumbled on the ground and the statues' feet sent up tiny dust storms when they moved.

"I've got this!" yelled Brynne.

She brandished her wind mace but only succeeded in kicking up the dust and sending it swirling around the plant-nursery bed. A chorus of wails sliced through the air. The statues towered over the babysitters, casting a cold shadow over everything. The Potatoes couldn't leave the baby plants, but they'd be killed if they stayed put. The mongoose statues slowly raised their fists as each lifted a foot to take the final step....

"Almost have it!" yelled Nikita. "Just make it quiet!"

Aru was torn. Any movement from her would only make her plants scream louder and the statues move faster. Vajra, equally torn, kept shifting back and forth between a spear and a bracelet.

A sound cut through the plants' crying and the statues' creaking movements....

A song.

Aiden was singing a lullaby. All the baby plants began to nestle contentedly in the dirt. Some of them propped clumps of soil behind their fronds like loamy pillows. The yali statues stepped back.

Aru wasn't even sure the song had lyrics. Aiden's singing was like Rudy's gift with the jewels. It summoned a feeling of contentment, like spending the whole day out on the lake or at the pool, drowsy with sunshine.

Brynne's warning rang through Aru's head: *Don't look at him. He's using one of his apsara powers.*

Aru tried her best, but the lure of the song was too strong.... She couldn't help herself. She looked.

Aiden appeared backlit by the sun. An invisible wind stirred his dark hair, and the plants beneath him glowed.

She knew the stories about apsaras. How they were not just beautiful, but capable of drawing the whole world's focus. It made them dangerous and sought-after. All this time, Aru had thought it was all just poetic exaggeration....

But when she gazed at Aiden now, the nursery fell away. Aru imagined the world was frosted over, snow spangling like diamonds, and she and Aiden were dancing the way people did in movies. Not a movie where the wind was blowing her hair and all the landscapes kept changing and people could somehow dance and sing at the same time, but dancing the way she imagined it should be... where you're held close and the music is the humming of hearts and—

"*Okaaaaay*, gonna reel you back in now," said a voice.

Aru blinked to find that she had her arms lifted as if she were dancing a waltz. Brynne gently brought them back down to her sides.

Rudy was laughing. Mini was shaking her head in pity. And

Aiden? He was staring at her. The plants beneath him cooed in sleep, and the yalis had reclaimed their spaces against the wall and gone still.

"Next time, just set me on fire," Aru whispered to Brynne, her face flaming.

"I told you not to look when he does his apsara thing."

Aru scowled.

"How come you didn't do that earlier?" Mini asked Aiden.

"I didn't want Nikita's plant to fall asleep."

"Oh."

Unfortunately for Aru's wounded dignity, that made sense. At the other end of the nursery table, Nikita gently lowered her now-slumbering plant back into the earth. When she looked up, a huge grin split her face.

"I got it," she whispered.

"Where's the tree?" asked Brynne.

"The Atlanta Botanical Garden," said Nikita. "It's the only place in the mortal world that has direct access to something called the Botanical Pavilion of Lost Cities? Kinda like the Otherworld, but with more plants."

"What?" said Aru. "It's been *there* all this time?"

Aru had been to the Atlanta Botanical Garden often. Around Christmastime, her mom would take her to see the holiday lights show, where the whole garden got dressed up in shimmering colors and the air smelled like cocoa and cider.

She'd seen all the exhibits, and there was no way a ginormous wish-granting tree was hiding in one of them. How would that even work? Statistically, there *had* to have been one visitor who offhandedly said, *I wish I had some ice cream right now,* only to have a huge vat of it land on their head. Wouldn't someone report that? Or maybe they thought it was so awesome they didn't want to share the news, and kept it to themselves. . . .

That's totally what she would've done.

"Let's go!" said Brynne, but Rudy stood frozen, still stunned. He flailed a hand at Aiden.

"You can *sing*?" asked Rudy, awed.

"Sometimes," said Aiden cagily.

"Wait, with my music and your voice—"

Aiden winced. "Please don't—"

"We—"

"No."

"Should start—"

"Rudy. *No*."

"A BAND."

FORTY-FOUR

Who Is Groot?

The five Potatoes and Nikita—who refused to let the others call her a Potato—climbed out of a Lyft and stood outside the entrance to the Atlanta Botanical Garden. The gardens weren't open yet, and there were no other people around. Even the cars ambled by sleepily, no one honking or rolling down the window to ask what the six kids were up to so early in the morning.

Everything about the gardens looked familiar to Aru. She recognized the wide bronze entrance gates, the scent of cut grass and distant roses, the wide banners proclaiming the exhibits that lay inside.

What she did *not* recognize was the smaller gate, just to the right of the official entrance, hidden in the shade of a myrtle tree and positively radiating with magic.

Aru waved her hand across it, feeling the air warp around her skin as the smaller gate's enchantments pushed back at her.

"Okay, I was wrong," said Aru. "Maybe this place really *is* hiding the wishing tree."

"Told ya so," chirped Nikita brightly.

"So how do we get in?" asked Brynne.

"I really don't want to use that key again," said Aru.

"Me neither," said Aiden.

"Weird," Rudy said, poking the asphalt on the street. "You don't use crushed stars in your pavement?"

"Rudy, please get back on the sidewalk," said Mini.

"I'm exploring!"

"You'll be roadkill," said Brynne.

"It has a sort of decrepit charm to it," said Rudy. "I'll buy two streets. Who do I pay? Hello?"

Everyone ignored him as Nikita walked right up to the tree next to the silver gate and knocked on the bark twice.

"Knock-knock," said Aru jokingly.

"Who's out there?" came a voice from inside the tree.

Aru jerked back. Even though she now knew that plants could speak, she hadn't expected the tree to respond to a knock-knock joke.

Especially not with a deep Southern twang.

Nikita lifted her chin. "*We* are the—"

Aru waved her hands, mouthing, *Don't say our names!*

As much as possible, they had to keep their mission secret.

"Y'all have to give me a name if you wish to enter the Botanical Pavilion of Lost Cities," said the tree, annoyed.

"Potatoes?" tried Mini.

"Y'all are obviously not taters. But if you are, bless your hearts."

"First compliment I've gotten all week," said Aru.

"If I don't have me a name in the next five seconds, I am shutting—"

"No!" said Aru.

"Your name is No?"

"No," said Mini.

"Is that a yes?"

"GROOT," said Aru, running with the first thing that popped into her head. "I am... Groot."

"We're all... Groot?" said Aiden.

The tree went silent, and Aru mentally kicked herself. *GROOT? That* was the name her brain supplied at the last second?

Bad brain, thought Aru.

Her brain instantly reacted by putting "Escape (The Piña Colada Song)" into her head.

"We gave you a name, now let us through," said Aru.

"All right, all right. No need to pitch a fit. No one wants to come out here today anyhow. It's Holi." The tree sighed, bowing its top and shaking down leaves.

The silver gate swung open, and they filed in as quickly as they could. As the entrance shut behind them, Aru heard the tree muttering:

"Awful names... Imagine introducing yourself like that. 'I am Groot,'" grumbled the tree. "Almost as inane as 'I am the Sleeper.'"

"Did you hear that?" asked Aru. She snapped her fingers and Vajra lengthened into a full-size spear.

Brynne had already drawn her mace, and Mini's Death Danda was at maximum length, too. Aiden's scimitars peeked out from his sleeves, and even Rudy had his messenger bag full of enchanted jewels unzipped and ready.

"The Sleeper is here," Aru said, keeping her voice hushed.

"Does that mean Sheela is here, too?" asked Nikita. Her

fingers flew to the little green heart at her throat, probably hoping to feel her twin nearby, Aru guessed.

"Nikki, I'm sorry, but your tracker was turned off back at the House of the Moon?" said Mini gently. "For your safety."

Nikita removed her hand, her expression hardening.

"If she's here, we'll find her," said Brynne firmly.

They stood on a wide pebbled walkway lined with waterfalls that stretched high above them. Huge plumes of steam and fog rose in the air, hiding the tops, so it kind of felt like walking through the middle of a parted ocean. Beneath their feet the polished river stones stretched out a good three hundred feet before disappearing into mist. A small sign to the right read:

UP AHEAD: BOTANICAL PAVILION OF LOST CITIES

"Mini and I can take the lead," said Brynne.

Mini nodded, unleashing a violet force field in front of the two of them.

"Aiden and Rudy, you guys take the middle," said Brynne. "Aru, you and Nikita guard the rear."

"Can I guard from there, too?" asked Rudy.

"No."

While the others took off, Aru hung back. Nikita was lagging even farther behind. The girl's hand was pressed to her chest, and there was a look on her face that Aru recognized instantly. Loneliness.

"Hey," said Aru, nudging her a bit. "We're going to find her, okay?"

Nikita looked up. She usually seemed much more composed than a typical ten-year-old. But in that second, her eyes welled with terror. It was the same expression she'd worn in the nightmare, when she'd stretched out her hand to the mother who was leaving her behind just to keep her safe.

Nikita took a deep breath before saying in a small voice, "I believe you. I'll always believe you now."

That made Aru stop short. What a strange burden, she thought, to be depended on like that. It made her feel like she was somehow ten times taller, and only for the purpose of protecting the twins who looked up to her. Nikita took her hand, and Aru felt a surge of warmth and fear. Was this what being an older sister was like? Wanting to yell at someone most of the time but still being willing to jump in front of a car for them?

If so, it was awful.

"You're not alone," said Aru, squeezing Nikita's hand.

"I know," said Nikita. But even as she said it, Aru noticed that her nature powers kept manifesting as a twist of vines wrapping around her dress like armor. "It's just...new."

"Better get used to it," said Aru.

Nikita beamed. She dropped Aru's hand and tugged at the faded T-shirt Aru wore, wrinkling her nose in disdain.

"You need some fashion tips."

"It's not that bad," grumbled Aru.

Nikita fixed her with a pitying look.

Up ahead, Brynne called out, "Uh, guys? We might need some help here...."

Aru frowned as she and Nikita made their way to the others. *What's the big deal?* she thought. Why couldn't they just walk into this pavilion and—

Oh, wait. Never mind.

The Botanical Pavilion of Lost Cities wasn't a gazebo in a

courtyard—it was an entire island. The Pavilion floated in the air within a ring of silent waterfalls that each made Niagara Falls look like a water fountain. Huge plumes of steam cast fractured rainbows around the landmass, and wispy clouds veiled it from every side. Nearly a hundred feet in the air, the island hovered within two beams of light—one of sunshine and one of starlight.

How are we supposed to get to it? wondered Aru. The walkway of river stones ended abruptly at a steep drop into churning water filled with sharp black rocks.

"Are we supposed to fly there?" demanded Rudy.

"*I* could . . ." said Brynne.

"If the Sleeper's up there, we *have* to go together," said Mini. "But if he *is* in the Pavilion . . . how'd he even get there?"

"I expect he used *that*," said Aiden, pointing down.

That's when Aru noticed two sturdy posts on either side of the path, both looped with rope. She looked over the edge of the cliff to see one end of a rickety wooden bridge dangling like a ladder, its other end floating in the water.

"Welp," she said.

In a flash of blue light, Brynne transformed into a turquoise falcon. She cawed once, dove toward the rapids, gathered the other end of the bridge in her beak, and flew back to them. The moment she transformed into her normal self, the planks fell in a pile at her feet.

"Plah!" said Brynne, spitting. "Wet rope tastes awful."

Aiden knelt by the ends of the rope and held them up. "Someone cut these deliberately."

"So how do we get to the Tree of Wishes?" asked Rudy.

"I can repair the bridge," said Nikita, moving to the front.

"I'll keep up the shield," said Mini.

"And if there's anyone waiting for us on that island"—Brynne's grin turned savage as she thudded her mace against her palm—"they won't know what hit 'em."

"I'll, uh, just, you know, stay here," said Rudy, ducking behind Mini.

"Not a chance," said Aiden.

Nikita raised her palms, and huge green vines manifested around her wrists. She extended her arms and the vines grew outward, entangling with the severed ropes and weaving themselves in between the planks. The vines kept lengthening until the bridge spanned the chasm again, and then they wrapped themselves securely around two posts on the island. Nikita snapped her fingers and the vines fell off her wrists, slithered over to the two nearby posts, and took a firm hold.

Brynne tugged the rope a few times and then nodded. "It's ready."

"I'll go first in case it needs any strengthening," said Nikita.

"If I go next, I can anchor the force field better," said Mini.

"And if I go behind Mini, I probably won't die," said Rudy.

"Move out!" said Brynne.

"What about—?" started Aru and Aiden at the same time.

"You guys have a lightning bolt and two scimitars. On a bridge made of *vines*," said Brynne, shaking her head. "Keep your weapons close to your body. And, Shah, please don't set anything on fire."

"I resent that," muttered Aru.

As they marched across the bridge, Aru felt her stomach

swoop with every movement. The bridge might have been strong, but it swayed with their steps. And with each sway, Aru felt fresh terror climbing up her body.

To distract herself, she looked over her shoulder at Aiden. "So . . . you sing, huh?"

"Don't start with me, Shah," said Aiden, rolling his eyes. "Rudy won't stop asking me to be part of his band. He wants to call it 'Rudy Rocks.'"

Aru snorted, imagining Rudy running around a stage, strategically placing his enchanted stones and gems.

"Honestly, it's so bad it's almost great," said Aru, grinning.

Aru was possessed by a sudden terrible urge to add a *wink.* The muscles in her left eyelid were going rogue. *What are you* doing? she mentally screamed at them. *Stop that!* Slowly, her left eyebrow flattened like a depressed penguin.

"Um, is there something in your eye?" asked Aiden.

"Delusions of grandeur," she muttered.

"What?"

"Eyelash," she said, rubbing furiously at her eyeball.

"We made it!" called Mini.

Aru kept her gaze straight ahead as they stepped onto the floating island. The ground beneath them was lush and green. Thick curtains of fog and steam from the waterfall slowly parted to reveal what could only be called a paradise. Or rather, *paradises,* for there were several.

In the sky above, a cluster of flowering trees hung upside down next to a winged-lion statue holding a sign that read FOR THE HANGING GARDENS OF BABYLON, TURN RIGHT. A few feet beyond that, the greenery gave way to a desert landscape with a palm-tree oasis and different instructions: FOR ZERZURA,

TURN LEFT. Aru also saw a path of clover that wound its way to Tir na Nog, the Irish fairylands, and signs that pointed the way to vast world trees that could hold whole cities in their branches.

Directly in front of them, in the center of it all, was a small white sign:

FOR THE GROVE OF ARANYANI,
STAND PERFECTLY STILL.

FORTY-FIVE

Please Don't Say You're Inevitable

Everyone stayed put as thin glowing roots shot out from the earth, wrapped around their ankles like chains, and *tugged* them downward. Aru flinched, not knowing what to expect, but the next thing she knew they were standing in the middle of an enclosed grove the size of an Olympic swimming pool. Silvery rivulets of water streamed down the rock walls, and wisps of fog curled overhead, letting in a few rays of sunlight.

Before them towered trees unlike any Aru had ever imagined. They had gold and silver bark, silk leaves, and jewels instead of blossoms. Some trees were laden with musical notes like clusters of berries, and there were parchment oaks covered in fine print that grew book fruit beneath their inky branches. She even saw a tree that looked as if it were made of actual paint, with daubed apples and violet-smudged plums.

Aru stared around at the place, drinking in the smells, feeling the light warm her face. She nervously weighed the two beads inserted in her necklace. They were so close to completing their mission. So close to stopping the Sleeper from hurting their families and damaging their homes. When Aru closed her eyes, she pictured Boo staring up at a false wishing tree, hoping for freedom. The twins holding back tears and wishing to be back with their parents. The Otherworld she loved going up in flames...

And yet, there was still a hollowness inside her as she touched the necklace. Every piece they'd found told her that she'd been robbed of something she didn't know how to miss, and it made her furious. Surely, Suyodhana hadn't made it to this grove before he became the Sleeper. Because if he had, things would've been different.

Maybe Aru would never have had to grow up without a dad. Maybe they would've come to this little island of paradises not to stop the Otherworld from being ripped apart... but because they wanted to have a picnic.

Maybe, maybe, maybe.

It was a cruel chant at the back of her thoughts.

"The tree's not here," said Nikita.

That snapped Aru out of her thoughts. "What?"

"But we're out of time! Today is Holi!" said Brynne. "If we don't find the wish-granting tree, the whole Otherworld—"

"It's not in this grove," said Nikita, holding up her hand. "But I can sense it nearby, the way I can sense Sheela."

"But I thought your gift from your soul dad was deactivated," said Mini, pointing to the little green heart.

Nikita waved away her concern. "I don't need that to know when my twin is nearby."

"She's here?" asked Mini, whirling around.

"Close . . . She's hidden somehow," said Nikita.

Aru's pulse raced, and she found it hard to breathe. If Sheela was here, then that meant the Sleeper was close, too.

"So let's search the place," said Rudy. "How hard can that be?"

Aiden frowned, squinting into the distance. He released his scimitars and turned in a slow circle.

Small rocks came tumbling down the walls, spraying up dirt when they hit the ground. Aiden raised his scimitars only for something to hurl him backward, slamming him against a boulder.

"Aiden!" yelled Rudy, running over to him.

The Pandavas instantly fell into battle formation.

A huge *rrrrip* sounded right behind them.

They whirled around to see the earth tearing open as though someone were rending cloth. Roots, dirt, and rocks flew up from the hole as shadows poured out of the ground, blanketing the grass. Something was coming for them, and they were too out in the open.

"Head to the back wall!" yelled Brynne.

They sprinted to the designated spot as Rudy half carried, half dragged Aiden after them. The rip in the earth chased him, as though a huge worm were burrowing under the dirt.

Aru felt the ground tremble. "Shields up!" she yelled.

Mini used Dee Dee to form a protective dome. Nikita plunged her hands into the earth, and pale roots as thick as iron bars sprang up, forming a fence around them. She whispered something, and thorns like white knives shot out from the roots, their sharp ends pointed outward.

But just as fast as the commotion had started, it stopped. The rip ended a mere five feet from where the Potatoes were huddled together. The shadows that had poured out of the ground were quickly sucked back into the tear, leaving nothing behind but trampled grass.

There were footprints . . . but no one was there.

A weighted silence fell over the grove, broken only by a soft groan from Aiden.

"You okay, Wifey?" whispered Mini.

Aiden managed a weak nod, dropping his arm from around Rudy's shoulder. "Thanks," he mumbled.

"You're my lead singer," said Rudy proudly. "*Nothing* is happening to you."

"I'm also your cousin!"

"Second priority, honestly," said Rudy, but he smiled like he'd just won a prize.

"What *was* that?" asked Brynne, staring out at the rip.

Mini's force field started to waver. Sweat sheened on her forehead, and Aru could tell she was getting tired. Aru's gaze darted from the rock walls to the trees on either side of them—one of them made of paint, the other a weeping willow from whose branches fat diamonds hung like tears.

Something had definitely tried to attack them. . . .

So why had it stopped?

Nikita was still crouched, her fingers spread on the dirt. She pulled back her hands with a shudder.

"What is it?" asked Brynne anxiously.

Nikita turned to them slowly, her eyes wide. "Heartbeats," she said. "The ground hears *dozens* of heartbeats."

A chill ran down Aru's spine. Heartbeats meant people. But there was no one here....

Thud.

Thud.

Thud.

In front of them, Mini's shield began to crack. Aru, pressed to the outside of the group, heard a low panting sound right by her ear. She whirled around, Vajra springing to life in her hand. Nothing. Her gaze fell to the ground.

The grass was flattened.

Someone had been standing there.

"I—can't—maintain—this—much—longer," said Mini, her arms trembling as she held up Dee Dee.

"Then we'll fight them," said Brynne, raising her wind mace.

"We can't even *see* them!" said Aru.

"Get ready!" yelled Mini.

From there, everything happened at once. The shield snapped in half. Nikita spread out her arms, and the fence of roots and thorns exploded outward. Something yelped in pain. For a split second, one of Nikita's thorns seemed stuck fast to the air. But whoever it had caught quickly ripped it out and flung it to the ground.

Brynne spun out her wind mace, zooming it back and forth. The far side of the rock wall trembled as bodies made contact, loosening stones. The grass was crushed by a sudden weight.

In Aru's hands, Vajra quivered like a strung bow, prickling with energy. *Why are you hiding, you cowards?* she thought, her fingers tingling.

In front of her, Mini was casting force fields left and right.

Sometimes no one was there, other times there was a loud thud, and saliva dribbled down the edge of the shield. Nikita pulled roots out of the earth and whipped them around like spiked snakes. Aru cast out a net and caught...

Nothing.

Vajra flew back into her hand just as a gust of warm breath stirred the hair behind her neck. Aru yelped, pivoted, then aimed Vajra like a javelin. Her lightning bolt hit the ground, then bounced back to her hand.

In the air around her, Aru heard a low cackle.

Aiden, now fully recovered, beat his scimitars together. He paused for a moment, then jabbed them up....

A metallic clang sounded. He must have made contact. Aiden almost grinned, but then fell flat on his face, groaning. Someone had hit him from behind.

Rudy caught one of the falling scimitars and slashed it in the air over Aiden. Rudy made a sharp hiss.

"All right, that's it," he said.

He looked down at his jeans, then let out a sigh, murmuring, "I can do this...I *can do this.*"

The scales on his wrist gleamed bright green. In a flash of light, he shot up to well over six feet. His legs fused and twisted into a red tail with bands of yellow.

His eyes glowed green as he slithered around Aiden, his powerful tail swiping the air. Something hit the wall, dislodging stones, and Rudy grinned.

Aru thought she caught a shadow on the ground, and she threw her lightning javelin at it. Before she could tell whether it landed, she doubled over in pain as an object caught her around the middle like a hook, snapping her backward. She fell to the ground, clawing at the earth, scrabbling to get back to her sisters. But whoever caught her was stronger. And faster.

"Aru!" screamed Nikita.

Aru was dragged back nearly twenty feet before the hook released her. She slumped to the ground as Vajra zoomed around her, surrounding her with a lightning net. She pushed herself to a standing position, her heart racing. Shadows poured out of the torn ground once more, but this time they blanketed the grove in a poisonous-looking fog. A low laugh filled the sanctuary, and the trees quivered.

Aru knew that laugh. She heard, even, the traces of what it had once been—the kind of deep belly laugh that warms the people who hear it.

Not anymore.

Aru jerked her head around but saw nothing.

The fog floated toward her. She had to act. *Now.*

Aru snapped her fingers, and Vajra flattened into a hoverboard beneath her feet. Something grazed her wrist, but she was quick. One leap and she zoomed over the fog, back to her family. She tumbled to the ground, and when she righted herself, Vajra was a powerful spear in her hand.

The Pandavas formed a tight circle. Rudy hissed, slapping the earth with his tail. Brynne whirled her mace. Mini held out her Death Danda. Nikita crouched on the ground, her fingers in the earth. Aiden had his scimitars at the ready.

But no fight came.

Nothing barreled toward them.

A low, dark voice spoke:

"You see what I can do? What I can take from you?"

Aru squeezed her eyes shut, willing herself not to recall Suyodhana's memories. His pain. His *love.*

It's not him anymore, she told herself.

But she hated the part of her that wished it was.

"It's almost impressive how far incompetence can take you these days," said the Sleeper.

"Thanks," said Aru, steeling her voice. "We try."

"And you will fail," said the Sleeper, simply. "You see, children, this war is mine to win. It always has been. If I have to spill your blood, I will not hesitate. But I will give you an option to live a little longer. For I am—"

"Inevitable?" asked Aru.

The Sleeper paused. "What?"

"Please don't tell me you were going to steal your villain line from Thanos."

A different voice, off to the left, asked, "Do we know him—?"

"Quiet," said the Sleeper.

There was a sharp *smack!* followed by a whimper.

Brynne pointed out a shadow to the left and some newly trampled grass. The walls surrounding them groaned, as if being pressed by hundreds of heavy shoulders. Aru's gaze flicked to the tree of paint and the willow tree closest to them, looking for any signs of movement among the branches.

"The truth is I *am* inevitable, Aru Shah," said the Sleeper. "I am war. And I am destiny. Now *give* me the girl."

From behind her sisters, Nikita hollered, "There's *NO* way I'm helping you!"

The air rippled. Sheela appeared, gagged with a shadow and bound with silvery ropes. Her eyes looked frantic, but she held up her chin.

"And what about her?" asked the Sleeper.

Nikita faltered. She looked to Aru and Brynne, torn. Aru set her jaw.

"Use your powers to bring me to the wishing tree, and I will return your sister to you," said the Sleeper. "After all, you cannot win a fight against an army you cannot even see."

Aru's hands balled into fists as she stared at the ground, the Sleeper's words running through her mind. Only one word caught hold: *see.*

The time for the prophecy had run out. Today was Holi. People would be celebrating. Feasting. Throwing colored powders at one another. . . .

Aru's eyes darted to the paint tree on her left. Brilliant colors dripped from its boughs. There was a smudgy quality to it, its bark made with daubs of paint. The branches were slender paintbrushes, and from their bristled ends hung wet fruit of every shade imaginable.

An idea took root.

Aru caught Aiden's attention. He looked at her questioningly, his scimitars still raised in anticipation of a fight. She subtly pointed to the tree of paint, and then to him and Rudy. Their eyes went wide.

Next, Aru tapped into her sisters' minds.

Get ready. We're going to celebrate Holi.

FORTY-SIX

Green Is *Not* Your Color, Trust Me

Aru tightened her grip on Vajra.

The six of them had lined up next to each other. Nikita's lip trembled as she stared at Sheela. Aru squeezed her shoulder, and Nikita looked up at her, her eyes shining, before her eyes searched the grove full of twisting black shadows.

"First... give me my sister," said Nikita. "And then... then I'll help you find the tree."

"Come and get her," said the Sleeper.

His voice seemed to come from everywhere—the ground, the rocks, the trees themselves.

Nikita took one step forward.

To Aru's left, just beyond the weeping willow, there came a low growl that made the hairs on the back of her neck prickle. She swung out Vajra....

The shadows twisted anxiously. Invisible hooves dug into the earth. Brynne jumped, smacking the back of her neck as if a bug had landed there. Her mace whipped the air beside her, which made Aiden slash out his scimitars. Rudy reared up on his tail, adjusting his grip on the short dagger Aiden had given him.

"Now, now," said the Sleeper. "None of that. We have a deal, don't we?"

Aru faltered, wanting to grab Nikita and pull her back to safety, but the youngest Pandava stepped outside her grasp.

Nikita squared her shoulders. The crown of flowers around her head glittered like jewels. Her daisy-patterned dress suddenly seemed like a child's Halloween costume, and Aru almost couldn't bring herself to watch as Nikita took one step . . . then two . . . then five . . . until she had reached her twin.

Sheela trembled as the fog writhed around her ankles like chains.

The twins stared at each other wordlessly, and then reached out. They touched fingers for barely an instant before Nikita whirled and dropped to the ground, plunging her fist into the dirt.

"NOW!" she shouted.

The fog twitched beneath Sheela, but Nikita was stronger and faster. A mesh of white thorns knitted itself around both twins, forming a spiked spherical cocoon. A green glow lit it up from the inside as tufts of cotton blossoms poked through, cushioning them. As one, the Pandavas launched fruit from the nearby tree into the air. Brynne swung her mace like a baseball bat, and the produce arced in the air, landing with heavy *splats*.

Colors burst from the fruit and dribbled down invisible forms, exposing various enemies. Not ten feet away, they saw the furred haunch of a rakshasa with the body of a wolf. Brynne blasted him backward with a powerful swing from Gogo. Paint splatter from the impact revealed a row of horns marching toward them. Aru threw Vajra like a javelin, and the demons fell to the ground. A pink pod splashed the face of a naga, and Mini took him out with a sharp twist of her shield. Aru reached for another paint fruit and pitched it forward. It burst in midair, coating a knot of demons. Green dripped down the horns of an asura, who bellowed in fury. Aiden dashed forward, knocking the sword from the asura's hand and jabbing him in the forehead with the hilt of his scimitar.

"Keep throwing!" yelled Aru. She looked around frantically for the Sleeper but didn't see him anywhere. What was he up to?

More fruit volleyed through the air....

Soon the army, which seemed to fill the whole grove, was dotted with color, as though the soldiers had been playing a game of paintball.

A wash of white from a giant apple splattered on the ground before the Potatoes, catching the tails of a pair of nagas who were trying to snake toward the group.

"For *shame!*" said Rudy.

He borrowed one of Aiden's scimitars and skewered the ends of their tails to the ground. They screamed and hissed, coiling back on themselves.

Rudy dumped out the contents of his messenger bag and began tossing darkly gleaming gemstones into the horde. Howls and moans filled the air as the troops scattered.

"Nightmare stones," Rudy explained.

It was something.

But it wasn't enough.

The writhing mass of the Sleeper's army recovered and they marched and slunk, ran and dove toward them. There had to be dozens of the Sleeper's soldiers, whereas there were only six on Aru's team. There was no way they could win. The words of Sheela's prophecy set fire to Aru's nerves.

No war can be won without finding that root. . . .
In five days the treasure will bloom and fade,
And all that was won could soon be unmade.

Only Kalpavriksha could bring an end to this fight. And Aru knew she couldn't find the tree by herself. With Vajra, she blasted back another stretch of foggy shadows. Once the air had cleared, the thorny cocoon holding the twins rolled toward them.

Mini forged a protective shield over the twins. While Brynne, Aiden, and Rudy handled the enemy, the cocoon broke open. Sheela and Nikita stood inside, with one tiny difference:

They'd switched clothes.

"I know where the Tree of Wishes is," Nikita whispered breathlessly to Aru. "I heard it in the ground."

"You have to take me," said Aru.

"Nikki," said Sheela, clutching her twin tightly.

"It's okay . . ." said Nikita. "We'll be right back, I promise. You're safer with these guys."

Aru fought back the panic rising inside her. "We *will* protect you," she said firmly. "Trust me."

Sheela looked up at her, a flash of silver lighting up her blue eyes. "I do."

"Go!" yelled Mini. She lowered the protective shield and turned the Potatoes—plus Sheela—invisible instead.

Nikita tugged on Aru's hand, and together they sprinted through the chaos, weaving in and out of the trees, until they squeezed through a crack in the wall.

FORTY-SEVEN

We're Not Lost, Are We?

"Where are we going?" asked Aru. "Wasn't that Aranyani's Grove back there?"

Nikita pulled Aru along and summoned walls of vines to hide them. As they ran, the battle sounds behind them faded.

After a few minutes, Nikita stopped in front of a tall boulder. She breathed heavily as she conjured one last vine screen behind them.

"It's here," said Nikita.

Uh, Aru wanted to say, *this is just a big rock.*

The sound of whispering made her jump. With an invisible enemy, every noise was treacherous. But when she looked around, she saw no sign of the Sleeper—no trampled grass or shadow out of place. She sensed no hum of dark magic.

Another whisper skittered past. Vajra sprang off her wrist and sparked to life as a short spear.

"Listen," said Nikita, pressing her ear to the boulder. As soon as she touched it, silver rivulets ran down the rock.

Aru took a closer look and saw that it wasn't water, but an

endless skein of silvery threads. They looked like hammered pieces of ice that had been enchanted to flow smoothly.

A chorus of voices lifted into the air:

"I should have told her that I loved her. . . ."

"I should have returned home when Mother fell ill. . . ."

"I should have spent my life appreciating what I had, rather than always seeking more. . . ."

"I should have—"

"I should have—"

"I should have—"

The rock was weeping people's regrets. The moment Aru heard them, her necklace glowed softly, as if answering a call.

Nikita placed her hands on the boulder, and a crack split it down the middle. The sides swung in like doors. They stepped through, and the rock seamed shut behind them.

The Pandava sisters found themselves standing at the base of an enormous tree. It was so huge that Aru couldn't get a sense of how wide the trunk was. It seemed to disappear into the shimmery mist crawling in from every side. Huge silver roots bulged out of the ground, towering over them. A thick carpet of autumn leaves edged in frost crunched underfoot. The tree's bark looked like the surface of a mirror, and etched into it was script in a language Aru didn't recognize. But even though she couldn't read what it said, she somehow understood that the tree protected something important, as if the pulse of the universe flowed beneath its roots.

Aru looked up and *up,* and still she could not see where the branches started. The more she strained her eyes, the less she could detect beyond a feeling of incomprehensible vastness, as if the tree held not just leaves but forgotten civilizations and the names of dead kings, lengthy histories that had passed on to the realm of myth, and stories so numerous that they outnumbered the stars.

"Is this Kalpavriksha?" she asked in awe.

Nikita shook her head. "That's a world tree. Meant to nourish the universe and hold it up. But the wish-granting tree is close. . . . I can feel it. Maybe it's around the trunk—"

Crash!

The rock door burst open, and shadows poured through, rolling into a black shape that towered to nearly eight feet. Within the cloudy form, Aru caught the flash of two eyes: one blue, one brown.

The Sleeper.

He stretched out a hand cloaked in darkness. His fingers ended in sharp red-tinged claws and he curled them in a terrible summons:

"Show me the wish-granting tree," he growled. "It was always supposed to be mine."

Aru flung Vajra at him, but he batted it away as if it were a gnat. Vajra emitted an electrical yelp before bounding back to Aru.

"Run, Aru!" screamed Nikita. "Go!"

"I won't leave you!" said Aru.

Nikita slammed her palms together. Roses of every size and color cascaded down her body like a ball gown unfurling. Their branches reached for the shadows and grew around the Sleeper, trapping him in a net of thorns. He roared and thrashed inside, drawing the darkness around him like a protective cape.

"Go," choked out Nikita as she reinforced the cage. "I'll keep him busy here."

"I don't want to leave you," said Aru, her voice breaking.

Nikita looked at her, her blue eyes wide, her smile shaky and fragile. "But sometimes you have to. . . . I can fight. Fierce and fashionable, remember?"

Her chin wobbled, and Aru hated that she'd dragged Nikita into this. Every part of Aru wanted to stay with her sister, but if she didn't find the tree, none of them would make it out and the Otherworld would be destroyed. Tears pricked at her eyes, but Aru needed to be strong. For both of them.

"I'll be quick," said Aru. "I'll fix this. I swear it."

As she turned on her heel and sprinted off, she heard Nikita's voice carrying over the air.

"I believe you."

Aru raced around the vast trunk of the world tree, feeling foolish. There were no other trees in plain sight. Where would you even hide a miracle as magnificent as Kalpavriksha?

The silvery fog rolled to her right. Part of her was tempted to run into it and see if the tree was hiding there, but something stayed her impulse. Whenever she looked too long at the silver mist, her necklace burned.

As if telling her, *No, not there.*

Aru slowed to a stop. She risked a glance over her shoulder. She couldn't hear the Sleeper anymore. Or, she thought with a pang, Nikita. It was as if Aru had stepped into another realm entirely.

Around her was nothing but fog, and the massive mirrored trunk and . . .

Aru paused.

A golden tree no taller than a book nestled against a bulging root. She'd almost missed it as her eyes swept over her surroundings, but now she thought she could detect a faint glow around it. Aru stepped closer. Waves of magic poured from it, thickening the air.

Aru took a deep breath and touched her mother's necklace for luck.

Then she closed her eyes and wrapped her hand around the trunk of the tiny tree.

FORTY-EIGHT

Ignorance Is Bliss

Aru blinked.

Gone was the world tree. Gone was, well, everything. She was standing in a chamber filled with golden light. The ceiling above her looked like interwoven branches made of sunlight. And before her stood a woman.

Make that a *goddess.*

"So, you located Kalpavriksha," said the woman, smiling. "I must admit, even *I* am impressed."

Aru stared at her. The goddess wore a simple linen shirt and dark jeans. Her black hair was pulled into a high bun. Her skin was the color of rich earth, and her eyes looked like hardened sap beneath thick eyebrows. She had a hooked nose and a mouth that seemed made for smiling. She was beautiful, but in an unexpected way. Like raindrops on a spider's web—invisible unless you take the time to notice them.

"You… You're…"

"Aranyani," said the goddess, inclining her chin ever so slightly.

The elusive goddess of the forest, and guardian of Kalpavriksha.

"Not quite what you were expecting?" she guessed.

"I, um..." stammered Aru.

Yes seemed like the exact wrong thing to say.

"I see," said Aranyani, still smiling. "And you've come all this way to find Kalpavriksha because...?"

"Because of the war coming to the Otherworld," said Aru.

But as she spoke, the words didn't sit right on her tongue.

"Because of the war," repeated Aranyani. "Because wars are so often won on wishes?"

"But the prophecy—" started Aru.

"Ah, yes. Let me see if I can recall it.... *One treasure is false, and one treasure is lost, but the tree at the heart is the only true cost. No war can be won without finding that root; no victory had without the yield of its fruit. In five days the treasure will bloom and fade, and all that was won could soon be unmade.*"

"Yeah," said Aru weakly. "That one."

"And where does it mention wishing?" Aranyani asked.

Aru was stunned into silence. In her mind, she ran through all the reasons she had been sure Kalpavriksha was at the heart of the prophecy: the fake tree in the heavens; Opal's nasty words; the growing threat in the heavenly and mortal realms, even the fact that her own father had been after the treasure.

Aru swallowed hard. "But it *has* to be Kalpavriksha, because we found the fake one—"

"Let me ask you again, daughter of the god of thunder," said Aranyani. "Where does it mention wishes?"

"It... It doesn't.... But it was the only thing that made

sense!" said Aru, panic rising in her. "We need to win the war! And it mentions the 'tree at the heart.' I thought... I thought we needed it to win. Like... the victors would be the ones who made a wish?"

Aranyani's face softened. "Oh, child. You know so much and yet so little. I pity you for that."

Aru's heart sank. Her family was outside this place, *waiting* for her to complete the mission. Nikita might have sacrificed herself just to get Aru to this moment, and all the goddess had to offer was *pity*? Vajra flickered angrily.

"You have come here to make a wish, and you may do so," said Aranyani.

A spark of hope ignited in Aru.

"This is the last place all who seek Kalpavriksha must enter," the goddess continued. "It is called the Grove of Regret." Aranyani gestured at the space around them.

Only then did Aru notice the same kind of soft whispers that had run down the boulder. The repeating chant of *I should have, I should have, I should have.*

"Should you choose to make a wish, know that regret will follow it," said Aranyani. "See for yourself, daughter of the gods."

Aranyani swept her right hand across the air. A strong wind blew against Aru, causing her to shut her eyes and hold her necklace in place. The touch made Suyodhana's memories flash through Aru's head like a biopic—how he'd grown up alone and without a family, how his brilliance had won over his teachers, how he had named her to be a light in the darkness.

Aru opened her eyes and saw that she'd been plunged into

another vision. She looked around, familiarity jolting her. It was home—*her* home in the Museum of Ancient Indian Art and Culture.

Her mother, young and beautiful, stood at the bottom of the staircase. She wore a long black dress and her hair was done up fancily, as if she'd just come back from a date. A man stood before her, his hands behind his back. It was odd to see Suyodhana so nervous when he was usually so confident.

"I told you I don't want flowers," said Krithika Shah with a coy smile.

Aru knew that well enough. Every Valentine's Day, whenever someone sent her mother flowers, they always ended up in the trash bin.

"I remember," Suyodhana said.

He pulled a bouquet from behind his back. It was definitely not your average arrangement. It was a metal sculpture of a dozen roses made out of gears and clockworks.

"You asked me to give you something that I want but can't have," he said.

Krithika blushed. "I was only joking—"

"The only thing I want is more time with you," he said.

The vision jumped ahead, and this time Suyodhana was older, dressed in the dusty travel clothes he'd worn when he went to Mr. V for the impossible key, when he sacrificed the memories of his upbringing, and when he crossed the chakora birds and gave away the secret of Aru's name. There were lines around his eyes that hadn't been there before, and his face looked like it had never known a smile. He stood in the same place Aru was now, in a room of golden light before the goddess of the forest.

"If you choose this path," Aranyani warned him, "you will

miss the birth of your child. You will give up the memory of ever loving your wife. Is that what this wish is worth to you, Suyodhana?"

His shoulders sagged.

"I've given you almost everything," he said. "But what you ask for now…it is too steep a price."

Aranyani bowed her head. "Then what will you do?"

Suyodhana swallowed hard, raising his head for the first time.

"I will not be defeated," he said hoarsely. "I will find a way to avoid this destiny. Krithika will help me, and together, we'll stop this. But I'm not…I refuse to give up my family."

"Then go home," said Aranyani sadly. "Go to them."

Aru wanted the visions to stop. She didn't want to know any more. She certainly didn't want to *see* it.

But there was more.

In the next vision, Hanuman and Urvashi were sitting beside a very pregnant Krithika.

"I believe in him," said Krithika firmly.

"What you're doing is reckless.…The Council has been calling you selfish, Krithika," said Hanuman. "You know the danger he poses, what he is destined to do! He's fated to destroy this age."

"Prophecies are uncertain things," she shot back.

"Maybe so," said Urvashi. "But what are you willing to risk in order to find out if you're correct?" At this, the apsara's gaze deliberately dropped to Krithika's swollen belly.

Krithika's hand moved to her torso, and she glared at them.

Urvashi sighed, and she reached out to hold Krithika's hands. "I know more than most what we must sacrifice for the ones we love…but think of the greater good. And where has he been while you've had to tend to yourself and your child all alone? He's been gone for months. . . ."

"But he went to protect us—" said Krithika.

For the first time, her voice wavered with uncertainty.

"And if he fails?" asked Hanuman. "What then?"

The vision shifted once more. Aru wanted to fall to the ground, cover her head, and make everything stop. But Aranyani wasn't done with her yet. Aru didn't know how much more she could take. Already, something deep inside her felt pulled tight to the point of snapping.

Images swam before her—more recent this time—showing a dark alley in the human world. Boo fluttered to a lamppost, squawking anxiously. From the gloomy depths of the passage, shadows poured forth, coalescing into the murky shape of the Sleeper.

"I hear you have a proposition for me, old friend."

"I am not your friend!" said Boo angrily.

"Details . . . details." The Sleeper laughed. "I know how long you've been seeking a release from your curse. And now that you've learned the Kalpavriksha in the Nandana Gardens is a lie, you seem to be out of options. So speak. And do not waste my time."

Boo's feathers fluffed around him. He closed his eyes. "The Pandava twins are being moved to the House of the Moon for safekeeping," he said. "I will . . . I will loosen one of the carriage doors so you may take the one who can lead you to Kalpavriksha. If you don't wish to be followed, you must remove her celestial tracking device. But you must swear on whatever remains of your soul that you will not hurt her."

The shadows twitched. "And in return?"

"In return," said Boo, lifting his head, "you will share the Tree of Wishes with me should you find it."

The shadows paused. Deep within the folds of gloom, the Sleeper laughed. "Do you have such little faith in your charges, Subala?"

Boo puffed out in indignation. "They are young, but full of potential. Still...I do not know that they can succeed. And I would not lose the chance of regaining my true form, for only then can I protect them from *you*."

The visions finally came to an end.

And the part of Aru that had been stretched so taut finally broke.

FORTY-NINE

The Fury of a Pandava Scorned

The chamber walls melted away, and Aru found herself kneeling on the ground before Aranyani and Kalpavriksha.

Aru couldn't stop shaking. She couldn't stop the tears from streaming down her face. She wanted to pull herself together, but it seemed impossible.

It felt like all the air in the world had disappeared. And not just the air, but the world itself—the world she thought she'd known, full of people she loved and who had loved her in return, had been yanked out from beneath her feet like a carpet, so she didn't know where to step, where to turn....

Whom to trust.

Trust was the knife that had finally cut loose an emotion she hadn't realized she could feel:

Fury.

She felt it coursing through her veins like blood, thrumming in her body like a whole new pulse. She was more fury than girl. More fury than Pandava.

Aru heard her mother's broken voice: *When I saw how much he had changed, I didn't know what to do.*

Aru wanted to claw through time, to scream at Hanuman and Urvashi to leave her mother alone, to show them everything Suyodhana had suffered simply because he'd *loved his family.* He had loved them enough to sacrifice a wish that would have given him a future. Her father had been stolen from her through no fault of his own. It was the devas' fault. It was her mother's fault. It was everyone's fault *but* his.

She inhaled a shaky breath before her thoughts turned to Boo....

Boo, who liked to perch on her head, and eat Oreos from her hands, and sleep in her home, and nag her to floss every night and take her vitamins. Boo, who had loved her and taught her, but betrayed her sisters anyway.

Sheela's words from the dream took on a whole new light.

He's making a terrible mistake....

And you will hate him for his love.

"I do hate him," she choked out. "I *hate* him."

A bright glow fell over Aru. She looked up, almost shocked to realize Aranyani was still standing before her. She wanted to get out of here, return to her friends, but Aranyani's gaze held her in place.

"This is the price of your wish, child," said Aranyani, tilting up her chin with two fingers. "*Knowledge.* Do you understand? This will be your regret, the thing you must always carry should you decide to use Kalpavriksha's power." She pointed to the necklace. "You are too young to bear such burdens, and I can remove that last vision from your memory. I can take you back to your friends. I can even have the grove swallow up the Sleeper's army, though I cannot stop the war. It's up to you. If you choose to bear this weight, go ahead and speak your wish."

Aru didn't care if it was cowardly—she almost grabbed Aranyani's hand and begged her to take this piece of knowledge away, to hide it from her forever. It *was* too much to hold—her heart didn't have the room. Her friends would be okay. The Otherworld would survive. No one needed her to carry this. They'd all stay safe....

Safe for now, whispered a voice in her head. *And after that?*

Aru remembered the venomous words Opal had spat at them, telling them they weren't good enough, hadn't proven themselves yet. Aru thought of the doubt that had been growing in her heart—the doubt she'd pushed aside because she thought it made her untrustworthy, the "untrue" sister. All this time, it hadn't been *she* who was untrustworthy, but *them*. The devas. The Council. The teachers—Urvashi, Hanuman, and Boo—who had held her hand and promised not to let her fall.

She didn't want to fight for them.

But the Sleeper was no better. She'd seen the bleakness in his eyes, the ruthlessness of his army, and the pain and destruction they'd wrought on the mortal realm and the Otherworld. What had happened to Suyodhana wasn't his fault, but what he was doing now wasn't right either.

More than anything, she wanted the world to be uncomplicated, for right and wrong to be as easily divided as the black and white sections of an Oreo. But the world was not a cookie. And sometimes right and wrong was nothing more than a frame held up to the eye, the view always changing depending on who held it.

Only one thing felt *right* to Aru.

Her sisters and friends. Strong Brynne and her fragility. Shy Mini and her secret strength. Nikita and Sheela, who didn't deserve to be abandoned or treated like puppets by the Council. Aiden, who only tried to capture beauty in the world. Even Rudy, who had so much more to offer than what his family believed.

She would fight for them. She would wish for *them*. No matter what that meant for herself.

Aru wrapped her hand around the little golden tree once again. She looked up at Aranyani, her gaze unflinching and her voice steely as she said, "I wish we win."

FIFTY

The Word Aru Never Spoke

The Sleeper's army was winning.

Aru did not know how she had arrived back on the battlefield, but she was there. As she surveyed the scene, she fiddled nervously with her necklace and found that a third bead had been added to it, containing all that she had seen in Aranyani's Grove of Regret.

Beneath her, the ground was splattered with paint and broken tree limbs. She looked to her friends, her stomach sinking.

Brynne swiped at the air with her wind mace, but her movements were too slow. Mini cast a force field, the light weak and wavering. Aiden was limping and down to one scimitar. Sheela crouched on the ground, one hand on Nikita, who was slumped over unconscious. Rudy slithered this way and that, blocking onslaughts with his tail, blood oozing from his arm.

"STOP!" she called out.

At the center of all the destruction writhed the dark mass of the Sleeper. The shadows paused at her voice, twitching with awareness. His army of demons and rakshasas halted, panting and turning their gaze to her.

The shadows knitted themselves into a pillar, and then peeled back to reveal the Sleeper standing in a charcoal *sherwani,* with dark pants that ended in coiling wisps of smoke. The sight jarred her. She couldn't look at him without seeing Suyodhana, like two semitranslucent images stacked on top of each other. One was the father who had loved her. The other was her greatest enemy, the primary threat to the world she loved and the people in it.

"I was willing to let you all go...to let you *live,*" he said. "But I find my mercy has run dry." The Sleeper raised a hand, and Aru sensed that a part of him knew what she was going to do even before it happened.

She snapped her fingers, and Vajra flattened into a hoverboard beneath her feet.

Go, she urged.

The hoverboard zoomed forward, heading straight to the Sleeper.

"No, Aru!" screamed Mini.

But she didn't listen. She wasn't listening to anyone except herself. Aru wasn't sure what guided her in that second, but her hands seemed to move of their own accord. The Sleeper's army moved closer, and he was now ten feet away, now five....

With one sharp tug, Aru removed the necklace at her throat. The three beads of memories winked in the light.

The Sleeper spread his arms wide.

In another world—in another *life*—it would have looked like a hug.

Aru struggled to keep her eyes open as the shadows leaped up and wrapped around her legs and stomach, squeezing her like snakes. She flung her arms around the Sleeper's neck and cinched the pendant of memories in back. As the shadows overtook her and the world went gray at the edges, Aru found that she had the strength to say one last thing.

"I'm sorry, Dad."

EPILOGUE

Aru stirred.

Snatches of dreams and memories fluttered through her. Shadows. Darkness. The feeling of being gathered and held close…

Someone in the dark speaking her name as if it were a question…

"Arundhati?"

A sudden rush of cold.

Aru opened her eyes. She was in front of a dark cave. But she was not alone. There was another girl sitting across from her, the same age as Aru. She had long black hair, high cheekbones like a model, and catlike eyes. There was something uncannily familiar about her face. Aru felt as if she'd seen it before, only she didn't know where.

"I'm Kara," the girl said.

Aru raised her hands, struggling to break free, but her hands were tied and a steel chain attached her to the cave wall.

She dimly remembered Mini screaming *No, Aru!* and the sensation of slick shadows hauling her off the hoverboard….

Vajra! she thought. She looked down and was flooded with relief when she saw her lightning bolt firmly attached to her wrist.

"Where am I?"

Kara smiled sympathetically. "You're in the house of the Sleeper, Aru Shah."

"So, then, who are you?"

Kara lifted her chin. "*I'm* his daughter."

GLOSSARY

AHA! YOU'RE BACK! I knew it. Good job, me. As always, I'd like to preface this glossary by saying that this is by no means exhaustive or encapsulating of all the nuances of mythology. India is GINORMOUS, and these myths and legends vary from state to state. What you read here is merely a slice of what *I* understand from the stories *I* was told and the research *I* conducted. The wonderful thing about mythology is that its arms are wide enough to embrace many traditions from many regions. My hope is that this glossary gives you context for Aru's world, and perhaps nudges you to do some research of your own. ☺

Adrishya (UH-drish-yah) Hindi for *invisible* or *disappear.*

Agni (UHG-nee) The Hindu god of fire.

Amaravati (uh-MAR-uh-vah-tee) So, I have suffered the great misfortune of never being invited to/having visited this legendary city, but I hear it's, like, *amazing.* It has to be, considering it's the place where Lord Indra lives. It's draped in gold palaces and has celestial gardens full of a thousand marvels. I wonder what the flowers smell like there. I imagine they smell like birthday cake, because it's basically heaven.

Ammamma (UH-muh-mah) *Grandmother* in Telugu, one of the many languages spoken in India, most commonly in the southern area.

Amrita (am-REE-tuh) The immortal drink of the gods. According to the legends, Sage Durvasa once cursed the gods to lose their immortality. To get it back, they had to churn the celestial Ocean of Milk. But in order to accomplish this feat, they had to seek assistance from the asuras, another semi-divine race of beings who were constantly at war with the devas. In return for their help, the asuras demanded that the devas share a taste of the amrita. Which, you know, *fair.* But to gods, the word *fair* is just another word. So they tricked the asuras. The supreme god Vishnu, also known as the preserver, took on the form of Mohini, a beautiful enchantress. The asuras and devas lined up in two rows. While Mohini poured the amrita, the asuras were so mesmerized by her beauty that they didn't realize that she was giving *all* the immortality nectar to the gods and not them. Rude! By the way, I have no idea what amrita tastes like. Probably birthday cake.

Apsara (AHP-sah-rah) Apsaras are beautiful, heavenly dancers who entertain in the Court of the Heavens. They're often the wives of heavenly musicians. In Hindu myths, apsaras are usually sent on errands by Lord Indra to break the meditation of sages who are getting a little too powerful. It's pretty hard to keep meditating when a celestial nymph starts dancing in front of you. And if you scorn her affection (as Arjuna did in the *Mahabharata*), she might just curse you. Just sayin'.

Aranyani (UH-rahn-YAH-nee) The Hindu goddess of forests and animals, who is married to the god of horsemanship, Revanta. She is famously elusive, which means we might never know *what* her Hogwarts House is. Alas.

Ashvin Twins (ASH-vin) The gods of sunrise and sunset, and healing. They are the sons of the sun god, Surya, and fathers of the Pandava twins, Nakula and Sahadeva. They're considered the doctors of the gods and are often depicted with the faces of horses.

Asura (AH-soo-rah) A sometimes good, sometimes bad race of semidivine beings. They're most popularly known from the story about the churning of the Ocean of Milk.

Chakora (CHUH-kor-uh) A mythical bird that is said to live off moonbeams. Imagine a really pretty chicken that shuns corn kernels for moondust, which, to be honest, sounds way yummier anyway.

Chandra (CHUHN-drah) The handsome god of the moon, who often gets into trouble. There are a lot of myths about why the moon waxes and wanes. In one, it is said that Chandra had a favorite wife among the twenty-seven sister constellations he was married to. The wives' father, Daksha, didn't like the fact that Chandra wasn't treating all of them equally, so he cursed him to wither. But Chandra appealed to the Lord of Destruction (see **Shiva**) and the curse was softened. In another story, Chandra laughed at the elephant-headed god Ganesh, who was so offended he chucked a tusk at the moon god and cursed him "never to be whole again." Er, at least not for a very long period of time.

Daksha (DUCK-shah) A celestial king and one of the sons of Lord Brahma, the god of creation. Daksha had *lots* of daughters. Like at least fifty. And he was a super-protective dad. If a husband mistreated his girls, he'd curse him to the brink of extinction. Seriously. Just ask Chandra.

Danda (DAHN-duh) A giant punishing rod that is often considered the symbol of the Dharma Raja, the god of the dead.

Devas (DEH-vahz) The Sanskrit term for the race of gods.

Dharma Raja (DAR-mah RAH-jah) The Lord of Death and Justice, and the father of the oldest Pandava brother, Yudhistira. His mount is a water buffalo.

Draupadi (DROH-puh-dee) Princess Draupadi was the wife of the five Pandava brothers. Yup, you read that right—all five. See, once upon a time, her hand was offered in marriage to whoever could do this great archery feat, etc. . . . and Arjuna won, because Arjuna. When he came home, he jokingly told his mom (who had her back to him and was praying), "I won something!" To which his mother said: "Share equally with your brothers." The rest must've been an awkward convo. Anyway. Draupadi was famously outspoken and independent, and she condemned those who wronged her family. In some places she is revered as a goddess in her own right. When the Pandavas eventually made their journey to heaven, Draupadi was the first to fall down and die in response (PS: She loved Arjuna more than her other husbands). Mythology is harsh.

Dwarka (DWAHR-kah) An ancient kingdom ruled over by the god king Krishna. Dwarka is still a populous city in India, located in the state of Gujarat.

Gandharva (gun-DAR-ruh-vuh) A semidivine race of heavenly beings known for their cosmic musical skills.

Ganesh (guh-NESH) The elephant-headed god of luck and

new beginnings. In prayers, many Hindus often invoke Ganesh first to remove all obstacles. Ganesh loves sweets, is even-tempered and wise, and rides a tiny mouse. (It must be a very strong mouse, because Ganesh ain't a tiny elephant-headed god.) When I was a kid, I was always deeply curious about why he had an elephant's head. Turns out, he did the number one thing to ensure decapitation: ANGER SHIVA, THE LORD OF DESTRUCTION. Seriously, gods! When will you *learn*?! Weird twist, though: Ganesh is Shiva's son. It's just that, well, the god of destruction didn't know it. One day, Shiva left to go run errands, and his wife built a little boy out of turmeric to guard her while she took a bubble bath. Shiva came home, hauling all those bulky bags from Trader Joe's, and demanded to be let inside. His son, who had never met him, was like "Get lost, old man!" Shiva didn't like that. The grocery line had been very long, and he was tired! So. He. Chopped. Off. The. Boy's. Head. As one does. Then he strolled inside, where he had to face the wrath of one furious goddess. Panicked, he dashed into the jungle, where his eyes fell upon an elephant. He chopped off the elephant's head, stuck it on the boy to bring him back to life, and, voilà, you have an aptly named god of new beginnings.

Garuda (GUH-roo-DAH) The king of the birds and the mount of Lord Vishnu, the god of preservation. He's also known as the enemy of serpents.

Hanuman (HUH-noo-mahn) One of the main figures in the Indian epic the *Ramayana,* who was known for his devotion to the god king Rama and Rama's wife, Sita. Hanuman is the son of Vayu, the god of the wind, and Anjana, an apsara. He had lots of mischievous exploits as a kid, including mistaking the sun for a mango and trying to eat it. There are still temples and shrines dedicated to Hanuman, and he's often worshipped by wrestlers because of his incredible strength. He's the half brother of Bhima, the second-oldest Pandava brother.

Holi (HO-lee) A major Hindu festival, also known as the "festival of colors" or "festival of love," in which people feast and throw colored powders at one another. There are many different interpretations of the meaning of Holi and what the colors signify, depending on which region of India one's family is from. My family celebrates the triumph of good over evil, represented by the tale of Narasimha (see: **Narasimha**), who protected the devout son of a demon king.

Indra (IN-druh) The king of heaven, and the god of thunder and lightning. He is the father of Arjuna, the third-oldest Pandava brother. His main weapon is Vajra, a lightning bolt. He has two vahanas: Airavata, the white elephant who spins clouds, and Uchchaihshravas, the seven-headed white horse. I've got a pretty good guess what his favorite color is....

Kadru (KAH-droo) One of the daughters of Daksha (told you he had a lot of girls!); considered the mother of snakes.

Kalpavriksha (kuhl-PUHV-rik-shaw) A divine wish-fulfilling tree. It is said to have roots of gold and silver, with boughs encased in costly jewels, and to reside in the paradise gardens of the god Indra. Sounds like a pretty useful thing to steal. Or protect. Just saying.

Kashyapa (KUSH-yup-ah) A powerful sage and father of Garuda, king of the birds.

Krishna (KRISH-nah) A major Hindu deity. He is worshipped as the eighth reincarnation of the god Vishnu and also as a supreme ruler in his own right. He is the god of compassion, tenderness, and love, and is popular for his charmingly mischievous personality.

Kubera (KOO-bear-uh) The god of riches and ruler of the legendary golden city of Lanka. He's often depicted as a dwarf adorned with jewels. Pretty sure we haven't seen the last of him... hint-hint, wink-wink, nudge-nudge for any readers checking out this glossary.

Lanka (LAHN-kuh) The legendary city of gold, sometimes ruled over by Kubera, sometimes ruled over by his demonic brother, Ravana. Lanka is a major setting in the epic poem the *Ramayana*.

Mahabharata (MAH-hah-BAR-ah-tah) One of two Sanskrit epic poems of ancient India (the other being the *Ramayana*). It is an important source of information about the development of Hinduism between 400 BCE and 200 CE and tells the story of the struggle between two groups of cousins, the Kauravas and the Pandavas.

Maruts (MAH-roots) Minor storm deities often described as violent and aggressive and carrying lots of weapons. Legend says the Maruts once rode through the sky, splitting open clouds so that rain could fall on the earth.

Mohini (moe-HIH-nee) One of the avatars of Lord Vishnu, known as the goddess of enchantment. The gods and asuras banded together to churn the Ocean of Milk on the promise that the nectar of immortality would be shared among them. But the gods didn't want immortal demon counterparts, so

Mohini tricked the asuras by pouring the nectar into the goblets of the gods while smiling over her shoulder at the demons.

Naga (**nagas**, pl.) (NAG-uh) A naga (male) or nagini (female) is one of a group of serpentine beings who are magical and, depending on the region in India, considered divine. Among the most famous nagas is Vasuki, one of the king serpents who was used as a rope when the gods and asuras churned the Ocean of Milk to get the elixir of life. Another is Uloopi, a nagini princess who fell in love with Arjuna, married him, and used a magical gem to save his life.

Nakshatra (NUCK-shut-rah) The collective name of the twenty-seven constellations married to Lord Chandra, god of the moon.

Nakula (nuh-KOO-luh) The most handsome Pandava brother, and a master of horses, swordsmanship, and healing. He is the twin of Sahadeva, and they are the children of the Ashvin twins.

Nandana (NUN-dah-nah) A mythical garden located in the heavens.

Narasimha (NUHR-sihm-hah) A fearsome avatar of Lord Vishnu. Once, there was a demon king who was granted a boon. In typical tyrant fashion, he asked for invincibility, specifically: "I don't want to be killed at daytime or nighttime; indoors or outdoors; by man or by beast; and by no weapon." Then he was like "GOTCHA!" and proceeded to wreak havoc on the world. The only one who didn't fall in line with his plans was his son, Prahlad, who devoutly worshipped Lord Vishnu. To protect Prahlad and defeat the demon king, Vishnu appeared one day in the demon king's courtyard (not indoors or outdoors); at dusk (not daytime or nighttime); in the form of a man with the head of a lion (not by man or by beast) and then dragged the king onto his lap and ripped him apart with his claws (not a weapon)! And that, children, is why you should always have a lawyer review your wishes. Loopholes are persnickety things. Why the gods went to all that trouble is a mystery to me. After all, they could've just sent a girl. Bam! Riddle solved.

Pandava brothers (Arjuna, Yudhistira, Bhima, Nakula, and Sahadeva) (PAN-dah-vah, ar-JOO-nah, yoo-diss-TEE-ruh, BEE-muh, nuh-KOO-luh, saw-hah-DAY-vuh) Demigod warrior princes, and the heroes of the epic *Mahabharata* poem. Arjuna, Yudhistira, and Bhima were born to Queen Kunti, the first wife of King Pandu. Nakula and Sahadeva were born to Queen Madri, the second wife of King Pandu.

Rahuketu (RAH-hoo-KEH-too) The ascending and descending lunar nodes in the sky, responsible for eclipses. Originally, Rahuketu was one being... but when it tried to drink some of the immortal nectar, Lord Vishnu chopped off its head. They still got immortality—it's just divided between their two halves.

Rakshasa (RUCK-shaw-sah) A rakshasa (male) or rakshasi (female) is a mythological being, like a demigod. Sometimes good and sometimes bad, they are powerful sorcerers, and can change shape to take on any form.

Rama (RAH-mah) The hero of the epic poem the *Ramayana*. He was the seventh incarnation of the god Vishnu.

Ramayana (RAH-mah-YAWN-uh) One of the two great Sanskrit epic poems (the other being the *Mahabharata*), it describes how the god king Rama, aided by his brother and the monkey-faced demigod Hanuman, rescue his wife, Sita, from the ten-headed demon king, Ravana.

Ravana (RAH-vah-nah) A character in the Hindu epic the *Ramayana,* where he is depicted as the ten-headed demon king who stole Rama's wife, Sita. Ravana is described as having once been a follower of Shiva. He was also a great scholar, a capable ruler, a master of the *veena* (a musical instrument), and someone who wished to overpower the gods. He's one of my favorite antagonists, to be honest, because it just goes to show that the line between heroism and villainy can be a bit murky.

Sahadeva (SAW-hah-DAY-vuh) The twin to Nakula, and the wisest of the Pandavas. He was known to be a great swordsman and also a brilliant astrologist, but he was cursed that if he should disclose events before they happened, his head would explode.

Sanskrit (SAHN-skrit) An ancient language of India. Many Hindu scriptures and epic poems are written in Sanskrit.

Shani (SHAH-nee) The Lord of Saturn and also the Lord of Justice. One day, his wife was super annoyed that he wasn't bothering to look at her (#relatable) and cursed him so that his gaze would be forever devastating, thus forcing his eyes always downward. But the curse was eventually lifted when, based on his karmic actions, he took on the title Lord of Justice.

Shiva (SHEE-vuh) One of the three main gods in the Hindu pantheon, often associated with destruction. He is also known as the Lord of Cosmic Dance. His consort is Parvati.

Takshaka (TAHK-shah-kah) A naga king and former friend of Indra who once lived in the Khandava Forest before Arjuna helped burn it down, killing most of Takshaka's family. He swore vengeance on all the Pandavas ever since. Wonder why...

Urvashi (OOR-vah-shee) A famous apsara, considered the most beautiful of all the apsaras. Her name literally means *she who can control the hearts of others.*

Vimana (VEE-mah-nuh) A flying chariot or palace. I have inquired at many a car dealership as to where I can procure such a thing. Each time, I have been escorted outside and asked not to return. Hmph.

Vishnu (VISH-noo) The second god in the Hindu triumvirate (also known as the Trimurti). These three gods are responsible for the creation, upkeep, and destruction of the world. The other two gods are Brahma and Shiva. Brahma is the creator of the universe, and Shiva is the destroyer. Vishnu is worshipped as the preserver. He has taken many forms on earth in various avatars, most notably as Krishna, Mohini, and Rama.

Vishwakarma (VISH-wah-kur-MAH) The god of architecture, believed to be the original engineer who taught humans how to build long-lasting monuments. Some of his greatest hits include Lanka, the city of gold, and the city of Dwarka.

Yaksha (YAHK-sha) A yaksha (male) or yakshini (female) is a supernatural being from Hindu, Buddhist, and Jain mythology. Yakshas are attendees of Kubera, the Hindu god of wealth, who rules in the mythical Himalayan kingdom of Alaka.

Yali (YAH-lee) A mythical creature that can be a composite of all kinds of animals, like lions and crocodiles and antelopes. They are believed to protect and guard the entryways of temples.

Yamuna (yuh-MOO-nah) A highly worshipped river goddess and also the name of one of the largest tributary rivers in

India. Yamuna is the daughter of the sun god, Surya, and sister to Yama, the god of death.

Phew! Got all that? You definitely deserve a vacation. How does the city of gold sound?

Aru Shah has messed up. Desperate to impress her snooty schoolmates, and embarrassed to be living in the museum where her mother works, she lights the cursed Lamp of Bharata. It can't actually be cursed… can it?

After accidentally freeing an ancient demon and freezing her classmates and her mother in time, Aru must fix things before the Ancient God of Destruction is awoken. Accompanied by a wise-cracking pigeon and her long-lost half-sister, she must find the reincarnations of the five Pandava brothers and journey through the Kingdom of Death.

But how is one girl in Spider-Man pyjamas supposed to do all that?

Just when Aru Shah is getting the hang of being a Pandava, the Otherworld goes into full panic mode. The god of love's bow and arrow has gone missing, and the thief isn't playing cupid. Instead, they're turning people into an army of zombies.

If things weren't bad enough, somehow Aru gets framed as the thief. If she doesn't find the arrow by the next full moon, she'll be kicked out of the Otherworld. For good.

Now with two sisters to handle, and an annoyingly charming new friend, Aru must set off on a quest to save the world. Again.

Coming in 2021

ARU SHAH AND THE CITY OF GOLD